W9-BUD-631

Now *and* Then, Again

A Novel

by
Bonnie S. Hopkins

Walk Worthy Press

West Bloomfield, Michigan

Unless otherwise indicated, all scripture quotations are taken from the *Holy Bible, New International Version®*. Copyright © 1973, 1978, 1984 by International Bible Society. Used by permission of Zondervan Publishing House. All rights reserved.

Scripture quotations marked (KJV) were taken from the *King James Version* of the Bible.

Scripture quotations marked (ESV) were taken from *The Holy Bible, English Standard Version®*, copyright © 2001 by Crossway Bibles, a publishing ministry of Good News Publishers. Used by permission. All rights reserved.

12 11 10 09   10 9 8 7 6 5 4 3 2 1

Illustration and cover design by Tracy D. McCutchion

Now and Then, Again
ISBN 13: 978-1-57794-880-3
ISBN 10: 1-57794-880-7
Copyright © 2009 by Bonnie S. Hopkins

Published by Walk Worthy Press in association with Harrison House Publishers
Walk Worthy Press
P.O. Box 250034
West Bloomfield, Michigan 48323
www.walkworthypress.net

Harrison House Publishers
P.O. Box 35035
Tulsa, Oklahoma 74153
www.harrisonhouse.com

Printed in the United States of America. All rights reserved under International Copyright Law. Contents and/or cover may not be reproduced in whole or in part in any form without the express written consent of the Publisher.

Acknowledgements

To God be all the glory, honor, and praise! My writing journey thus far has been accomplished through nothing but His grace and power.

Family, you know you are the human instruments in which God uses to hold me up through thick and thin, ups and downs. I am so thankful for you.

To James and Brenda Jones, Clarence and Barbara Smith, Felicia Fontenot of Exhibit Hope Book stores, and my neighbor, whose words of encouragement and intention to be the first to buy a copy of this book have inspired me, God bless all of you for going the next mile. Of course, there are others too numerous to name (you know who you are) who have continuously prayed, encouraged, and supported me on this journey. To all of you, "Thanks", and don't quit now!

To Pastor John D. and Evelyn Ogletree, and the First Metropolitan Church, I have nothing but heartfelt love and appreciation for all of your wonderful support.

To Denise Stinson of Walk Worthy Press, I'm *still* so very grateful. God bless you! To editor, Monica Harris, I can't thank you enough! And to Harrison House Publishers, I have nothing but appreciation for your hard work and conscientious endeavors on this book.

To all the wonderful book clubs, churches, organizations, and bookstores who bought and read *Seasons,* and graciously provided wonderful opportunities for me to communicate, interact, and receive feedback and encouragement (as well as superb meals), words can't express how much I enjoyed meeting and fellowshipping with you and I continuously praise God for you.

To all my fellow writers who have inspired me through your wonderful literary works and especially those of you who have extended friendship, support, and shared invaluable knowledge, you will never know the extent to which God has used you in my life! Thank you!

And last (but certainly not least), praise God for each and every person who read *Seasons* and have patiently, but with great anticipation, waited for *Now and Then, Again.* This book, like *Seasons,* was written with much prayer lifted up to God for your abundant blessing. I fervently pray that as you read this story of forgiveness and new beginnings, you will be encouraged, inspired, and edified in your walk with God, yourself, and others. May this story also help to build your trust that *nothing is over until God says it's over!*

Blessings!
Bonnie

P.S. I would love to hear from you. Please say hello at: bonniehopkins08@yahoo.com.

Dedication

This book is dedicated to
the memory of my childhood Pastor,
Rev. Willie J. Boyd

His humility, integrity, and love for God and people
greatly influenced me, and provided a wonderful
example of what it means to serve the Lord.
Although he's been in heaven for many years,
he still holds a special place in my heart.
Memories of his joyful walk with the Lord
continue to stir a desire in me to follow
in his footsteps by being a blessing to
the Kingdom of God and to others.

chapter one

Judge Mitchell Langford was not in the best frame of mind. A fire in Houston's main court building had caused many of the pending cases to be rescheduled, and made it necessary for his courtroom to be relocated to the older annex building where mostly family cases were handled. During all the shifting, he had somehow been assigned to family court, which he hated. Hearing case after case of families in disarray and having to make judgments for or against family members fighting one another over children or possessions filled him with a hopelessness that came from knowing there was little he could do to stop what was, too often, a cycle of multigenerational dysfunction. Additionally, some of these cases were a reminder of his own family issues, which was why he had been happy to be in criminal court.

After taking his seat on the bench, he looked out over the courtroom, took in the press of people gathered, and knew it would be another rough session. It was an unseasonably hot day for December. The heat and humidity from the outside filtered into the small, inadequately ventilated courtroom, which was overcrowded with people who were already deep in the throes of anger and aggravation. Hostility simmered, tempers flared, and whispered taunts were already underway. He knew they would escalate into physical outbreaks if not for the presence and intervention of the deputies hovering around the room.

Heat rose beneath his robe and he wanted to remove the hot, uncomfortable garment. Every day, each of his sessions brought a seemingly unending stream of families in various stages of turmoil and conflict, all seeking legal retribution of some kind—husband against wife; parents battling over children; parents losing rights to children they had abandoned, abused and neglected; grandparents fighting parents over grandchildren; families battling caseworkers over custody issues—on and on it went. Many of the cases involved innocent children, which hit a vulnerable place near his own heart. To make matters worse, today his regular clerk was out sick, and the temp couldn't seem to get the hang of what was required.

His patience was already stretched to the limit when the obnoxious child advocate volunteer stood before him, about to push him over the edge. The advocate was obviously at odds with the birth mother and the caseworker over whom the children in question should be placed with. It was the caseworker's recommendation that the children be returned to the mother, who had lost custody due to neglect and abandonment, but who had since been through court ordered rehabilitation. The children's advocate argued against the mother, contending that the children were better off left in the care of the foster parents, who loved and provided a stable home for the two small children.

He ruled in favor of the mother and caseworker, which was routine in most cases. But the advocate would not give up, and her pushiness threatened the small fragment of tolerance he was trying to hold on to.

"That is my ruling, ma'am!" Mitch seethed as he recalled that this woman was the very reason he was against these child advocate volunteers. In his opinion, the caseworker handling the case was the best person to decide if a family was ready to be reunited. "Have you forgotten that your only responsibility here is to provide input to the court, and not to tell the court what to do?"

The woman's eyes flashed angrily and Mitch's attention was drawn to how attractive she was, even as she continued to annoy him.

"Your Honor," Savannah Sinclair pressed, "what you don't understand is that my job as a child advocate is to fight for what is best for the children...specifically their welfare and safety. I have provided you with information that clearly shows there is a history of abuse. To put these children back into that home will be a mistake and could lead to tragic consequences. Please your Honor, all I'm asking is that you read the case history and think about the welfare of the children before making a decision."

As Vann argued with the judge, she silently questioned her sanity. *What am I doing? I know I'm not standing here arguing with this judge.* From what she had always heard, judges were not to be messed with—ever. But the thought of those children going back into a potentially unsafe environment pushed thoughts of herself to the back of her mind.

"Ms?" The judge pushed his glasses up from the tip of his nose as he searched the file in front of him to find the name of the child advocate. "Ms…Sinclair," he said, wearily. "I'm just about out of time and patience. I'm sure I don't have to explain to you that we make every effort to keep families together. It's always the preference of the court to reunite children with their parents after the parents have received the required rehabilitation. Why is that so difficult for you to understand?"

"Your Honor, what *you* are failing to understand is that those children have been reunited with the mother a number of times," she retorted, a frustrated ring in her voice. "The children have ended up in abusive and neglectful circumstances each time. What is it going to take for the court to realize that the preferred course of action may not always be the right one, and in the process, you're putting children in danger? The last time these children were removed from the mother, they had been left alone for more than two days before someone found them, while the mother was off somewhere getting high. That is unthinkable for children six and three years old. Think of the children, your Honor!" She continued to glare at him.

The judge glared back. "Are you an attorney, Ms. Sinclair? A social worker? Do you know all the state laws and regulations regarding child custody matters? I don't think so. I'd appreciate it if you would restrict your comments to those of advisement and recommendation, and leave the rulings to those qualified to make them. The ruling stands."

As he reprimanded her, the judge couldn't stop his eyes from taking in everything about this woman. She was beautiful and passionate. He noticed that she wasn't wearing a wedding ring, and he couldn't help hoping that meant she was unmarried, because he didn't want to be guilty of coveting another man's wife.

Her reddish-brown complexion was flushed red with anger and as she tossed her head in defiance, thick, curly, auburn hair that was liberally sprinkled with gray strands bounced around her face, exposing a beautiful, classic, profile—high cheekbones, full, well shaped lips.... *Stay focused on the issue, boy!* He reminded himself. She stood no more than 5 feet 5 inches in her black two inch heels, and the forest green business suit she wore was a perfect compliment to her skin tone as well as her shapely figure.

Mitch controlled the temptation to let his eyes travel up and down her body, a habit men had which he thought was rude and contemptible. But this woman made him want to drink in every inch of her. He saw women of all ages dressed from every extreme from his perch on the bench; however, something about this woman spoke of grace, elegance, and class. He just wished he had met her in more favorable circumstances.

His ruling goaded Vann beyond sensibility. "Your Honor, I beg you to listen to someone who has seen firsthand what these children have suffered both physically and emotionally, and not to sit there and nonchalantly order them back into an unstable situation. I know they've been left alone, have gone hungry, and have been neglected. I've been on this case almost two years, and I've seen them shuffled back and forth too many times. They need...deserve...a safe, loving, and stable home environment."

"Ms. Sinclair!" The judge raised up in indignation, and rapped his gavel. His deep voice resonated through the courtroom. "You have far exceeded your court-given boundary. I'm very close to holding you in contempt and throwing you in jail. I order you to leave this courtroom. Now!"

Vann stared him down for seconds before reason took over. She was so angry she could have chewed nails, but she didn't want to go to jail. She turned and walked out of the courtroom with the foster mother following closely behind her.

"I am so sorry," Vann told her, "but you know that as a volunteer advocate, all I can do is report what I've observed and recommend what I think is best for the children. Sometimes we get a reasonable judge who listens, and sometimes we don't."

"Well, I hope you are finally getting the message!" a loud voice yelled. "Ain't nobody taking my kids away from me." The mother of the children stood before them, a challenging glint in her eyes. "You better go and find you some children somewhere else," she yelled into the foster mother's face. "Huh! You are just pitiful." She walked away laughing.

In tears, the foster mother said to Vann, "I just wish they would understand that my sister's only motive for wanting to keep the children is for the benefits she receives from the state. I've told the caseworker that time and time again. But my sister is able to convince family services that *I'm* the one in the wrong—that I'm only trying to take the children because I can't have any of my own. But that's not true. The system is full of adoptable children, but these children are my own flesh and blood who desperately need love."

They found an empty bench outside the courtroom and sat down.

Vann felt so bad for this woman who lovingly cared for her niece and nephew each time they were returned to her after another round of neglect and abuse by the mother. *Why?* she questioned, silently. Why are there so many people who want children and would make good parents who are unable to have them? But she was getting into God's business, and knew to leave that alone.

Vann empathized with this woman and her husband who had become certified as foster parents so they could assume responsibility for her sister's children. She observed how their nurturing restored the children back to physical and emotional health.

"I just regret we were assigned a judge who is so insensitive to the welfare of children," Vann said, with no thought as to who might hear her. If she had realized the judge was anywhere nearby, she would have definitely been more circumspect in expressing her frustrations.

On his way to lunch with his colleagues, Mitch's head snapped around and his steps came to a stop when he heard Vann's voice and knew she was talking about him. He turned and walked back toward her.

"Aw, Mitch, come on!" his coworker urged. "We don't have any time to waste."

Stepping close enough for her to hear, he spoke in an even tone, "Ms. Sinclair, you don't know anything about my heart or my sensitivity, so I suggest you keep your opinions about me to yourself."

Surprised for just a moment, Vann stood up, absently noticing how tall and how well built and muscular the judge was. She took in his hazel hued eyes, thick, neatly trimmed salt and pepper hair, and the handsome face the color of milk chocolate. *Good looking!...too bad he has to be so hard-hearted,* she thought to herself.

"You know what, your Honor, I know you have the power to overrule my argument and even throw me in jail, but I would ask that you remember that I have a right to my own opinion outside of your courtroom. Perhaps I did go overboard, but I can only hope that someday, someway, you will somehow have the compass...uh...the knowledge to understand that my only motivation is to protect the welfare of those children, and not to offend the court."

Their eyes battled in nonverbal warfare. Vann's reflecting her desire to apply a swift kick to his behind, his challenging her to try it.

"You have taken your volunteer status much too far, and I caution you to tone it down. The next judge may not be as lenient, nor will I, if you're ever in my courtroom again," he said in a soft voice.

Vann lowered her large, light brown eyes, and drew a calming breath. *I must have lost my mind,* she thought. "I'll remember that."

"Just don't ever come into my courtroom again with that kind of nonsense." He gave her another hard look before turning and continuing on his way.

"I can't believe I lost it like that with that judge," Vann said in a loud voice, as she entered the solace of her lovely home later that day. "I've never come face-to-face with the possibility of going to jail before." She kicked her shoes off, and collapsed with a sigh onto the soft burgundy leather sofa in her family room. The room itself was meant to be calming. Painted a serene blue and accented with varying hues of blue, mauve, and green, the tranquility of the room never failed to soothe her. Vann had lived in the house nearly ten years. She fell in love with the one-story, twenty-four hundred square foot house located in a beautiful subdivision when she first saw it. It was larger than what she needed, but she loved the spacious layout of the rooms, and was constantly adding little touches to improve it and make it more comfortable and attractive.

The house was an outlet for her need to nurture. She was single, middle-aged, and would soon be unemployed. She had no children of her own, although she did have TreVann, her godson, who was like her own but was the son of her best friends, Rubye and Thomas. TreVann had lived with her a good portion of his life, but he was now grown and had been living on his own for years.

A flash of excitement flowed through her as she remembered she was about to make a major life change, and although it had taken a while to make the decision to retire, she was now convinced it was the right one. In fact, she now thanked the Lord for pushing her out of the nest of comfort and familiarity and into the world of the unknown.

After her court case that morning, she had intended to spend the remainder of her day with the Lord...praying and praising Him for His goodness, and seeking His direction for this new season of her life. But her disturbing encounter in court crept back into her mind, robbing her peace. "Father in Heaven, what was I thinking about to argue with the judge like that? I lost all sense of wisdom and good judgment."

She reached for the phone to call Rubye. She needed to de-stress before moving on with her day, and talking to Rubye could always help her put things into perspective.

"Hey, Rubye, can you talk a minute?" Ruybe was a dessert caterer, and was usually either cooking or delivering her delec-table dishes to restaurants.

"I'm getting ready to make some deliveries, but I have a minute. What's up? You back from court already?" Rubye replied.

"Girl, it is definitely time for me to resign as a child advo-cate, because I lost it in the courtroom today. Rubye, the judge almost threw me in jail."

"What? What happened, Vann? What were you carrying on about?" Rubye asked.

She gave a summary of how the case went. "Had one of the regular family court judges handled the case, I have no doubt he would have listened to my recommendations. But the case was somehow reassigned to a man who was so unreasonable, he disregarded everything I had to say. And I tell you, girl, I just lost it in there."

"Maybe you need to try to understand why he ruled the way he did. It could be that he was adhering strictly to written policy. It sounds like you've gotten too personally involved, Vann. And I'm sure you know better than to mess with a judge."

"You are so right, and I don't know what got into me. But even after he threatened to put me in jail, somehow I felt I could speak my mind to him. Obviously, he didn't feel the same connection to me. Or maybe he did, because he could have right-fully held me in contempt."

"God was just with you, girl. And hopefully it'll work out alright for those little children. Anyway, don't worry about it, Vann. All you can do is pray for those children at this point."

"I know, and I'm doing that. I'll tell you though, I'm still shivering in my shoes. Lord, I hope I never see him again. I'd probably die of embarrassment...after I finished giving him a swift kick," she said with a chuckle.

"But you will see him again if you continue as a volunteer advocate. So you'd better be prepared," Rubye reminded her.

"Well.... As a matter of fact, he told me not to ever come back into his courtroom with my nonsense. And that's fine with me. I shall fervently pray that we won't ever end up in the same courtroom."

It was Rubye's turn to laugh. "Vann, you must have really acted a fool."

Vann's laughter joined in with Rubye's. "I'm sorry to admit it, but yes, I did. And to tell you the truth, I'd probably do it again. It is definitely time to give up my advocacy efforts."

"Well maybe you don't have to go to that extreme, but just keep everything in the right perspective," Rubye admonished. "To give it up completely would be a disservice to those little children who need your help. And now that you're retiring, you'll have the time and freedom to do more of this volunteer work."

"True. But it became clear today that I need to find another way to help the Child Advocacy Agency. The CPS caseworkers have their hands full trying to do what's best for the family, and sometimes the needs of the children get lost in the system. Although my heart lies with fighting for the welfare of the children, I can always help with fundraising or recruiting events. I suppose I should have given it up months ago when my new boss required me to use vacation time to carry out my advocacy duties. I did think about it then, but I hated to quit on those children."

"That was really low of him, especially since he knew you were representing the company at Cy's request and had been involved as a volunteer for several years."

Vann sighed and laid her head back against the cushions as she reflected on her thirty year career with Welch Mortgaging and Title Company. For most of those years she had handled a variety of responsibilities in her position as personal assistant to CEO, Cyrus Welch, whose failing health had made it necessary for him to be replaced by Sam Riland. That change had bought an end to Vann's satisfying work environment and ultimately convinced her it was time to leave. She pushed aside unfriendly thoughts about Sam and said, "Not that I minded using my vacation time for a good cause, but it was the principle of the thing that bothered me."

"The good thing is you don't even have to deal with him anymore, Vann. You worked hard for that company, and gave them many good years. Let God take care of them. That's what I hate about some of these companies today. They have no loyalty to their workers."

"Sam always felt I had too much freedom and too many perks, and he was determined to take them all away. Anyway, I know the Lord was just confirming that it was time for me to get on out of there. I truly believe the Lord let's us know when it's time to move on, and thirty years at that place was long enough. Especially with the working environment as it is now."

"That's exactly why I work for myself," Rubye stated. "So, are you ready for your retirement reception tomorrow? That's what you should be thinking about. Do you have your speech ready? You do know you're going to have to say something," she reminded. Although she did it often, Vann hated to speak in front of large groups of people. "Anyway, I have orders to get out so I'd better go. I'll see you tomorrow."

Later that evening, Mitch was relaxing in the family room of his spacious house situated on a large wooded lot in The Woodlands, Texas. The Woodlands was a growing community bordering the city of Houston where extensive efforts were made to preserve the forest-like environment. He liked the house, but had bought it more for an investment than anything else. He would have loved for it to be a true home with a wife and family he could look forward to coming home to at the end of the day, but as it was, it was just a place to crash. He hadn't even bothered to furnish all the rooms. Right now, he was satisfied with having the necessary furnishings for he and his son, Matthew, to live and function comfortably.

He thought back over the day and couldn't help smiling as he remembered the confrontation with the Sinclair woman. Her fieriness had pushed all his buttons, and he had certainly been annoyed during the heat of the moment. But he had also been distracted by his attraction to her. At any rate, he could have had her removed from the courtroom long before it reached the point it did. After cooling down, he had to admit she had a sincere and real concern for those children and had actually been doing her job as their advocate. He couldn't help wondering if perhaps his unusual attraction to her as a woman had fueled his forceful response.

In fact, after he'd thoroughly reviewed the case file, he saw she had made some valid observations about the mother's irresponsible parenting history. Cold chills of uneasiness ran up his spine when he thought about the very real possibility that the children could be seriously hurt because their mother couldn't seem to change her lifestyle. Now all he could do was pray that she finally had her act together, although Ms. Sinclair didn't seem to think so.

Thinking of the case also brought enticing thoughts about Ms. Sinclair's passion. From observing her during their explosive encounters, he had deciphered several traits that would probably come close to describing her character: compassionate, loyal, determined, intense, ...even loving. Just the thought fascinated and intrigued him, and he found himself smiling again. He couldn't recall the last time the thought of a woman had brought a smile to his face.

But the images were quickly overshadowed as thoughts of two other women invaded his mind. They were women he wished he'd never met. Unfortunately he was stuck with them for life because he shared children with them. How he wished the mothers of his own children fought as vigorously for their children as the Sinclair woman had fought for children who were not even hers. But instead, they used their children for selfish ends.

Her name, Savannah Sinclair, was burned into his memory. He wanted to know more about her and he looked forward to their next altercation with eager anticipation. Then he remembered. He had ordered her not to come into his courtroom again.

There has to be a way for me to find out more about this woman, Lord. He silently sent his desire to the Lord. "Yeah,

Father," he verbalized his prayer, "I really would like to know who Savannah Sinclair is, and I know You can make that happen. This woman intrigues me, Lord, and I can't get her out of my mind. So, I'm asking You to help me find out more about her. I'm lonely, Father, and I really would like to have a godly woman to share my life with, and for some reason, she's the one now monopolizing my thoughts."

As he sat there talking to the Lord, he noticed the message light blinking on the phone. He retrieved the message which turned out to be from Thomas Robertson, a frat brother, calling about their annual benefit affair. He hated those things, but they brought in scholarship funding for needy students, so he tried to participate. Mitch dialed the number.

"Hello, Robertson residence," a woman answered.

"Hello, this is Mitch Langford. I'm returning Thomas' call. Is he available?"

"Yes, he is. Hold on a minute, please." He heard the thud of the phone being dropped while the woman yelled loudly, "'T' telephone!"

"Thomas Robertson."

"Hello, Thomas, this is Mitch Langford. I'm returning your call about the fraternity event. What committee am I on this year?"

"Oh, so you know the drill? We are responsible for presentation of awards. So many brothers act like they don't know what I'm calling about," Thomas said, laughing.

"Yeah, I do understand. I've had your job before. It made me want to reach through the phone and shake them," Mitch said.

"Aw, man, you know it!" Thomas answered. "I don't know a lot of the younger guys...old ones either...because I haven't been active. Too busy trying to make a living. And I lived in the Middle East for ten years so I was out of the loop. I've been back a couple of years now, but it just hasn't been at the top of my list. But it's time to get back involved in some worthwhile projects, so I've volunteered for a lot of stuff this year.

"I'd like to meet with our committee as soon as possible so we can at least get acquainted and start making some plans. Do you happen to work anywhere near downtown Houston?"

"Yes, as a matter of fact, I do. I'm a judge and work in the criminal justice district."

"That's perfect man! My office is in the Shell building on Louisiana, and since several other brothers on our committee also work in the area, I thought we'd get together for a brief meeting after work tomorrow. Don't worry, it's going to be brief because one of my dear friends is retiring and a reception for her is being held at the Four Seasons Hotel at six. I have to be there at some point, or both she and my wife will have my head."

"I can do that," Mitch replied, as he scribbled the information he needed down on a pad.

"I'll probably have most of the meetings at my home on weekends," Thomas continued. "I live on the north side, in the Spring area. Is that okay with you? We can always change the location if it's not convenient."

"Hey man, that couldn't be more perfect. I'm just on down the freeway a little ways, in The Woodlands," Mitch answered.

"Good! It's turning out that most of us live on the north side of town."

"Alright, brother! I'll see you tomorrow," Mitch said, thinking Thomas sounded like he was an okay guy. He was actually looking forward to meeting him.

He didn't know meeting Thomas would be the entryway to changes in his life, and the answer to the fervent prayer he had just prayed.

chapter two

Hallelujah, I'm retired! Vann pushed all thoughts of yesterday's courtroom encounter to the back of her mind as she went from group to group in the large hotel ballroom, thanking people for sharing this very special occasion with her. It was the second week in December, near the end of the year, and to Vann, the fitting time to celebrate the close of a significant chapter in her life. Thanks to her former boss, Cyrus Welch, who had enlisted the help of her pastor and close friends, her retirement celebration was being held at the Four Seasons Hotel downtown.

The room had been decorated in a festive theme, with balloons and streamers in Vann's favorite colors hanging from the ceiling. Balloon bouquets in the same colors sat on each of the round tables, and large "Congratulations" signs were strategically placed around the room. Long buffet tables loaded with food stood on both ends of the room, attracting lines of people who came away carrying plates piled high with a variety of delicious looking foods. Cyrus Welch had spared nothing to make this a memorable occasion for Vann.

Vann was dressed in a burgundy pantsuit trimmed in gold piping, with matching shoes and accessories. Her jewelry included a gold shaped dove pin which she wore on her left shoulder as a reminder that the Holy Spirit was with her.

The room was full. Not surprising, since her entire church, coworkers, family, personal friends as well as friends she had met through her job, had all been invited. She noticed a table piled high with gifts and cards and her heart swelled with praise. "Oh Father! You are so good," she stated in a low voice. She spotted her family seated at tables up front, her girlfriends busily directing and coordinating things, and she caught sight of TreVann, her godson, who had arrived from Austin to attend the event.

Vann's intent to move around the room from group to group to hug and greet people was soon stalled by the crowd gathering around her. She was trapped in one spot where she was inundated with hugs and kisses along with joyful congratulations from the attendees, and she was just as generous in expressing her appreciation and in giving all the praise to God for His blessings. She knew the ceremony would start soon, but she wanted to personally greet as many as she could before it started.

It was still hard to believe she was actually retiring. It had been a long and interesting journey...perhaps not always enjoyable, but certainly a blessed and profitable one.

She couldn't help but reflect on that journey, even as she hugged and greeted those who had come to share her celebration.

She started her career as a lowly clerk in the company back when the slumping economy had made it impossible for the college diploma she had worked so hard for, to open the door to a professional level job—for African Americans anyway. So she had taken the clerical position because she was realistic enough to know any job was better than none. As it turned out, God had definitely been ordering the steps of her life. Cyrus Welch, the senior partner of the Welch Mortgage and Title Company, had quickly noticed her diligence and had taken her under his wing. Under his mentorship, Vann rose through the clerical ranks in record time, became a loan servicing officer, and eventually moved into administration to work in many capacities as personal assistant to Cyrus, including acting as the company's official liaison to other businesses and community service organizations.

Over the years, Cy had become much more than Vann's boss. In addition to being her mentor, he was friend, fatherfigure, and advisor, while she had also become much more than an employee to him and his wife, Sylvia. Under their tutelage, Vann had prospered in more ways than she could count.

"Hello!" She smiled as she greeted and hugged Sister Alberta Hairston, one of the church mothers, and one of Vann's favorite people at the church. The eighty-something-year-old didn't miss any occasion to dress up and to eat food she didn't have to cook, especially when it was free. "I'm so glad you were able to come and share this occasion with me," Vann told the elderly woman warmly.

"I wouldn't have missed it, you know that. I'm kind of surprised that you're actually doing this. I know you told me you were thinking and praying on it, but I just didn't believe you would go through with it." The old lady cocked her head to the side and asked, "Well, what are you planning to do with yourself, now that you'll be a lady of leisure?"

"Oh, I'm sure I'll find enough to keep me busy," Vann responded. "The truth of the matter, Sister Hairston, is that God has blessed me and granted me favor on that job for a very long time, but now, He has shown me that it is simply time for a change. Does that make sense to you?"

"It sho' 'nuff do, honey! I'm going to be praying, because I know God's going to take care of you. You just trust in the Lord, baby, and I just know He's about to give you a beautiful testimony that He wants you to share with others. God is known for working things out just for His glory, and I know this is going to be a doosey. Oh yes it is!" She moved on still chuckling and praising God.

Her conversation with Sister Hairston sent Vann's mind back to the past, even as she continued to mingle with the crowd.

Through the years, Vann had been called Cyrus' flunky, gofer, and worse. She hadn't cared. She had been taught while growing up in Georgia that any kind of honest work was nothing to be ashamed of. Cyrus and his wife had never asked her to do anything that compromised her integrity, and had treated her with respect and kindness. It hadn't bothered her to run their personal errands, plan and oversee their dinner parties, and stay on top of their business concerns. She did it for her grandmother, who raised her, and other elderly friends, so it was no big deal to do it for her boss.

She loved and respected the Welches, who had generously cosigned for her first bank loans, encouraged and guided her successful investment ventures in the stock market, and introduced and tutored her prosperous excursions into the world of real estate. They were also responsible for her involvement in volunteer programs like Child Advocates as a representative for the company.

Her grandmother, whom she called 'Mama', had been right when she'd frequently told her, "Baby, it's not just having a payday that makes a good job. Sometimes that job is just God's way of getting to you what He wants you to have. Don't pay no attention to what other folks say."

And so she had stayed, and prospered, for over three decades. *Lord! Where had the time gone?* She wondered as she accepted a hug from one of the young ladies in her Sunday school class.

But eventually, life had brought one of its inevitable changes. A year ago, Cyrus was forced to step down for health reasons. And although he was still the major stockholder and senior partner, his absence from everyday office routine meant life at work was not the same for Vann.

Without Cyrus' powerful presence in the office to protect her, those who had been jealous of her position and relationship with Cy were free to take vengeful potshots. Sam Riland, her new boss, wasted no time assigning the free parking space she'd always had in the building garage to someone else, leaving Vann with the ordeal of finding another space two blocks away that came with a hefty monthly fee. Sam had changed her work hours, requiring her to arrive an hour earlier, while having trouble with the fact that she would also leave an hour earlier. She no longer had specific job assignments or her own office, but was told to report to the clerical pool, where she became a floater and never knew where she would be working from day to day. This was frustrating to Vann, who was focused and used to planning and accomplishing goals.

Sam reassigned her administrative duties to others who had no knowledge of how to get them accomplished. They would then find Vann and inform her that Sam wanted her to handle these responsibilities. She often found herself in a conflicting position since she also had other clerical assignments to complete. She was still receiving calls from longtime customers she had dealt with for years as Cy's assistant; however, she was advised to forward such calls to Sam who, she quickly found, had no skill in customer relations and could not give the clients the service they had grown accustomed to. The firm was soon bombarded with disgruntled customers with no place to voice their complaints.

When Cyrus found out what was happening, he told her to resign. His advice sounded enticing, and Lord knows she was tired, but she had concerns that the amount of her monthly pension would be inadequate to cover her living expenses, and she was too young to receive social security. Even though the negative environment was pulling her down spiritually, emotionally, and physically, the prospect of looking for a new job filled her with dread.

She had managed, by the grace of God, to stay almost a year after Cy left. But after much thought and prayer, along with figuring and refiguring all the different 'what if' scenarios of her finances, she decided to retire. She had a nice bank account, had money saved in a 401K account, and she owned a healthy investment portfolio, as well as several pieces of valuable property. So where was her faith in God? Surely God would meet her needs! "Okay Lord, I hear You," she finally said.

The decision felt good, and peaceful. An enormous burden had been lifted from her shoulders.

And now here she was, in the midst of this crowd, celebrating a new start along the journey of life, confident that God was with her. Even now, she needed His help in fending off questions from inquiring minds wanting to know why and how she was retiring.

She was immediately tested as a question rudely brought her back to the present. "What are you going to do with yourself, girl? How are you planning to make it on just a pension check? I know you're not old enough to be drawing social security. You have another job lined up? Oh, you must have a lot of money saved up, huh?"

The questions came from Sister Coffner, who was not particularly one of her favorite people. Vann knew she was not only nosy, but a big gossip as well. *Patience, come forth, please!*

"You retiring on disability or something?" Sister 'Nosy' continued. "You know it's going to be a whole lot of years before you'll be drawing a social security check. Unless you're a lot older than you look. Just how old are you anyway, Vann? I never did know your age."

"*Okay!*" Vann whispered to Rubye who had walked up and stood next to her. "This is what happens when the entire church is invited to your celebration. You get the well-wishers, the curious, the hungry, and the nosy."

"You should have been ready for that," Rubye reminded her, speaking out of the side of her mouth.

Vann smiled at Rubye's words, as she said to Sister Coffner, "I'm old enough to be tired. I know you can understand that, can't you?"

"Oh yes! Chile, I know what you talking about for sure. Oh yes, I do."

"Excuse me," Rubye cut into the conversation. "We are getting ready to make presentations. Vann, you need to start toward the stage."

After their short, but productive meeting, Mitch Langford let his frat brother, Thomas, lure him to the reception of someone he didn't even know with the promise of some good food. He really liked Thomas and had enjoyed the meeting with his frat brothers, most of whom he already knew. He had learned through some of Thomas' comments that he was a Christian brother, and Mitch knew he needed to be in the presence of a strong Christian because he had let his life get into a pitiful condition.

He filled a plate and found a seat at a table in the back of the room, planning to eat and run. He was halfway through his food and thinking about visiting the desert table, when he heard someone at the microphone asking those scheduled to make presentations to the honoree to please come forward. He watched several people climb onto the stage and was glad he didn't have to stay to hear any long-drawn-out speeches. Thomas had told him it was only a two-hour event, but from the looks of things, it was going to be much longer.

He nearly dropped his fork when he heard, "Now, we need our honoree for the evening to make her way up here. Ms. Vann Sinclair! You need to come this way!"

Can't be! Mitch thought. But sure enough, the lady who hadn't been far from his thoughts over the last twenty-four hours walked onto the stage. *Thank You, Father.* He forgot all about eating and sat back to listen, because he knew he was going to learn more about the woman he was so intrigued with.

Sam Riland was brief and to the point. He thanked Vann for her years of faithful service to the company and handed her a certificate, along with a small wrapped package, that Vann knew was a watch with the company logo, which was the usual parting gift. Two clients she had formed a relationship with spoke, followed by someone from Child Advocates and a representative from the Christian television station where she also volunteered. She was able to smile through them all until her pastor, then Cyrus and his wife, took the podium. That was when she lost a valiant battle with the tears that swelled up and overflowed.

"I'm Rick Travis, Vann Sinclair's pastor. When I became pastor of the church about twelve years ago, I looked around for some unique and special people that I could depend on to pray and help me stay on the right path. God led me to select Sister Vann as one of these people to become one of my personal prayer warriors. Every Tuesday night, my office is turned into a spiritual war room, as Sister Vann and eleven other people gather there with me to do some spiritual warfare. Sister Vann Sinclair is a mighty prayer warrior.

"But she's also an encourager. I can call Sister Vann anytime, and she'll have an encouraging word from the Word of God that I need to hear. Additionally, she's a wonderful teacher of the Word. I almost caused a riot a couple of years ago, when I asked her to teach a single women's class. That meant she had to leave the class she was already assigned to teach, and they didn't take it well. But I needed her wisdom and her example of what a Christian woman should be, as well as her ability to pass this insight on to the single women of the church. You see, I truly believe that if we can flood the world with godly women who are strong in the Word of God and living to honor Him, we'll see more men coming to the Lord. I am seeing that slowly happening. And I have to keep looking for a larger room for her class, because more and more women, including many married ones, are crowding into her class to sit under her teaching. She is an exceptional woman of God, and she can make some slamming sweet potato pies, too." He paused as the audience laughed loudly.

"I am happy to see such a great woman of God honored in this way, and I can't wait to see what God has in His plan for Sister Vann's future. I just hope she'll keep our church on her list of things to do. God bless you, Sister."

There was loud applause, as Vann smiled through her tears. She knew her turn at the podium was coming soon.

Cyrus walked slowly to the podium, accompanied by his wife, Sylvia, and spoke in his slow, methodical way. "My wife and I never had any children of our own, and Vann is like a daughter to us. She has been a model employee. She's loyal, conscientious, dependable...," he paused to wipe his eyes. "She's loving, hardworking, and goes above and beyond in ways that are not in her job description.

"I'm not ashamed to admit that over the years, she's been my spiritual advisor. I'd see her reading the Bible before she started work every day, and I'd often jokingly ask what she found that was so interesting in that 'book'. I don't mind telling you that she's helped me make some decisions that led to my personal and business growth. One of the few things we always disagreed about was Vann's penchant for wanting to help everyone. It was not unusual for her to bring me a file and ask me to give someone another chance. And it usually worked out well. But she was also just as quick to come back and let me know if she discovered she had made a mistake. I appreciate that kind of integrity and over the years, every time she talked about leaving, I made it worth her while to stay.

"These are tears of joy I'm shedding because Vann deserves this kind of celebration," Cy paused, as he looked around the room, "and I'm so glad you all came to share it with her." He wiped his eyes again. "Vann, I want you to know how much we love and appreciate you. And I'll still be looking for my pie every week just like the pastor." He waited as Vann walked up to the podium and handed her an envelope. "Congratulations!" he said, as he and Sylvia hugged her.

Vann had to take a minute to collect herself before she could speak. "Thank you. I've been sitting there wondering who these people were talking about," she said to much chuckling. "The door is closing on what has been a large and very significant portion of my life. I've heard many comments and questions this evening on why I decided to retire. Well, the main reason is that I'm old and tired." The audience laughed again. "But I want to share something with you that might satisfy your curiosity, or if doesn't, take it up with the Lord.

"There is a passage of scripture in 1 Kings chapter 17 that tells of an experience a man named Elijah had. In that passage, God told Elijah to go and dwell by a brook. Then God commanded the ravens to bring him food in the morning and food in the evening, and of course he had the water from the brook to drink. All his needs were supplied because he was at the place God wanted him to be. But after a while, the brook dried up because it didn't rain and the ravens stopped coming with food. God told Elijah to go to another place where He had already made arrangements for him to be sustained. Now, had Elijah been disobedient and remained at that brook, praying for rain and for the ravens to come by with some food, he would probably have died of hunger and thirst. You see, our blessing is in obedience to God and His appointed place for us."

Applause at her words broke out, as well as many 'Amens', 'Praise the Lord', and 'Thank You Jesus.'

"Well, I believe my brook dried up at Welch Mortgaging. I also believe that God has already made arrangements to sustain me in other ways. But I must be obedient and follow the path He's leading me on."

Amens resonated around the room again, and Sister Hairston stood and yelled loudly, "You talk, Sister. You sho' 'nuff right!"

Vann smiled, wiped her eyes and continued. "At certain points in life, God sends us the message that it is time to move on, and for those of us who are hard of hearing, He causes things to start drying up around us, just so we get the message. So I solicit your prayers as I make this transition into a new year and a new life. I thank each and every one of you for coming and sharing this occasion with me, and for all the kindnesses that have been extended to me. May God bless you all. Thank you!"

Vann was again swamped by people wanting to wish her well, and she was graciously trying to speak to everyone, when she saw her friends discreetly removing some of the decorations as they prepared to leave for the private celebration planned after this one. Rubye's husband, Thomas, rushed up to her, interrupting someone trying to congratulate her. "Vann Jo, give me the keys to your car so we can load all of your gifts."

"Oh, thank you, Thomas," she said, searching through her small handbag for the key and valet parking ticket.

When she looked up to hand Thomas her keys, she noticed TreVann and another man beside him. At first, the identity of the other man didn't register, but when it did, her mouth fell open. Standing before her was that hateful judge. *Oh Lord, why is he here?* The thought rushed through her mind, as her heart started a double beat.

"Congratulations, Ms. Vann Sinclair," the judge said in his deep voice.

Her mouth was still hanging open as TreVann stepped closer to give her another hug. "Auntie, I am so proud of you!" He told her in an emotional voice. "I'm going to load what will fit in my car and take it home," he said. She knew TreVann drove a BMW two-seater, so not much was going to fit.

"Okay, sweetie, if you're going straight home." She struggled to recapture her runaway thoughts. "Otherwise, I'd better take it." She didn't dare look at the judge.

"I'm going straight home," he said with a smile. "It's been a long day, and I'm beat."

"Come on, guys! Let's get this done," Thomas called to them as he hurried away.

"I'm glad I know how to find you, Vann Sinclair," Mitch said softly before he turned and left.

Vann's mouth was hanging open again.

An hour later, at another celebration with some of her closest friends, Vann was still hyped. She hadn't eaten a thing at the hotel, so she was also hungry. She sat quietly and half listened as the others made comments about the earlier reception.

They were in a small private room at an upscale bistro that was managed by her friend Katherine's husband. When Vann arrived, she found the room filled with balloons and decorations her friends had confiscated from the hotel ballroom, and spotted another pile of gifts on a small table, waiting to be opened after they finished eating.

"The reception was very nice, and I think everyone made very nice comments about Vann," Estelle said, after placing her order. "I wasn't planning to eat anything at the hotel because I knew I would be eating here, but that food looked so good that I had to get a taste of it." Estelle was only about 5 feet and always fighting a battle with her weight.

"Me too." Katherine, also a little overweight, agreed. But I'm ready for some of my favorites that they serve here. You know, I never thought I'd see old man Cyrus crying, but Lord have mercy, he just boohooed. That man has always been crazy about Vann...and his wife is too. I thought it was sweet how she just stood there smiling and letting Cy do all the talking."

Vann smiled, knowing it was usually the other way around, and Cyrus was the one who couldn't get a word in edgewise. Her eyes moved from one to the other as the other five women around the table discussed her reception, and she silently thanked God for giving her good friends like these.

Vann, Rubye, and Estelle had been friends since their freshman year at Texas Southern University. Rubye and Estelle had both grown up in Houston, although they were from different areas of the large sprawling city, and were the first friends Vann made in Houston after she moved from Georgia to attend Texas Southern University. Their friendship had strengthened over the years, and they were her best and most loyal friends and confidants. Roxanne and Katherine were coworkers and had been her closest friends on the job. However, unlike Rubye and Estelle, they were not privy to a lot of Vann's most personal information, because though she loved them, she had found out they were not as discreet as Rubye and Estelle.

And Annette...well, Vann didn't know a lot about the latest addition to the group who had joined Vann's church a few months ago and had literally latched onto Vann for some inexplicable reason. The other ladies had also tried to figure out what Annette was about. It was obvious she was determined to be wherever Vann was, so they accepted her because Vann did.

With the exception of Annette, the women around the table had been doing things as a group for years and had shared many of the joys and sorrows that life inevitably delivered.

Katherine and Roxanne, who worked in the Human Resources department at Welch Mortgaging and Title Company, admitted they couldn't help feeling a little envious that Vann was retiring and leaving them behind, even though they understood why she had decided to leave. They knew the pension and benefit plans provided by the job, and had a good idea of the dollar amount of every benefit Vann would have.

However, they wondered if it would be enough for Vann to maintain her beautiful home and pay for that new SUV she had just bought. They loved Vann, valued her friendship, and certainly wished her well, but their curiosity was about to send good judgment out of the window.

"Vann, I know you have to have some idea about how you're going to make it financially," Katherine remarked as she cut into a spicy chicken dish. "I know you were tired of dealing with that mess, and you said you're not going to look for another job. You know there are all kinds of rumors floating around at work about it. So, have you been keeping us in the dark about the 'old geezer' and you're getting ready to get hitched up with him?" She said it jokingly, but her expression was of the seriously seeking variety.

"Girl, please! If I were planning something like that, y'all would know to take me on to a padded room and lock me up," Vann answered, laughingly. The group had a running joke about the man they called the 'old geezer' who sneakily tried to date Vann, since he was snobbish and considered her to be beneath his social status.

Roxanne, the most outspoken one in the group, was more direct. "Some people are saying that old man Cyrus is probably going to take care of you, just like he always has. I don't know about that, but honestly, Vann, I do know I wouldn't have let those jerks run me off my job until I was ready to go."

"Huh! Me neither!" Annette said, huffily. "Nobody's running me off from any place I want to be." *Not until I'm ready,* she thought, as her reason for attaching herself to Vann flashed through her mind.

"Well…" Vann hesitated as she sought an answer that would tactfully, but effectively banish any further digging into her private matters. "You know, God has been good. I've worked very hard, and y'all know I don't waste a lot of money, and will squeeze every penny until it hollers. I hunt for sales and bargains, make most of my clothes, and do my own hair and nails. So I won't have a problem surviving with God's help." She paused for a minute and looked around the table before continuing.

"The way I see it, you either sacrifice on the front end or the back end. I've sacrificed on the front end so that my back end would be easier."

"But really, Vann!" Roxanne pressed. "Aren't you tired of having to sacrifice? Wouldn't you like to walk into a store and buy a beautiful outfit rather than having to make it yourself? And what about treating yourself to a salon visit every now and then? I think everyone should be able to treat themselves occasionally. Are you taking your 401k account out?" She fished nosily.

Rubye and Estelle exchanged annoyed looks.

"Roxanne," Rubye said, struggling to hold her irritation in check. "You're getting mighty personal with the questions. I know shopping and going to the salon every week are important to you (Roxanne always looked as if she stepped off the page of a fashion magazine), but if I could sew as beautifully as Vann can, I wouldn't be in those stores either. And I don't have to even mention her hair. I would love to be able to just run a brush through my hair every day and have it look that good."

"Oooh! I would die for hair like hers!" Annette put in. "Some people just have all the luck," she said, looking with envy at the thick loose curls that were pulled back and cascading down Vann's back. In fact, she felt Vann had too much good luck—and not just with her hair, but in everything. Not only did she have an abundance of material possessions, but she also had love and respect from others. Annette recalled the beautiful reception they had just left, and tossed a look at the table piled high with gifts and a stab of jealousy hit her. Never in her life had she been the recipient of so much love. She struggled to keep her disparaging thoughts from showing on her face.

"Roxie, how do you know I haven't always been able to walk into any store in Houston and buy whatever I want? The same goes for the salon. I just don't like sitting there for hours when I can easily do my own hair. At any rate, let me worry about that, okay?"

"Watch out!" Estelle, who owned several beauty salons, yelled. "Don't judge all salons by your limited experiences," she said, tapping Vann playfully on her hand, before letting her eyes rest briefly on the other women. "As Vann's friends, we're here to celebrate her victory, not sit here trying to rain on her parade by digging into her business."

"You are absolutely right, Stelle!" Rubye vehemently added. "And you know what, Roxie?" Rubye was still stinging from the comment about Vann letting people from the job run her off. "Nobody is running Vann off of that job. Didn't you hear her say that she knows it's time to leave, and believe me, they'll miss her before she misses them."

"Wait a minute!" Vann stretched her hands out to both sides. "Let's pray before this goes any further. I'm not going to let the devil get in and destroy this victory." She bowed her head and began praying.

"Heavenly Father, we come in the name of Jesus this evening thanking You and praising You, because we know that You are worthy above all else to receive the glory and honor. We acknowledge, Father, that we have sinned and come short of Your glory, and we ask for Your forgiveness right now. And Father, we thank You that You are faithful to forgive us and cleanse us from all unrighteousness.

"Father, I can't thank You enough for this wonderful victory, and as we celebrate that victory tonight, Lord, I invite Your presence and peace around this table. Yes, Father, fill each of us with Your precious Holy Spirit, and let us not lose sight of Your love, grace, and mercy. Lord, let us do nothing but worship You and celebrate Your goodness around this table tonight, realizing that You are the source of every victory, and every good and perfect gift. Bless this food, and this fellowship, dear God. In the name of Jesus, we pray. Amen."

Roxie's head dropped into her hands, as the tears that had formed as Vann prayed slid down her face. "I'm so sorry, Vann. I don't know why I let the devil get in like that." She rambled in her purse for a Kleenex and handed one to Katherine who was also crying.

"You're so right, Vann, and I hope you'll forgive us," Katherine said, softly. "The pastor was right. You always know what to do and how to do it to pull us back on the right path when we wander off into the wilderness. So let's get on with this celebration."

In an emotionally filled voice, Vann said, "Ladies, some of my greatest joys in life have been the times I've shared with you all. We've shared many victories as well as sorrows." She looked at each one as she began recalling some of those things. "When Estelle had a heart attack; when Katherine's twin sons graduated from the navel academy; when Roxie went through major surgery; when we went on the cruise together; when we got together and prayed after we heard the place where Rubye and Thomas were living in the Middle East had been bombed and we couldn't get in touch with them; when Rubye's son, TreVann, who is really my son—Rubye just had him for me," she laughed—"honored me in such a beautiful way on my birthday a few years ago. These and other things were significant events in our lives where joys were increased, and burdens were made easier to bear because they were shared.

"Now, y'all know I'm not saying this just because I happen to be in the spotlight this time, but we've been through too much together and we're too old—both chronologically and spiritually—to let the devil steal this victory."

With the exception of Annette, tears were flowing down all of their faces. "Y'all, God... has... been... so good... to all of us!" Rubye said, weeping openly. "I am so thankful to God for keeping us together over the years."

"Me too, Ruybe," Vann stated. "Let me just say this, because as my friends, I think you should know my thoughts about this transition." She took a deep breath. "I'm just simply changing lanes so I can do things my own way. I've worked hard all my life for other people, and I want to spend the years I have left doing something I enjoy on my own terms. I have prayed to see this day, and I am so thankful to God for answering those prayers."

Annette, who had been quiet through all the emotion, spoke up. "Well, I know I'm the new kid on the block, but I appreciate being here and hearing about some of the things you guys have shared. I hope I get to share some of those things with you all in the future." But inside she was thinking, *Corny, boring and depressing. I'd cry too if nothing more exciting happened to me. Sure hope I'm not wasting my time, but I know the type of men who are attracted to these dull women are the ones with the money, who I can easily manipulate.*

Vann didn't know how to take Annette's comments. Shortly after she joined the church, Annette had attached herself to Vann, and no matter how hard Vann had tried to shake her, the woman held on tightly. She joined every ministry that Vann participated in, always wanted to go out to eat with her, and was in the habit of showing up uninvited at Vann's house. Vann tried to be a friend to her because it just wasn't in her nature to be unkind to others, but Annette made it difficult by being so pushy.

"Vann, I offer you my best wishes for many happy years of doing whatever the heck you feel like doing. I say, 'you go, girl'!" Estelle lifted her glass of iced tea toward Vann in a salute, and the others followed suit.

"Amen to that!" Rubye said. "So please, Vann, do yourself a favor and take off six months or a year to just rest, relax and enjoy yourself. God knows you deserve it. I know that's what I'm going to do when my day comes."

"That is most definitely in the plan," Vann answered with a smile. "But one thing I've found out about life is that even the best laid plans will find a way to get messed up. I'll probably just play it by ear for a while."

"Well, lock your doors and make good use of your caller I.D. because you do know that people are going to be hunting you down," Rubye laughingly told her.

Vann looked around the table with a smile. "The really great thing is that I now have options. The only thing I know I'm definitely going to do now is go to Georgia to see Mama. She's not getting any younger, and I'm going to start spending more time with her now that I can. And another thing I plan to do is go down to my beach house more often. As a matter of fact, girls, we need to plan a get-away down there sometime soon."

"Count me in!" Roxanne quickly said. "And I ain't even gon' ask about your sugar daddy paying for that house." They all laughed because every time they went to the beach house, Roxanne tried to find out if it belonged to Vann's sugar daddy.

"The only thing we need to be concerned about is whether she'll continue sharing that place with us," Estelle said. "Anything beyond that is in the category of 'mind your own business'. But if she does have a sugar daddy, I gotta tell you, I hope he has a friend," she laughed, "because I'm certainly looking for one." Estelle was in the middle of a nasty separation from her husband of over thirty years.

"Just let me know when!" Katherine stated. It was a known fact that she was always looking for ways to get away from the husband she claimed to be thoroughly sick of.

"Well, all I want to know is, what beach house? And why am I just now hearing about it?" Annette asked, huffily. Annette had a personal agenda. After learning that there were several well-to-do widowers at their church, Annette had joined, determined that one of them would become her next husband. While fluttering around two of the well-known widowers one Sunday, hoping to get their attention, Annette overheard them discussing Vann. When Elliott Shaw, the one they called the 'old geezer', stated his intentions to pursue Vann, Annette had decided to stick close to Vann. Who knew what opportunity would arise by being in the right place at the right time? Sister Sinclair wouldn't be making too many moves without her, Annette had resolved. She desperately wanted to marry a high echelon man, and Vann might be the avenue to accomplish that, whether she knew it or not.

"Annette, you hadn't heard about it because you haven't been around when we've gone before," Vann answered, now realizing her mistake. She regretted saying anything about the beach house in front of Annette, since she couldn't invite her because there was no more sleeping space for an extra guest. She would have to explain all that to her when the time came.

"Where is this beach house anyway?" Annette asked, thinking of all the times she and Vann had spent together recently. Annette knew if she owned a beach house, she would have brought it up at some point.

"In Galveston," Vann answered shortly, hoping to end the discussion.

"And when are we going?" Annette wanted to know.

"Didn't you just hear her say her only definite plan right now is to go to Georgia to see her mama?" Rubye answered with impatience. Rubye had little patience for Annette, and didn't trust her. As far as she was concerned, something didn't add up and she had told Vann more than once to watch her back with the woman.

"Oh well, then I think I'll tag along on your trip to Georgia, Vann. I've never been there, and I always love traveling to new places. How long are you planning to stay?" Annette asked. *She probably has something else there that I need to know about,* she thought.

Katherine jumped in to answer this time. "Now, Annette, don't you know to wait for an invitation? It's simply not good manners to invite yourself. You're way old enough to know that."

"Sorry, Annette," Vann said, shaking her head. "My trips to Georgia are filled with taking care of things for my mama and spending time visiting with her." Vann's grandmother, who she called 'Mama' after her mother rejected and abandoned her, was the most important person in Vann's life, and she did whatever she could to make her life comfortable.

Vann quickly changed the subject. "Well! I am ready to enjoy my food without all this conversation, and then open my gifts."

It was late when Vann got home that night, and she was happy to see that TreVann was already home and in bed. Her gifts from the hotel were stacked on the dinning room table, and although tempted, she decided to wait until she was rested before unloading the others and opening them. She reflected on the events of the day and thanked God for His goodness. But something was disturbing her spirit. "What is it, Lord?" she asked, seeking to identify the source.

She knew she was a little apprehensive about the big change in her life. After all, she was stepping onto a new path into unfamiliar territory. But she knew she wasn't stepping out alone, because God was with her. So what was bothering her?

As she prepared for bed, she prayed and pondered until the reason for her apprehension crawled out from its hiding place. The hateful judge's face floated before her. "Uh, uh, uh!" she said with distaste. She had pushed his presence at her reception to the recesses of her mind so she wouldn't have to deal with it earlier. But now it stood front and center, demanding attention. How had he even known about the reception? Why had he come? What had he meant when he said he now knew how to find her? A vision of being handcuffed and taken off to jail for contempt flashed through her mind. But something unimaginable also floated into her mind. That judge was the first man to make her heart flutter in a very long time. And that scared her.

chapter three

A few days later, Vann flew to Georgia to spend the Christmas holidays with Mama, with plans to remain until after the first of the New Year. She fought off arguments that she should move back to Georgia, knowing the house was already too full of women. Beside Mama and great-aunt, Rachel—sisters who were both in their nineties,—her great-aunt's daughter, now well into her seventies, also lived there.

After getting a good look at Mama she was troubled. Although just as feisty in spirit, Vann noticed alarming signs of physical deterioration. Vann recalled in the past how Mama had always been up and doing something in or around the house. She had only recently given up raising her own chickens and planting a vegetable garden. Now she moved only when necessary, and then very slowly.

While there, Vann enjoyed sitting on the front part of the wrap around porch where she had a view of the fields across the road where the neighbors grew corn, peas, and tomatoes during the summer months. If she tired of that view, she could move to the back porch where she had a view of the open meadow that stretched for miles. The house sat on a hill and the panoramic view of the countryside with its lush greenery, and cows and horses grazing lazily, always filled her with peace and love for God's creation. On cold days, she relaxed on the glass enclosed sun porch on the side of the house and listened to the outrageous stories about the old ladies' youthful escapades. Although these women had been strong disciplinarians during Vann's childhood, they had now turned into old age children whose minds spent more time in the past than in the present.

"In my courtin' days, I was a pistol!" Aunt Rachel declared one day. "Chile, any man I wanted, I could get. One time, this other girl tried to beat my time with a fella by calling me out to show him she could whip me. I tell you, by the time I got through with her, that heifer didn't have a strand of hair nowhere on her head! Naw! You just didn't mess with Rachel. Tell her, Becky."

"Um hmmh!" Mama quickly backed up her sister's words, then added, "Well, I wasn't no slouch myself. Rachel, 'member that time my husband thought he was going to play around on me? Well, he came home one night after he'd been out...you know...anyhow, he woke up over in the night thinking that the part of his body that he'd been out catering to was on fire!"

Vann hollered with outrage and laughter, as thoughts of her loving Papa came to mind.

"Mama! No, you didn't!"

"Oh yes, I did! He jumped up and shot out of the house like lighting, and headed straight for that old water well we had in the backyard. Kinda scared me then, cause I thought he was about to jump in. But he had sense enough to go to the big water barrel we kept out there to catch rain water and jumped in that. He was screaming louder than any woman I ever heard."

Tears of laughter were streaming down Vann's face. "What happened?" she asked, wiping at her eyes, and imagining the worst.

"Nothing." Mama answered succinctly. "It wasn't nothing that caused no permanent damage. But he didn't never think about doing that again, I'll tell you! I told him if he did, it wouldn't be no need for him to ever worry about it 'cause I was gonna fix it so he wouldn't be no use to nobody."

"Mama! You did that to Papa? I don't believe I'm hearing this. You both were terrible!" Vann wiped at the tears. "Tell me more!"

In their old age, the women, whose minds were still as sharp as tacks, had lost all constraint and decorum. Whatever came up, came out. Colorful stories about boyfriends, husbands, and rivals, most of whom had been dead twenty or thirty years, were recalled and talked about in a way that seemed to bring them just as much joy to hear as to tell.

Then there were the ghost stories that even in her adulthood, had the power to chill Vann's blood. Ghost stories were plentiful in the South, and during her childhood, wherever people gathered at night, it was inevitable that ghost stories would be told as a pastime and form of entertainment. Whether it was on a cold night, while they were sitting around a hot wood burning stove, or on a summer night sitting on the porch, trying to catch a cool breeze, the story tellers would pull stories from a seemingly unending imaginative arsenal and soon have others laughing or shivering from fear. They had a natural flair for telling the stories in such a dramatic and truthful way that they sounded real, with many declaring they were. Whether they were real or not, they scared the heck out of children and adults alike.

Sometimes, Vann had to calm herself by remembering her Papa's assurance that ghosts didn't have the power to hurt you, but they could sure enough make you hurt yourself.

While she was visiting, Vann hired someone to come in and take care of some needed repairs around the house, paid the telephone and other utility bills up for several months, and stocked the freezer and pantry, to make sure Mama didn't have to worry about anything. Years ago, she had bought the house and surrounding acreage from the family estate to assure that Mama would always have a place to live without hassles from someone else in the family trying to stake claim to it.

❖ ❖ ❖

"Dad, can we please go to the Kids Zone and play some games? We haven't done that in a while. Please, please, please," Mitch's nine-year-old son, Matthew, begged.

They were just leaving Thomas' house after another meeting on the fraternity benefit event.

"Now, son, you've had a great time playing with the other kids here, and I thought you wanted to go see that new movie. We can't do both, because then you'll be too tired to go to the golf course in the morning. Right?"

"Oh, okay I guess." Matthew was quiet for a few minutes, thinking hard. He proudly looked at the new watch his dad had bought him that morning which featured one of his favorite cartoon characters. "But Dad, after the movie, there'll still be time to do something, 'cause it won't even be dark. Do we have to go home?" he persisted.

Trying to hide his exasperation, Mitch spoke calmly. "Matt, what did I just say? We've already had a busy day, and it's not over yet. I tell you what—we can go to Kids Zone after the movie if that's what you want to do. But that means golf is out in the morning. If you're up late tonight, by the time you wake up tomorrow and get packed and ready and we go some-place to eat, it'll be time for you to go home. Now, what's it going to be?"

After a slight pause, Matt answered in a dejected voice, "Golf, I guess."

Mitch sighed with relief. He was enjoying teaching Matt how to play golf and had even bought him his own set of golf clubs and gave him a Tiger Woods video. And the kid was pretty good, even if he had to say so himself.

Helping Matt into the car, he looked back at Thomas and Rubye's house and felt a twinge of disappointment. He had hoped that on the off-chance he would run into Vann Sinclair there. He had mentioned to Thomas that he had met Vann

Sinclair, but didn't go into the circumstances of that meeting. For some reason, he feared it might hurt his chances to really meet and get to know her. He knew she and Rubye were very good friends, and although tempted, he resisted the urge to ask Rubye anything about Vann.

The most encouraging thing was that he believed the Lord was working on answering his prayers. The very fact that he was getting to know Vann Sinclair's friends was reassuring.

He was already convinced after their courthouse encounter that Vann was a woman he wanted to know,, but after observing her at that reception and hearing all the wonderful things people said about her and after hearing her inspiring speech about God's faithfulness, he was anxious for it to happen. He knew, however, that he would wait on the Lord and trust Him to bring them together.

Mitch drove straight to the movie theatre, where he and Matt visited the refreshment stand before taking their seats. He wasn't looking forward to sitting through a kiddie movie, but that was okay. He knew his son would enjoy it. He was supposed to have Matt two weekends a month and some holidays, but Matt's mother, Katrina, rarely followed the schedule. He tried not to let it aggravate him because he loved having Matt whenever he could. During the summer months, they took drives to different parts of Texas, mostly to places that had lots of activities for children, which he tried to make educational as well as fun for Matt.

Katrina had tried to invite herself along on some of those trips, but he had been firm in his refusal. The fact that he had messed up and had a child with her without benefit of marriage only gave fuel to Katrina's persistent hope that they would have a future together. He'd been telling her for years that marriage would only add to the mistakes they had already made. He truly felt they were opposites when it came to beliefs and values, although he didn't discover that until after Matt was on the way. That was when he'd found out that if Katrina believed in God at all, she certainly didn't believe in living a Christian lifestyle. He loved his son, but regretted his sinful actions with Katrina that had produced a child. His guilt over that, as well as his refusal to marry her caused him a lot of anguish, and made him go overboard with the time and money he provided toward Matt's well-being.

But Mitch still had a strong desire to find and build a life with the right woman. And as he sat in the darkened movie theatre, his mind replayed everything he had observed and heard about Vann Sinclair.

chapter four

Vann returned home from Georgia the second week in January, ready to get on with the life called *retirement*. For the next few weeks, she did nothing but relax and read the Christian novels stacked up on her nightstand. It was a hard choice trying to decide which one to read first. Would it be *Forgivin' Ain't Forgettin'* by Mata Elliott; *Good to Me* by LaTonya Mason, *Soul Matters* by Yolanda Sanders, *Like Sheep Gone Astray* by Leslie Sherrod, or *What a Sister Should Do* by Tiffany Warren? She had been assured by the women in her class that they were all good reads, and very inspiring. She closed her eyes, grabbed one, and started reading. Her eyes were suffering from fatigue brought on by almost nonstop reading when she laid the last book down. Her voice mail was full, and she was tired of the frozen dinners she had been living on, but she was enjoying herself.

"Wow!" she told Rubye and Estelle. "Y'all have got to read those books so we can get together and discuss those stories."

She had enjoyed a nice hiatus, but when the first Sunday in February arrived, Vann was ready to get back into worship services and her Sunday school class. However, she put off returning to the Christian television station where she volunteered as a prayer counselor and the Child Advocates Agency where they were already trying to assign a new family to her. She decided to take a few more weeks off, just to relax and take her time dealing with some of her own affairs, which needed attention.

In addition to the house she lived in, Vann owned eleven others—some multi-units—that she leased out for sums above the mortgages. It was a nice supplementary income, which she usually put into a savings account for maintenance and emergency needs.

Although she had a management company who collected rent and maintained the properties, she planned to start keeping a closer eye on everything because she would have to determine if she needed to use any of the rental income to supplement her pension. Or she might decide to sell one or two of the properties. If she added the profits from the sale to the large retirement gift Cyrus and Sylvia had given her, she could probably pay off the mortgage on the home she lived in. It was a decision she would make after she saw how things went financially.

She planned to put all of her financial information on the computer to make it easier to keep track of everything. She was also eager to do some work on her house, even if she only painted a room.

Since returning from Georgia, Vann had taken the time to visit Cy and Sylvia a few times to check on them and arrange doctor and other appointments for them. She would always come bearing one of her mouthwatering sweet potato pies, which they loved but had absolutely no business eating. Whatever the reason for the visit, they would always slip a large check into her hands before she left, telling her how much they appreciated her love and care for them. They knew she didn't do it for the money, and this made them appreciate her all the more.

But before Vann could settle into a comfortable routine, her plans quickly went awry as people realized she was back in circulation. It began with an early morning telephone call the second week in February, that came before 7 A.M.

"Sister Vann, this is Sister Coffner. I hate to call so early, but I was trying to catch you before you got busy. You know I talked to you about helping out in the church pantry."

"Yes, Sister Coffner, I remember," Vann said, trying to get her eyes open to look at the clock. She groaned when she saw the time. "Oh how quickly we forget," she mumbled to herself, thinking that just a few weeks ago, she would have already been on her way to work. "But Sister Coffner, I think I told you I would help out when I could."

"Now, chile, you know I can't sit back waiting on you to decide when you gon' come. I need to put you on a schedule, so I'll know when you're coming. You a business woman...you know that's the way it s'pose to go."

Vann was wide awake now. "Sister Coffner, you caught me at a bad time. I haven't had my cup of coffee yet, and my brain is not working. So I'm going to have to call you back on that."

"You sho' you gon' call me back? 'Cause if you don't, you know I'll be calling you back. Well you go on and drank you some coffee and wake up. We'll be talkin' soon. Bye, now."

Vann struggled out of bed and stumbled into the kitchen to start a pot of coffee, realizing for the first time in her life that she might not be a morning person. "Now, Father, You know I don't mind helping out at the pantry. But I told her...! And Lord, why did that old woman have to call me this early in the morning?" she grumbled. For decades, she'd formed the habit of rising early and putting on a perky face and attitude because that's what she had to do. But now, visions of wringing Sister Coffner's neck flashed through her mind. "Oooh, Father! I know I need to pray!"

She was finishing her second cup of coffee and reading Genesis chapters 12 and 13 as her morning devotional. Points started jumping out that would be beneficial to her Sunday school class. She was about to grab pen and paper to develop an outline when the telephone interrupted her. "It's barely eight o'clock in the morning for goodness sake!"

"Vann? This is Aunt Lu. How you doing?" It was her biological mother's sister, and one of her favorite aunts.

"I'm fine, Aunt Lu. Is anything wrong?"

"No, nothing is wrong. I'm just calling you before you start running around. I sure do need some fresh vegetables and fruit from the Farmer's Market. I thought if you were going anywhere near there, you could pick some up for me."

"Aunt Lu, why are you calling so early? If some other person hadn't already called and woke me up a little while ago, I'd probably still be asleep. But yes, I'll go by the Farmer's Market for you. What do you want?" She scribbled the list of things her aunt needed and hung up. She tried to get back to her Bible study, but was interrupted a few minutes later by another call.

"Sister Vann, this is Sister Hairston. Baby, I sure would appreciate it if you could pick my medicine up for me today. My grandson was going to do it, but he has to work, and can't get to it. I told him that was alright. I knew you would do it for me, since you're a lady of leisure now."

Thirty minutes later, she was relieved the phone hadn't rung and finally had an outline for her Sunday school lesson. She was pleased when she reread the verses and her outline. The focus would come from Genesis chapter 13, verses 14 through 17: "The Lord said to Abram after Lot had parted from him, 'Lift up your eyes from where you are and look north and south, east and west. All the land that you see I will give to you and your offspring forever. I will make your offspring like the dust of the earth, so that if anyone could count the dust, then your offspring could be counted. Go, walk through the length and breadth of the land, for I am giving it to you.'" Vann's main point would be to not focus on your present condition, but to always look from where you are to see what the Lord has for you. She saw many other points in the passage that could be developed and would inspire a lively and beneficial discussion.

Before she could think about starting on the errands she had agreed to run, the phone rang again. "Sister Vann, this is your church calling," the church secretary's cheerful voice said. "I was wondering if you could help me out with the Women's Day programs this afternoon. Just a couple of hours I expect."

Before she could respond, the phone beeped to indicate another call coming through. She put the secretary on hold and answered.

"Good morning, Vann. First Lady Travis, calling. Vann, one of the speakers for our Women's Day program is flying in a few days early, and I need someone to pick her up from the airport. Are you available to do that for me? Her plane lands at two o'clock."

Vann hung up after saying yes, she would go to the airport. But before she could get back to the secretary, the phone beeped again. This time it was Sam Riland from Welch, needing to ask her something. She told him she would call him back, and finally got back to the secretary.

"It'll be late, but I'll be there to help you," she told her. It was barely eight o'clock and her day was full.

The next day was almost a carbon copy. This time it was Sam Riland, who she had failed to call back the day before, who woke her up at seven o'clock. He was calling her to find out where old records were archived. Evidently he had managed to run off everyone who would know, and no one there even knew the procedure that had to be followed to retrieve anything. She hurriedly told him and hung up.

"I'm going to monitor my calls today because yesterday was ridiculous," she resolved.

But she didn't. Child Advocates called and wanted her to meet the new family they had assigned to her, even though she had told them she didn't want another family right now but was willing to help out with other things. Aunt Bernie called to check in on her; thankfully, her calls were always short, sweet and to the point.

But her mama's call a little later wasn't. "Baby, I sure do miss you. When are you coming back home? No reason in the world for you not to come and spend more time here since you're not working."

Little did she know. "Mama, I told you, I can't just up and leave anytime. I still have things here to do. Now if you needed me there, you know I would be there."

"I know, baby. I know."

And just when she thought things were about to settle down, the television station's volunteer coordinator called, wanting to know if she could come in and work the prayer counseling phone lines because they were shorthanded.

The next day, as she sat at her computer trying to figure out the software she had bought to help manage her accounts, the phone rang, interrupting her. Vann looked at the caller I.D. and groaned. "The 'old geezer'. Lord, You know I really don't want to talk to him today." She picked up the phone and answered unenthusiastically. She knew he would keep calling until he got her.

"Hello, Sister Sinclair." The pleasant sounding voice said. "I wasn't sure I would catch you at home. I figured you would still be out celebrating your retirement."

Professor Elliott Shaw: retired Dean of Student Affairs, deacon, highly visible as a mover and shaker in community affairs, and widower of several years. He flaunted his self-proclaimed esteemed status like a banner, which he deftly used to exploit and take advantage of silly, desperate women. He had perfected his smooth, debonair, widower persona to an art form, and his main line when trying to really impress a woman was: "I'm looking for another good wife to live out my days with. I believe you could be that woman."

Elliott was in his sixties, still handsome, a snazzy dresser, and drove a big car. Admittedly, he appeared to be a good catch for any woman, and a particularly plum prize for a woman above fifty. But Vann had heard horror stories from several women who had been misled by Elliott, and she had been quick to pick up on his disparaging assessment of her.

Elliot Shaw was a part of the era in which teachers, especially college professors, were revered. With Ph.D. behind his name, he was accustomed to a certain amount of deference and respect from others, and truly believed his social status put him out of the reach of someone of Vann's class. He needed a society woman. Elliott put women into two categories. There were women for marrying—these included those who simply by virtue of who they were, increased his standing in the community—and then there were women for playing around with. His next wife would have it all—looks, class, sophistication, and the proper social status. In spite of her good looks, Elliott thought Savannah just didn't have it all.

"Elliott." Vann answered in a dry, unexcited tone, scolding herself for answering the phone. "I've been celebrating, that's for sure. God is so good. It's been wonderful to share my victory with all my family and friends. And I know you're not calling my house talking about my celebration when you didn't even show up."

"I told you I wouldn't be there," he told her arrogantly. "I don't agree with this decision to retire, Savannah. I think it indicates a lack of wisdom and foresight. You could have easily worked another five or ten years. Maybe by then you would've had a halfway decent pension and wouldn't have to scratch around to survive. Some folk just don't know how to pull themselves up out of the commonplace. As soon as they reach a certain level, they jump off the ladder."

"That's a condescending, small-minded attitude, don't you think?"

"In what way is that condescending and small-minded, sweetie? I'm just telling you the truth."

I need to hang up right now because this is not headed to a nice place, Vann thought. "Elliott, you've made your feelings about this apparent, first by your mistaken assumption that my decision to retire needed anyone's approval except my own, and by the fact that you think there's a rule about the correct time a person should retire, and finally by your refusal to come to my celebration because you disagree with my decision. All of this says to me that yours is a mind that refuses to think outside of the box."

"Now see…" he blustered.

"Furthermore, Elliott," she interrupted him. "Since I'm not going to be asking you for anything, you don't have to worry about me scratching to survive, do you?"

"I was merely…" Elliott tried again to get a word in but Vann was on a roll.

"And you know what, Elliott? If you're not calling to congratulate me, I don't have time for anything else you have to say. I'm too busy praising God for my victory to let the devil get in to destroy it."

"Wait a minute!" Elliott said hurriedly. "I know you're not trying to call me the devil!"

When she remained quiet, letting his question hang between them, he waded into a long and rambling explanation of why he felt the way he did.

Vann sighed, letting the phone hang in her hand while her mind meandered during his long-winded commentary. He was dangerously close to toppling her last nerve. "Why do I punish myself by even talking to this man?" she mumbled to herself, and wasn't surprised when the answer popped into her spirit. *I guess I keep hoping to get a word about the Lord into his pitiful thinking.*

Elliott. Vann's mind sauntered through the issues his calls never failed to awaken. Although he didn't have the depth to appreciate her as a strong Christian woman and only wanted to use her for his own selfish purposes, she had to acknowledge that she did have those days when she wished for what *could* have been. She closed her eyes and gave a brief nod, admitting to herself that when those bad days... those lonely and empty days...came along every now and then, Elliott Shaw didn't seem quite so bad. Perhaps that was the reason she put up with him the way she did. Because there were days when she looked back on her life and saw only failure and fruitlessness. Those were the days when being unmarried and childless made her want to run out and grab any bum off the street and rush to marry him just so she could be Mrs. 'Somebody'. Those were the days when she cried out to God for answers.

Elliott. His voice droned on, as her mind sought and tried to grasp the unthinkable fact that yes, there were days when putting up with Elliott's condescension and snobbery were preferable to being alone. Those were the days when Satan told her that Elliott was her last chance, so she'd better be jumping on him for all she was worth because there would be no one else. And tragically, those were the days when she wished she could be more of what he wanted in a wife, and that she...maybe...could be a little more accepting of his snobbishness and arrogance because after all, Elliott *was* a good catch...wasn't he?

Absolutely, positively no! no! no! She had seen too many women—men too—make the mistake of settling for a person they knew was not right for them, only to live in a constant state of misery and regret.

Elliott's words finally caught her attention and she tried to capture her wandering thoughts.

"...and I said all that to say that you just misunderstood what I was trying to say. See, you're always trying to put words in my mouth, thinking you understand who I am," he finished in a whining, offended tone.

"Oh really?" Vann asked quietly. "And exactly what words did I put into your mouth, Elliott? And believe it or not, I understand more about you than you give me credit for." Her bluntness caught Elliott off guard, causing him to hesitate a moment before continuing.

"You know what, Savannah? You have a real problem!" She could hear the anger ringing in his voice at her cool assessment. "You're totally out of touch with the real world. You need to come on down off of your high horse and face reality. You should be trying to catch every train coming your way, because you never know when it'll be your last chance."

That did it! The nerve he had been leaning on, crumbled, taking the last shred of her patience with it. "Elliott, I'm going to say this, and then I'm going to hang up because I'm trying very hard not to say anything rude, because Lord knows, what I need to be doing is praying for you. But let me give you a little reality check. If you *were* my last chance, what gives you the idea that I'd even want you? Furthermore, it's not your call as to what I need to do with my life, because nobody but God has that right. And let me give you a little advice. It wouldn't hurt for you to take a long look at yourself through the eyes of the Lord."

But Elliott had more in his arsenal. "Savannah, you're walking around with this 'holier than thou' attitude like you're not human like the rest of us. I've told you before, God knows we have physical needs, and there's nothing wrong with fulfilling those needs. God wouldn't have put Adam and Eve in the garden together and told them to be fruitful if He hadn't wanted men and women to get together."

"Well, now we get to the crux of the matter. You always manage to work the conversation around to that, don't you, Elliott? Well, like I said, it's time to end this conversation. Goodbye Elliott." She disconnected the line.

"I know, Lord. I'm just a glutton for punishment," she said, shaking her head.

chapter five

"Hey girl, what are you doing with yourself over there?" As busy as Rubye's catering business kept her, she always found time for regular telephone conversations or visits with Vann. Rubye was one of those people who decided at first meeting, whether they liked or disliked a person. If she didn't like you, it was best to stay out of her presence. If she did, there was nothing she wouldn't do for you. Rubye had liked Vann when they met decades ago and had grown to love her like the sister she never had.

Vann spent the next several minutes telling her about how busy she had been. "It's like everyone decided I'd had all the leisure time I needed, and started calling."

"It sounds like you might as well have a job to go to," Rubye replied. "If so, you can always help me out with the catering business."

Vann laughed. "You never give up do you? I have told you, I don't want to be messing with no food. I get enough of that dealing with Cy and Sylvia's occasional dinner parties, even though they pay me well."

"Well I hope you won't keep letting other people set your agenda. If you're going to work, then you sure ought to be getting paid for it. Don't you know people will use you up, then complain when you can't go anymore?"

"Yes, I'm starting to find that out. The only difference between now and before I retired is that I'm not being paid for waking up early every morning and running myself ragged. And girl, I've found out that I'm definitely not a morning person. I'm as grumpy as a sore-tailed cat the first thing in the morning."

Rubye laughed. "Vann, that's messed up! I know you want to do good and give some time to the Lord and helping others, but girl, you have to draw the line. It's not as if you've lived self-ishly up to this point. You've been giving of yourself all your life. Take some time for yourself. You don't have to answer that phone every time it rings, and you certainly don't have to say yes to everyone who calls. Just answer me this…what have you done that you really enjoy? There ought to be something that really satisfies you and makes you happy to be doing it. And when was the last time you had a date? Not with us girls, but with a man?"

"A date? What's a date? Girl, it's been so long, I hardly remember. The 'old geezer' is starting to look good, so you know it's been way too long."

"Oh Lord have mercy! Vann, please tell me you don't mean that!"

Vann laughed at the absurdity of her own statement and Rubye's response to it. "Just joking, girl. But to be honest, Rubye, I'm not too concerned about dating at this point in my life. Face it, girl, I'm old and set in my ways. I have a peaceful life and I'm reasonably content. I don't know if I want to give that up to deal with some old cantankerous coot. I get a little lonely sometimes, but I'm probably better off by myself."

"Oooh Lord, help her!" Rubye yelled into the phone. "Vann, age is a state of mind. And you're not content…girl, you're just in a rut. Just don't equate having a man in your life with losing your peace. If it's the right man, you can have both. God can bring the right man into your life and give you the ability to enjoy each other, even if He has to whip him into shape!" They laughed uproariously, with Rubye having the last and very potent word.

"Vann, remember that God is faithful and His mercies are new every morning. That's why it's always too soon to give up. God can do new things in places where we think there's no hope.

In the meantime, me and 'T' are gonna fix you up with someone you'll want to hold on *to* rather than run *from*."

Strangely, when Vann tried to conjure up the kind of man she could enjoy and be content with, the face that popped into her mind was that of the judge who had threatened to put her in jail. She shuddered and quickly blotted out the ridiculous vision.

After hanging up, Vann took stock of her life. Rubye's comments bothered her. Truthfully, she *was* in a rut, and maybe she *had* given up on God's desire to bring new life into old, hopeless places in her life. Yes, she decided, it was time for change in some areas of her life. Financially, she was doing okay, but not so well in other areas. She had not taken any time to renew her spirit, soul, and body, or to simply relax, reflect and plan. She was over her head in busy work, but how productive was she?

There *was* that feeling of discontent—so subtle she could hardly detect its presence, but strong enough that she knew something was not right.

A scripture came to her mind and she grabbed her Bible, turned to Isaiah 43:18–19, and began to read. "Forget the former things; do not dwell on the past. See, I am doing a new thing! Now it springs up; do you not perceive it? I am making a way in the desert and streams in the wasteland."

Vann meditated on the verses, reading them several times. Then she began to pray. "Father, thank You for the former things and for bringing me to this point in life. But now, Father, it's time to move on from the former things to the new things You have for me. The only thing is, I've been so busy that I've not taken the time to seek You and to perceive what new things You want to spring up in my life, or to look for the new streams that You want to flow into my life.

"I ask Your forgiveness for my ingratitude and thoughtless-ness as I consider the negative forces that have kept me in a comfortable rut of thinking and doing." Vann cringed as some of these things ran through her mind: past hurts, lack of courage to explore new possibilities, failure to pray for wisdom, lack of faith to expect more, failure to ask for more, fear of the unknown, unforgiveness, doubt, unbelief....

"Oh Father," she cried out. "No wonder I've settled for so little when Your plans are for so much more. So now, Lord, I seek You with my whole heart, and I thank You for Jeremiah 29:11 that tells me that Your plans are to prosper me and give me a hope and a future. I give You praise for what You are about to do in my life. In Jesus' holy name. Amen."

She wiped away the tears that had come from her self-examination, and knew she wouldn't be satisfied to remain in the rut any longer. Vann pulled out a tablet and wrote 'New Things' at the top of the page. Excitement and expectation filled her and she said, "Okay, Lord, send forth the new streams."

Immediately questions popped into her mind. What had she done to let herself get in the rut? Why had she remained there and what must she do to get out? She went on an extensive Bible study before she began writing.

When she looked back over her list, she was surprised at some of the things there. *Wow! This could get interesting,* she thought with a smile, as she considered what she had written— the characteristics of some of the notable women of the Bible. The wonderful attributes of the Proverbs 31 woman; the love, loyalty, and commitment of Ruth; the courage, favor of God, and faith of Esther; the bold leadership of Deborah; the wisdom of Lois and Eunice; the worship-filled prayer, praise, and faith of Hannah; the transformation of Rahab and her desire to become a part of the Lord's redemptive plan. They were all traits she needed as she went forward to explore what life had to offer from this point. "Father, let the characteristics of these women be developed, expanded, and appropriated in me as I go forth."

Her list also included some desires that had been buried in her heart for a very long time. But how was she to know there were things coming that she never imagined? Things that would test her quest for new things, bring deep anguish, and cause her to question God, herself, and the depth of her Christianity?

chapter six

Mitch always enjoyed his visits to home improvement centers. He would arrive with a carefully thought out list of things he needed, only to leave with a basket full of stuff he didn't need, but wanted.

Today wasn't any different. He had things in his basket that just seemed to leap off the shelves on their own and he still didn't have what he had come to get. He turned the basket into the paint aisle to look for the wood stain that was on his list and noticed a woman at the booth where they customized paint colors for customers. She and the man behind the counter were laughing as he mixed different colors of paint to get the color she wanted. She was giving him a hard time about some paint she was trying to match with a piece of cloth.

"I told you, it's the same color. You'll see when you get it on the wall," the guy told her. "If not, just bring it back."

"I don't want to have to bring it back," the woman responded. "I want you to get it right the first time." She told him with a smile.

The woman's appearance from the side, and the voice...that distinctive voice that was low, sultry, and provocative, with a breathless quality to it, and which caused all kinds of sensual thoughts to parade through his mind... reminded him of Vann Sinclair. *I have it bad for that woman if I'm starting to imagine I see and hear her in other women,* he thought. Trying to distract himself, he grabbed a can of stain off the shelf, backed up and went to the check out counter.

He hung around near the exit until the woman came out of the store, just to see if his mind had been playing tricks on him.

Dressed in a red jogging suit and tennis shoes, Vann Sinclair looked comfortable and attractive. Her hair was pulled back in a ponytail and her beautiful rich toned skin glowed with health and vitality. He had to say something to her...but what? He was suddenly tongue-tied and unable to produce a coherent thought. "Come on, Father! Help a dude out," he prayed silently.

It was obvious she didn't recognize him. He had a ball cap pulled down over his eyes and was dressed in well worn jeans, a polo shirt, and a lightweight blue jacket. He saw her eyes flash with concern when he approached her. "Hello, Vann Sinclair. Fancy meeting you here! How are you?" Mitch watched as recognition dawned on her face, but the concern was still there.

"Well, if it isn't the judge popping up like a persistent weed," she said. "What are you doing here, Judge? Do you live in this part of town?"

He laughed, feeling like a nervous schoolboy. "No, not exactly. But I like this store and have gotten to know a lot of the people who work here. They're always willing to help me when I get stuck," he explained. Clearing his throat, he tried to regain his footing. "What about you? You live near here?"

"Yes, as a matter of fact I do." She answered in a cool voice, her expression clearly indicating her desire to leave. She turned to walk away.

Mitch couldn't let her leave without saying something to turn things in a more positive direction. "Look," he took a couple of steps to hinder her progress. "I am so sorry we got off on the wrong foot. I've been thinking about you and that fiasco in court, and praying for the opportunity to meet and talk to you again."

She shifted the weight on her feet. "Why do you want to talk to me? So you can make more threats?"

"No, no," he said, laughing. "That's the furthest thing from my mind—and I certainly don't want to give you the opportunity to act on your desire to do harm to my behind."

He was thrilled to see her eyes light up with humor at the memory. "Well, what did you want to talk to me about?"

Mitch cleared his throat like he was about to audition for a play. "I believe the Lord has already answered a prayer, first by letting me meet Thomas, then by leading me to your retirement reception, and now by arranging this meeting here. I am fascinated by what I have seen and heard from you and about you. You seem to be the kind of woman I've always wanted to meet, and I would really like to get to know you personally, if that's possible."

She looked away to hide her face, but not before he saw the flash of emotions running across her features.

She turned back to face him. "Everything is possible, Judge. But why?" she said, still in that cool voice.

He was surprised by the vulnerability, uncertainty, and fear that slid over her face before she could hide it. It didn't fit the image of the strong, self-assured woman he had observed on other occasions. His reaction also surprised him. Tenderness touched his heart for her and made him want to hold her close and tell her everything was going to be okay.

"Because like I said, I'm interested in knowing more about you. So don't prevaricate, Ms. Sinclair. I know you to be a direct and upfront person who speaks her mind. So, is it possible?" He reached into his wallet and pulled out a card and tried to hand it to her. "Will you call me or can I get your number?"

She didn't take the card, and after a pause, said, "No, I don't think so."

"I hope you're not holding that courtroom incident against me," Mitch said. "That really has nothing to do with either one of us. We should be able to move past that."

She quickly looked away from him again, then spoke after a few seconds. "And why wouldn't I hold it against you,

Judge? Tell me why I would want to know someone who I feel is insensitive and callous, and who threatened to throw me in jail for trying to defend helpless children? Look, I have to go." She turned and walked away from him.

He watched her leave and accepted the disappointment that clutched his heart. He knew a good relationship was possible because he had seen it in other marriages, beginning with his parents. He just couldn't figure out why it eluded him. He had tried with his wife, Beverly, but that had failed due mostly to his absence from the home while on military assignments. Years later, he had briefly hoped of finding it with Katrina. But as much as he wanted it, he had quickly discovered Katrina was far from the woman he wanted as his wife. He knew Katrina had no career aspirations, but she did want to reap the benefits that a job and a career would provide. She figured the only way to get it was to marry it. Mitch had come closer than anyone else she had been involved with to providing it.

Mitch had no desire to get into another bad marriage. He figured that he might be able to live the life he dreamed of with a woman like Vann appeared to be, but it didn't seem to be a part of the plan.

chapter seven

One of the things on Vann's list was to redecorate the inside of her house. Since she had always been good at sewing and decorating, Vann looked forward to this new adventure.

She spent the next several weeks taking a class provided by a craft store to understand the techniques she needed for furniture refinishing. She had decided to start with her bedroom furniture, which was old enough to be disposable if it didn't turn out right.

After completing the class, and with the help of a neighbor who was a carpenter, she refinished the dresser and nightstands and redesigned the headboard. It was a fulfilling process, and she was loving every minute of it.

She decided to deviate from her favorite colors, and selected the color scheme of lilac, lavender, and deep purple, with splashes of yellow. She found fabric that she liked in these colors, and got to work on the sewing machine making pillow shams, accent pillows, drapes with matching valance, and a duvet. She also decided to try her hand at covering her old lamp shades. She had watched enough room makeovers on home improvement television shows to figure out how to do it.

She groaned as uneasy thoughts which she tried to ward off entered her mind. Running into the judge at the home improvement store had thrown her off balance, and she knew she hadn't handled it well. She had fled like a foolish teenager, driven by fear that prompted her to do nothing except get away from him. She only hoped that would be the last time they met because she made a fool of herself every time they did. Seeing him again and recalling what he had said brought back unpleasant memories and sent her into an introspective mood. Her illustrious list of gaffes ran through her head, and she knew she was sliding back into the rut she was trying so hard to escape.

When it came to relationships, she sometimes felt like she was under one of those Georgia curses her great aunt loved to talk about. When she chronicled her life up to this point, she admitted that the devil had done his work to bear that out. So many significant relationships had been lost to her one way or another.

She had been abandoned at birth by her mother and she had never even known who her father was. At eighteen, she had been devastated when her beloved Papa suddenly died shortly after she had left home to attend college.

She smiled as she remembered that had been the first time Rubye had come to her aid, just after they had met as freshmen in college. She had been surprised when the tall, light skinned, attractive, and self-assured girl with reddish hair had befriended her, and after learning about her grandfather's death, had jumped right in to help her get ready for the long bus ride back to Georgia for the funeral. Rubye had been a blessing to Vann ever since.

At twenty, Dennis, the first man she had been in love with, was killed in a car accident. She and Dennis had been together since junior high school. How she had wished over the years that she had married him when she finished high school, instead of going away to college. Maybe it would have made a difference in the way her life had turned out.

Again Ruybe, along with Estelle who had become a part of the group, helped her get through it. Although Vann had joined a church at a young age, she had never learned how to trust and lean on the Lord to see her through trouble, mostly because her grandparents tried to shield her from as much hurt as they could. But after Dennis died, she began praying and reading the Bible to find the comfort only God could give.

At twenty-five, she met, fell in love, and got engaged to Billy. But before they could get married, she discovered that Billy was a player, and that while he had been engaged to her, he had also been busy having a baby with another woman. While Billy didn't think it was a big deal and wanted to go on with their marriage plans, Vann recognized his lack of integrity and loyalty and swiftly kicked him to the curb. She grew closer to the Lord and prayed for His strength to help her endure the hurt and confusion she felt.

That had been the year Rubye gave birth to TreVann and in her effort to comfort Vann, had told her she would share the baby with her. In fact, TreVann's name was a mixture of Thomas, Rubye and Estelle's initials added to Vann's name.

At nearly forty, and feeling the desperate effects of old maidism upon her, Vann decided she would get married at any cost. She settled for Alfred, a quiet, timid man who looked as if he would run if someone said 'Boo!' But he was loving and loyal to her. However, before they could marry, he was shot and killed in a freak hunting accident that came simply from being in the wrong place at the wrong time.

At that point Vann decided God must want her to remain alone, but the hope that God would eventually send her the man who would be her husband refused to die. Other men briefly entered and left her life, never staying long enough for anything to develop.

She eventually reached the point where she trusted that God knew what He was doing and she threw all of her energies into people and activities where she could make a difference. She made sure Mama was always comfortable and doing well, assumed guardianship of TreVann, who had been left in her care while his parents were in Saudi Arabia on a long-term assignment for a large oil company, and stayed heavily involved in church activities. Add her job, various volunteer projects, and maintaining her own affairs and she stayed extremely busy.

She flourished. Cy gave her significant increases in salary and bonuses on a regular basis, so although her job title wasn't impressive, she actually made a decent salary. And certainly, the fringe benefits had been worth staying.

She'd taken some long leave of absences from work when her aging Mama had gone through lengthy illnesses. How thankful she had been for the latitude Cy gave to her. Of course, she'd had more than enough time on the books, but it was a blessing not to have to beg for it when she needed it.

Now, Vann wondered where the years had gone. How had she gotten here? She was unmarried, childless, with too many hopes and dreams in ashes. But she'd made up her mind years ago that she wouldn't become a bitter old woman nobody wanted around.

As she thought about it, she had to acknowledge that she'd had a reasonably happy life. Yes, there were disappointments and some unanswered prayers. And yes, she wished some things had worked out differently. But she was thankful for what the Lord had done and tried not to focus too much on what He hadn't.

Now the handsome judge was causing her to face one of the enemies on her list—fear! She was afraid...afraid she was too old for the feelings he stirred in her, afraid of being hurt again, and afraid of losing another man she loved and cared about. She had no problem interacting with men who posed no threat to her heart (like Elliott Shaw), but she already knew Mitchell Langford was another story. The man made her heart flutter, her stomach tingle, and her throat dry. And frankly, she didn't know how to deal with it. It was as if a wide chasm stood between her and what she knew was possible, but closing it was impossible for Vann. *But fear is not from God, and nothing is impossible with God*...she heard in her spirit.

chapter eight

Mitch was finally back at his rightful place in criminal courts. All morning, he had listened intently as first the prosecutor, then the defense attorney made opening statements. The father and son defendants had originally begun a legitimate towing and storage business, but had somehow gotten off track. They had been arrested and charged with numerous counts of trespassing, theft, and extortion. They would enter private parking lots after the lots were full, put up their own no 'parking signs', and then tow the cars away for parking on private property. The owners of the cars would then be contacted and charged excessive amounts for the towing costs, storage, and retrieval of their cars.

Mitch tried to keep the emotion off his face as he sympathized with the young defense lawyer, who basically had no viable defense against the charges. Unless the attorney pulled a rabbit out of the hat, Mitch knew the defendants would be spending a significant number of years in prison.

He was glad when it was time to recess for lunch. He called his lunch buddies to see if they were ready, and headed out of his chambers to meet them. A group of people who had been called as potential jurors had also been released, so the corridor was crowded. He was concentrating on making a path through the throng of people and trying to watch for his friends when he collided with someone.

"Oh, excuse me, I'm so sorry." He said, reaching to steady the woman he had almost knocked over. "Oh my goodness! Ms. Sinclair? What are you doing here?"

Vann looked back at him, just as stunned. "I'm here for jury duty. What are you doing here?" she said in a breathless voice.

"I work here, remember?" He grinned down at her. As usual, she looked gorgeous in casual black slacks, a white blouse, red v-neck sweater, and low heeled black shoes. She wore little or no makeup, but with her smooth, radiant skin she didn't need it. Her brown hair, mixed with strands of gray, was a jumble of curls that attractively framed her face.

"I was so right," she said, a small smile on her face.

"Right about what?" he asked, still surprised at literally running into her again while trying to find a way to use it to his advantage.

"Right about you being a persistent weed that keeps popping up everywhere. It's almost comical. Anyway, let me get out of your way, so you can hurry on to wherever you were going."

"Would you have lunch with me?" he blurted out, already knowing what the answer would be.

"No, but thank you. I've been released, so I'm getting out of here."

"Then there's no reason you can't join me for a quick lunch is there? If you want me to beg, I will. Please, please have lunch with me."

"You just never give up do you, Judge?" Humor flashed in her eyes. "Is it that you can't stand rejection? For the life of me, I just can't understand why you keep messing with me like this. But the answer is still no." She turned and started walking away.

"One of these days, Ms. Sinclair. One of these days," Mitch said to her back.

Mitch stood back and looked with satisfaction at the large media cabinet he was building. Smiling, he said, "Not bad! Not bad at all."

Finally, all the money he had spent attending woodworking classes and on woodworking tools was paying off. His only problem was finding the blocks of time needed to give to this hobby. He took special care and time to do everything right because he wanted to be proud of anything he made. The cabinet would hold his fifty-two-inch television and all the other media toys he and his son, Matthew, thought they needed to enjoy life. He already knew exactly where it would stand in his family room. Now, all he had to do was choose the right stain for it. He wished he had someone to help him decide. Putting the wrong color on it would detract from its beauty.

Who would have ever thought he would be spending his weekends in his garage, designing and creating things from wood? He couldn't believe how enjoyable it was. He remembered when his time had been spent out clubbing with the guys and chasing women. But that had lost its appeal after he'd gotten serious about serving the Lord. Now, he longed for quiet and peace and the company of someone special.

Immediately, Vann Sinclair came to mind. No matter how hard he tried, the woman was never far from his thoughts. Although tempted to try and forget her because it was obvious she wasn't interested in him, he kept recalling the vulnerability and fear he had glimpsed on her face in the parking lot of the home improvement center and the way she almost ran away from him at the courthouse. He wanted to know why.

His efforts to find love on his own had failed miserably. He looked around the garage and decided he was at a good stopping place, and he had some calls to make before it got too late. "I need Your help, Lord," he prayed again, as he began the routine of putting his tools away.

Vann was in her element. She was having so much fun with her decorating project that it was a struggle to keep other commitments, especially when unexpected things like jury duty kept popping up. She had managed to change her volunteer duties with Child Advocates to only helping out with fundraising and recruitment events. Of course her church responsibilities and prayer counseling duties at the television station remained constant. But she had finally learned to make use of caller I.D. and although it was hard, to say no.

It was a great and fulfilling moment when she stood back and admired her finished bedroom. It had been a strenuous process and she was dog tired. Her fingers showed numerous signs of splinters and needle pricks, and she had suffered through days where she could barely move from all the stooping, lifting, and moving heavy furniture. But it had all been worth it, and the twice a week visits to Curves that she had previously signed up for were no longer necessary.

Her bedroom had been transformed into a tranquil, luxurious place of comfort. The lavender colored walls looked great with her other color choices and the bedroom furniture looked almost new. Her success encouraged her to tackle another room in the house.

Over the next weeks, she decided to take a class in floral design and started experimenting with arrangements. It helped that she'd always had a natural flair for decorating and creativity, as well as sewing. Soon, exquisite creations were added to her rooms, and the home improvement centers and the Home & Garden Television channel had become her regular companions.

The end of April rolled around, and after redecorating another bedroom including matching floral arrangements, she invited her friends over for Saturday brunch to belatedly celebrate her April 3 birthday and show off her work. When her friends saw her creations and wanted to buy, or at least duplicate them, she knew she was on to something good. She told her church folk and all her neighbors what she was doing, and she was soon getting calls requesting specific pieces or asking for her help with projects. She began searching used furniture stores and flea markets for unique pieces which she knew could be refinished or redesigned into something new.

Estelle came by one evening a couple of weeks after the brunch to check on her. "Girl, what's going on? You don't half answer the phone, and you look like something the dogs dragged out of the trash. Why are you working yourself like this?"

"No, girl," Vann beamed. "What you don't understand is that this is not work to me. It's fun, relaxing, and satisfying. I'm enjoying myself."

"Well, if that's the case, then go for it. But me and Rubye and them are trying to find you a significant other. I just hope we can find him before you work yourself to death," Estelle said, laughingly. "Vann, everything you make is so beautiful," Estelle said, walking around the house and looking at the new pieces in various stages of completion. "You can see the love and care you put into everything. I need new drapes for several rooms in my house, and I'm thinking about buying that bedroom set you're working on." She spoke of an antique headboard with matching night stands Vann had found at a garage sale. "And I want a duvet and all the accessories for it too."

"Too late, girl. My neighbors already have dibs on it."

"What!" Estelle said, looking disappointed. "Well, save the next one for me. I want to redo my daughter's old room, and one like that would be perfect. Or maybe I need to put an order in," she said with a wink.

What had started as a hobby was turning out to be a profitable venture for her. She was surprised by how many people who didn't have the time or inclination to do what she did, gladly paid her to do it for them. "You know," Vann answered, thoughtfully, "as a matter of fact that would probably be a good idea. That way, you'll be sure to get what you want, because I can start keeping an eye out for one."

"Umm," Estelle thought aloud. "That works better anyway. You know all this emotional upheaval takes so much out of me that I can't concentrate on anything else right now. It's probably wise to wait and do that after I get through this mess with that jerk husband of mine."

Concern prickled through Vann. "Stelle? What's going on now? I thought everything had been settled, that he was going to go on with his woman, get a quiet divorce, and leave you alone."

"Yeah, I did too until I found out he wants to take half of my salon business. Vann, you know how hard I've worked building up my business while he was out chasing after every skirt in town. I can't even tell you how angry this is making me. I don't care about the girl. Heck, she's welcome to him. But I have too many years of prayer, hard work, and sacrifice tied up in my salons. I just can't let him walk off with a part of me."

"Girl, why hadn't you said anything?" Vann said, giving her a hug. "I could've at least been praying for you. You know better than to carry a burden by yourself when you have friends to help you bear it."

"I know, Vann," Estelle said, with her head down. "I've just been hoping he'd catch a little decency and move on with his young woman and leave me in peace. But I'm starting to think she's the one pushing him to do this because I know this man well enough to know his mind doesn't flow like that, and with all of his faults, he's not a vicious person. That girl has had an issue with me ever since she worked in one of my salons and I had to let her go. I have no doubt she's doing this for spite. Heck, I'd be willing to bet she doesn't even want his old crazy behind, but just wants to take what belongs to me."

"Well, keep me posted, okay? And let me know if I can help you," Vann said.

"I sure do appreciate that. I'll let you know how things go."

"Okay. You'd better! And Stelle, don't let this get you down. There is a bright side to this. Just trust God to get you through the darkness," Vann said, as they walked out to the car where she stood and watched as her friend drove off.

"Lord, Stelle needs You to rebuke Satan's strategies to rob and destroy her life. Please don't let this weapon that has formed against her prosper," Vann prayed as she walked back into her house.

While she had been immersed in her decorating projects, Vann had also been in prayer, asking God to enlarge her borders, to guide her into His purpose, establish the work of her hands, and manifest her list of 'new things'. Amazingly, unexpected things began to happen.

She had been a volunteer telephone prayer counselor for the Christian television station for several years, and it never crossed her mind to stop doing it because she knew she was meeting the needs of the people who called in asking for prayer. The burdens many carried made her feel guilty for complaining about her minuscule concerns.

Over the years, she had gotten to know the people who ran the station, produced shows, or worked in some capacity there. One of the people she had become friendly with was Francis Frazier, who hosted a community affairs show called *High Point*.

One Saturday in May, the scheduled guest failed to show up, leaving Francis frantically looking around for someone to fill in. Her eyes landed on Vann, who was busy answering calls in the glassed-in phone room.

She motioned for Vann, and when she came out of the phone room, said, "Vann, the person who was supposed to be on my show is not here, and I need someone to fill in. Will you come on the show and talk about your retirement—why you decided to do it, how you're adjusting, what you're doing—and all of that?" Francis pleaded. "I know people would love to hear about that because it gives them an opportunity to dream about their own retirement."

Apprehensive, Vann looked down at her casual clothing and shook her head. "Francis, I'm not dressed to be on television, and I'd be really nervous since I haven't had time to pray and think about what to say. I'm here to work the phone lines, and nothing else. I'm sorry, but I'm afraid I'll embarrass both of us."

But Francis finally convinced her to do it, so Vann spruced herself up as best she could and appeared on the show as a guest, comforted by the fact that it was not being aired, but taped. During the first few minutes, Francis graciously welcomed her to the show, and explained to the television audience how Vann happened to be the guest. Vann soon got over her anxiety, and talked comfortably with Francis about how retirement was definitely a high point in her life. "Tell us about retirement, Vann. Exactly what made you decide to retire at this time?" Francis asked.

"I prayed hard about it, because I wanted to be sure it was what God would have me to do. I know the most blessed place for us is always at the center of His will." Vann relayed the Elijah story about the brook drying up and God's plan to sustain him in a new place. As she talked, her face lit up, and her enthusiasm was captured by the cameras and communicated to the television audience. "One of my greatest concerns was that I would have trouble making ends meet financially. But I've lived conservatively and made wise financial decisions over the years, and that story reminded me that with God's blessing, I'd be okay." She went on to talk about how her hobby in decorating had turned into an unexpected business venture and how much she was enjoying it, and about her efforts to get out of a rut and try new and different things.

"Well, do you miss going to work every day?" Francis asked.

Vann answered with obvious sincerity and passion. "Absolutely not. My ultimate desire is to be in God's will, and that whatever I do will be for His Glory. I have such joy and contentment in what I'm doing now that I haven't missed it at all. Of course, my biggest challenges are to get out of familiar ruts and let go of old ways of thinking, and to say no to others when I have to."

To Vann's total amazement, she received many compliments. "Vann, you were wonderful on the *High Point* show," Hayden, the station manager, told her the next week. "You captured an audience and that show experienced good responses. We've even had requests for it to run again."

"That's all well and good, Hayden. But in front of the camera is not on my list of favorite places to be. I'd just as soon spend my time answering the phone lines from now on," she had told him laughingly.

"I understand that, Vann," Hayden said. "But seriously, you're very photogenic and have a wonderful presence and personality on camera. In fact, I think you may have missed your calling." She waved him away and got busy answering the phones.

In June a few weeks later, Francis got sick and had to go home before doing the show. The guests had already arrived and Hayden needed someone to host the show for Francis. Again, eyes landed on Vann, and again, she was coerced into substituting. Thankfully, Francis already had the show outlined, with questions and comments for each guest, and the pressure was relieved a little when she found out they would be taping the show, rather than going live.

When Vann received compliments this time, she was not so surprised, but was unnerved when Hayden asked her to act as Francis' official backup. Reluctantly she agreed, but prayed fervently that Francis would never miss another show.

As the end of June rolled around, Vann felt like she owed herself a few days off. For several months, she had been working day and night every day except Sunday, and was amazed and pleased at all she had accomplished in the six months she had been retired She decided it was time to do nothing but sleep late and watch the home and garden shows on television.

Her plan was interrupted on the very first day. The phone rang, and she was tempted to let the call go to voice mail. But when she saw who it was, she decided she might as well answer now. She had been ignoring the 'old geezer's' calls and knew he would only continue to call and disturb her peace and quiet.

"Sister Savannah?" Elliott's voice came over the telephone.

"Elliott," she stated coolly. "How are you?"

"Fine, fine. I've been calling quite often, but you're obviously too busy to return my calls. I'd still like to take you out to celebrate your retirement. So what about tonight? Or do you already have plans?" he asked.

"Thanks, but I'm planning on doing absolutely nothing. I've decided to give myself some well deserved days of rest."

"Well, can I persuade you to change your mind? I promise I won't keep you out too late, unless you're ready to change your mind about some things, *heh, heh, heh*."

"I don't think so, Elliott."

"Wouldn't a nice meal be a good way to top the day off?" he persisted. "That's all I'm talking about. Surely you're not too holy for that."

A few minutes later when Vann hung up the phone, she could have kicked herself. She had no desire to go out with

Elliott. However, much to her annoyance, Elliott had turned into a very determined pest lately. She had been too busy to give him much thought, but now that she was taking a breather from her projects, her brain must have also taken a breather, because she hadn't been able to concoct a viable excuse to overcome his persistence. She rationalized that maybe if she went out with him once and let him know exactly where he stood with her, he would leave her alone. And she *had* decided to get out of her rut and do things differently, she reminded herself. She could use this as practice.

As she was getting dressed for her date, still questioning her decision to go out with Elliott, the phone rang, and she saw it was him. "Good! Maybe he's calling to cancel."

"Savannah? I failed to get directions to your place. Where exactly do you live? Somewhere in the Acres Homes area, if I'm not mistaken."

Vann wasn't surprised by Elliott's assumption. Acres Homes was the oldest African American community in Houston. Although there were sections with beautiful, well-kept homes, unfortunately, as many proud property owners grew older or passed on, and their children and grandchildren chose to move out, the community had been left with an overabundance of rundown homes, neglected rental properties, and abandoned houses with overgrown lots. Elliott would automatically focus on the negative attributes and not the positive ones about the historical community, and conclude that she lived there.

"Well, not exactly, although I am near there," she answered. "But let me give you the directions."

She could hear astonishment in Elliott's voice when she gave him directions on how to get to her home. He knew exactly where it was, and stated that he had several friends who lived in her subdivision. Vann lived in an older upscale, predominantly

African American subdivision that was one of the most beautiful and well-kept in the city.

But it was his reaction after arriving that had Vann chuckling.

"How long have you lived here?" he asked, looking around in wide-eyed wonder at the beautifully decorated home. "You live in this big house by yourself? Why are you living way over here on the northwest side of town and going to church across town in Third Ward? There are no churches closer around here that you want to attend?"

She ignored most of his questions and answered, "I lived in Third Ward for years, which is why I joined that church. When I moved, I saw no reason to change my church membership."

"Where in Third Ward did you live?" he asked curiously. "You know I live in Third Ward," Elliott stated proudly. "I've lived there many years." The Third Ward, located in the South Central part of the city was where Texas Southern University was located, and where Elliott had worked for many years.

"I didn't know that," Vann answered in a tone that indicated she was not impressed. "I lived on Rosedale not far from TSU for several years. Then I bought a house in the South McGregor area."

His eyes got wider. "South McGregor? Where in that area did you buy a house? Those are some pretty high priced properties for a single woman in your income bracket."

Vann pushed back her annoyance, deciding to enjoy the reaction she knew was forthcoming and to have some fun with Elliott's snobbishness. Just because she didn't wear expensive, flashy clothes, and didn't walk around bragging about what she had didn't mean she was destitute. But church folk were often just as bad as people in the world when it came to making judgments based solely on appearances.

"Yes, those are some pretty expensive properties, and my property is a very nice one. But I've always loved the north side of town and this particular subdivision." Without waiting for an answer, she went on, "Anyway, when this house came on the market, I liked it, so I decided to buy it."

"You sold the houses in Third Ward?" He gave a know-it-all smirk. "Bad move. You should have held on to them. Property values in that area are skyrocketing."

"No, I didn't. I still own both of those properties. In fact, I've converted one of them into a multi-unit."

His baffled look returned. "And you say you're buying this one as well?"

"Of course. Paying rent is a waste of money as far as I'm concerned." She decided not to tell him about the other houses she also owned. It wasn't his business anyway.

"Well, this is certainly nice," he said, looking around again. "It's beautiful in here. You did all the decorating yourself?"

"Yes, I did. I'm in the middle of redecorating the entire house. That's one reason why I've been so busy lately." Thinking it would make for pleasant conversation, she continued. "I've discovered a new business venture. Do you know people actually want to *buy* my creations? I've already sold several items that brought a nice profit, and I have orders for more. I've discovered I love bringing new life to old things. Being able to sell them just makes it that much more enjoyable." She knew on some level that telling Elliott of her successes might not have been a wise thing to do. However, she kept hoping that somewhere in his inflated mind, there was a man astute enough to appreciate what she was doing.

But Elliott, true to form, couldn't wait to insert a bit of negativity into her enthusiasm. "You have to be careful with that. You know how people are. They'll take the fruits of your hard work and then won't pay you."

Vann cringed, realizing she had opened herself up to his pessimistic comments. She decided to ignore them, and again questioned her decision to go out with him. *What was I thinking?* "Well, I'm ready to go if you are."

"Girl, you won't believe what I did last night!" Vann gushed into the phone.

"What? Let me hear it! I can use some exciting news right now," Rubye answered.

"I went out with the 'old geezer'," Vann calmly announced, knowing what reaction she would get.

"You what? Please tell me you're lying." When Vann didn't say anything, Rubye sighed and said, "Well, where did y'all go?"

"Rubye, I'll give you three guesses at where he took me."

"I don't even want to try," Rubye answered, irritably. "Just tell me."

"Rubye, you're taking all the fun out of this, doggonit. Anyway, do you know...*(laugh, laugh, laugh)*... that old cheapskate took me to *Happy's* for my retirement celebration?" She could barely get the words out because of the laughter choking her. "*Happy's,* girl! And then he made sure I ordered a budget plate."

"*Happy's?* Girl, I know you didn't just say that man took you to *Happy's?*" Rubye asked, barely holding on to her laughter. "You telling me that this self proclaimed, upper crust, high society, cream of the social strata, think he's God's gift to all women jerk, took you to *Happy's* Cafeteria to celebrate your retirement? And then made you get a budget meal?"

"Yep!" Vann said around hilarious laughter. "That's what I'm telling you." *Happy's* was a buffet style cafeteria that served good, but ordinary food.

After she calmed down from laughing, Rubye said, "Well, I admit it's funny in a way! But it also makes me angry. Is he just stingy and cheap, or does he think that's all you're worth? You know, I'm about ready to call your mama and aunt and get one of their spells to working on him. He deserves it. Vann, that's insulting!"

"Yes, but I'm not mad at him. He confirmed a lot of things I'd already guessed about him. And now, I know exactly who I'm dealing with. He's a stingy, status seeking, manipulating snob, and a carnal, selfish, woman chasing devil disguised as a God-fearing deacon. I actually feel a little sorry for him. He's too old to be so hung up on superficial facades and chasing after shadows when he should be looking for substance."

"But *Happy's?* Vann, you will never convince me he didn't do that in meanness. Even Elliott knows there's nothing special or celebratory about *Happy's*. That was meant to be nothing but a put down."

"I'm not worried about it, girl. God will repay him according to the motive of his heart, whether he did it out of meanness and snobbishness or good intentions. Anyway, I like *Happy's* and had a good meal. And I guess another reason I'm not too upset is that his eyes nearly popped out of his head when he saw my house, and my SUV which was sitting in the driveway because my garage is full of my projects. Now girl, you know I don't get excited about materialism, but I did have to chuckle at his surprise and shock," Vann said, laughing.

"Vann, you deserve so much more. Why did you go out with that jerk anyway?"

"I don't know!" Vann answered in an agitated voice. "I guess sometimes loneliness gets flavored with a tinge of desperation and causes you to do stupid things. Or maybe he just caught me at a weak moment, or perhaps I did it because I'm all caught up in getting out of that rut you accused me of being in. But you know, I think I might have a really hard time getting rid of him now. I'm sure he's thinking hard about how he can lower his standards just a little to make me *worthy* of him." She laughed.

"Vann, before I let you get hooked up with him, I'll pack you up and send you to Georgia to sit on the porch with your mama." She paused a moment before adding, "and he deserves *everything* God is going to pour out on him."

They had another good laugh before hanging up.

chapter nine

Mitch got off the plane anxious to get to his car and head home. The week he had spent at the judicial conference attending boring sessions of updates on laws and legislature, followed by even more boring speeches from colleagues, had seemed never-ending. The few rounds of golf he had managed to get in hadn't been enough to make up for having to endure all that boredom. Now, he couldn't wait to get home and relax.

His cell phone rang. When he saw the number, he was both happy and leery. He looked forward to talking to his son, Matt, but he hated the hassles he often had to go through with Katrina.

When he had first met her, Katrina had joined his church and immediately became deeply immersed in several ministries. Her beautiful smile had captured his attention. Although he hadn't been exactly looking for a serious relationship, he was taken in by her pretty face, shapely body, and award winning performance as a sincere Christian woman. Not wanting another man to get to her first, he had swiftly made his move to ask her out. They had only gone out a few times when Katrina pushed for a closer relationship.

"We're both mature Christians," Katrina had crooned. "And I'm ready to settle down with someone special." She had looked at him with eyes that said he was the most 'special' someone she knew. "And Mitch, I know you are, too."

He still cringed in shame at how easily he had capitulated. He'd ignored the red flags that a man of his age and Christian maturity should have recognized. He had honestly started out respecting her and appreciating what he thought was her love for the Lord, and had had every intention of doing things God's way, but he had been too weak and pitiful to stand against temptation. It was a fact he wasn't proud to admit.

It was only after they'd gotten involved physically that her true colors started to show. She began to constantly demand money to pay some bill or to meet some need. She insisted on moving in with him, and when he said no, she became angry. Then she began to push for marriage, accusing him of taking advantage of her. Soon, her church persona disappeared completely and was replaced by the type of manipulative woman he had learned to give a wide berth. By the time the truth about her was becoming apparent and he was ready to end the relationship, she was gleefully informing him she was expecting his child.

Now, he had to live with the fact that not only had he failed himself, he had also failed Katrina because he should have attempted to bring her to the Lord, rather than join her in sin. His biggest failure had been to the Lord. He could only bow his head in shame and condemnation. Gradually he stopped going to church where word had spread like wildfire of his dirty, lowdown ways.

"Hey, Matt," he answered the phone warmly. "How's it going, fella?"

"It's going okay, and this is not Matthew," Katrina smugly answered. "So are you at home? I need to drop Matthew off for the night. I have a date," she announced proudly.

Frustration flared through Mitch. This wasn't his weekend to have Matt. The court ordered agreement was that Matt would come every other weekend and they would rotate holidays. But Katrina never adhered to the schedule. One month Matt would be at his house every weekend, and the next, he had trouble getting him for one. It aggravated him, but he didn't fight it because he was too happy to have Matt with him.

"Katrina, I'm just getting back from a trip. I'm tired and have a lot to do when I get home. This is really not a good time for Matthew to come over. Maybe tomorrow night, after I get caught up on my work, and get a good night's rest."

"No! Tonight, Mitch! I have responsibility for this child twenty-four-seven. The least you can do is keep him when I need you to."

"Katrina, you know doggone well I don't mind having my son with me. Heck, I'd have him all the time if you would agree to it. It's just that I'd already made plans and tonight is not a good time."

"Well you can tell whoever you have plans with to forget it because I can't find anybody else to keep him tonight, so you're it. We're on our way." The phone went dead.

Mitch pushed the disconnect button on his cell phone in disgust. For more times than he could count, he wondered why he hadn't seen through Katrina's act. She had to be the devil's sister, straight out of hell. Now, at nearly fifty and a grandpa, he was the father of a nine-year-old son born out of wedlock If only he had maintained his own Christian standards.... How many times had he reminded himself of that? His guilt over that fact had caused him to examine his double standards and luke-warm adherence to the Word of God. He had conceded that getting off on the wrong road wasn't an excuse to keep going the wrong way.

He groaned in frustration. "Now I've got to think about what I'm going to feed the kid, who seems to be half starved every time he comes over, and how I'm going to entertain him until I can get him to bed," he said resignedly.

❖ ❖ ❖

Before she knew how it had happened, Vann was not only selling customized floral arrangements and accessories, she was also helping people select fabric, paint, wallpaper, and flooring. Surprisingly, her flair for decorating had led into a flourishing business. Plus, she was enjoying herself! The new venture was fulfilling, and her only problems were finding time to fit everything into her schedule. Her friends began bugging her about working too hard.

"What you really need is a significant other," Rubye had told her. "But don't worry, we're working on it. 'T' has a friend he wants you to meet. It's one of his frat brothers, and he's sure you two will hit it off."

"Is he a Christian?" Vann asked. "I'm not even interested if he's not. I don't have time for any more foolishness."

"Vann, I don't know!" Rubye answered in an aggravated tone. "But I'm sure you'll find out and run him off real quick if he's not. You have to give people a chance, girl. He may not be in church every Sunday, but that's not to say he's not a good man. You ought to know by now that you can't judge a book by its cover."

Vann laughed. "Yeah, girl, I know you're right," she replied, as memories of recent experiences with men invaded her mind.

Amazingly, another new thing had happened to get her out of her rut. Evidently, she had been going to the wrong places because since she had been working on her projects and making frequent trips to the home improvement stores, she was starting to meet men—three of whom had asked her out. Sadly, all of them had been big disappointments.

The first guy picked her up for a dinner date, but before Vann realized it, he was headed to a city two hours away to a gambling casino. After sitting and watching him for hours, she told him she wanted to leave.

"Sweetie, I work hard and party hard, and this is one way I do that," he said, grinning widely. "And I've booked a room so I can show you another way I like to do that, *ha, ha*. We ain't leaving until I'm ready."

Vann had called Thomas and Rubye to come pick her up and left him there.

A nice, soft-spoken man, who told her he was a Christian was the next one she accepted a date with. But as they talked over the meal in a nice restaurant, she found out they had different concepts about Christianity. He did not believe in organized religion or preachers. He said he was his own pastor, and could read the Bible for himself. His odd interpretation of the Word almost tempted her to call her friends to pick her up again, but other than the differences in their fundamental beliefs, he seemed nice enough. Before the night was over, she had come to two conclusions: she would not go out with him again, and she would drive herself to the next date.

The third man owned a used furniture store and told Vann he was divorced. They had a pleasant dinner and a movie date that Vann enjoyed. She was a little hopeful about this one, until she went by his store to see some new items he told her he had. As they walked through the store, a woman with a fierce look approached Vann and told her to leave the store *and* her husband alone. Vann quickly left the store—and the husband.

As she pushed the memories of these bad experiences away, she said, "Rubye, I'm just tired of these old men who ought to be somewhere trying to get close to God, but instead are somewhere trying to get a woman in the bed, or are just plain messed up."

"You can't let a few bad dates discourage you, girl," Rubye told her. "God is just getting you ready for the right one."

Later, during her praise session, Vann rejoiced at the peace and contentment she felt with her life. "I don't have that 'significant other' that my friends are so concerned about, but Lord, I'm grateful for what You are doing in my life. I don't take these good things for granted, and I thank You for them all. In Jesus' name. Amen."

Elliott had been idly flipping the channels while he talked on the phone and degraded low class women to his friend, Seth. He first heard the familiar voice, then looked closer to see none other than Savannah Sinclair on the screen. He lost whatever thought he had been trying to convey to his friend, as his mind struggled to comprehend what he was seeing.

"Hello, and thank you for joining us for High Point. I'm Vann Sinclair, sitting in for Francis Frazier. Welcome! Today our show is about staying healthy. The information we'll be sharing with you is something we all need, so listen with purpose in your heart to be a doer of what you'll be hearing. Our special guest today is Dr. Harvey Whitely from the City of Houston Health and Human Services Department. He'll be giving us some high points to good health and informing us about the services his department provides to help us stay healthy."

"Elliott? Elliott! You there?" Seth's voice called to him.

"Seth, I'm going to have to hang up now. I'm getting another call," he lied. "I'll talk to you later, okay?" He swiftly hung up the phone, his eyes riveted to the television.

"Well I'll be doggone!" Elliott said to the room. "What is she doing on television?" He settled back in his chair, listening intently.

Elliott didn't understand how he had missed so much about Savannah Sinclair. "Why am I just learning all this stuff about this woman? All these years, I've been thinking there was nothing to her. Now all of a sudden, every time I turn around, I'm finding out something new. How in the world did she get herself on television?" he wondered again, while admiring the beautiful woman on the screen as she comfortably conversed about health issues.

Each new glimpse Elliott got into Vann's life brought a bigger surprise. He prized himself on knowing everything he needed to know about every member of the church, especially the women, but somehow, he had missed some vital details about her. Elliott realized that Savannah herself helped to foster that deception by giving the false impression she was ordinary, simple-minded, and broke. It puzzled him that she had plenty to boost her image and show she wasn't run of the mill, but she didn't use it. The woman dressed well, but not expensively, and generally kept a low profile. There had been no hint that he needed to take a closer look at her life.

He had already asked a friend who worked in the county tax office to check on the properties she claimed she owned. He'd enjoy getting into her face with the knowledge that he knew she had lied about owning any property. However, much to his amazement, his friend had told him that she actually owned a dozen pieces of valuable property.

Now, here she was hosting a television show and looking beautiful under those lights. No wonder she had such a cavalier attitude toward him. His life and home might be an attractive lure for other women, but they didn't mean a thing to Savannah.

Mitch Langford had also seen Vann Sinclair on television. He, too, had enjoyed seeing her beautiful face on the screen, but he hadn't been surprised. The way she aptly handled the interview made it seem more like a friendly conversation, but she made sure important points were stressed. Somehow he had known there was a lot more to the woman than met the eye. That was probably the reason he was so fascinated by her. He prayed again that God would send him a special woman, but this time he was praying about a specific woman. He wanted Vann Sinclair.

Vann didn't complain about the hot and humid temperatures the month of July brought because she knew August would be worse. As usual, she was spending July 4 at Rubye's house where she was dancing around the large family room with her godchildren and having no problem keeping up with them.

"Go, Aunt Vann!" they urged her on, while also trying to create more difficult moves for her to follow.

"See, I don't know when you kids are going to realize y'all can't outdance me! I'm the dance champion," Vann boasted, as she bumped hips with one of them, laughing and adding some steps they had never seen.

"Dancing is more than jumping around shaking your butt. You're supposed to move your feet, too." She whirled around, demonstrating steps she had perfected decades ago, and came face-to-face with a man leaning against the doorjamb, arms folded across his chest and a huge smile on his face.

Vann almost fainted, as embarrassment flooded her from head to toe. She froze, as all thoughts of dancing flew out the window, and she took a hard look at Mitchell Langford's face. She stumbled her way to a recliner in the corner of the room so she could sit down and get air into her suddenly depleted lungs.

"You okay, Auntie?" TreVann questioned. He ran across the room and grabbed her hand. "You need some water? What happened? You look like you just saw a ghost or something."

She looked cautiously toward the door again, and her heart beat faster. There's no way that hateful judge could be standing in her friends' home watching her make a fool out of herself.

"I'm alright," she said nervously.

She took another wary look at the man. Again, he wore a baseball cap and tinted glasses covered his eyes. He was dressed in brown casual slacks and a tan golf shirt that looked *very* good on his tall muscular frame.

Vann struggled to pull herself together. She said in a whisper, then, in a voice loud enough for everyone in the room to hear. "I've got to go. Tell your mother to come here."

Roderick, Rubye's youngest son, went flying out of the patio door, yelling, "Mom! Mom, come quick! Aunt Vann's sick!"

TreVann, his girlfriend, Reneé, and his sister, Kia, all stood over her, concerned looks clouding their faces. "Aunt Vann, what's wrong?" Kia asked.

"I'm alright, baby, just got a little winded that's all. I guess that's what I get for trying to keep up with you youngsters." She tried to smile reassuringly at the group huddled around her chair, but could tell she hadn't convinced them.

Rubye came rushing into the room from the backyard, where she and Thomas were grilling meat for the barbecue they were having that evening. She looked around the room trying to decipher what was wrong.

"Boy! Why are you yelling like somebody crazy? What did you say?"

"It's Aunt Vann! All of a sudden she looked like she was going to faint," Roderick explained to his mother.

Rubye looked down at her. "What's wrong, Vann? You feeling okay?" Concern showed on Rubye's face when she looked down at her friend.

Vann was starting to feel a little silly and her embarrassment increased. "I'm alright Rubye, but I think I should leave. Those famous hot flashes are hitting I guess."

"You think?" Rubye asked, looking at her strangely, knowing if it had really been a hot flash, her friend would never admit it to a room full of people. "Well, come on, let me get you something cold to drink."

Vann stood up on shaky legs and followed Rubye into the kitchen, careful to keep her eyes averted from the source of her trouble. But Rubye stopped in front of him. "Mitch, Thomas said for you to come on out if you want to."

Mitchell Langford wasn't going anywhere. He was too busy looking down at Savannah Sinclair, the woman who had haunted his thoughts for months, and thinking, *God does answer prayer!*

"I...uh...think I may have startled your friend here," Mitch told Rubye. "I caught her in the middle of showing the kids how to dance." The amused smile was back on his face.

Rubye looked from one to the other. "Oh, y'all haven't met have you? Vann Sinclair, this is Mitch Langford. He's the guy we wanted you to meet. He's one of 'T's frat brothers. Mitch, Vann is a very dear friend of ours."

Vann's head was buzzing. *Mitch Langford. Judge Mitchell Langford!* Thousands, millions even, of men in this city, and they had to drag this one in front of her! Vann could hardly bear to look into his face. "The judge and I have met," she mumbled softly.

Mitch's amusement was back full blown as he took in everything about the flustered woman.

"Yes, Ms. Sinclair and I met the first time several months ago. How are you, Ms. Sinclair?" Mitch said, smiling down at her. "I didn't mean to embarrass you, or to interrupt your little groove."

Lordy! Vann thought as she peeked a look at him and noticed that when he smiled, it accentuated the cleft in his chin and the dimples on both sides of his strong masculine mouth. And yes, he had the most beautiful smile she had ever seen on a man. *I've got to get out of here,* she thought

"No, I, uh… just feel a little foolish having a virtual stranger witness it." She looked at Rubye. "Do you mind if I take a rain check on this evening? I am feeling a little out of sorts, so I think I'd better get on home."

"Aw, Vann! Do you have to? You know Trevie is going to be so disappointed if you leave. They're driving back to Austin tonight."

Vann's heart dropped. The last thing she wanted to do was disappoint TreVann. She had planned to visit with TreVann and smoke his new girlfriend over. Trevie had met the girl in Austin, where he now lived and worked, and although it was only three hours away, they hadn't had a chance to meet her.

"I know, and I'll have to make it up to him another time," Vann mumbled. Trevie had held her heart since the moment he was born, but he had really become hers when he had walked up to her when he was about two, looked up at her with big brown eyes, and arms stretched high and said, "Can you hold me, Au-tie?"

Vann had been a goner. "Yes, baby, Auntie Vann will hold you for as long as you want." That had only strengthened the already strong bond between them, and though she loved his brother and sister, they all understood that TreVann held a special place in her heart.

"Just sit your butt down for a minute. You'll be okay," Rubye admonished her. "Anyway, if you're not feeling well, it's better to stay here than go home where you'll be alone. Come on y'all, sit down." She motioned Vann and Mitch to the alcove where the kitchen table sat. "I'll get you something to drink."

"No really, I think I'll feel better at my own house," Vann answered, suddenly feeling like a deer trapped in the glare of headlights.

"Vann, I know you don't want to be rude, but Mitch is the guy 'T' has been wanting you to meet. You're both from the same area down in Georgia. You need to sit down and talk to him. You probably know some of the same people."

Vann looked at Mitch with distaste. "I don't think so."

Mitch noticed the look she gave him, and disappointment hit the bottom of his stomach. Darn it! The first woman to really spark his interest in years, and he had blown it with her.

"That's alright, Rubye," Mitch said, looking straight at Vann. "Vann and I can talk another time. If she's not feeling well, it's probably a good idea for her to go ahead and leave."

Rubye gave Mitch a questioning look, then said, "No, I think she's just embarrassed. Vann, come on! Mitch is not going to hold it against you for making a fool out of yourself dancing with the kids."

"Like I said, I'll make it up to Trevie, even if I have to run up to Austin one weekend to see him," Vann stated.

Vann went into the family room to get her purse and kiss the kids goodbye. She fought back tears as she hugged TreVann tightly. He was the closest thing to a child she'd ever had. Rubye had given him a part of Vann's name when he was born, and told her she would share him with her until Vann had one of her own. That had never happened. But God had been gracious enough to give her the opportunity to love and care for TreVann for a good portion of his young life.

Vann didn't even glance in Mitch's direction when she came back into the kitchen. "I'll talk to you later, okay?" she said, hugging Rubye. "And you better save me some food! I'll come by and get it after church tomorrow."

chapter ten

On the way home, Vann gave herself a good talking to. "I'm far too old to let this affect me like this," she told herself. But she knew it would take hours for her to get that handsome face with the amused smile out of her mind. Of all the men to show up at her friends' home!

"I'm not taking this into my house. Lord, help me!"

She entered the house, determined to get her mind off of the man who seemed to be dogging her steps, and headed to the kitchen to make a cup of tea. She carried her tea into the family room where she clicked the TV on and started flipping channels. Then she noticed the message light on her phone blinking.

"Now who is bothering me on a Saturday afternoon?" she said as she struggled out of the recliner to walk over to the small table holding the phone. She scrolled through the caller I.D. and found out she had six calls.

The call list included the 'old geezer', Sister Coffner *(I guess it's time to put in another appearance at the food pantry)*, Aunt Lu, Estelle, Annette, and Rubye. She was not surprised to see that Rubye had called. She'd known Rubye wouldn't be content until she found out what was going on with her.

She dialed the number to retrieve her messages, and clicked past all of them until she got to the last one.

"Savannah Jo Sinclair!" Rubye's voice came over the line. "I want to know what in the world got into you today to make you go rushing off like that. We are going to talk before this day is over. By the way, Mitchell Langford is a very nice man!"

Hanging up the phone, Vann went back to her recliner and her tea, which was now tepid. She sat in the recliner and looked out on the restful scene of her backyard. Large elm trees and magnolias that bloomed in different colors were surrounded by an assortment of flowers in beds and pots. How she loved her yard with its constantly blooming flowers, even though she didn't have time to take care of it now. Thank goodness for her yardman. As she looked out through the window, two squirrels ran back and forth from tree to tree, and then, because of the quietness that surrounded her home, were brave enough to enter her deck to continue their antics.

She smiled. "It would have been better for me if I had stayed at home today and watched the squirrels play. At least I would still have my peace of mind."

Her mind catapulted back to Mitch Langford. Rubye had said they were from the same area in Georgia. Rubye and Thomas probably thought they had hit a homerun in their matchmaking effort.

She let her thoughts roam free, and they took her to where she didn't want to go—straight to Mitch Langford. "Uh, uh, I'm not going there," she exclaimed. She knew the one sure way to get past every low place was through praising God, so to get her mind off of the disturbing man, she started praising God for the good things in her life.

"Lord, I have so much to be thankful for. I have a reasonable portion of health and strength in my body and soundness in my mind. I have good friends, and I'm able to be a blessing to Your kingdom and to others. I'm thankful for the new streams of blessings flowing into my life, and Lord, most of all, I'm thankful for the peace and hope that fills my spirit each and every day.

"Father, I...Arrrgh!" The phone rang, interrupting her praise.

She wasn't surprised to see it was Rubye. "Hello," she sang into the phone. "Why are you on the phone calling me, when you have a house full of company to see to?"

"I told you I was going to call. And for your information, you spoiled the party. When you left, everyone else decided they had other places to go, too. This was after they ate all they could hold, of course. Now, you need to come clean, missy. I want to know what caused you to split like that."

Vann hesitated for a minute, recalling again her embarrassment and amazement at coming face to face with Mitchell Langford. "Well..., remember when I told you about that disastrous episode in court, and how the judge threatened to throw me in jail?"

"Yes, but what does that have to do with Mitch? He's in criminal, not family court."

"Rubye," she said impatiently, "if you recall, I told you that the judge I acted a fool with wasn't one of the regular Family Courts judges." She paused again. "Well, believe it or not...but that judge was none other than...ta! da!...Judge Mitchell Langford!"

Total silence from the other end.

"Rubye?"

A few seconds passed before she heard her friend say, "Vann, how in the world, in this big city with millions of people, could that have happened?"

"Rubye, I might as well come clean with everything," Vann continued in an agonized voice. "Since then, he just keeps popping up every time I turn around." She recounted the times she'd seen him. "He told me he had been praying about us getting to know each other, and tried to give me his number, but I wouldn't take it. To turn around today and find him standing there watching me act a fool with the kids was more than I could take. I had to get out of there."

"Yeah, I can understand that," Rubye said slowly. "But you know what, Vann? He's one of the nicest people I've met in a long time. I bet if you had stayed, he wouldn't have even brought up that courtroom incident. I know he's very intrigued by you. He kept asking all kinds of questions about you, like whether you're seeing anyone, why you retired, what you're doing now, and other things. He even said they needed more advocates like you."

"You're lying! Not the way he ripped into me in court that day! I can't believe that."

"Well it's true." Rubye paused for a minute. "But Vann, why didn't you take his number? Why won't you talk to him? Anytime a man tells you he's praying about you, you know he has to be interested."

"I really don't know, other than I guess I'm still a little upset with him about the child advocate case. But I guess the biggest reason is that I'm afraid. I think I could be attracted to him," Vann admitted in a quiet, subdued tone.

"Ohhh," Rubye's voice brimmed with enlightenment. "Vann, you know I know your history, and I understand why you would feel a little afraid, but don't let the past rob you of your future. Vann, you know what? I see God's hand all over this, because it's so far-fetched that only He could have orchestrated it. Girl, you need to keep an open mind and heart about this man. You never know what God has in the works."

After hanging up, Vann thought about what Rubye had said, and knew she was right. Her recent dating fiascos aside, she hadn't seriously dated in so long that she didn't know how to respond to a man who admittedly had the ability to make her heart flutter. Could he be another new and wonderful stream flowing into the desert of her loneliness? At her age? The very thought of it blew her away. She pressed her hand to her chest as she recalled the women in the Bible that she had listed as examples of the kind of woman she wanted to be. "Lord, make me more than a conqueror over the spirit of fear and help me appropriate the faith, wisdom, boldness, and courage You have given me so that I can open my mind and heart to everything You have for me. If it is Your will for me to get that man's number from Thomas and let him know I'm ready to talk..." The ringing phone interrupted her again.

"Vann? I'm so glad you're home. I...I...need to talk to you!"

"Roxanne? Hey, girl, what's up?"

"Vann...I...uh..." The next thing Vann heard was the sound of Roxie crying hysterically.

"Roxie, what's wrong? Calm down, tell me!" Vann said in a worried voice.

"Vann, I just found my husband...in our bed with someone else. And...oh Vann, it was a man. My husband was in *our* bed with a man! Vann, what am I going to do? I don't know what to do!"

Oh Lord! Were the only words that came to Vann's mind. She didn't know what to say. Roxanne was the kind of woman who had to have a husband to feel good about herself. Vann had witnessed two previous husbands being pushed to the curb before this third one had come on the scene. After Roxanne and the second husband had broken up, it had only taken her a few months to hook up with this one. Vann had wondered how Roxanne kept finding husband after husband, when she hadn't had her first one. Roxanne would sing her husband's praises to Vann one day, and be cursing him the next for his shortcomings.

Vann was at a loss, because nothing like this had ever crossed her path before.

But she had to help her friend. The one thing she did know was that Roxanne needed a friend, and definitely didn't need to be alone. "Roxie, I'm coming to pick you up, okay? You throw some clothes into a bag and get whatever else you may need and we'll come back to my house. Can you do that?"

"Y-y-yes!" Roxanne answered tearfully.

"Lord, You've got to help with this," Vann prayed as she hung up. "I don't know what to say to her, so give me the words to comfort her, Father. I don't know why she called me...I would think she would have called her family...but maybe it's because You want to use me to help her get through this. It's going to be a long night, of that I'm sure."

It was a very long night as she tried to help Roxanne sort through her shock, and decide what to do. Roxie's devastation over her husband's unfaithfulness was made worse by the fact that it was with a man.

"I've suspected he was seeing someone else," Roxanne confessed. "And finding out it was another woman would have been bad enough. But a man! And in my house...in our bed! That just makes me sick."

"What if it had been a woman?" Vann asked Roxanne. To her way of thinking, man or woman, it was still a ruthless disregard and violation of the marriage vows.

"It would have been more bearable to me if he'd lost his head over another woman. Another woman I could have dealt with, but when it comes to this homosexual stuff, I never would have guessed that he...." She started crying again. "It's just unimaginable that he would do something like this to me, to us! Our marriage wasn't the best by any means, but I thought...."

They talked until an exhausted Roxie finally fell into a troubled sleep, only to wake Vann a couple of hours later screaming, "Vann! What if I have AIDS?"

There had been no more rest for either of them the remainder of the night, or the next day either. Vann ended up missing church, and while she prayed and tried to console Roxie in her fatigued state of mind, she thanked God for what, in His mercy, He might have saved her from.

chapter eleven

Mitch was involved in one of his favorite activities, puttering around in his garage with his woodworking projects. Nothing relaxed him more than creating something beautiful out of a piece of wood. The hours that he spent there soothed the loneliness he often felt.

After spending over twenty years in the military, the last ten of those years assigned as Judge Advocate General, it had been an easy move from that to a local judgeship eight years ago. Now, he planned to work another five or ten years and retire from there as well. But then what? He had once dreamed of moving back to Georgia, building a home, practicing a little law, and doing a lot of golfing and fishing. But that dream had faded. Moving back to the small town near Savannah, Georgia, held no appeal to him anymore. If he was going to be alone there, he might as well stay here to be near his children and grandkids. At least they brought some excitement into his life. Sometimes too much excitement, he admitted.

His two older children were grown, and though not married, were involved in relationships that had produced babies. He hated to see them following in his footsteps with one bad relationship after the other, but with the kind of example he and Beverly had set, they'd had nothing to inspire them to do better. He met Beverly shortly after going into the military, and they had quickly become close. When he was scheduled to be transferred to another base, they'd decided to get married, and he left with a wife and the first baby on the way.

With him away so much, the burden of parenting was left to Beverly, who resented it, as well as the loneliness she felt. She was soon leaving the child with a sitter and going out to party.

The marriage limped along a few years and produced another child before Beverly told him she was tired of moving all over the place and needed her husband at home with her all the time. Mitch, reluctant to abandon his career goals at the time, refused to leave the military, which was what she wanted him to do, and it wasn't long before she told him she wanted to end the marriage. So his children had grown up in an unstable home that soon fell apart. He just prayed they would eventually get their acts together.

"Oh Lord, please bless my children," he prayed. "I seem to be praying a lot these days," he said to himself. He knew he needed to stop procrastinating about getting back into church, but couldn't decide where to go. After the mess with Katrina, he had let guilt and shame drive him away from his former church, and it hadn't taken long before he was out of the habit of going, even though he had never stopped praying and reading the Word. He had eventually made Christian television his substitute for attending church, but he knew by doing so, he was being disobedient to God's command to gather with other believers. Besides that, he was not getting any younger, and the thought of dying without a church home or pastor who knew him, made him sick in his spirit. Not that it would matter at that point, but he would want the kind of homegoing services that he remembered from his youth...the kind that would make others think, *I want to live the kind of life he lived.* In reality, sometimes he wondered if he was even going 'home' anymore.

Mitch shook his head. "I've got to get that straight! How can I point my kids in the right direction if I'm lost?" Thomas had invited him to visit his church, and he decided then and there that he was going.

Thomas and Rubye were down to earth and genuinely good people, and he certainly enjoyed each visit he had made to their home. It was the kind of home where you felt the love the moment you entered. The kind of home he wanted.

"It sure doesn't hurt that Ms. Sinclair is a close friend of theirs, either," he mumbled to himself. The woman made his heart sing and brought a smile to his lips. And the next time, he resolved, she wouldn't run from him.

chapter twelve

August hadn't arrived yet, but the temperature was oppressively hot. Vann had managed to help Roxanne get situated in an apartment until she could settle up everything with her husband. Then, supporting her through the AIDS test and agonizing days of waiting for the results had been another traumatic experience. Thankfully, everything had been okay.

She finally got back to her projects, which had been neglected during the days she spent with Roxanne, and was making progress on a bedroom ensemble when she had to stop again to go help out at the church pantry, make a visit to Cy and Sylvia's, and go to the television station. "Am I out of the rut yet?" Vann asked herself.

As soon as she walked into the television station, Hayden and Francis cornered her and asked her to consider sharing hosting responsibilities for the community affairs show, *High Point.* They explained that their request was due mostly to the good reviews Vann had received from the two shows she had done, and partly because of Francis' uncertain health issues. They would each host two shows each month on alternate weeks, giving them both two weeks to prepare for each show. Francis said it would take some pressure off of her, and Hayden believed it would bring variety and thereby an increase in viewers.

Vann agreed, but only after thinking and praying about it. She decided to give up the telephone counseling, as much as she enjoyed it, and devote that time to preparing for the shows. She also decided to go on a much needed shopping spree. She would even spring for the works at the beauty salon! If she was going to be a television personality, she had to dress and look the part.

For her first show as an official host, she blew everyone away when she walked into the studio wearing a red designer suit, three inch matching sling backs, and silver accessories. Estelle had cut her hair into a flattering new style and expertly applied her makeup. She had to admit—she looked the part of show host even though she may not have felt like it when the camera lights went on, and she smiled and said, "Hello, everyone. Welcome to *High Point*. I'm your host, Vann Sinclair."

In addition to the many phone calls she received after the show, the following Sunday she could barely move around in the church because of all the people stopping her to comment on how much they enjoyed her show, and how beautiful she looked. Pastor Travis embarrassed her by saying over the pulpit, "Church, we have a star among us in the person of Sister Vann Sinclair. The show is a real delight, Sister Vann. It appeared as though you have been doing that for years. But that's how it happens when the Lord puts you somewhere."

"Wow, another step out of the rut," Vann said to herself. "Lord, I thank You, and praise You for every victory."

Mitch was nervous. More nervous than he had been in a long time. He looked at the number written on the piece of paper in front of him, and rehearsed what he planned to say in his mind.

"This woman has been on my mind for too long, and I've got to get her to talk to me." He fiddled with the paper with the number written on it, still working to get his nerve up. "Oh well! If I'm going to do it, I might as well get it over with." He started punching in numbers. "Hello, Ms. Sinclair. This is Mitch Langford. How are you?"

"Fine, thanks." He could hear the surprise and puzzlement in her voice.

"I know I'm the last person you expected to hear from."

"That's the truth. What can I do for you?"

"Well, uh...for one thing, I hope you don't mind that I got your number from Rubye."

"No, as a matter of fact, I had planned to call you to apologize for my rude behavior during our previous meetings."

Wow! He hadn't expected that. "Well, I want to apologize for the way things went in court. I had forgotten all of the different ways those kinds of cases can go bad. Anyway, Vann,—I hope you don't mind if I call you Vann?"

"No, that's fine," she said with a smile in her voice.

He began smiling himself. "Anyway, that's one reason I'm calling. It's been brought to my attention that some new developments have taken place regarding the children you were advocating for in my court. Unfortunately, your predictions have come close to happening. The family is back in court already because the mother has been picked up for writing hot checks, and the grandparents have asked for custody of the children. I read through your notes in the file, and I saw where you advised against this. Can you talk to me about why you are against the children living with their grandparents?"

"Sure. But I should first tell you that I'm not involved in that case, or in any case right now. But if you go back far enough in the file, you'll find that the grandparents' household is very unstable. They move about every three months, probably because they don't pay their rent. They have a pillar-to-post lifestyle that I don't think is good for the children. That's why they have been denied custody before."

"I'm sorry you're no longer involved, and hope our little run-in in court that day didn't bring that about." His voice dropped an octave. "Vann, it's obvious to me that you're one of the best things that ever happened to those children."

"Thanks, but no, their foster mother is the best thing that's ever happened to them. She was heartbroken when you ordered the children back to parental custody. She and her husband are the ones who have to nurse them back to emotional and physical health after they've been with their mother. And as far as the advocacy thing, I've had to rearrange a few things in my life, and that happens to be one of the things I let go."

"So, would you recommend that the court rule against the grandparents getting custody? I'm now back in criminal courts where I belong, but I still have some input in that case."

"No. Since it's not my case, I can't recommend anything. But I suggest the court read through the entire file and talk to the current advocate and caseworker...have a home investigation done, if one hasn't already been done, then make the decision based on those findings."

"I'll see that it's done. And I'd like to do something to express my apologies for not understanding your pleas that day. Would you let me take you out to dinner some time?"

He heard her take a long steadying breath.

"I would love to, Mitch. I had already decided I was going to stop running from you. There has to be some reason God is suddenly causing our paths to cross."

A gigantic smile covered Mitch's face. "How about tomorrow night? Where would you like to go?"

"Tomorrow's fine. And why don't you surprise me? I like just about any kind of food, but I do prefer a nice, quiet atmosphere."

"I'll see you at seven, and I'm really looking forward to it. I guess I need to get your address." He wrote it down and said, "Oh, and I promise I won't threaten to throw you in jail, if you promise not to do damage to my backside."

Vann laughed nervously. "Okay. I'll see you then, but I'm not promising anything right now."

"I'm sorry, Elliott. I already have plans."

"Why is it that you always have plans when I invite you out, Savannah? I just don't believe you're all that busy. I think you're just trying to play hard to get."

"Like I said, Elliott, I stay pretty busy, and I really need to go."

"Oh, so now you don't even have time to talk to me on the phone? I wouldn't get too uppity if I were you, because the day may come when you'll be glad to get a call from me," Elliott said huffily.

"Oh, I think I'll be able to survive, Elliott. I really don't enjoy talking to people who love to put me down. Nor do I like being in their company."

"Are you trying to say I'm one of those people?"

"I'm glad you understood what I said. I really have to go now. Maybe I'll see you at church sometime."

Vann hurriedly disconnected before Elliott could say anything else. She needed to check on Estelle, whose situation was evidently not going well. And her aunt had called asking that she call her back as soon as possible. She decided to call Estelle first.

"Estelle? I am so sorry for not calling sooner! But girl, its been hectic. How are things with you?"

After a long pause, Estelle said, "I uh...I really need to talk to you, Vann. But I don't want to talk over the phone. I'm not working so can you come by sometime today? I'd come to your place but I'm waiting on a repairman to come by and check my washing machine."

"Sure, honey, I'll make time." Vann answered cheerfully. "How about after lunch, around two? My aunt has been calling too, so I'll swing by her house before coming to your place. Is that good?"

"Yes. That's fine." Estelle said in a low voice.

Vann hung up, feeling burdened for her friend. Estelle sounded like she had received some really bad news, and Lord, she didn't need that right now. Her husband seemed to enjoy inflicting unnecessary pain when he continuously flaunted his much younger girlfriend in Estelle's face by parading her through Estelle's salons.

Vann knew she needed to strengthen herself in the Word so she could lift her friend's spirit. She grabbed her Bible and read the twenty-seventh Psalm, which was one of her favorites. Then she prayed on behalf of her friend.

"Father God, Your Word says that because You are our light, our salvation, and the strength of our lives, that we need not be afraid of anything. I thank You for the privilege and opportunity to come before Your throne of grace and mercy to let my requests be made known. And Father, I come interceding on behalf of my friend, Estelle. I know I don't have to tell You what's going on in her life because she's Your child, and You know everything about her. All I know is that she needs You, Lord. She needs Your light, Your strength, and Your protection. Your Word also tells us that this battle is Yours, so I thank You for fighting this battle for Estelle. I thank You that Your grace is sufficient for her, and that Your strength is made perfect in her weakness, and I thank You for making Estelle more than a conqueror over every attack that comes against her. We know that if You are for her, nothing and no one can stand against her. And so I praise You right now for the victory in Estelle's situation. In Jesus' name. Amen."

Later, as she headed to her aunt's house, she was totally unprepared for the news that would change her world.

"Hey, Aunt Lu!" she greeted, as she entered the house. She never failed to thank God for the aunts—her mother's sisters—who had been so kind to her over the years. "How're you doing?" Vann gave her aunt a brief hug.

"I'm tolerably well, honey. Can't complain. How are you? I saw you on television the other night. You looked so good! I got my grandkids to tape it for me. I'm going to send it to Mama and them. They will get such a joy out of seeing that."

"Oh, Aunt Lu, it's not a big thing. I just hope I'm helping someone," Vann said with sincerity.

"You *are* helping people. My friends are all calling me, telling me how much your show blesses them. I am so proud of you."

"Aunt Lu, shame on you for exaggerating like that," Vann said jokingly, to get the conversation moving away from herself. "So, what did you need to talk to me about?"

"Sit down a minute, Vann. I have something serious to tell you." Aunt Lu wrung her hands, a distressed look on her face. "I don't know how to say this other than to just come out and say it, because there is just no easy way." She stood up again, after sitting down, and began walking around the room.

Vann frowned. "What is it, Aunt Lu? What are you talking about?" Vann felt uneasiness grow as she took in her aunt's nervousness. It was totally out of character for her outspoken aunt to beat around the bush.

"It's your mother, Vann. She's sick."

Alarm shot through Vann. "Oh Lord! Mama's sick? Why didn't you tell me sooner? I need to get myself together and get there," Vann said, starting to get up to leave.

Aunt Lu caught her hand and pushed her back down. "No, not your grandmother. Your mother, Vann. Rosetta. And she ain't got nobody to help her. She's up there in Dallas, sick and by herself. She's been asking...wanting to know if you could possibly help her, maybe put her up for a while until she can decide what to do. I already have a house full otherwise she could stay here with me. And you know Mama's not able to do anything for her. Rosetta really needs you, honey. And she is your mother."

Stunned. That was the best word to describe how Vann felt about what her aunt told her. But it didn't take her long to snap back. She jumped up and walked away from Aunt Lu, her emotions running rampant.

"My mother, huh?"

Vann thought of the woman who had rejected and disowned her, and remembered every timid overture she had made to connect with her. Every wound from each one of those rejections now stood painfully open. The last time Vann had tried to reach out to the woman was when she wanted to let her know that she now lived in Texas. That had been thirty years ago. The woman hadn't responded, and to Vann, that had been the last nail in the coffin. All hope to establish some type of relationship with the woman who had given birth to her died. She had finally accepted that this woman wanted nothing to do with her.

Why? From the quiet and hushed conversations she had managed to overhear through the years from her aunts, it was because Vann had been kept a secret from the well-to-do man Rosetta had married. And there was no way Rosetta would let the secret of an illegitimate child ruin her life.

Anger, hurt, and resentment settled in her heart. "No, Aunt Lu. I can't do that." Vann fought threatening tears, and moved closer to the door. "She might be the woman who gave birth to me, but she is not my mother. My grandmother, the woman I call Mama, is the only mother I know. The person you're talking about is a stranger to me. She made sure of that."

Vann's heart and mind were doing double time as she tried to get her thoughts and emotions back in line. "She has other children, I'm sure. Children that she loved enough to keep and raise. Where are they? Why can't they help her?" Her relatives had been very closemouthed when it came to details about her birth mother, so she knew very little about the woman's life.

"From what I've been able to find out, your two brothers are all over the place. Rosie can't keep up with them most of the time, so they may be in jail for all she knows. And your sister won't even call her."

"You know what?" Vann said, as sadness grew within her. "I'm in my fifties, and this is the first time anyone has ever told me how many siblings I have."

Aunt Lu bowed her head in shame. "Baby, we didn't want to hurt you any more than you were already hurting by talking about them. And Rosetta has kept them away from her family, so we know very little about them. I honestly don't know why they're not taking care of their mother, but I want you to pray about this, Vann. Don't let your emotions get in the way of you doing the right thing. I know your mother hasn't done right by you. She's my sister, and I have never agreed with the way she's treated you. I know you don't owe her a thing, but look upon her as you would anybody in need, and make your decision based on that. Would you do that for me?"

"You know what, Aunt Lu?" Vann said, with tears in her eyes. "Of all the things you could ask of me, that's probably the one thing I won't even consider. I just can't do it." She walked out of her aunt's house. She was in a daze and barely managed to get into her car, before the tears she had been holding back slid down her face. Some hurts you don't get over, no matter how old you are. She sat there long enough to calm down before starting the car and driving away.

She drove slowly as she left the Greenspoint area where Aunt Lu lived, and headed up I-45 North, toward Farm Road 1960 and Champions, where Estelle lived in a large two-story home.

When Estelle opened the door, she looked as if someone had stuck a pin in her beautiful round face, and let out all the air. As the owner of several beauty salons, Estelle was able to change her look as often as the mood hit her. One week, she would have long, blonde hair; the next week, she would be a redhead; and the next, sporting a short, sexy style. Today, the weave was nowhere in sight and her own hair stood out all over her head. Vann quickly pushed her own problems to the back of her mind.

"Stelle! Honey, what's wrong? What happened?"

Estelle motioned for her to follow her through the large house. They ended up in the sunroom.

"Vann, you'll never believe this," she said, shaking her head sadly. "Not only does that jerk husband of mine want half of my business, he also wants this house. And he had the nerve to bring that little...that woman...over here with him to drop that bomb. While he was telling me he needs the house because they're thinking about having more children, she was walking around planning how she was going to redecorate. Honestly Vann, I..." Estelle broke down, sobbing out her hurt and pain.

Vann left her for a minute to go to the kitchen to get them glasses of tea. When she returned, Estelle was struggling to get her emotions under control.

"Go ahead, girl. You have every right to be upset," Vann told her gently.

"I was about to agree to let him have a couple of the salons just to get rid of him. But when he came in here demanding my home, and disrespecting me by bringing that woman with him, I just lost it. Vann, you know how much I have put up with from that man. He's never held a decent job, refused to even help me run the salons, and was always out partying on the money I work so hard for. I'm angry at myself for not kicking him out years ago. If I would have, I could have saved myself this aggravation."

Rather than respond to Estelle's hurt, Vann decided to focus on practical things. "Stelle, do you have a good divorce attorney?"

"No, I'm using the same attorney who takes care of my business affairs."

"Well, I think it's time for you to think about getting one that specializes in divorce cases. Because if you don't fight this man with all you can muster, he and that woman are going to run over you and take everything you have."

"I know you're right," Estelle said, sadly. "He's always been able to bully and manipulate me. Do you know a good lawyer? I have no idea how to go about finding one."

"No, I don't know one, but I think I know someone who might," she said, thinking of Mitch Langford. "I'll work on it."

They sat in silence, sipping tea for a few minutes, each burdened with heavy issues. "Enough about me," Estelle finally said. "What about you, Vann? You still over there working like crazy? How are things going? Ruybe told me they had a man for you to meet. Did you meet him yet? The TV show going okay? Bring me up to date, girl," Estelle said.

"Everything is going okay, and yes, they introduced us, but guess what? I already knew the guy." She gave Estelle a brief rundown of how she and Mitch had met—not once, but several times.

"Oh my goodness! It sounds like a greater power is definitely at work to bring y'all together. So when are you going out with him?"

"Well, as a matter of fact, we have a date tomorrow night. I decided to stop running and see what happens." She hesitated, wondering if she should tell Estelle about Rosetta. She hated to add to her friend's already heavy burden, but it occurred to her that her friends never hesitated to bring their burdens to her.

"I'm kind of preoccupied with something that happened at my aunt's house today, and I sure wish I had a little time to put it into perspective because I don't want it to spoil my date with him. I need all my wits and positive thoughts at maximum levels for this, because I don't mind telling you that the man makes my heart tingle. But don't you dare tell Rubye and Thomas!" she said smiling. "I need you to be in prayer, girl. I don't want to mess things up again," Vann said.

"Now, you know I'll be praying, but what happened at your aunt's house, Vann? And I don't want you to let my troubles get you down. One of us down in the dumps is enough."

Vann smiled, gratefully. "No, Stelle, your troubles have nothing to do with this trouble. When I stopped by Aunt Lu's house, she told me that my mother—not my grandmother—is sick, and needs my help. Now, Stelle, you know how hurt I've been all of my life over that woman's rejection of me." Vann set the glass of tea down, and covered her face with her hands. "How? Please tell me how she can now think she has the right to ask me to do anything for her. I tell you, girl, it's blown my mind. The only reason I came on over here was because I knew you needed me. Otherwise, I'd probably be at home cursing her out."

"Oh, Lord!" Stelle said, a look of unbelief on her face. "Well, you're free to curse her out right here," she offered with a laugh. "And I'll happily join you. But I think the best thing we can do is to pray and ask the Lord to give you peace and guidance in the situation."

"You know what, Stelle? That's why God puts godly people around us. It's so we can keep each other on the right path. It's really funny how we can always come up with the right solution to someone else's problem, but when it comes to our own, we lose all perspective," Vann said, with a smile. "You are absolutely right. Come on, girl, pray!"

They joined hands and Stelle began to pray. "Gracious Master, we come to You today, thanking You for the privilege of prayer. We acknowledge that You are God Almighty, and in control of everything. We ask that You forgive us, Father, for the ungodly thoughts and desires we have toward other people, because You have told us to love, and to forgive, and to do everything we can to live in peace with others. Well, Lord, I don't have to tell You how hard that is to do sometimes. So, Father, we both come heavily burdened with the wrongs and hurts that have been thrust upon us. Father, we know that it is only because of Your mercies that we have not been consumed. So all we know to do is to keep trusting in Your mercies, Your grace, and Your power to help us deal with these hurts.

"Lord, strengthen us where we're weak, and build us up where we're torn down. We thank You that the same mercy that has kept us, and brought us this far is surely a refuge in this time of trouble and will help us to keep going, and so we praise You for the victories that are to come. Now Lord, bless Vann as she goes on her date, and let it be a refreshing and enjoyable occasion, and most of all, Lord, let Your will be done regarding Vann and this man, and Vann and her mother, and in my own life as well. In Jesus' name, we ask these and all other blessings. Amen."

Vann hugged Estelle, and wiped at the tears running down her face. "Thank you, girl. I needed that."

"We both did," Stelle replied. "Like you said, we spend too much time focusing on the problem, when we should be focusing on the Problem Solver. Now how many times have you told us that in Sunday school class?" Stelle asked, wiping at her own tears.

"So true. But it's understandable that we're knocked off balance when something unexpected hits us in the face. That's why I am so thankful for good, godly friends. Thanks again, girl, and now I'm going home and start getting ready for my date."

Vann walked out of Stelle's house a little lighter than when she had first arrived. Funny how prayer changes things. The issue with Rosetta was still hanging over her like a dark cloud, but she had been reminded that God's mercies endure forever. And it helped that she had her dinner date with the judge to look forward to. She prayed it would turn out differently than her recent disappointing dates.

The minute she walked in the door, her phone started ringing. "I hate it when that happens!" she said, running to grab it. "Hello!"

"Vannie, baby? Aunt Bernie here."

Oh no! Vann thought, sure her mother's other sister was calling to add her comments to Aunt Lu's. Aunt Bernie was another aunt who lived in Houston, and who had opened her heart and home to Vann when she had moved to Texas over three decades ago. She would always love her aunts for trying to make up for their sister's failure.

"How're you doing?" In her usual way, her aunt didn't give Vann a chance to respond, but rushed into why she was calling. "Now I just talked to Lu and Mama, so I know all about what's going on. I'm just calling to put in my two cents for what it's worth. Now listen! Don't you let them push you into doing something that you don't want to do. They can't say anything to justify you taking that woman into your home and taking care of her." She talked as though 'that woman' wasn't her own sister.

"Yeah, I know she's my sister," she continued as though she had heard Vann's thoughts, "but I told her years ago that until she made things right by you, I wouldn't have anything to say to her. And I haven't spoken to her since...until now. She knew not to even call me, but when I found out what was going on, I called her and gave her a piece of my mind. As far as I'm concerned, she made her bed, now she ought to be woman enough to sleep in it. She has no business trying to turn her problems into your problems. None whatsoever! I've told Mama, Luberta, and Rosetta that, in no uncertain terms. You don't owe her anything. You don't have any responsibility to do anything for her. You hear what I'm saying, Vannie?"

"Yes ma'am," Vann answered.

"Well, now you know you're not alone. I'm getting ready for my trip, but you call me if you need me to back you up. I'll get 'em off of you lickety split." She paused a minute, then said, "Bye now," and like a whirlwind, she was gone.

Vann was smiling when she hung up. Aunt Bernie was the black sheep of the family—never doing what was expected— never conforming to tradition. When Aunt Bernie's husband died, leaving her financially stable, she hadn't lost any time getting her hair dyed, buying a new wardrobe, and joining a senior travel club. Her children were swiftly corrected when they mistakenly made plans for her. Aunt Bernie put her house on the market and moved into a condo. She made dates to see her children and grandchildren. Showing up unexpectedly at Aunt Bernie's house could mean hurt feelings.

chapter thirteen

"I recently bought a new house, and I'm kind of floundering on how to furnish and decorate it. Thomas and Rubye told me about your decorating business and I thought you might be able to help me," Mitch told Vann over dinner.

"I wish they hadn't done that!" she said vehemently.

"Why? You don't want to work for me? I can afford it."

"No, that's not what I mean. It's only a hobby, and one that I just started. I have no training or real experience for that matter. I just kind of go with what I like. I wouldn't want you to be disappointed, so I really think you should look for a true professional with experience."

"Well that's just it," Mitch explained. "I don't want my house to look like its been professionally decorated. I'd rather have a comfortable, inviting look. I'm afraid I may not be able to get that across to a professional. I really wish you would consider it. And I wouldn't worry about disappointing me, because I'll be right with you every step of the way. I'm not going to let you do anything I don't agree with. Will you at least give it some thought? Let me give you my number," he said, handing her a business card with his home and cell numbers written on it. "You can feel free to call me at any of these numbers anytime, okay?"

They were having dinner in *'The Americas'*, a beautiful restaurant in the Galleria area. The atmosphere was quiet and relaxing, and the food was excellent. Surprisingly, any discomfort she thought she would feel in his presence was absent, and conversation flowed freely between them as they shared stories and experiences about growing up in Georgia. She surprised herself—she was actually enjoying his company, and noticed that they were both smiling at each other a lot.

"Now don't ask me why I bought such a big house when I live alone for the most part," Mitch told her. "My son is there quite a bit, but it's still too big for just the two of us. It has five bedrooms—two downstairs, and three upstairs—three bathrooms, not counting the one in the master suite and a powder room, formal living and dining rooms, large kitchen, family room, study and game room. It's well over five thousand square feet. But you know, I've always wanted this kind of house. I was in the military when my older children were growing up, and a house like this was out of the question because we moved around so much. Now, as foolish as it seems, I decided that I might as well get the kind of house I wanted while I'm able to enjoy it. I can always sell it with no problem."

"You only live once, so you should go for all the gusto you can," Vann agreed.

"So, are you enjoying retirement?" Mitch asked, changing the subject.

"Yes, I am," she answered with enthusiasm. "Although I still work just as hard, the difference is, I'm enjoying it more. And I still see all the people who matter."

She told him a little about Cyrus and Sylvia. "I try to get by as often as I can to check on them. They've been very good to me, and I don't take kindness lightly."

"I remember Cyrus crying at your reception. It's apparent he thinks a lot of you. So, I guess you're living out all your dreams, huh?" he asked, smiling. "A hobby that you enjoy that has turned into a business, and I've seen you on television, hosting your own show. You're a very busy lady."

"Well, not all of my dreams. Not yet. I still have some things on my list that I haven't gotten around to" she confessed.

"Like what?" he asked.

"Like doing a little traveling, and believe it or not, I've always wanted to learn how to play golf. I think it has more to do with the beautiful scenery and serene atmosphere of the golf courses than the game. But I'll get around to it one of these days."

"I play golf. I'm teaching my son how to play, and I'd be happy to teach you. When do you want to start?"

"Oh!" Vann said, looking embarrassed. "I wasn't trying to...uh...you know...hint around that you teach me to play or anything. I was just sharing some things I still would like to do."

"If I know nothing else about you, Vann, I do know you wouldn't hint around about anything. I hope you'll accept my offer in the spirit that it was given." He hoped desperately to get to know this woman better, and he would grab any straw he could. "What about relationships? Where does that fall in your future plans?"

"It's...uh...its been so long since I ...uh...have been seriously involved that I don't really have any plans."

Mitch smiled widely. "So am I correct in assuming that you're not involved with anyone right now?"

"Yes, much to the disgruntlement of my friends," she answered.

"Is there a particular reason?"

"No. Other than the fact that available men in my age range are kind of scarce, and the ones who are single have so many women after them, or have other issues, that I just choose not to deal with it all. At any rate, I'm pretty content with my life as it is."

"Your age range?" He looked puzzled and she could see the burning question in his eyes that he wanted to ask, but wouldn't.

"I'm in my fifties, Mitch, and have never been married. I suppose I'm the classic example of what the world calls an old maid."

Surprise flicked in his eyes and he smiled. "I would never have guessed it. You look good! By the way, when is your birthday?"

"April 3," she answered, and laughed. "Can you believe I was so caught up in my projects that my birthday passed without me realizing it this year?"

"Now that's too busy," he said, making a mental note of the date. "I'm fifty, and for some reason have trouble finding women I'd like to spend time with. All I can say is that it's too bad we haven't met before now, because I was interested in you from the first moment I saw you in my courtroom when we were going at it with each other. I was wishing, even then, that we had met under better circumstances." He looked directly into her eyes and spoke softly, but intensely. "And as you know, I'm still interested. But you can't make me believe you've never had a man interested in you, not a woman as beautiful as you are—both inside and out."

A shadow crossed her face, and Vann lowered her eyes. "As a matter of fact, I've been engaged a few times, and have dated quite a bit. It just never worked out for one reason or another. That's a whole new story that would take too long to get into tonight."

Mitch noticed her body language and said, "We can both share our stories another time. When can you come out to my house and look around? What about tomorrow afternoon? Then we can go to the driving range and I can start teaching you how to hit balls."

She hesitated before answering. "I had to think for a minute about whether I had made plans to help someone after church, or if there's something going on with my family or my friends that I'm needed for. But you know, it's time to stop thinking

121

about the needs of others all the time and start doing some things I want to do some of the time. That sounds like fun, so yes, I'll plan to come over after church tomorrow."

Mitch let out the breath he'd been holding. But he knew that even if she had said no, he would have asked her to go out with him again. "Good. I'll have dinner ready for you."

"Oh, do you cook?"

"Like I said, I'll have dinner ready. I'm not promising that I'm going to cook it."

She laughed. "At least you're honest. By the way, I have something to ask you. Would you happen to know a good divorce attorney? Two of my closest friends are in need of one right now."

He thought for a minute. "Yes, I happen to know a very good one." A frown appeared between his eyes. "I hope you're not going to let their marital troubles influence you to not take a chance on a relationship though."

"Ha! That's the same thing Rubye told me," she said, laughing again. "And no, I'm not going to do that. I know that just like people, every relationship is different. Rubye and Thomas, for instance, are on the positive side of the equation. Unless I'm way off in my observation, they will be married forever."

"I agree. They have the kind of marriage I've always wanted, but which has evaded me." Mitch now had painful shadows running across his face.

"What's his name?" Vann asked, digging into her purse for a pen and paper.

Puzzled, he asked, "Whose name?" Mitch quickly pushed the unpleasant thoughts to the back of his mind.

"The attorney. I need his name and number."

"Oh. As a matter of fact, it's a woman. I'll have to give you the number later, since I don't have it with me."

"Good. Can you do that as soon as possible? My friends really need help fast."

"I'll have it for you tomorrow when you come over."

"That'll be great."

Vann came down quickly from the euphoria she felt after her date with Mitch. She had a message from Mama, demanding that she call her right away. She knew what that would be about.

"Savannah Jo Sinclair! I know how I raised you, and it wasn't to be uncharitable. You were taught to love others. Now, I know your mother has caused you a lot of hurt and disappointment and I can't even say I know how you feel. But I do know me and Papa did the best we could by you. You was raised up in the fear of the Lord. Now, I can't tell you what to do because you're a grown woman, but I am asking you to do what's right for Rosetta.

"I want you to think about this hard before you go saying no to helping her. I ain't proud of what Rosetta did. But I am proud of you and the woman you turned into. I know you're a Christian woman. All I'm asking you to do is to look upon Rosetta like you would anybody else that you wouldn't hesitate to help. I want you to let love be your guide and peace be your umpire. Now take it from me baby, that's the only way you're going to have any joy. You got to do the right thing."

The pain that Vann had managed to push to the back of her mind returned, fortified with anger. "Yes, the woman gave birth to me, but I have never even laid eyes on her as far as I know. Mama, I think you're asking too much of me. As much as I love you and Aunt Lu, and you know there's nothing I wouldn't do for either of you, I can't take care of this woman. I don't have that much love in me. You need to be talking to the children this woman apparently loved enough to keep and raise. They are the ones you need to be laying a guilt trip on, not me. Aunt Bernie agrees with me. Have you talked to her?"

"Yes, I've talked to that heathen!" the old lady replied harshly. "You know Bernetta ain't never had a kind word to say to her sister. She put herself up as judge and jury, and you know what the Word of God says about judging others. It ain't her place to judge her sister. And she ain't got no business telling you to do wrong either. Rosetta is your mama, child! Your mama!"

Vann tried to hold the anger she felt in check. "*You* are my mama. In every sense of that word, you are the one who holds that place in my heart. But right now, I'm feeling like Aunt Bernie is the only one who is considering my feelings. And you know what else? That woman has talked to everyone about it but me. If she needs my help so badly, why is she still treating me like a nonentity? I'll tell you why. I'm just a nobody to her. A baby she had, threw away, and now wants to come back and use because she happens to need me for her own purposes."

"It's guilt, sugar!" Mama said, forcefully. "She's ashamed to call you. And well she should be. But baby, you got to love her with the love of Christ and honor her as your parent so that all will be well with you."

Vann sighed. "Mama, you know I love and respect you, so I don't mean any disrespect when I say I think you're the one telling me wrong. I'm hurt that you're demanding something of me that could destroy the life I've worked so hard, and waited so long for. I'm not sure this is something God Himself would expect of me. And Mama, I don't think y'all are being fair about this."

"Sugar, this ain't about being fair. This is about doing the right thing. And everybody gon' have to give an accounting before the Lord for themselves. You can't get weary in well doing...even if it means doing good to somebody who wronged you in the worst way. You have to trust the Lord to make things right for you. Now, I'm tired, baby. It's late, and time for this old woman to lay down."

But Vann couldn't leave it alone. "What about her, Mama? Where does reaping what you sow come in for her?"

Her grandmother sighed tiredly. "Baby...how many times have you heard your pastor say that we shouldn't let anyone make us have a hard heart against them? That it'll only make you sick, or shorten your life? Just think and pray about what I said. That's all I ask."

"Lord!" Vann had to try several times before she could get the phone back into the base. Tears streamed down her face as she sank into a chair, confusion swirling in her mind. "I don't know what the right thing is, Father, and worse, I don't even know if I want to know."

A few days later, Vann reflected on all that had happened since her retirement. Most of her experiences were new and wonderful things that brought much joy, but the situation surrounding the woman who had given birth to her had only brought agony, and that made her want to clutch the good things close, and lock the door to anything else.

She looked down at the ensemble she was making. It was coming together nicely she thought to herself. "Beautiful!" she said, holding the fabric up and looking at the rich royal blue color that she had coordinated with a floral pattern. "I might have to use this in one of my rooms."

This was all a part of her determined effort to keep thoughts about the troubling situation with her mother at bay. As long as she filled her mind with other things, she wouldn't think about her...the woman who had finally called Vann...the woman she had spoken to for the first time in her life. She threw the fabric down in frustration and jumped up from the sewing machine as the disturbing conversation she'd had with Rosetta demanded center stage of her mind.

"Vann? Is this Vann?" a woman's uncertain voice asked.

"Yes," she answered, already knowing the identity of the caller.

"Uh, Vann...uh, this is your mother, Rosetta. How are you?"

"I'm fine, thank you," she responded with a deep chill in her voice.

"I, uh, know you're surprised to be hearing from me."

"No. Mama and my aunts told me about your situation."

"Well, I hope you don't mind me calling. I'm really happy to finally be talking to you. And I sure hope you're going to help me out."

Vann gave a disgusted grunt. "Let's just lay it on the line, Rosetta. If you didn't need my help, we wouldn't be talking now. And would you tell me why you think I should even consider helping you out?"

Rosetta sighed. "I don't blame you for being angry. And I want to tell you that I'm so sorry for the way I've treated you. I know nothing I can say will change things, and I am sorry. But I knew my mama and papa and my sisters would make sure you were taken care of."

"No, you didn't," Vann shouted into the phone. "But thank God they did, otherwise, there's no telling where I'd be. Maybe dead for all you cared."

"Naw. I knew you would be alright. Mama was going to see to that."

"Uh huh!" Vann said, sarcastically. "Is that also why you've made sure that you kept yourself and your other children away from me like I had the plague or something?"

"Naw, it wasn't like that," Rosetta said quickly. "See, you don't understand how it was back then. If a woman wanted to get a good man and keep him, she had to present herself in a certain way. I just couldn't let it be known that I'd had a baby out of wedlock. The man I married would have never forgiven me."

"And where is your husband now, Ms. Rosetta?" Vann asked, sarcasm still ringing in her voice.

"Oh. He's dead. He's been gone about five years now."

"And what about since he died?" Vann asked curiously. "You didn't think about calling me in all of that time? And what about your children? Do they know about me?"

"Well, so much time had passed that I felt I should just let sleeping dogs lie. After all, finding out about you at this point would only hurt and confuse them, and frankly, I didn't want to tell them about you because...well...I just didn't want them to think badly of me...you know...as a mother."

"Well, Ms. Rosetta, I suggest you call those children who must think very highly of you, and ask them for the help you need. I certainly wouldn't want you to be tainted in their eyes at this point. It was interesting to finally hear your voice, but I really have to go now."

"Wait, Vann! You're not even going to ask what's wrong with me? I'm a very sick woman and..."

Vann quietly hung up the phone without saying good-bye.

Coming back to the present, Vann wiped at the tears she hadn't realized were sliding down her face.

Mitch was still basking in the joy he felt about the budding relationship with Vann. Their dinner Saturday night, followed by Sunday afternoon at his home, had been the most enjoyable experiences he had had in a very long time. They had talked about so much, and actually found they had a lot in common. But most importantly, their time together was comfortable, restful, peaceful, and sweet. He made himself remember the mistakes he had made with Katrina and Beverly, and cautioned himself not to get too caught up in this woman before he knew where the relationship was heading.

He wanted so badly for things to work out well between them that even the thought that it might not, filled him with agony. She was an exceptional woman, full of softness and tenderness, but hard as nails when she felt the need. She was just what he needed to keep life interesting and exciting, but he vowed to at least try to tread slowly and prayerfully.

They had walked through each room of his home and made notes on the kind of décor he wanted in each one. Some didn't have a stick of furniture yet, which was good. It gave him a reason to spend more time with her, shopping for furniture, or getting together with her to make it, since they both enjoyed doing that. Just being in her presence was enough. And although they talked on the phone at least once a day, which was difficult some days because the woman was busier than he was with a full-time job, he could hardly wait to see the joy in her beautiful smile, hear her sultry voice, touch her silky skin, and imagine what it would be like to really kiss her inviting lips—which he planned to do soon. She had quickly become very important to him.

"Slow your roll, dude!" He kept telling himself, but he soon realized it was already too late. She had mentioned more than once that they needed to talk about relationship issues before they got too deeply involved, to make sure neither one ended up getting hurt. He agreed, but he sure didn't want to rock the boat in any way. So, he kept putting her off when she mentioned the serious talk they needed to have.

Vann was in a continuous wrestling match with herself—knowing the right or moral thing to do for Rosetta, but unable to get past the hurt the woman had caused her. If peace was her umpire, her troubled spirit told her she had lost the game. And love? Love hadn't even played in the game. So of course, joy was nowhere to be found, and guilt was furiously eating away any justification she felt she had a right to feel.

"I know I need to spend some serious time in prayer, Lord. But I'm so confused right now I don't even know how or what to pray for. Have mercy upon me and this situation dear Lord, and lead me in the path of righteous."

Remembering her list, she suddenly decided to get away and do something different and to see the woman who had always been 'Mama' to her. In spite of their disagreement, she knew that just seeing Mama and soaking up the love and comfort she was sure to find there, would soothe her mind and spirit. She excitedly went into preparation.

"Rubye, in case you're looking for me, I'm going to Georgia to visit with Mama for a few days. And since it's on my list of new things to do, I'm going to spend a couple of days in Charleston first and do a little sightseeing, then I'll rent a car and drive on to Savannah. Charleston is an interesting city, and maybe that old historical place will restore something I've lost, or help me see things in a new perspective. A change of scenery will do me good right now, and I need to check on Mama anyway."

"What's going on, Vann?" Rubye asked, with concern. "Is it this situation with your mother, Rosetta?"

"Please don't insult me by calling Rosetta my mother," Vann snapped. "And yes, I suppose that's at the root of it. She finally called, after Mama got after her about it I'm sure. She said she was sorry, but I think the thing she's sorry about is having to come to me for help. Otherwise, I don't think she'd be giving me a second thought."

"Well, don't beat yourself up because you're not able to welcome her with open arms," Rubye sympathized. "Vann, she had choices. She made them and went on her way. Everybody makes mistakes, but she's never even acknowledged her mistake or made an effort to correct it. You didn't ask to be born, whatever the circumstances. No, it's on her. I'm sorry she's sick, and I'm certainly not happy to see her in need, but Vann, why should her problem suddenly be your problem? I guess I need to be praying too if that's not the right attitude. But I know how wounded you've been all your life because of this woman's rejection. I think your family is wrong, and expecting way too much from you."

"Rubye, I gave up all hope of ever even seeing this woman over thirty years ago. That's not to say the hurt over her rejection went away, but I moved on as best as I could. And now that I've started a new chapter in life, I don't want to complicate it. I'm happy and satisfied with my life and the good things happening now."

Rubye sniffed on the other end. "Yeah, Vann, I know, and you shouldn't have to deal with the complications this woman is bringing into your life. This is your time to enjoy and savor all you have accomplished. And I truly believe God has more blessings in store for you. You just go on and do what you need to do for your own peace of mind."

"Will you tell the other girls where I am in case they're looking for me? I've called the church already, and arranged for someone to teach my class for me. I don't have anything else pending that can't wait until I get back. And Rubye?"

"Yeah, honey."

"Thanks. You have always been there for me. You're such a good friend."

"Oh come on! I know who has always had my back, so don't even go there. Listen, be careful and stay in touch so I'll know you're okay."

"Will do. You and Thomas keep me lifted up in prayer please. What I'm really wrestling with is feeling guilty about failing in my Christian walk. I've talked and taught love and forgiveness to others for many years. And now, here I am, unable to extend either one to the woman who brought me into the world." Vann's voice broke as she admitted her own shortcomings.

"Oh, Vann," Rubye choked out. "I'm so sorry you're having to deal with this at a time in your life when things are going so well. It just doesn't seem fair."

"Well, like Mama told me, it's not about fair, it's about doing the right thing."

"Now you know I love your mama, but I'm fighting the temptation to go to Georgia and kick her old behind off the porch!"

Vann laughed. "Rubye! Shame on you, talking about a ninety-something-year-old woman like that!"

Rubye didn't join her in laughing. She was too angry with Vann's family for trying to take advantage of her. "Vann, I'm not the only one who ought to be shamed; in fact, I'm way down that shame list as far as I'm concerned. And I wouldn't mind telling your family that."

"Bye, Rubye. I'll stay in touch." Vann hung up feeling better knowing she had friends who loved and supported her—right or wrong.

chapter fourteen

Vann caught a flight out two days later and flew into Charleston. She rented a car and drove to the hotel where she had reserved a room on her computer the night before. After checking in and realizing she was hungry, she ordered a meal from room service and settled down for the rest of the day to pray.

She prayed like she had never prayed before. Never before had she fought a battle where she wasn't sure what outcome she wanted. "Oh God, Your Word says that a double minded person is unstable in all their ways. Help me, Lord."

She hated the indecisiveness she was feeling. She had always desired in her heart to do the right thing; however, this time she was confused about what exactly was the right thing. There were so many negative emotions involved in the situation that Vann had to conclude nobody but the Lord could guide her through them. If taking her biological mother into her home was the right thing, Vann knew in her heart that she might be fighting a losing battle because she just didn't know if she could do it. But could she live in disobedience to the Lord?

The next morning she was up early, preparing to do the tourist thing. As she was sitting in the hotel lobby, waiting for the tourist bus to pick her up, an older gentleman sat down near her and struck up a conversation. "Hello, I'm Ben Edmonds." He introduced himself with a friendly smile. "Are you staying here at the hotel? I love this hotel, and stay here often. Are you enjoying your stay so far?" His questions were more gracious and friendly, than nosy. "I'm from a little town outside of Atlanta, and I'm here to attend the festival going on this week." He was of indeterminate age and ethnicity, with weathered light brown skin, straight black hair sprinkled liberally with gray, and piercing blue eyes. She thought she detected a slight accent, but couldn't pinpoint it.

Vann was drawn to the warmth and friendliness of the man, and figured he must need someone to talk to. "Hi, I'm Vann Sinclair, and yes, I am staying here a couple of days. I'm from Houston, Texas, and no, I'm not here for the festival. It's been many years since I spent any time here, and truthfully, I had forgotten about all of the festivals they have so I haven't made any plans to attend."

"Aaah, that's too bad. I come for several festivals every year, and I always see something I haven't seen before."

"I know. I've been to some of the festivals before, and always enjoyed them. So, I'm sure you'll enjoy them this time," she said. "But I've made plans to do some sightseeing and to just soak up some of the historical ambiance of the city. In fact, I'm about to go on a tour now."

After hearing that Vann was about to go on a tour, he decided to go as well. "Since the festival won't be starting until later today, do you mind if I join you on the tour? I could use the company."

"Certainly. It'll be much more fun having someone along to take in the sights of the city. Have you done any touring here lately?"

"No, no, I haven't. I have friends here, and I usually spend time with them, but they're all busy preparing for the festival or working at their regular places of employment. I keep telling them they need to retire," he said, with a sparkle in his eyes.

"Oh? Are you retired?" Vann asked him.

"Yes, yes I am. It's been many years ago. It's a good life, retirement. I can just go, and do things when I get ready. It's wonderful."

They continued the conversation as they got on the tour bus. "I recently retired, but I'm just as busy as I was when I worked on a full-time job," Vann shared with him. "I think I made a mistake, telling everyone I was retiring. They all think I'm a lady of leisure now, and think all I have to do is whatever they need me to do," she said, laughing.

"You must change that perception. Perhaps you are sometimes taking responsibility for what someone else is supposed to do. It's good that you are busy. It keeps you young and filled with vitality, but it must be on your own terms, you understand?"

"I'm still learning how to do that," she confessed. The tour guide directed their attention to various points of interest, but Vann barely noticed, she was so engrossed in her conversation with the stranger.

"You must learn this, or people will take advantage of you. So I challenge you to be selective in what you choose to do and tell the others to leave you alone—in a nice way, of course. You've paid heavy and expensive dues to be at this place in life."

"Oh, Ben! I'm so glad to hear you say that, and I know you're right, but I still feel guilty about saying no. But it's true, I have paid my dues."

Ben's piercing eyes gazed directly into her light brown ones. "Something tells me that you always put the needs of others before your own. Am I correct in my assumption?"

Surprised by his intuitiveness, Vann answered slowly, "I don't know how, but you have certainly assumed correctly."

He smiled again. "It's not hard to see kindness in your eyes. But you must also remember to be as loving and kind to yourself as you are to others. There is nothing selfish about that. One does not preclude the other. Love is action in the spirit of sacrifice. Whatever you do must always be rooted in love. You do things sometimes for the sake of peace, sometimes for the sake of need, sometimes for the sake of kindness, but always for the sake of love—love for others as well as yourself. Always remember, if you keep pouring from your own bucket of love without replenishing it, soon there will be nothing left, and an empty bucket won't do anyone much good."

Surely the Lord arranged this meeting, Vann thought. She was fascinated by his wisdom and kindness, and amazed at how easy he was to talk to. Her curiosity about who he was, and what made him tick prompted her to ask, "What about you, Ben? Who are you? What do you do when you're not attending festivals and entertaining strangers?"

He smiled widely. "Aaah! Curious about me, I see. I am a widower of many years now, and I loved my wife very much. I still miss her smile and her gentle ways. That is why I spend the majority of my time traveling around from place to place and meeting new and interesting people. It pours into my bucket and helps me to pour into others, and it keeps me from sitting and thinking about missing her so much. As soon as I return from one trip, I am planning another. I have made many good friends in my travels, so wherever I go, there is someone to spend time with. And you? Do you have a special person?"

Vann found herself telling him about Mitch, and how much she was beginning to like him. "We met by yelling at each other in a courtroom, so the fact that we are now friends who are growing closer is almost a miracle."

"But that is the wonder of miracles," Ben exclaimed. "They happen in unexplainable ways. Ways in which we have to acknowledge the touch of a higher power."

"Strange you should say that, Ben, because this man told me he prayed that God would bring us together. And it's come about through a series of coincidences."

"Then you must always keep that miraculous element in your relationship. What has brought you together will be what keeps you together. But make sure he is a man of honesty and integrity who is the right recipient of your love, and is capable of loving you as you desire and deserve."

"From what I have observed, he's very hard-nosed and opinionated, but as a judge, I suppose he has to be. Yet he has also shown me that he's willing to admit when he's wrong and to try to right any wrong he's done."

"He sounds like a man of principle, and they don't come along very often. Hold him close and find the way to touch his heart and mind."

"I don't know if I know how to do that, Ben," she said softly to the stranger.

"By being true to who you are, and letting love rule in your heart. Love never fails."

Vann was amazed that she was having this kind of conversation with this stranger and that he had been able to put his finger on the pulse of her concerns. Her mind immediately went to Rosetta. So much of what he had said shed light on the dark places in her heart where hurt and bitterness lived.

Throughout the day, Ben was the perfect gentleman companion. "You must let me buy you something cold to drink," he frequently insisted as they traveled around the city. "You must tell me when you are ready to eat. I know many interesting places where the local cuisine is excellent." They left and then rejoined the tour several times.

They ended the tour at the Market, which covered several blocks and had a vast array of handcrafted items that were locally produced. Vann had been there before, but it had been years ago. Ben made it seem as though it was her first time there and kept her laughing as he regaled her with funny stories about the history of some of the things they saw. Vann was able to almost forget about the situation she was running from. She enjoyed his company so much that she agreed to have dinner with him. "Oh, that is wonderful!" he exclaimed. "I will cancel dinner plans with my friends, so I can enjoy it with you. My friends and I will have plenty of time to enjoy one another."

After dinner, Ben tried unsuccessfully to persuade her to accompany him to the festival that evening, but she was tired and begged off. After making plans for the next day, she returned to her room where she showered and began turning the situation with Rosetta over and over in her mind. Ben's words kept returning. *Love is action in the spirit of sacrifice. Sacrifices are always rooted in love, sometimes for the sake of peace, sometimes for the sake of need, but always for the sake of love.*

"Oooh, Gracious Master," Vann began to talk to the Lord. "Ben's words have made me face up to some things that I already know. Father, Your Word tells me that without love it is impossible to please You, and that love never fails. I've read and heard and even taught this most of my life. But now, because of hurt over Rosetta's rejection of me, I'm unwilling to meet her need for help, and Father, nothing but Your love in me can help me to do what will be a great sacrifice.

"I'm enjoying my life and the new and good things that are happening: my decorating venture, becoming a television host, and most importantly...Mitch. Am I to sacrifice these things for the sake of this woman?" *One does not preclude the other.* More of Ben's words flowed into her mind. "In my heart, I want to do the right thing, Father, so Lord, forgive me for my sins of unforgiveness, disobedience and selfishness that are rooted in hurt, anger, and bitterness against this woman. Cleanse me and fill me with Your love, heavenly Father. In Jesus' name. Amen."

She was almost happy when she heard her cell phone ringing. She needed a distraction from the painful acknowledgment of her own shortcomings. "Hello?" she answered.

"Vann, this is Mitch. How are you? I've been calling you at home and not getting an answer. I finally called Rubye and she told me you were dealing with a serious family issue. Can you tell me about it?"

"Well, so much for the discretion of friends!" Vann exclaimed, but pleasure at hearing his voice swelled up in her. "Actually, it's good to hear from you. I didn't tell you I was leaving town because I'm so mixed up in the head that I didn't think you would appreciate being drawn into that confusion. I felt like a change of scenery was what I needed to keep from going crazy."

"What is it, Vann? I'm a good listener, and I do know how to be discreet."

Vann decided that since he was asking, there was no reason not to tell him. "It's my mother, Mitch. My birth mother. I was raised by my grandmother after my mother abandoned me. I won't go into everything now, but suffice it to say that my mother never wanted anything to do with me. She got married, had three more children, you know, the perfect little family. Now, her health is failing and her other children evidently don't care, or at any rate aren't offering any help. So what does the woman do? She finally remembers that, oh yes, there is this other child. Now she wants this thrown-away child to graciously take her in so she won't have to go to a nursing home."

"I can hear the hurt you're feeling, and I don't blame you for being angry about it," Mitch responded in a sympathetic voice. "That's a tough situation, honey. What are you going to do?"

"I don't know!" Vann literally wailed. "That's why I had to get away for a few days to pray and think. The confusing thing is that I know what I would like to do, but I'm having trouble because I don't know if I could live with that choice. I was praying just now, confessing my own sins and asking God to fill me with His love, because…" Vann's voice grew faint as she spoke.

"You don't want to take her in," Mitch surmised. "Nobody can blame you for that, Vann."

"Nobody but me and the Lord. Mitch, I've come face to face with my Christianity, and you know what? It's demanding that

I put my heart where my mouth has been, that I walk the walk I've been talking for so many years. All the love, forgiveness, grace, and mercy that I've claimed to believe in all my life is now being tested in a way I never imagined, and frankly, it's distressing to realize that I'm flunking the test."

"Well, don't be too hard on yourself, because we all flunk that test at some point in our walk," Mitch said. "This is a very difficult decision, Vann, and it's one you'll have to make alone because nobody but you knows the depth of your feelings about it. Take consolation in the fact that the Spirit of God is so strong in you that it's causing you to struggle with this decision, because it wouldn't even bother some people to tell that woman where to go, and not give it a second thought. If it's any help, I believe you'll do what's right. Not right for you, or what your mother thinks is right for her, but right in the eyes of God. Is there anything I can do for you? Do you need anything?"

"Just pray," she answered. "It's between me and the Lord. It'll be interesting to see who'll win, because right now, I honestly don't know what I'll choose, and won't know anytime soon from the looks of it," Vann answered wearily. "Otherwise, believe it or not, I'm having a great time. I met a very nice gentleman, who has been extremely kind to me. He escorted me on one of the tours today, and we really had a wonderful time. Tomorrow, we're going to tour one of the plantations near here, and he wants to go to one of those ghost shows...I don't know about that," she said, chuckling. "Then the next day, I'll drive on to Savannah to visit my mama for a couple of days. I'll have to get on back home then, because duty calls."

"I don't know if I like the idea of you picking up strange men," Mitch said, surprised by a sudden tinge of jealousy. "But I suppose you know how to take care of yourself, huh?"

Vann laughed. "Of course I do. And he is one of the most kind, gentle, and wise souls you could ever meet. Actually, he's gone out of his way to entertain me and take care of me. It's almost like he knows I'm in a painful dilemma and he's trying to help me through it. It's very curious, but I believe he is the reason God brought me here. He's said some very enlightening things that have helped me. But I do know to be careful, thank you," she said, smiling.

"I'll be praying, but I miss you…miss talking to you, miss you not being close enough to see you. Do you mind if I call from time to time and check on you?"

"Yes, that's fine. It might help me hold on to my sanity."

"Vann?" Mitch hesitated, not wanting to come on too strong. "Will you let me help you with this? Whatever decision you make, I want to be there to help you get through it. Okay?"

"Uh, of course." Vann struggled to hide the fact that she was all choked up, but that was exactly what she was feeling. "Uh… I…uh, appreciate that, Mitch. It means a lot to me. And God is already working through friends like you, Rubye, and Thomas to express His love and faithfulness to me. Thank you."

"I mean it, Vann," Mitch said softly. "And I'll be upset if you don't let me help you." He paused for a moment, then asked, "Will you let me take you to dinner when you get back?"

"I suppose."

"Well, I look forward to it," Mitch answered before hanging up.

Vann spent another pleasurable day with Ben, who she had started thinking of as her guardian angel. They exchanged contact information and promised to stay in touch. She left the hotel after a very enjoyable stay, but still with a heavy heart. She felt the burden of the situation settle onto her shoulders again as she drove from Charleston to the rural area near

Savannah, where her mama lived. The burden grew heavier when she saw how much more frail her mama had become. She had to struggle to keep tears from falling, as no amount of questioning would make the old woman admit to feeling anything but old age.

They had a lengthy conversation about Rosetta. When Vann repeated what Rosetta had said to her, the old woman wiped at the tears that quickly filled her eyes and slid down her winkled face. "I can't hold with anyone with the kind of heart that would let her say that to a child she's mistreated all of her life. She has no right to expect anything. I don't blame you for hanging up on her, baby. And I'm not going to say anything else to you about it. You just let the Lord lead you, sugar. I know you'll make the right decision. In the meantime, you go on and enjoy your life." She quickly changed the subject, showing that her frail body didn't equate to a dull mind.

"What's this Luberta's been telling me about this man you're going out with? You know I want to hear all about him, and I sho' 'nuff would like to meet him. If anyone deserves to have something good happen, it's you. You just make sure he's the right one. I know you're wise enough to know everybody smiling at you is not seeking your good. And oh, child! I sure do love seeing you on the television, looking so pretty, and talking so intelligently. I'm glad the Lord let me live to see it. I'm just so proud of you." The old woman's weak eyes glowed behind her eye glasses with unshed tears.

Vann left three days later. Her mama's words warmed her heart, but Vann knew that just because she was off the hook with Mama, she was far from being right with the Lord regarding Rosetta.

She couldn't dispute the fact that Ben and her mama were right about the love and peace assertion. In spite of her justifiable hurt, the continuous pricks of guilt on her conscience meant she had no peace, even if she did feel she was warranted in her actions. In an attempt to ease her guilt, she decided to send Rosetta some money. "That's probably what she's after anyway," Vann said, as she dialed Aunt Lu's number.

"Hey, Aunt Lu. I'm calling to see if you have Rosetta's address. I'm going to send her a little money to help her out."

"Hi, Vann. How you doing?" Luberta asked in a chilly tone. "I talked to Rosetta. Did you really hang up on her when she called you? I'm really disappointed in you, Vann. The Lord expects better from you."

Anger burned through Vann, and she had to count to ten before she answered her aunt. "Yes, I did hang up on her. First, she told me that she rejected me because she knew her husband would never forgive her for having a baby out of wedlock. Then, she told me that she didn't contact me or tell her children about me after he died because she didn't want them to think badly of her. Well...it felt like a knife turning in an open wound and I just kind of lost it. I mean the woman must think I'm a fool! In so many words, she's basically telling me, 'I want your help, but even after all these years, I'm still ashamed I gave birth to you.' Anyway, I told her I certainly wouldn't want her children to start thinking badly of her at this point. That's when I hung up. Now, Aunt Lu, please tell me what you would have done in that situation, because as much as I've prayed and thought about it, I can't come up with another response."

"Oh my goodness! I don't know what she was thinking to tell you something like that, and she'll hear from me about it. But Vann, just remember that she's sick and she needs help."

"You're right, Aunt Lu, God does expect better of me. But He also expects better of you, Rosetta, and anybody else who refuses to understand why this is so hard for me. I'm doing the best I can right now. That's why I'm sending her some money.

Now can I get the address?" Vann's tone indicated that if her aunt didn't give her the address, that would be fine with her.

She wrote the check and stuck it in an envelope with a note that said, "I hope this helps you in some way," then drove to the post office to mail it. "Now, Lord, will you please give me back my peace and joy?" Somehow, she knew...the prayer didn't make it beyond the roof of the car, not when love was a missing ingredient in her action. "I'm sorry, Lord. This is the best I can do right now."

chapter fifteen

Elliott and his date arrived at the Annual Fraternity Banquet a little later than he had planned, but they were still early enough to select a table that was placed in the huge ballroom so that he could watch the door to see who was arriving. Hopefully he hadn't missed the arrival of too many. He would later walk around to see and be seen by everyone, but for now, he would sit back and watch. He felt good about attending his fraternity's annual event where he knew many well-known, high profile people would be in attendance.

He smiled proudly at his date, Madeline Maddox, who was just the right woman, with the correct social connections. And she seemed to be just as proud to be with him as he was to be with her. She knew how to handle herself, and knew nearly everyone there. She would have been a perfect candidate for Elliott's consideration as a wife, but unfortunately, her influential husband had died and left her almost penniless. It was obvious she was on the hunt for another husband who could provide the life she was accustomed to. Elliott already knew it wouldn't be him, but she was the perfect date for this kind of event.

Savannah Sinclair, on the other hand, would be totally out of place at this kind of event. He didn't know exactly how he would handle that fact after he married her, but he would cross that bridge when he had to. He might just have to attend these events without her because he couldn't have her embarrassing him.

Elliott's mind was working, even as he smiled and greeted people from his table. He was thinking about the good time he was going to have tonight with his date, especially after the event, and he was making future plans for Savannah. Tomorrow after church, he would ask Savannah to go out to eat with him.

He might even spring for *Pappadeaux's Seafood Restaurant* this time. That might really impress her. Although she did get around more than he had originally thought, she hadn't had the privilege of being escorted by a man of his standing. She would have to realize how advantageous it was to travel in the right circles. That was something she couldn't do for herself. She needed him, although she didn't realize it yet.

"Hey, Elliott!" His frat brother and friend from church called to him and motioned for him to join him across the room. "Honey, I'm going to speak to Seth for a second," Elliott told his date. "I'll be back in a minute." He walked across the room to where Seth stood.

"Elliott. Man, how is it going?" Seth asked. "I thought you told me you were serious about Vann Sinclair, that you two had something going on?"

Elliott laughed. "Yeah, that's right. But that doesn't keep me from enjoying myself with some other pleasant company, now does it? Man, you know this is not the kind of event to invite Savannah to." He laughed again.

"Elliott, how in the world did you get to be such a snob?" Seth asked, coughing to hide his amused smile. "I'm just curious that's all," he said.

"Curious about what, brother?" Elliott asked with a sly smile. "About how I can have a little fun with another woman while I'm keeping Savannah on the back burner?"

Seth's smile got wider. "Nope. About how *Savannah* can have a little fun with another man while you're keeping her on the back burner." His smile became a loud laugh.

"What're you talking about, Seth?" Elliott asked, all signs of amusement gone.

"Have you looked over on the other side of the room? Looks like she's cooking pretty nicely."

Elliott's shocked gaze followed the direction Seth was looking and pointing. There, at a table across the room, was Savannah, looking up into the face of none other than well known criminal judge Mitchell Langford, who looked back at her with the kind of look that told Elliott the man was very interested in the woman. As he watched, they laughed at something someone at their table had said. Then the judge caught Savannah's hand as he leaned over to whisper something in her ear. Whatever he said brought a big smile to her face.

Elliott's mouth literally hung open with shock and surprise as he stared at the couple laughing and talking as though they were the only ones in the room.

"Surprised?" Seth asked. "You shouldn't be. I told you a long time ago that you were wrong in the way you were thinking about her. Vann Sinclair is a very nice woman, who has had some toughs breaks. She's decent, man! A genuine Christian woman. But you're so hung up on impressing other people that you can't tell a good woman from a bad one."

"If you know so much about her, then why didn't you tell me, man? I could've…"

"Could've what, Elliott?" Seth said, chuckling. "Now that judge, he knows a good thing when he sees one. And I don't think he has a problem being seen with her."

"You low-down,…!" Elliott snarled at his friend. "You're enjoying this aren't you? You had information that could have helped me get to her, and you kept it to yourself! Some friend you are!"

"Elliott, hold on a minute," Seth said, his back straightening. "Just listen to yourself. You just don't get it do you? That woman belongs to God. And God is not going to let you or anybody else use her for selfish purposes. And I'm certainly not going to be a part of anyone trying to use her. You need to check yourself, Elliott. It's time for you to get real with the Lord and the world we live in. You can't go around looking down on people simply because you think they fall below your ridiculous standards. You better listen, man."

Elliott watched as Seth walked away from him. He was seething with anger, both at Seth and at Savannah. His anger increased when he remembered that Savannah had told him something similar to what Seth had just said about checking himself. He looked across the room to the laughing Savannah and decided she was going to marry him, whatever it took. Nobody dumped him!

He went back to the table where his date sat, talking to the people there, but his eyes never left Savannah. A little later, he saw her leave the table and immediately excused himself and followed her.

"Savannah!" he called to her before she could disappear into the ladies' lounge. "What are you doing here and what are you doing with that judge? Why didn't you tell me you wanted to come to the banquet? If I had known, I could have brought you."

Vann looked at him pleasantly although she was fighting the urge to slap him silly. "Elliott, I'm having a good time with my friends. Now, I'm going to walk away and go about my business, and I suggest you do the same."

He grabbed her arm to keep her from leaving. "Can't you talk to me for a minute? I mean after all, you've stepped out with another man when I thought you and I had an understanding. The least you can do is act like somebody with a little sense," Elliott demanded.

Vann looked him steadily in the eye. "I suggest you let go of my arm or I'm going to remind you of what is socially correct." He let her arm go like it was on fire. She gave him an angry look before leaving him standing there.

"What did that old geezer say to you? I saw him follow you," Rubye asked as soon as Vann returned to the table. Vann proceeded to tell them about her conversation with Elliott. Rubye laughed and raised her hand for a high five when Vann finished.

Mitch looked a little puzzled. "What's the deal with the guy anyway?" he asked.

Rubye was more than happy to fill him in. "That creep actually thinks he's so much better than Vann that he doesn't think she should even be at an event like this, but he's always trying to talk to her on the sneak and get her into his bed."

"You don't need to be bothered by the likes of him," Mitch said.

When Mitch left the table to take care of his assigned responsibility of making presentations to award recipients, Elliott pulled him aside for a little talk. "Uh, brother," Elliott said in a low voice. "I don't know how to tell you this, brother, but the woman you're with tonight, Ms. Sinclair? Well, she and I have a sort of understanding between us, if you know what I mean."

Mitch looked at him coldly. "No, I don't. Explain exactly what you mean by 'understanding'."

"Well, I mean we've been talking and seeing each other for a while now. We attend the same church, you know, and things are pretty tight between us, so much so that it's understood that we'll be married some day in the near future. I don't believe she didn't tell you."

Mitch took a step forward. "If things are that tight between you and Vann, why is she not *your* date tonight?"

"Well, you know how it is, Judge. There are women you invite to certain things, and those you don't. And Vann kind of falls into the last group...you know what I mean?" Elliott swallowed hard when he saw the look on Mitch's face. He sought for the right words to explain himself. Surely the man understood what he was saying!

"No, Mr. Shaw, I don't know what you mean. I have the highest regard for Ms. Sinclair, and I don't believe she would have accepted a date with me if she had any type of commitment to another man. And I certainly don't believe a man with any sense would step out on her with another woman. So please explain."

Elliott bristled. "Wait a minute, brother. You don't talk to me like that! *I've* been over the road you're coming over."

"Evidently you didn't learn much on your road, mister," Mitch told him. "Everyone knows that the woman you apparently feel honored to be escorting tonight happens to be looking for the socially acceptable connection that you are. You two obviously have a lot in common, so why don't you stick with her and leave Ms. Sinclair to me. Goodnight."

Elliott sputtered as he tried to process what the judge had said.

Mitch walked away from Elliott with his mind made up. Even if things didn't work out the way he wanted them to with Vann, he would make sure she didn't end up with a creep like Elliott Shaw.

Mitch was spending as much time with Vann as he could manage. He coerced her into having dinner with him several nights a week and he began attending church with Thomas and Rubye, where Vann was also a member. Afterwards, he and Vann would spend the rest of the day shopping for things for his house, taking drives along one of the scenic farm roads, or at the miniature golf course where he had a lot fun teaching Vann the game of golf.

One weekend in October, Mitch had all of his children over so they could all meet Vann at the same time. Mitch had never considered bringing another woman around his children, but he wanted them to get to know Vann and that he was serious about her. Vann fixed a roast at home and brought it to his house Saturday afternoon, then made mashed potatoes and a green salad after she got there. She had also brought along a couple of sweet potato pies. Mitch's contribution to the meal was store bought rolls and fruit punch.

"Kids, I've met a special person I would like all of you to meet. This is Ms. Vann Sinclair. Vann, this is Mike and Alicia, children from my marriage years ago to Beverly, and this is Matthew, my youngest son, whose mother is Katrina. The little one is my granddaughter, Robyn, who belongs to Alicia, and I also have a grandson that belongs to Mike."

"I'm happy to meet all of you," Vann said, with a wide smile. They smiled back, but she could tell they had reservations about her, which she definitely understood. "Why don't we sit down and get acquainted?" They followed her suggestion, while watching her with curious eyes. They all looked a lot like Mitch, and seemed a little uncertain about her presence.

"Do you have any children, Vann?" Alicia asked, her large brown eyes filled with curiosity.

"No, none of my own; however, I do have a godson that I call mine. He lived with me for several years and still has a room at my house that he uses whenever he's in town."

"Does he have any children?" she asked.

"No, but I tell him all the time that I wish he would hurry up and get married and have some," Vann said, laughing. "Well, the food is ready, so why don't we eat while it's hot?"

Mitch led the way to the table and got everyone settled. "You are in for a treat," he told his children, as he smiled proudly at Vann.

It took only a few mouthfuls for Mike to say, "Umm! This food is good!" while licking his lips in appreciation. "If there's any left, I'm taking it home with me for later. Dad, you need to keep this woman."

"Why, so she can cook, and you can come over and stuff your face?" Mitch asked, laughing.

Mike finished chewing the mouthful of potatoes before answering, "Yes, that too. But I'm also glad to see you with a significant other to spend time with, Dad."

"Me too, Dad." Alicia said, smiling shyly.

"What's a significant other?" Matthew asked around a mouth filled with food.

"Don't talk with your mouth full, man," Mitch scolded. "A significant other is someone you like spending time and sharing things with."

"And who cooks good food?" Matthew said, cramming more food into his already full mouth.

"Matt, how many times do I have to tell you not to speak with your mouth full of food?" He often wondered just what Katrina fed the child. He suspected it was a lot of junk food because when Matthew came to his house, he was always starved for some nutritious food. Mitch didn't do a lot of cooking, but took him to good restaurants with a variety of healthy selections.

Mitch was glad to see that his children liked Vann, although it would have made no difference to him if they hadn't. But Vann's loving and outgoing kindness to them won them over. As they ate, she talked to them, asking questions about their jobs, and their lives in general. Mitch knew she was trying to show them that she wasn't a threat to their dad's love for them. It made him feel really good when she smiled at him in her special way, or said something to show how much she appreciated him in front of his children. They hadn't ever witnessed their mothers doing that.

After Mike, Alicia, and the baby left and Matthew was in bed, Mitch took Vann's hand and led the way into the family room. "I can't tell you how much I appreciate you, Vann. And I can tell that my children like you, too. I am so blessed to know you, and have you in my life, and I plan to do everything I can to keep you."

Vann was quiet for a few seconds before she responded. "Well, I'm blessed to know you, too. And I'm really enjoying all the time we're spending together."

Mitch leaned over and kissed her—really kissed her—for the first time. They had shared little pecks on the lips, and hugs, but not a real, passionate kiss that took her breath away and made her heart pound.

"I've wanted to do that for so long," he murmured, hugging her close. "But I've held off because I didn't want to scare you off. I think I'm falling in love with you," he whispered. "No, I know I'm falling in love with you," he said, and kissed her again.

Vann was filled with mixed emotions. She backed away from him and stood up from the sofa. "I, uh...think it's time for me to go," she said in a shaky voice. "I've enjoyed you and your children tonight." She quickly gathered up her things and left.

Vann was smiling when she hung up the phone. Admittedly, she had been nervous about meeting Mitch's children, and whether they would accept her as part of Mitch's life. But she'd never had a problem relating to young people, and apparently didn't with Mitch's children. That had been a major hurdle in Vann's mind, and she was extremely relieved that things had gone so well.

The kisses they had shared and Mitch's statement about falling in love with her stirred feelings that were exciting, but scary. She wanted to admit how she felt, but somehow, couldn't take that step. "Help me, Father. If Mitch is a part of Your will for my life, then give me the wisdom and strength to accept the love he's offering."

Mitch had called and invited her to attend a jazz concert with him next weekend. She had heard about the concerts they held on the boardwalk in Kemah, a seaside town that bordered the south side of Houston, but had never attended one, so it would make the occasion all the more special to go for the first time with Mitch. Only in the last ten or so years had Kemah been developed into a major tourist attraction. Somebody had finally woke up and smelled the coffee, or the tourist dollars, the city could bring in. Now it was one of *the* places for tourists to visit, and they did so in great numbers, drawn to the well-planned attractions and activities, as well as the diverse eating places. Besides that, it was on the water and provided a great seaside experience.

After eating at one of the restaurants that looked out on the water, Mitch and Vann sat on the boardwalk listening to music that was reminiscent of the good old days, and held hands as they swayed to the music.

The night had to be one of the highlights of Vann's life, and one she wished could go on forever. In addition to her delight with the Kemah experience, she looked forward to more of Mitch's kisses, and she was not disappointed. His kisses grew bolder and more passionate and took her breath away. She knew it was time for them to have a serious discussion about where they were headed. They were both professed Christians, but nothing could be taken for granted. Elliott said he was a Christian, too, but he was constantly harping on how God gave us needs and wanted us to satisfy them.

They were sitting in her family room, sipping on glasses of tea, after a passionate session of kissing. She avoided direct eye contact as she spoke, and knew her face was flushed with embarrassment, but this had to be said. "Mitch, I think we need to talk about how we both feel about how far we're going to take our physical involvement. I believe that as Christians, we are to abstain from any sexual involvement until and if, we're married." She took a drink from her glass of tea. "We, uh...need to be in agreement before this goes any further."

Mitch laughed at her embarrassment. "Well, look at my little sweetheart, acting all timid and everything. I know what you're saying, sweetheart, and I totally agree with you. I know you realize how much I enjoy holding and kissing you, and I believe you enjoy it as well, but I know what the Word of God says, and I plan to obey it. I disobeyed it in the past, and still live with the consequences, so although I'm not going to stop kissing you, I do want us to be diligent in not going too far. You do realize it's going to take both of us to stay on track, don't you?"

She smiled. "Yes, I realize that. Now, kiss me and get out," she said, punching him in the arm.

Everything was going so well with Mitch that she had to forcefully hold back the fear when Satan whispered to her that, like the other men who had been through her life, Mitch too, would leave one way or another. "Please God, keep him safe, and keep him close to me, and let me enjoy this time with Mitch just a little longer." But the issue of Rosetta lurked in the background of her mind, and she knew she needed to tell the woman something.

She continued to send money every week, and kept tabs on Rosetta through Mama and her aunts, but continued to put off making a decision.

A couple of weeks later, Vann and Mitch were sitting together in her family room half watching a senseless television sitcom while exchanging kisses between conversation that was just as nonsensical. They were so involved that a sonic blast could have exploded and they probably wouldn't have heard it. Vann was actually astonished that she was experiencing the eruption of feelings she hadn't felt in a very long time. And was just as amazed to realize that yes, there was still life in old places she had believed to be dead.

"Man, I know you better get your hands off of my mama," TreVann stated in a loud voice, as he stood over them with an outraged look on his face.

Even with the surprise interruption, the couple was so caught up in the moment that they were slow in moving away from each other. It took a minute for Vann to remember that TreVann was at home for the weekend, but had gone out with some friends earlier. She was startled to see him back so early and that he had entered the house without her hearing him.

"That's just Trevie messing with you," Vann quickly explained to Mitchell, who seemed to be frozen in place.

Mitch looked at Vann, then at TreVann, a puzzled expression on his face, and Vann said, "Trevie! Don't mess with Mr. Langford like that."

She smiled at Mitch and said, "He's just acting crazy, don't pay any attention to him."

Mitch's eyes returned to TreVann, who was now laughing uncontrollably. "I had you going for a minute didn't I, Judge? But do you know how traumatic it is for a child to find his mama indulging in this kind of scene?" He laughed harder. "Seriously though, I do want you to know, I don't play when it comes to this lady. You mess with her, you mess with me. You treat her right, you alright with me. Got it?"

"Yeah, man, I got it," Mitch said, slowly. "And you can call me Mitch," he added, relief evident in his face. TreVann stood about 6 feet 3 inches and had the muscles and bulk of a linebacker.

"Auntie, did you bake my cake?" TreVann asked as he headed for the kitchen. "Do you have any ice cream?" Vann heard him rummaging around in the refrigerator. "Gotta have some of that to go with the cake," he continued, as he searched the freezer compartment.

"Oh, baby, I might have some around here somewhere, but have you eaten anything? You know the rule. No desserts until after you eat."

"Aw, man! I came all the way from Austin just to see her and get some cake and she's talking about rules. I'm a grown man, I don't wanna hear about rules, I just want my cake. And she didn't even get any ice cream to go with it," TreVann grumbled from the kitchen.

Vann smiled at his grumpiness. "Grown or not, you heard me. There's some leftovers from last night in there. If you don't want that, I made some chicken salad. You can make a sandwich."

TreVann's crankiness quickly vanished. "Oh, good! I love your chicken salad. I'll eat some of that. You have any of those croissants you used to buy to go with it?"

"Yes, and you know where to find them," Vann answered, smilingly. "If I'm not careful, he'll have me up and fixing his plate for him with his spoiled, grown self," she told Mitch.

Mitch observed the interchange between them with curiosity. They sounded and acted like parent and child, but he had been under the impression that TreVann was Rubye and Thomas' son. But why was he here?

"Hey Mr....uh, I mean, Mitch? Would you like to join me in a sandwich and then some of the best lemon pound cake you've ever had? I guess I need to go to the store and get some ice cream. Auntie, are you sure you don't have any?"

"Look in the freezer in the garage, Trevie. And you're going to have to eat every bit of it, and that cake too, because I don't want any left here to tempt me."

"Now, why are you making me trip like that? You knew you had some." TreVann scolded her with a smile.

"Mitch, come on and join me if you can pull yourself away," TreVann offered. "I guarantee, you don't want to miss this."

Mitch stood slowly. "Okay." He headed to the kitchen. "You convinced me."

"Oh, oh! I'm really gonna have to watch you. You're letting the lure of food pull you away too easily. I wonder what else you give in to so easily?"

"Trevie! Stop teasing Mitch," Vann smiled at him. "Go on, join him, help yourself to whatever you want," she said to Mitch.

Mitch smiled eagerly. He knew her cooking was something he didn't want to miss. He went into the kitchen and, like TreVann, started digging around in the refrigerator. He pulled out the leftover grilled steak and potato salad and felt his mouth start to water when he put the steak in the microwave to heat it up. TreVann was already eating the gigantic chicken salad sandwiches he had made.

Vann was debating whether to join them or not, when she heard the doorbell. "I wonder who that can be?"

"Elliott! What are you doing here?" she asked in an annoyed tone when she opened the door.

"I was just in the neighborhood and thought I'd stop by." He pushed past her and stepped into the foyer. "It looks like you might have company," he said, looking around.

"Two cars sitting in my driveway that you know don't belong to me, Elliott, and it looks like I *might* have company? It's very rude for you to come to my home uninvited like this."

Elliott planted his feet. "We need to get some things cleared up, and since you won't return my calls, and when I see you at church, you're always busy or with somebody else, I figured I'd come over so we can talk. It's getting so I have to watch television just to see you. I'm getting tired of waiting, and the least you can do is show me the courtesy of talking to me. Is everything going alright with your little business?" he asked in a condescending tone. "And that's another thing we need to talk about. I can probably help you manage that and all this property you own around the city, and we can increase your profits. You're most likely letting people rip you off."

Help me manage my business? I don't think so! "Everything is going well, Elliott." Vann said, in an irritated voice. "You need to leave. I know you're astute enough to know I don't have time to have a conversation with you now," Vann told him with an angry voice.

TreVann had come into the room and heard from the tone of her voice that she was not happy. A curious and questioning look covered his face as he asked, "Who is this dude?" He took in everything about the older man standing there.

Vann turned to him. "Nobody, Trevie. Go on, finish eating. I'll be back in a minute."

TreVann didn't move. "Well, you do have company, which you are rudely ignoring," he told her, looking suspiciously at Elliott. "Who are you, anyway?" TreVann directed his question to Elliott.

"Boy, just go on back in there and finish eating and stop being so nosy," Vann said.

"I might ask the same thing about you, young man," Elliott replied, huffily. "Who exactly are you? What's this boy doing here, Savannah?"

"I'm her godson, I live here. Now who are you, and what are you doing here? She's already told you we have company and that you need to leave."

"Godson?" Elliott's face reflected surprise. "Does he live here with you, Savannah? You're just full of surprises, aren't you?"

"None of which is your business," TreVann answered rudely. "I'll see this guy out while you go back to your guest," TreVann offered in an overly solicitous voice.

"I told you, I'll be there in a minute. Now you go on, please!" She gave him a stern look and a gentle shove. She could tell TreVann didn't like Elliott at all, and there was no telling what might come out of his mouth next.

"You can leave anytime, dude," TreVann said to Elliott as he slowly left the room.

"Who is that, Savannah?" Elliott said, as laughter exploded from the back of the house.

"Like my godson said, it's not your business, Elliott. And I do have to get back to my company so...," she opened the door and firmly pushed him out. "You need to leave now, and I'd advise you not to come to my door like this again. It's very rude."

"It seems to me that you're the one who's rude. I drove all the way over here to see you. Who is that back there? Is it that judge? And what do you mean keeping company with other men when I thought I had made it clear th..."

Vann slammed the door before he could finish and went back into the kitchen.

"I can't believe that jerk had the audacity to show up here uninvited and to ring my doorbell when he saw I had company. I bet he won't do that again," Vann fussed. "That man gets on my last nerve."

"Who was it?" Mitch ask curiously.

"Elliott."

Mitch's face darkened with a look Vann hadn't seen since that day in his courtroom. "What was he doing here?"

The doorbell rang again. "I'll get it this time," TreVann said, jumping up and hurrying toward the door. "If it's that dude again, he's not going to like what I say to him." He snatched the door open, and saw a woman he didn't know standing there. "Can I help you?" he asked.

"Yes, is Vann in? I'm Annette, a friend of hers."

"Is she expecting you, Ms. Annette? She's here, but she's busy right now."

"Oh, really?" Annette looked him over. "Are you a relative or something? I'm sure she would want you to invite me in."

TreVann gave her a measured look. "I'm her godson. Can I give her a message for you? Like I said, we have company right now."

"Who is it, Trevie?" Vann called from the family room.

Before TreVann could answer, Annette called out, "It's me, Vann. Annette."

Vann came to the door, a puzzled look on her face. "Annette? What are you doing here?"

"Oh, well I just thought I'd drop by," Annette replied. "Looks like you're entertaining."

"Yes, Annette, I sure am." She was irritated again. "I wish you had called before coming. I would have told you it wasn't a good time."

"Well, I was over this way and thought I'd just drop by, and I'm a great party crasher. Can't you at least offer a friend something to drink?" Annette asked with a hopeful look toward the family room.

"My godmother just told you it's not a good time," TreVann said, a look of distaste on his face.

"Uh, Trevie, let me handle this please," Vann said to him. "Annette, I really need to get back to my guest now, okay. I'll have to talk to you later." She opened the door and gave the woman a strong look that said 'go now'.

"I didn't know your godson still lives with you, Vann," Annette stated as she reluctantly stepped through the door to leave. "It was worth the trip over here just to find that out," she said, throwing an odd look at TreVann before she walked out.

"Weird people. Really weird people!" TreVann said, shaking his head. "Didn't like old dude, and don't like Ms. Lady either. Where are you getting these crazy people?" TreVann asked, leading the way back to the kitchen.

"Believe me, it wasn't any effort on my part. They just kind of latched on to me, and I can't seem to shake them."

"Don't worry, honey. I'll be glad to help you shake them. Especially 'old dude'" Mitch said, smiling, and continuing to devour his plate of food. "TreVann, I don't know who the woman is, but I do know Elliott Shaw. He and I have already had some words."

"Auntie, you need to start telling these people where to go, or I'm going to do it for you," TreVann said. "They need to be sent packing real quick."

After they finished eating, TreVann stood to leave the room. "I need to make some calls, so I'm going to say goodnight." He stuck his hand out to shake Mitch's. "Nice seeing you, man. I hope I can depend on you to look after this lady here," he said, kissing Vann on the cheek.

"Yep. You can do that. And I won't let you down," Mitch assured him with a smile.

"Tell Reneé 'hello' for me." Vann called to TreVann.

"Okay. I guess you can pickup from where you were when I came in. I promise not to disturb you again," TreVann said, winking at Vann with a mischievous grin covering his face, as he covertly let her know he approved of Mitch. "Good night."

"Night, sugar. Night, Trevie," Vann and Mitch answered.

After he was gone, Mitch looked at her inquiringly. "Let me get this straight. TreVann lives here? I thought he was Thomas and Rubye's son."

Vann started laughing. "No, he lives in Austin, he's just here for the weekend. And I can see how you would be confused. He *is* their biological son." Her laughter faded as familiar sadness invaded her heart. "I never had any children of my own, Mitch." She summoned strength to get past the difficult moment. "I wanted them, but it just wasn't in the plan. But God, in His mercy, touched Rubye and Thomas' hearts and they have always graciously shared TreVann with me. Rubye says that all she did was give birth to him for me. So, he's always spent a lot of time with me and had his own room in my house. In fact, I became his legal guardian when his parents lived in the Middle East for ten years. They asked me to keep him when TreVann cried and begged them not to take him because he wanted to stay in the states and finish school. I got him through high school and then college. I've sweated blood and tears over that boy."

Mitch saw the sadness in her eyes and grabbed her hand, squeezing it. "So he stays with you when he comes to town? Even though his parents are back?"

"Most of the time. This is more home to him than where they live because he never lived in that house with them. By the time they returned, he was already grown and living on his own."

"It seems you guys have a good relationship," Mitch told her.

"Yes, we do. I couldn't love him more if he were mine. But trust me, he knows who his parents are. He was just calling me mama tonight to get a reaction out of you." She didn't tell him that TreVann had come to Houston just to check him out, and to check on her after hearing about the situation with Rosetta.

"Well, I like him, and appreciate his obvious love and concern for you," Mitch said, pulling her into his arms to follow TreVann's suggestion.

chapter sixteen

Vann left the church parking lot after Wednesday night Bible study with an unsettled feeling in her stomach. She had just had an argument with Elliott.

"Lord, forgive me, but that man pushes every one of my buttons," she prayed.

She had only gone a block when she looked into her rearview mirror and saw, what looked like, Elliott's car following closely behind her. She speeded to the next stop sign, then made a left to enter the freeway ramp. The car stayed behind her. She moved into another lane and slowed down. The car stayed with her. She sped up and moved toward the exit lane. The car followed.

Frightening stories she'd seen in the news ran through her mind. Why was Elliott following her? Alarmed, she pulled out her cell phone and punched in Mitch's number.

"Mitch, this is Vann. I'm a little unnerved because something weird is going on. I just left the church after having words with Elliott Shaw. Now he's following me. I just got off the freeway and he's right behind me."

"Get back on the freeway and come to my house. I hope he does follow you here."

Potential scenarios ran through her mind. "You know, I wasn't thinking. I shouldn't have called you, because the last thing I'd want is to get you mixed up in a mess," she said. "Maybe I should just go on home and call the police."

"No, I'm glad you called me. Why don't you drive real slow and take a few detours before going home? I'll meet you there."

"I don't know Mitch, maybe I should just let the police handle it?"

"I'll meet you at your house," he insisted. "Is he still there?"

She looked in the rearview mirror. "Yes, he's right on my tail. This makes me so angry." Coming to a sudden decision, she said, "I'm going to do what I should have done at first—ask him what the heck his problem is." She signaled to make a right turn off the feeder road. Elliott's car followed close behind her.

"Vann, what are you doing?" she heard Mitch asking through the earpiece. "You don't need to be confronting that jerk by yourself, honey. Just come on home, slowly. I'm leaving for your house right now."

"I'll call you back." She pushed the end button on the telephone and made a few more turns. Elliott still followed close behind her. She finally pulled into the parking lot of the police sub-station not far from her neighborhood. She jumped out of her car, happy to see a few officers standing around the lot, and walked quickly toward Elliott's car.

"Elliott, why are you following me?" Vann demanded.

"We didn't finish our conversation, Savannah," he said in an aggrieved tone. "I agree that the church is no place to have this discussion so I figured we could go to your house and talk. Why are you stopping at this police station?"

"Well you figured wrong, Elliott. We have absolutely nothing to talk about, and I have asked you several times to leave me alone. Now just what part of that are you not understanding?"

"You're the one with the messed up understanding, Savannah. Here I am, a decent, upstanding man trying to give you a chance at a little respectability and you don't even appreciate it. I'm trying to get you to understand that we could have a good life together, but you're running around with that judge like a foolish person. That judge doesn't mean you any good. He's just using you."

"And what about you, Elliott? What are you after? My best interest? I don't think so."

"Of course I am! I can forget all about this foolishness you're coming up with if you'll just straighten up. I have a lot to offer a woman, Savannah, and if you had any sense you would be jumping at the chance to become my wife."

If she weren't so angry, she would have laughed. "And what if I'm not interested in being your wife, Elliott?"

"Then you definitely have a problem because you're even more stupid than I thought you were."

Vann saw red. "I am about to go inside and file a complaint against you, Elliott. I will not tolerate your foolishness anymore. Now, is that what you want? If so, I will certainly do it." She turned and started walking toward the entrance to the station.

"Woman, what are you doing? I know you're not trying to put the police on me?"

"Evening, Ms. Sinclair." A young police officer who patrolled her neighborhood and worked with her civic club came over to her. "Is there a problem here? Do you need help?"

"I'm not sure yet, Officer. This man is trying to follow me home, but I'm trying to talk some sense into him."

"I'm right here," the officer said, folding his arms and giving Elliott a stern look, "and there won't be anymore problems, right, sir?"

"You crazy woman! Who do you think you are?"

"I know who I am, Elliott. I have always known who I am. It's you who have a problem. Now unless you want to get arrested, you'd better be getting away from here. I have a camera in the car, and at this point I'd love to get a picture of them handcuffing you for the church newspaper. Let's see, the headline could read..." She knew something like that could never happen, but Elliott was so arrogant that just the thought of it would alarm him.

Elliott jumped into his car and was quickly burning rubber out of the parking lot. Vann and the officer both bent over laughing. She thanked him, then got back into her car and headed home. She called Mitch to tell him everything was under control, but he told her he was almost to her house.

Mitch pulled into her driveway right behind her. "Well? Did he turn around?" he asked her, jumping out of his car and running to her.

She started laughing. "Yes, he turned around after I drove to the police station and told an officer what was happening. I'm so sorry I bothered you with this mess."

"Well, I'm happy you thought about going to the police station. If that jerk was following you like that, there's no telling what else he might have done. I was afraid you were going to confront him alone, and that would have been..."

"Foolish?" she inserted laughingly. "What would you have done, Judge? Hold me in contempt and throw me in jail?" She opened the door and motioned for him to come in.

"That's not funny, Vann. Yes, it would have been a very unwise thing to do. You never know what people are capable of these days." He followed her into the house, and hugged her tightly.

"Well like I said, I regret calling you and causing you to drive over here for nothing, but I handled it myself. I told him I had my camera in the car and would happily take a picture of him going to jail for the church newsletter. He couldn't get away fast enough."

"Good riddance," Mitch said, kissing her. "I hope he's finally gotten the message. But this indicates I need to start going to Bible study with you."

Mitchell was again visiting Thomas, Rubye, and Vann's church. He knew it was time for him to get back into church and serving the Lord, and he had come with his mind made up to join. The only down side to this church was that Elliott Shaw was a member. He could handle that though. He had been a Christian all his life, but had let his weakness with Katrina condemn him and get between him and the Lord. But today...he was going to get it straight.

When he looked down at the program and saw the sermon topic, "Are You Ready?" he knew God had led him to church today to hear this sermon. It was a question that had been troubling him for a long time. He wasn't in a right relationship with the Lord, but he knew, even before hearing the sermon, that it was time for him to get ready.

The pastor stood and immediately jumped to the heart of the sermon. "We all know Bishop T.D. Jakes' popular phrase, 'Get Ready! Get Ready! Get Ready!' But you know, each time I've heard it, I've had some questions.

"Get ready," the pastor paused, dramatically. "Brothers and Sisters, we all have countless scenarios that require intense preparation. We get ready for work, school, medical procedures, weddings, church events, oooh...the list of things we get ready for is endless. But when we hear Bishop Jakes telling us to get ready, some of us are probably just thinking...get ready for big blessings! And hey, I'm just as ready for that as anyone," he said smiling. "No, there's certainly nothing wrong with getting ready for that."

"Amen, Pastor! I'm getting ready, too."

"I know you right, Pastor."

"However, today Brothers and Sisters, I want to talk about the *number one, paramount, foremost, primary, initial,*" ...he placed emphasis on each word, "you get the idea. There is one thing we must do—*first*—before we get ready for anything else." He walked around to the front of the pulpit, and looked over the sanctuary, as though he was trying to make eye contact with each person. "I want every person here to honestly answer these questions within your own spirit. Are you ready for the ultimate event that we are all moving toward? Are you ready for your exit from this world? Have you made Jesus the Lord of your life? Are you living a life pleasing to Him? Do you know for sure that your name is written in the Lamb's Book of Life?

"You do know there are only two choices, huh? You're either going to enter into the eternal joys of His kingdom, or you gon' burst hell wide open and suffer eternal damnation. What are you getting ready for? That's a question you should be asking yourself right now. Will your loved ones suffer in agony, unsure about your destination? Or will there be rejoicing because they will know where you are?" He spoke to a silence so quiet you could hear the proverbial pin drop.

"Oh, Lord have mercy!" a sister cried out in the stillness.

The pastor continued, "Are you ready? I don't care who you are, preacher, deacon, Sunday school teacher, choir member...if you're following the devil and doing his bidding every day, who do you think you're getting ready to spend eternity with? Some of you are saying the right words, but your actions are saying something else. Some of you are acting like you're going to be here forever. Well, Brothers and Sisters, I've got a newsflash for you. You are going to leave this world one day. So now is the time to choose where you want to spend eternity. Are you ready? You may have been in the church for fifty, sixty or seventy years, but if you know you're not ready, you need to get ready today!

"Jesus died to save us all, but He's a gentleman, and He's not going to force His way in. He's knocking on the door to your heart right now. He's waiting for you to open the door and invite Him in. There is no other way. Don't put this off! Don't count on doing it another day because tomorrow is not promised. All you have is right now. Now is the acceptable time. Are you going to make this your day to get ready? Why don't you come today?"

The pastor and deacons stood in front of the church, hands outstretched, while the choir softly chanted, 'Come to Jesus, He will save you, Come to Jesus right now.'

Mitch almost leapt from his seat. With tears in his eyes, he quickly walked to the altar and shook the pastor's hand. The message was definitely for him. Ringing through his spirit was the knowledge that indeed, God's mercy had kept him. He had never stopped praying and depending on God to guide him, even as he sat on the judge's bench making rulings on the cases presented before him. He never wanted to be without God's wisdom in his personal issues, but he had lost his way and wandered away from his heavenly Father. Now, he thanked God for the grace that gave him another chance.

After service, Mitch took Vann out to lunch to celebrate his 'getting it straight'.

"I feel about a hundred pounds lighter," he told her as they ate. "It was a burden knowing I was living in disobedience to God. Frankly, I don't know how anyone can stay in a backslidden condition, because I certainly didn't have any peace in my spirit about it. I knew I was wrong when I violated the Word of God, but I went ahead and did it anyway. I know God forgave me, even though I still have the consequences."

"I'm glad you did it too." Vann said, looking at him with a smile. "You're too good a person to be living life apart from the body of Christ. I don't care what we're going through, if we can find our way to the house of the Lord where we can worship Him and hear a Word from Him, the burden will be made lighter. Consequences are one thing, but condemnation is another, Mitch," Vann said, thoughtfully. "Christ took care of that when He died for us. So we don't ever have to feel condemned about falling short. We know God has made provision for us through Jesus. So when Satan comes to condemn us, we can remind him of that."

"That's why I appreciate you so much," Mitch said, smiling. "You always know the right thing to say to keep my focus on the Lord."

She smiled back. "Ironically, I can always say and do the right thing where others are concerned, but when it comes to myself, I'm just plain pitiful. I'm still messing around with the decision I have to make about Rosetta, and I know God can't be pleased with that." She didn't want to admit to him that one of the reasons she was procrastinating was because she didn't want to interrupt the time she was enjoying with him. But God was about to turn up the heat to get her moving.

It met her at the door. The minute she said good-bye to Mitch after a sweet kiss and closed the door, the phone began ringing.

"Vann?"

She cringed as she recognized the voice. "Yes."

"I just wanted to tell you again how sorry I am for everything, and thank you for the money you've been sending. It sure is a big help."

"You're welcome," Vann managed to choke out.

"Well, that's all I wanted to say, really. I, uh...I'm still not doing any better, but I'm holding on and doing the best I can.

The doctor wants to put me in the hospital to run some tests, but I've been putting off going. I..."

"Well, I think you should do what the doctor wants. Do you need more money? Is that the problem?"

"No, no. That's not it. Look, I know I hurt you when I said what I did to you about my other children. I wasn't thinking right, and I'm so sorry about that."

Vann fought the sudden tears that threatened. "You don't have to apologize. I know how you feel about me, and I've accepted that. So you don't have to beat yourself up on my behalf. I just hope your children appreciate you."

"I do need to apologize. Since I've been sick, I've had time to face some facts about my life. I'm not proud of myself and some of the things I've done. Maybe if I'd done right by you, I wouldn't be sitting up here alone like I am. My other children just don't seem to care about anything except themselves. They don't even call or come see me," Rosetta admitted

"That's too bad. Maybe they'll come around one day soon. Was there anything else?" Vann asked, really wanting to end the conversation.

"Well, I hear you're a Christian woman, so would you please pray for me? And will you take down my number and call me? I get so lonely sometimes, and I sure do need help."

Vann closed her eyes, sighed, and accepted the guilt that accompanied what she was about to say. "Ms. Rosetta, I'm going to be honest. I'm not going to promise that I'll call you, but I'm already praying for you. I'll tell your sisters and mama that they need to call you more often. And you should keep trying to reach your children. Who knows, it might just be the right time to get through to them. But I'm not the one you need right now. You need them."

"Naw, I don't think so," Rosetta answered, sadly. "My children don't have the same thing inside them as you do. Mama and Papa did a good job raising you. I evidently didn't do so well with them."

"You never know. They might come through. Don't give up on them. I really have to go now. I'll send some more money soon."

Vann hung up and wiped at the tears running down her face. Strangely, she didn't even know why she was crying. *Lord have mercy on that poor woman!*

"Oh my! Where did that come from?" she asked. But she knew. She had always known.

She walked through her house, praying, "Lord, help me!" But even as she walked and prayed, she looked around and in her mind, planned how she could rearrange her home to accommodate the woman.

Still, she walked. She prayed. She cried harder, cried because she was finally accepting that she had to do the right thing for a person who had done her wrong. She cried because she didn't know the effect doing that would have on the new and good things that were happening in her life. She cried from relief as the weight of guilt and unforgiveness began to lift from her shoulders.

Most of all, she cried because she didn't know this woman who had rejected her all of her life, but she knew the hurt, bitterness, and anger she felt so strongly in her heart. Though she knew what the love of God required of her, and wanted to feel that love, she was unable to, and so she cried harder over her inability to do so. But she did finally feel compassion.

"Thank You for the compassion I feel for her, Lord. At least that's a step in the right direction."

She picked up the phone and called Mitch. "Mitch, I just spoke to Rosetta, and I think I've finally made a step in the right direction. I can't not do something to help her, there's just no way around it." She broke down and started weeping, and when she could speak again, said, "I don't know when I'm going to work my way around to doing it...my heart is ready but my mind is not. And there are some things I want and need to do before I take further steps."

"Vann, baby, I know what this is costing you, and I want you to know that I love you, and I am here for you in whatever way you need. And don't worry, God is going to direct your steps."

She was boo-hooing in earnest now. "I love you too, Mitch," she told him tearfully. "But I have to also tell you that I'm afraid of what that means. There are issues...serious issues that I haven't told you about. I've been enjoying our time together so much but..."

"Vann, your plate is full with this Rosetta situation right now. At least we know that we love each other. We'll work everything else out, okay?"

The tears continued after they hung up. "Lord, just give me a little while longer with him," she prayed.

chapter seventeen

The following weekend, Mitch planned an evening of perfection for them. He had reservations at the same restaurant he had taken her to on their first date, a ring in his pocket, and his proposal ready. From the first time he saw her that day in his courtroom the better part of a year ago, he had known she was the woman he wanted. The few months they had dated and grown close had only confirmed it. He knew they both had issues, but he was certain nothing either one was dealing with was more powerful than the love he felt for her and hoped she felt for him. They could handle it.

He saw the sadness in Vann's eyes and heard it in her voice all through dinner as she talked about her struggle to do the right thing for Rosetta. He had planned to propose to her during dinner, but changed his mind and decided to wait until they were alone. They were back at her house when he finally spoke what was in his heart.

"Vann, every morning when I wake up and thank God for letting me see a new day, you are the first person I think about and want to hug and say good morning to. And at night, after I thank God for bringing me through the day, I think about you, and want to hug you and say good night to you. You blew into my life like one of our famous Texas hurricanes. I prayed that God would navigate the paths of our lives and cause us to meet again, and He kept doing that until it finally worked, so I truly believe it is God's will for us to be together. I knew from the first time I laid eyes on you... when your eyes told me you wanted to kick my butt,... and each time I've seen you since then that I wanted you...your depth, your compassion, your strength, your beauty...like I've not wanted anything before.

"I love you, sweetheart, and I need you. I want to spend every day of the rest of my life with you. You add something to my life that I don't want to live without." He pulled the ring box from his pocket and opened it to reveal a beautiful emerald cut diamond ring. "Vann Sinclair, would you do me the honor of becoming my wife and making me the happiest man alive?"

"Oh, Mitch!" How long she had waited to hear those words again. But today she was totally unprepared to respond to them.

His proposal filled Vann with immeasurable joy—for just a minute. Then, as fears of another failure flooded her mind, the joy disappeared. Twenty years ago—even ten, she would have been overjoyed that a man like Mitch Langford wanted to marry her. But now, all she could think about were all the reasons why she couldn't or shouldn't marry him.

"Vann? Are you going to answer me?"

While she sat there speechless, all sorts of craziness did summersaults in her mind. Admittedly, some place deep within her, the longing to share her life with someone had lingered a long time, but as the years passed, the actuality of that happening had become so unlikely that she had stopped seriously considering the practical aspects of actually being married.

Singleness had it's perks. Was she willing to give them up? And what about him. Didn't he deserve more than she could give him?

"Oh, Mitch, there are things running through my mind that I have to consider. I'm an old lady, Mitch. You are a healthy, vibrant, energetic man and you don't need a wife who is dealing with old woman issues. You're just fifty years old, Mitch, and you could even entertain having other children, while that is beyond the realm of possibility for me. I love you, and I can't stand the thought of hurting or disappointing you in any way. I just can't do that."

Mitch looked down at her, confusion covering his handsome face. His decision to ask her to be his wife hadn't been made lightly. In fact, he had prayed and agonized over it before coming to the conclusion that his life would be incomplete without her. Mitch shook her shoulders gently. "Honey, you'll hurt me if you say no. Vann, I want you to be my wife. I know plenty of younger women and none of them appeal to me. Vann, please marry me."

What would he do if she said no? He didn't have a backup plan because no other acceptable option existed. Spending the rest of his life alone wasn't an option—at least now that he had met her—and no other woman would do. Although lonely, he had been prepared to live out his remaining years alone...until he'd met Vann. He touched her face gently, and forced her to look at him.

Needing to get away from his touch and the intensity of his eyes, Vann stood and walked across the room to stand in front of the fireplace mantle. She kept her back to him as she pondered everything he had said. Her fear of another failure was too ingrained for her to make a quick decision. "Mitch, I told you before that I've been engaged three times. Each one of those engagements ended in disaster. Two of the men were killed and one of them cheated on me before we could get married. I've been able to move on, but I don't know if I ever truly got over the fact that every serious relationship I've been in has failed, and that caused me to question if marriage is God's plan for me. And I admit to having a deep rooted fear that if I ever do step out and try again, something horrible will happen to stop it."

"Vann, are you telling me that you're afraid to even try again? Somehow, that just doesn't fit the woman I know you are."

"Mitch, it's not just that. There are other things as well." She still refused to look at him as she listed the things weighing on her mind. "I'm old and set in my ways. I do what I want, when

I want. There's no one to have to cook for, clean up after, or answer to about my lifestyle, or to question how I handle my financial affairs, or where I go. I don't have to worry about bumping into anyone when I toss and turn or stretch horizontally across my bed. There's no one to complain when I throw off the covers to ease the ever increasing hot flashes that have me wanting to rip the covers off one minute and reaching for them a few minutes later to ward off the chill. There's no one to witness or complain when my hormones are running rampant and I just want to be left alone, or to hide the cellulite on my thighs from. I don't even know if I ...you know... the intimacy aspects of marriage."

Vann's face burned in embarrassment as she ran through her list. Mitch grunted impatiently at various points, but remained quiet until she finished.

"Vann, don't you think I've thought of all of that, and it's all hogwash as far as I'm concerned. Do you think other women faced with the same issues stop living, getting married, or having sex? I don't think so. Vann, the few years difference in our ages is not significant. We're at a time in our lives when there are so many things much more important than what you're concerned about: serving the Lord together, loving each other, companionship, peace and joy that comes from just being together, just to mention a few. I know the things you mentioned come into play, but I believe that with God's help, we can work through them. And I don't know how you could possibly think I'd want any more children. I've got Matthew, *and* grandchildren. Vann, nothing that you mentioned is an obstacle that can't be overcome. Nothing!"

His words brought only a little joy to her cluttered and confused heart. "Mitch, there are other considerations as well. My...Rosetta is another big issue..."

"Vann, I can't promise what the future holds, but I can assure you that I will do everything humanly possible to be the best husband that I can be. I will never dishonor you. We'll remove as many of the pitfalls as we can, but honey, there are no guarantees. It'll still take work and commitment to keep our relationship on a strong foundation and thriving. So say yes," he prompted. "Please."

"Oh, Mitch, you're such a precious man, and I love you." Stress filled her face. "But honey, just understand that I've gone through several major life changes just this year—retirement, a new business venture, becoming a television show host, and now dealing with my long lost mother. I know you mean everything you've said, but my own issues about the past coupled with the weight of these recent transitions makes it difficult for me to tackle another major change right now. Please forgive me, but I can't say yes because the last thing I want to do is hurt you."

Disappointment consumed him. He walked to the other side of the room, away from where she was standing by the unlit fireplace. "Well, I am hurt," he said quietly. "Because Vann, none of those things have anything to do with how we feel about each other. We love each other, we have fun together, we enjoy the same things. All I understand is that you are trying to find every reason you can not to marry me. Are you going to let past hurts, fear of the unknown, and other people keep you from enjoying the life you have left with someone who loves you and wants to share that life? Are you going to turn your back on the fact that this could very well be God's will for us?"

"Mitch, sweetheart, I just can't say yes *right now*. But give me some time. I promise you I'll think and pray long and hard about this," Vann said in a low shaky voice. "You must consider that we've only been seeing each other a few months. I think it's wise to take the time to really get to know one another better. For all we know, our first meeting could be a true gauge of how we'll really relate to each other."

He walked over to where she stood and looked down at her with love shining in his eyes. "I told you, I knew from the minute I saw you that you were special, and I'm not deluding myself, I know there'll be many more of those scenes between us. But honey, nothing can overcome the love we feel for each other."

"I kind of liked you too," she said, smiling up at him. "But I still think we should take our time. I'll let you know when I'm ready."

"Promise?" he asked softly, catching both of her hands with his own. "I'm hurt and disappointed, but I love you, and I'm willing to wait."

"Yes," she said with a wobbly smile. "I promise."

He pulled her into his arms and they hugged each other close for a long time. "Just know this, lady. I'm not going to give up. Once I set my mind on something, it's hard for me to turn around. So lady, you're in for a fight that I plan to win," he told her, with a smile. "Will you still see me while we sort this out?"

"Just try to stop me."

He hugged her tightly—almost desperately—then kissed her as he never had before. "I've tried to hold off on the hot and heavy stuff because I know we both want to honor the Lord in all we do. But woman, you can't put this off too long, okay?" The emotion in his voice and on his face showed the depth of his feelings.

The next day, Vann was getting ready to start working on her Sunday school lesson, hoping there wouldn't be any interruptions. She wanted to lead a discussion with the women on how to make godly decisions and was searching the concordance for some appropriate Scriptures. With all the decisions before her and as hard a time as she was having, the lesson would be invaluable to her as well. "I'm going to ask Pastor for some insight on this," she said to herself. She was making a list of the Scriptures that might be helpful when the telephone rang. "Oh well, there's no such thing as no interruptions in this house."

"Hey, Vann, this is Katherine, how you doing?"

"Hi, Katherine, I guess I'm okay, what about you? I haven't talked to you in a while."

"I'm so-so. Are you busy? I need to talk to someone, and you're it. I know you'll give me some sound advice."

"Huh! I don't know about that, Katherine. I can't seem to handle my own troubles, so I'm not promising that anything sound is going to come out of me today."

"Well, can you meet me at that sandwich place we like on the Beltway near Greenspoint, so we can talk? I really need a listening ear."

"Okay, Katherine. But aren't you at work?"

"No, I'm not at work today. I'm using a mental health day to make a big decision. Can you meet me before the lunch crowd floods the place?"

"Okay, I'll be there at ten-forty-five." She hung up with *now what?* ringing in her mind. "Lord, help," she said, looking at the clock and realizing she only had an hour.

After ordering several appetizers along with iced tea, Katherine started talking. "Vann, I'm seriously thinking about leaving my husband. I'm just sick of him with his slow, boring, never-want-to-do-anything-but-sit-in-front-of-the-television-self. I've figured out how I can make it financially, and not have to put up with him. I can travel like I want to, go stay with my kids and grandkids when I feel like it, go home when I want to, and cook when I want to. Can you believe he works at a restaurant, where he can eat all he wants, but he still wants me to cook every day. I want freedom...like you have, Vann."

Vann put her head down and laughed until tears were running out of her eyes, while Katherine looked at her like she had lost her mind. "I'm sorry, I'm not laughing at you, Katherine, just at how ironic life is."

"What are you talking about, Vann?" Katherine asked, a puzzled look on her face. Katherine was tall, heavy set, and nice looking. She was always dressed in the most current fashions, and had thick, gorgeous gray hair which she wore in a short style.

Vann had been awake most of last night, angry at herself for focusing on the reasons she shouldn't marry Mitch instead of focusing on reasons to marry him, and now here Katherine was, with a long list of reasons why she wanted to leave her husband.

"You know what, Katherine? The grass always looks greener on the other side of the fence. So never make a decision based on what you perceive about another person's life. There are millions of women who would give anything for what you're trying to get rid of. Have you prayed about this, Katherine?"

Katherine frowned. "Well, not really. I just know what I want, and it's to be free of him. I want to live, do fun things, go fun places while I'm still able, and he's just not going to do it. He goes to work, and comes home, day in and day out. And he's happy with that."

Dear God, give me the right words, Vann silently prayed. "Katherine," she said in a soft voice, "I can't tell you what to do. What I will do is remind you of what God's Word says about divorce. It tells us that God hates divorce and that there are very few instances where divorce is acceptable to Him. And I'll ask you to consider some other things. You've been with this man over thirty years, have children and grandchildren with him, and he's coming home to you every day. He seems like a good man, and take it from me, they are not easy to find. Of course I don't know what's going on in your marriage, and don't want to know, but I do know you want to be in God's will. So pray about it before you make your decision. Maybe you guys could go to a Christian marriage counselor and try to fix the issues. Just don't make any rash moves. Okay?"

Katherine had a disappointed look on her face. "I know you're probably right, Vann, but I really wanted to hear you say you understand how I feel, and that it's okay to leave him and move on like you did with Stelle and Roxie. I guess I should have known better, huh?"

"Sorry, chick, but you won't hear that coming out of my mouth. That's a decision you should make with nobody but God directing you. And Stelle and Roxie's situations are very different, but I certainly didn't tell them what to do."

"You're right, girl," Katherine said, softly, a downcast look on her face.

All had been said on that subject that she intended to say, so Vann changed the subject. "Hey, I haven't forgotten about our getaway to the beach house. But so much has been going on with everyone that the time just never seems right. Why don't we get with the others and start planning to go before the holidays?"

"That's a great idea, Vann. I'll call the others and arrange a date and get back to you. We need to make the time to do that," Katherine said, excitement shining on her face.

Katherine brought Vann up to date on what was going on at work while they finished off the appetizers, then they went their separate ways. But for the rest of the day, Vann was shaking her head at the irony of her and Katherine's places in life.

chapter eighteen

Vann was loving the brisk November air. She had just returned from taping three holiday related shows: a Thanksgiving show in which she talked to a class of fifth graders about their understanding of the holiday and how it is observed in their families, and two Christmas shows—staying safe while shopping, and establishing family traditions. Hayden told her they would probably air all the shows more than once before the season was over.

She visited Cy and Sylvia and returned home to find a message from Katherine, who was busily planning the getaway for the Veterans Day holiday. It was no surprise to hear that the women were excited—they always were—but Vann knew it was only a diversion for her. She was only running away from the decisions that loomed over her head, waiting....

"Father, I know I'm blowing it," she confessed. "Have mercy on me, and help me to get out of this rut of indecision. Rosetta is waiting and You've already told me what I have to do. Mitch is waiting and I'm convinced that it's Your will for us to be together, but here I am, rolling around in this rut again." She dropped her head into her hands as sadness enveloped her. All of the enthusiasm for her decorating projects and the talk show was disappearing, and if Mitch hadn't been so persistent, she would probably feel the same way about him.

"When was the last time I had a good praise session?" Her head popped up as she realized she had not spent any quality time with the Lord in prayer and praise in a long while.

"So many new and good things have happened over the last several months, Lord, that I actually thought I was free of the rut and its negative influences. But I have lost sight of a vital truth in Your Word found in 1 Peter 5:8 (KJV), that says, 'Be sober, be vigilant; because your adversary the devil, as a roaring lion, walketh about, seeking whom he may devour.'

"I know I haven't dealt with the hurt and unforgiveness caused by Rosetta's abandonment, or my fear of serious relationships caused by losing three men I cared about. So the devil has entered these doors that I left open and is devouring my joy and enthusiasm.

"Father, I've lost my perspective since this thing with Rosetta started, but I know that according to Lamentations 3:22–23 it'll be alright. This Word tells me that because of the Lord's mercies, I won't be consumed because His compassions never fail, and are new every morning and that His faithfulness is great. Father, forgive me for the sins that have so easily overcome me. I thank You and praise You, Father, for never leaving or forsaking me. I thank You and praise You for making me more than a conqueror over these sins. And I thank You, Father, for working in me and helping me to keep pressing toward the mark of the high calling of God through Jesus Christ. I thank You that even in these weaknesses, Your strength is made perfect. So Lord, I look to the hills from whence cometh my help. Because I know that all my help, my strength comes from You. I'm not giving up, and I refuse to stay in the rut. So that means I'm coming out, in the name of Jesus."

She was wiping at her tears when the phone rang.

"Vann, this is Aunt Lu. I just talked to Rosie, and she said she was feeling a little better. The doctor put her on some different medication that seems to be working. Her neighbor came while we were talking and invited Rosie to Thanksgiving dinner. I'm so glad because I was worried that she would be by herself. So let's just keep praying that things are going to work themselves out."

"I'm glad too, Aunt Lu," Vann said, as the weight of guilt lightened a little. "I'll keep on praying," she promised before hanging up.

Vann had been thinking about Thanksgiving and trying to decide what to do. She and TreVann usually spent the holiday together, and of course for the last several years since his parents' return, they had gone to Rubye and Thomas' house.

But this year Vann was torn. Mitch wanted her to spend the day with him, since she would be going to Georgia for Christmas. Of course, Mitch was welcome to go to Rubye's house with her, but he was waiting to find out if his children would be in town or with their mother. If they stayed, they would expect to spend the day with him, and he would want her there as well. At least she didn't have to feel guilty about Rosetta since she had already made plans.

"Well, I have time to make that decision," Vann said to herself. "Things will probably work themselves out, but now I've got to do some planning on this getaway." She got back to her list and making plans.

The phone rang again, and she was expecting it to be Mama, calling about Rosetta. But when she answered she discovered the call was from Georgia, but not from Mama.

"Vann?" Aunt Rachel's quivering voice came across the line. "Becky done fell and hurt herself. She's in the hospital and wanting you to come see about her."

"I'll be there as soon as I can," Vann said through a choked up throat. Everything else was out the window. She made some phone calls, then went about preparing her life, her home, and other responsibilities for what she knew could be a long absence. After making reservations for a flight and rental car, she started packing.

Mitch drove her to the airport. "Baby, now don't forget to stay in touch with me, and be sure to take care of yourself while you're there. Did you pack some heavy clothes? It may be a little colder there than it is here. And do you know if you'll be able to come back before Christmas? I know you were planning to spend that holiday with your mama, but that may have to change now. Have you talked to the hospital and received a report on how she is? I sure do wish I could go with you."

Vann was worried and Mitch wasn't helping any. "Honey, just calm down, I'll be okay."

Hours later, she was relieved to be in the rental car and on her way to the hospital. When she arrived and ran in to see Mama, she was so exhausted she could hardly see, but she knew rest was a long way off. She talked to the doctor who told her that her mama was resting comfortably. "She has a hairline hip fracture that she got when she had a dizzy spell and fell. Of course at her age, any kind of fracture is serious. But I'm more concerned with the cause of the dizziness," the doctor told her. "So we'll be running some tests and prescribing treatment for the dizziness, as well as taking care of the fracture. She'll be here awhile, so see if you can make her understand that. She's already asking to go home."

Reconciled to the fact that she would be in Georgia for at least the next two months, Vann sat down beside the bed, took her mama's hand in hers and began praying. "Father, thank You for this woman and the blessing she has been to us. Now, Lord, I ask that You touch her with Your healing power, and restore health to her body. In Jesus' name, amen."

Mama squeezed her hand to let Vann know she had heard the prayer. "I'm ready to go home, baby," she said in a weak voice.

"Mama, the doctor told me that you'll be here awhile because they plan to run some tests. You're going to have to be patient, okay? But I'll be here with you, and when they tell me I can, I'll take you home. Then we can start planning for Christmas."

"Alright, baby. I guess I don't have a choice." She sighed heavily, and drifted back into sleep.

As Vann sat beside Mama's bed on Thanksgiving Day, she thought about the plans she'd been making before she got the call from Aunt Rachel. Her friends had been disappointed, but understood why the getaway had to be canceled. Mitch and TreVann were both at Rubye's, enjoying what Vann knew was a wonderful meal. Aunt Rachel and her daughter had cooked and her uncle and aunt had brought food, but Vann didn't have much of an appetite. Mama didn't seem to be getting better, and was depressed over not being able to go home.

Vann decided to use the hours to remember and reflect on the good things God had done for her since last Thanksgiving. Indeed, it had been a full year. She pulled out her journal and started writing.

The weeks slid by as Vann sat beside the bed every day, praying and talking to Mama about the goodness of the Lord. A bout with pneumonia extended Mama's stay in the hospital, but she was finally released a few days before Christmas. Although frail and weak, she insisted that Christmas be the same as always. Vann rushed to do Christmas shopping for both herself and Mama, and then helped with holiday cooking. Her aunts in Houston, as well as other relatives were flying in to spend the holiday, and Mama was overjoyed and looking forward to it. Vann, however, was exhausted, depressed, and homesick. She missed her home, her life, and Mitch.

After learning that Aunt Bernie was planning to stay through the New Year, Vann quickly made plans to fly home. Hoping to surprise Mitch and spend a part of the holiday with him, she managed to get on a flight on Christmas Day. After helping to prepare the Christmas feast and visiting with her relatives, she grabbed her bag and left for the airport.

Mitch could barely contain his excitement as he made his way to Vann's mama's house. He had spent Christmas Eve with his children and grandchildren, and managed to get on a flight out of Houston Christmas morning. He missed Vann so much and wanted to share at least a small part of the day with her. He wanted to surprise her, so he had been dodging her calls for the last two days for fear of spoiling his surprise. He made his way to the house after parking, and ran into a man just leaving the house.

"Uh, hello. I'm Mitch Langford from Houston. I'm a friend of Vann's and I'm hoping to surprise her."

The man laughed, shaking his head. "Well, I'm Vann's uncle and I'm afraid the surprise is on you. Vann left to catch a plane to Houston a couple of hours ago. Y'all crossed paths with each other at some point."

Mitch was so disappointed he couldn't say anything. He stood there with his mouth hanging open and his heart crashing around his feet.

"Do you want to come in for a bite to eat? I know you must be hungry," Vann's uncle offered.

"No, uh, I think I'll drive over to see my parents, then try to get a flight back to Houston. I can't believe this," Mitch mumbled as he made his way back to his rental car.

Rubye picked her up from the airport, and after assuring that everything was okay in her house, Vann said, "Lord, it's good to be home." I could kiss the floor I'm so happy to be here."

"I know that feeling," Rubye said, laughing.

"Have you or Thomas heard from Mitch? I've been trying to reach him for a couple of days. I've left several messages, but he hasn't called me back. I'm getting a little worried." She went to the phone and dialed his number. No answer.

After several more attempts to reach Mitch failed, Vann accepted Rubye's invitation to a late Christmas dinner. She rested a while, showered, dressed, and drove over to Rubye's. Since she had asked Mitch to return her call on her cell phone, Vann never bothered to check the messages on her home phone. She questioned her judgment after arriving at Rubye's house, thinking she should have stayed home. She was tired, travel worn, and worried about Mitch, but she made a valiant attempt to join in the festivities. It was better than sitting home alone on Christmas.

"Vann Jo, telephone!" Thomas called to her above the music and chatter of people enjoying themselves.

Vann went to a quieter part of the house to answer, and was relieved to hear Mitch's voice. "Honey, where *are* you? I've been trying to call you for days," she complained.

"Sweetheart..." Mitch said, wearily. "I'm in Georgia. I was trying to surprise you by coming and spending Christmas with you."

Vann screamed in frustration. "Oh, honey! I was trying to do the same thing. We blew it, and I want to see you so bad."

"I'll be back as soon as I can get a flight, babe. You're not planning to leave anytime soon are you?"

"Not until next week. Aunt Bernie is staying with Mama until after New Year's Day."

"Don't go anywhere until I get there. Do you realize it's been nearly two months since we've seen each other? That is totally unacceptable, Vann."

"I know, honey. I feel the same way. But we could have saved ourselves this frustration by just communicating. So no more surprises, okay."

Mitch laughed. "It would have been good if one of us had stayed put." He laughed again, then said, "I'll be home as soon as I can. By the way, when I couldn't reach you on your home phone, I started calling you on the cell. Why aren't you answering your cell phone? I had to call you on Thomas' number to get you."

"Oh! It's in my purse...and my purse is upstairs in the bedroom. Sorry!"

After celebrating New Year's Day with Mitch and taping several *High Point* shows over the next week, Vann returned to Georgia and stayed with Mama until the end of January, when Aunt Lu came back to spend some time with her.

chapter nineteen

Vann spent February resting and getting her life back on track. Mama was doing okay, although still frail and weak. Rosetta's health seemed to be holding steady, and Vann had not received any more calls from her. She called her friends and suggested they try for the getaway again the second weekend in March. They might catch some of the Spring Break crowd, but hopefully the weather would be pleasant. Annette had made it a point to inquire regularly so she would know when they were going, so Vann called her to explain the situation.

"Annette, this is the deal with the beach house. It's pretty large, but there are only four bedrooms. I have one, Rubye and Estelle each have one, and Katherine and Roxanne share the other. I know you want to go, but you would have to stay at a hotel or sleep on the sofa, and that's really not a good thing because we're often up late laughing and talking."

"Why can't I share with you?" Annette asked.

"No, not possible. That place is a special haven for me, and that includes being able to retreat to my own bedroom. Look, Annette, I don't want to tell you that you can't go, but I do suggest that you wait and go another time—maybe when one of the other ladies can't go. That happens sometimes."

"No, I really want to go this time," Annette insisted. "And if I have to take the sofa, then I'll do it."

Disappointed Annette refused to take the hint, Vann continued. "As long as you understand what the arrangements are, then okay. So, here's what will happen. The others already know all of this. The beach house is often rented out to others, and would be now, if the people hadn't cancelled. Everyone must bring their own towels, bedding, and toiletries, and we all chip in on the food and snacks. Rubye is our official cook, but we all help out with food preparations, cleaning up, and all that. I keep basic items like cooking utensils, dishes, and other household things stocked in the house. Rubye, Estelle, and I will ride down together, with all the groceries and other necessities, and Roxanne and Katherine will drive down when they get off work. So you'll have to drive down on your own."

"No problem, I can do that," Annette didn't argue. She knew to choose her battles, and she was determined to see this beach house and perhaps discover if a man she needed to know might own it.

Annette's mouth fell open when she turned onto the long driveway that lead to the large beach house. "Look at this!" She exclaimed. "I need to find out who really owns this place. Watch out Vann Sinclair because you are about to be moved." She continued to take in everything as she slowly drove toward the house. Tropical trees lined both sides of the driveway and colorful flowers were in bloom all around the house. A view of the beach and the seemingly infinite Gulf of Mexico could be seen from every direction. A long flight of steps was the only way to reach the living quarters of the dark blue house with white shutters, that sat on tall concrete blocks, high above sea level.

"I don't understand why I can't share with one of you? The rooms are very spacious," Annette complained, after looking around the house.

"Let me explain it to you like it was explained to me and Roxie," Katherine answered. "Vann, Rubye, and Estelle all have squatter's rights. They don't have to share. That's why me and Roxie don't complain about having to share with each other. We know we don't have a choice."

"Yes, but changes can always be made," Annette shot back. *These women are really getting on my nerves.*

"No changes, Annette," Vann stated impatiently. "I explained everything to you and you said you didn't mind sleeping on the sofa."

"Okay, that's fine," Annette said, but her facial expression indicated she didn't like it.

In keeping with their usual routine, they had fun pigging out on seafood at one of the excellent island restaurants, then walked along the beach, people watching and trying to walk off some of the food they had eaten. After tiring of the crowds, they returned to the beach house and settled in for a night of girl talk. Of course, Roxanne and Estelle had the most traumatic issues. They cried as they talked about their pending divorces.

"Vann's got a boyfriend y'all," Rubye announced proudly, after the tears had dried. "A *young* boyfriend. Can you believe that? Vann's got a young, fine man seriously pursuing her. Yes, I said *young*," she said again to the astonished expressions of the other women.

"Yes, young!" Estelle kicked in.

"Vann! You've been holding out on us! Shame on you!" Katherine said.

"Rubye is just exaggerating," Vann tried to downplay the situation. "We've just been going out and spending time together. He's teaching me how to play golf and I'm helping him decorate his house."

"Sounds serious enough to me," Roxanne said. "But take it from me girl, tread very carefully. It's treacherous out there with men these days."

"No, you just go with the flow, girl," Estelle said. "I don't care how carefully you tread, you can still end up in a mess. Just enjoy the ride as long as it's fun, then jump off when it ceases to be fun. Don't hang around in it when you realize it's time to get to stepping."

Vann knew there would be just as many opinions as there were women, and took everything they said with a grain of salt.

Saturday, they went shopping, played tourists, and strolled the beach with the crowd of swimmers, surfers, and sand and sun worshippers. That evening, they enjoyed the sunset while eating the delicious grilled chicken salad that Ruybe prepared. Later, they drove over to Moody Gardens and walked through, admiring the large array of flowers and other attractions, then watched a movie. Sunday, they ate a big breakfast and lazed around, not really trying to find anything to do other than relax.

"I wish 'T' was here. I'd make him fry up some fish," Rubye said lazily.

"Yeah, and then you wouldn't have to cook," Vann teased.

"What's wrong with that?" Rubye asked. "You love 'T's fish as much as I do."

Around two o'clock they heard a knock at the door. Rubye went to answer since she was already up and making preparations to fix dinner. "What are you guys doing here?" they heard her exclaim. A minute later, the door leading to the back deck opened and Thomas, followed by Mitch, stepped out, both smiling broadly. Immediately, Vann's heart escalated and she couldn't stop the smile that covered her face.

"'T' you read my mind!" Ruybe said. "I was wishing for some of your good fried fish."

"Woman, I didn't come down here to be cooking no fish."

"Please!" the others all chorused.

He grinned widely, unable to resist their pleas. "Oh, alright! Do y'all have the fish already?" Seeing their blank expressions, he groaned. "I should have known better than to ask. Come on Mitch, we have to go shopping."

Mitch, who was comfortably seated on the extended part of Vann's lounger and was holding her hand and looking at her with a smile, looked reluctant to leave. "Come on, Judge Langford!" Thomas insisted. "I ain't having all this fun by myself."

As soon as the men left, Rubye went into high gear. "Okay girls, let's get busy!" she said, leading the way into the kitchen. "We can have everything ready when they get back. Vann, you can get the stars out of your eyes. We know Mitch is the reason they showed up down here, and you're the reason for him coming. But you're going to have to work, too." The others laughed, as they moved into action.

Nobody noticed the look on Annette's face as they peeled potatoes for potato salad and prepared a green salad.

Judge Langford? Annette thought. *I knew if I hung around Vann long enough, I would hit the jackpot.*

After they enjoyed the mouth watering fish dinner, Mitch, who was anxious to get Vann to himself for a few minutes, volunteered to clean up the kitchen. When the others gladly thanked him, he grabbed Vann's hand. "Come on honey, help me."

In the kitchen, and out of sight of the others, he hugged her close and kissed her the way he had wanted to since arriving. "So is this one of the places you run to when you need to get away from things?"

"Yes," she answered. "It's a perfect place for thinking and praying. If I hadn't wanted to check on my mama when I first started dealing with the Rosetta issue, I probably would have come down here instead of going to South Carolina and Georgia."

"No, you wanted to go some place and pick up strange men," he said jokingly, then added, "it's a nice place. Just too many people here right now," he said as he leaned over and planted a light kiss on her lips. "So have you ladies enjoyed your weekend?"

"Yes, we have," she answered. "But we always do. We really should do it more often, just for the therapeutic value."

"So what have you been doing?" Mitch asked, as they worked.

"Well, let's see," Vann began to recount the weekend's events, but they were interrupted.

"Vann!" Annette rushed into the room with a distraught look on her face. "I have managed to slit my finger on one of your bamboo chairs. Do you have a first-aid kit around here?"

Vann threw down the dish towel she was using. "Oh Annette, I'm so sorry. Is it bad?" She asked, walking toward the other woman to inspect the cut.

"I don't believe it's too bad," Annette said, holding her index finger with napkins tightly wrapped around it. "But I do need to clean it and put a bandage on it."

"Well, check in the upstairs bathroom cabinet. There should be a first aid kit there. I'm sure you'll find whatever you need in it."

"Vann, I really hate to poke around in somebody else's house. Would you mind getting it for me?"

"Sure, Annette. I'll be right back," she said over her shoulder.

Annette slid toward Mitch as soon as Vann left the room. "Judge." She eased up close to him, a seductive smile on her face and all signs of an injury thrown into a nearby trash can. "I hear you are seriously interested in Vann. Is that right?"

Mitch's eyes narrowed, and he backed away from her. "Yes, that's true. Why are you asking?"

"Well, because I know for certain that Vann is not interested in anything serious with you. I mean, not only is she older than you, for goodness sakes, but she also has too many serious issues to deal with. A man in your position shouldn't be saddled with that kind of baggage."

"What serious issues?" Mitch's heartbeat quickened in concern. Vann had promised him she would be praying about his proposal, and if he didn't know anything else about her, he knew she was a woman of her word. "I know she has some things to work out, but nothing that can't be overcome."

"Well, you know she has a sick mother to take care of, a sick grandmother, a grown man who calls himself her godson who lives with her off and on, and I happen to know that she's in a relationship with one of the deacons at our church."

Mitch smiled at the woman's exaggerations and intention to mislead. "Dang, lady! I thought you were Vann's friend. Why are you telling me all this?"

Annette shrugged. "I am, don't get me wrong. But a girl has to look out for herself, and I know a good, decent man when I see one. I'd hate to see you waste your time when there are available women—like me for instance—who could do so much more for you. At our age, we can't beat around the bush. I would like to know you better. I believe there are all kinds of possibilities for us."

Mitch glanced nervously toward the door. Obviously, this woman had some loose screws to be standing in her friend's house and coming on like this to her friend's man. She was very attractive he thought, taking in her light skin, pretty face with high cheek bones, full lips, and large eyes. But he knew looks were deceiving, and this woman's whole demeanor screamed deceitfulness.

"With friends like you, Vann doesn't need any enemies," Mitch said, shaking his head. "You need to back off, lady. Even if I were the least bit interested in you—which I assure you, I am not—this is not the place or the time to be having this conversation. It's disrespectful to Vann, and I think it's in very bad taste."

"I believe in striking while the iron is hot. In any case, all is fair in love and war." Annette pressed a business card into his hand. "Call me next week. You won't be sorry."

Mitch backed away from her again. "I don't particularly care to be a part of this conversation, and like I said, this is not the time or the place." He knew Vann would be returning any second and he didn't want her to hear any part of this conversation and get the wrong impression. He had to get the woman away from him without drawing attention to them. His memory kicked in, and he was certain this was the woman who had shown up uninvited at Vann's house that night, insistent on coming in. TreVann definitely had her pegged right.

Annette stalked as he backed away, a determined smile on her lips. "Well, Judge, you have my number so give me a call anytime and we'll talk, or do anything your heart desires. But if you don't call me, believe me, I'll look you up and call you."

Mitch looked at the card in his hand, and looked around for the trash can. "I can't say what I'd like to say to you the way it needs to be said." He heard a noise, and knew he had to end the conversation before Vann returned. "Doing it now will only cause confusion and hurt Vann," he said, pushing the card into his pocket. "But if and when we do talk, I have some choice things I'd like to say to you, and I need to be able to say them to you without the chance of being overheard."

"Talk to me now, Mitch," Annette cajoled, stepping closer and smiling, obviously missing the disgusted look on Mitch's face. "I welcome anything you want to say and do to me."

"I really have things to do, and I think you should go," Mitch said, and turned his back to her to start running water in the sink.

"I suppose you're right about this not being the time or the place, but personally, I really don't care if someone sees or hears us," Annette said, as she walked toward the door.

"I do," Mitch said, still with his back to her.

Just around the corner, Vann, in her rush to get back to Annette with the first-aid kit, dropped it, spilling some of the items. When she stopped to pick them up, she overheard the last part of Mitch and Annette's conversation. She felt her heart shattering into more pieces than she could have imagined. *Oh no! Not him too!* she thought.

She walked slowly into the kitchen, but Annette had already returned to the deck. She could barely look at Mitch. "I think we're finished in here. If not, I'll finish later. I'll just take this out to Annette," she said in a stiff voice. "And I know you and Thomas will want to be getting back home before it gets too late."

Mitch frowned. "Don't worry, I think that woman is okay. Are *you* okay, honey?

"Yes, I'm fine," she answered. But she didn't know if she'd ever be fine again as her mind took her back over the journey of her life to revisit all the other disappointments she had endured.

Vann was unusually quiet during the next hour or so that Mitch and Thomas were there, and as soon as they left, she escaped to her bedroom, pleading tiredness. She actually wanted to pray—about Mitch, about Annette—and her desire to throw the woman head first off of the balcony. But if Mitch had instigated that incident in the kitchen, why blame Annette?

Later that evening, Katherine rushed out onto the deck of the beach house where Rubye, Estelle, and Roxanne were relaxing and enjoying the sight and sound of the powerful waves pounding against the seawall from the vast body of water that reached as far as the eye could see.

"Ladies!" Katherine's abrupt interruption of their peaceful interlude brought groans of protest, as they forced their eyes away from the scene in front of them to the obviously upset woman.

"Ladies! A big ole yellow-bellied, sneaky, deceitful, traitorous, low-life snake has crawled into the house!"

"What! Where? Oh Lord!" were the simultaneous responses as the women jumped up, looking around at the floor nervously.

"No, no, no, this is a two-legged snake I'm talking about! I went in to use the bathroom and heard Vann and that snake talking. I heard that two-legged snake, Annette, telling Vann that she needs to step out of the picture and let her have Mitchell. She said she had talked to Mitch and that he agrees with her. Can y'all believe that?"

Rubye was headed to the door, Estelle and Roxanne close behind her. "It's on!" Rubye announced.

"I knew something was wrong. Vann hasn't been right since the men left," Estelle said. "Yeah, it is definitely on."

Rubye flung the screen door open so hard it banged against the wall. "I've always known that woman was up to no good!" Rubye huffed.

They arrived in the living room just in time to hear Vann saying, "I've been puzzled by how you have dogged my steps since you joined the church. Always wanting to be where I was, go where I went, and even trying to get in the ministries I'm a part of. I've treated you with kindness, invited you into my inner circle of friends, and all this time, you've been waiting for a chance to do something like this to me? To my knowledge, we've never met before, so why, Annette? What did I ever do to you?"

Annette's lips curled in contempt. "Everybody *loves* Vann Sinclair. Everybody *respects* and *appreciates* the esteemed Vann Sinclair. All the women look up to you, and the men are always standing around talking about you, and how good you look for an old chick, and how they want to get next to you. I've been struggling all my life with one no-good man after another, and one dead-end job after another, but everything comes *easy* to you. Just look at you—already retired from one job, and a business just opens up for you. Your own television show just drops into your lap, and just look at all of this," she waved her hand around the room. "And you say you haven't had a man in years, but I happen to know that beach houses like this don't come cheap. So you had to do something to get it, with your holier-than-thou self!"

"You mean this is all about *jealousy?* You come into my home and try to get between Mitch and I because of some misconceived notion that I haven't had to work and struggle for what I have?" Vann's expression showed astonishment and disgust. "Annette, you know little about my life and have no idea how hard I've worked to get where I am. All of your conclusions about my life are ludicrous."

Annette seemed to grow angrier. "That's what you say. But I've been trying to find a decent man all my life, and you get a man like Mitch running after you, and don't know how to appreciate him and snatch him up. Well, I do. You have everything I want, and I'm taking everything I can," Annette said with an ugly laugh.

Vann shook her head as though to clear it. "Lady, you get your messed up behind out of my house right now. If Mitch wants the likes of you, he's welcome to you, but I don't ever want to see you again."

When Annette didn't move fast enough, Rubye said, "Do you need any help? You act like you didn't understand."

Annette, seeing the looks on their faces, picked up her half packed bags, walked a few steps, and set them down near the door to toss parting words at Vann. "You can give it up, honey. I talked to Mitch, and he totally agrees with me that you have way too many issues, and frankly, he doesn't want to deal with them. He's going to tell you as soon as you get back to Houston."

"Out!" the women all yelled, pointing toward the door.

Annette ran through the door, past her bags, and didn't stop until she reached the bottom step. Realizing she had left them, she looked up in time to see the open bags flying down to the ground, spilling the contents.

Rubye ran to Vann's side and put her arm around her shoulders. "I know now why I've never liked that woman. Don't you pay any attention to anything she said, Vann. You know she has to be nuts to be a guest in your house and do some crazy stuff like this."

"But she's right, Rubye. Mitchell does agree with her. I heard them talking," Vann said in a flat emotionless voice. "Anyway, I have a headache." Vann turned and wearily walked up the stairs and into her bedroom, closing the door firmly.

Rubye went to her room, got her phone, and called her husband's cell phone number.

Thomas answered, "Yeah woman! What's up? Can't I be out of your sight just a little while without you tracking me down?"

"Listen 'T'!" Rubye said. "Your friend is in big trouble and has a lot of explaining to do. Vann is devastated, and we just threw Annette out of here. Annette has informed Vann that she needs to step aside so that she and Mitchell can get together; and she insists that Mitch agrees with her. Now, I'm telling you 'T', if Mitch did that, he's got trouble coming. Vann doesn't deserve that."

"What?" Thomas was shocked to hear how quickly things had gotten crazy since they had left the beautiful beach location. "Mitch, pull off at the next exit. Something's going on."

When the car came to a stop in front of a business on the freeway feeder road, Thomas handed him the phone. After listening for several minutes, Mitch too, yelled, "What?!"

Several more minutes passed as he listened. "That's not true! Yes, that woman did get in my face talking some kind of foolishness. But after I realized what she was about, I politely told her that it wasn't the place or the time to have a discussion like that. The only reason I was polite was because I didn't want to tell her off in Vann's house, and I most certainly didn't intend for Vann to hear and misinterpret that conversation."

"Well, that's exactly what happened," Rubye answered.

"Rubye, do I need to turn around and come back?" Mitch asked.

"If you want to straighten things out with Vann, yes! Vann's been through some things that you probably don't know about. I can't tell you how badly this has hurt her."

"We're going back," Mitch told Thomas after disconnecting the call. He headed down the feeder road and made a U-turn. "I'm glad we stopped and messed around at that gas station and didn't get any further down the road. Hopefully, I'll get back before Annette can get away," he said, praying he wouldn't get a speeding ticket.

Mitch turned onto the street that would lead them to the beach house. He prayed Annette was still there, so he could tell her in Vann's presence, just what he thought of her. He saw there were still several cars in the circular driveway, so maybe God was with him. They quickly jumped out of the car and finally saw Annette down between the cars gathering up clothes and other belongings, putting them into bags.

"Good! I'm glad you're still here, lady." He told her in a hard tone. "I don't know what you said to Vann, but we're going to get it straightened out right now."

Thomas had gone into the house and a few seconds later, Mitch followed a mutinous Annette through the door. He looked around the room.

"Where's Vann?" he asked.

"She's upstairs," Rubye answered him. "You need to talk to her and explain yourself, Mr. Judge."

Mitch saw the look on Rubye's face and knew she was prepared to protect Vann's interest at all cost.

"Alright, but please, don't let this woman leave. I have some things to say to her and I want to say them in Vann's presence."

He ran up the stairs, knocked on the closed bedroom door, then went in, closing the door behind him.

The group downstairs all turned and glared at Annette.

"Vann? We need to talk, honey." Mitch walked over and sat down on the bed beside her. "Surely you don't believe I would be low enough to come on to one of your friends under your own roof! I know you know me better than that. To be honest though, that woman did approach me in the kitchen and try to talk to me. There was nothing wrong with her hand, that was just a ruse to get you out of the room. She had it all planned out.

"I know now I should've confronted her in your presence, but I was trying to protect you from a bad scene. I didn't want to spoil the good time everyone was having by letting something as despicable as that upset things. But I had every intention of telling her off in no uncertain terms, and telling you about her later. I know you didn't have any idea what kind of person she really is, and just so you know, I detest women like that. Vann, honestly, I have absolutely no interest in that woman. I hadn't given her a second look or thought before she got in my face. You have to believe that."

Vann gave him a cold look. "Then why didn't you tell her that at the time, Mitch? Just like you told her you would talk later, you could have just as easily told her you had absolutely nothing to talk to her about. You could have stopped it right there." She flung her hand out as she talked. "And so what if it caused a scene? It's done that anyway. That woman actually got in my face and boasted about how she was going to take you, and anything else she can take. And in my house! She was shown the door real quick."

"I wish now I had handled it differently," Mitch said, softly. "I've had some experience with devious women before, Vann. They're not satisfied unless they're destroying someone and they're very determined to do it, one way or another. The only thing I could think of was my fear that Annette was going to try to destroy what we have if I had tried to reject her then and there. I was also afraid that if you heard any part of the conversation, you might jump to the wrong conclusion about what was really happening. But whatever she told you about me and her getting together is a lie. I only said we would talk later because at the time, I was just trying to get her away from me before you came back. I swear to you that's the truth."

Vann covered her eyes with her hands and sighed wearily. "Will you just go?"

"No, not until we get this settled. Come on, let's go downstairs." He pulled her with him through the door and down the stairs, where he faced Annette.

"Lady, you owe it to Vann to tell her the truth and I'm asking you to try to find it within yourself to do that." He looked at Annette coldly, waiting for a response.

"You did say we would talk later," Annette said. "That is the truth."

"Yes, I did say that. But what else did I say?" When she didn't answer, Mitch continued. "Did I not say that what you were doing was distasteful to me, and disrespectful to Vann?"

"Yes, I suppose," Annette admitted. "But I thought you just meant it was distasteful because we were in Vann's house. Not about us getting together," she looked at him hopefully. "We can still get together, Mitch," she brazenly suggested.

"Lady, what rock did you crawl out from under?" Mitch said scornfully. "If I thought it was distasteful for Vann's friend to come on to her man in her house, don't you think I'd also find the friend distasteful?" All of a sudden an odd look dawned on Mitch's face. The woman's need to get what she wanted at any cost reminded him of some of the women he had seen in his court. "Annette, who are you, really? What do you do for a living? How long have you lived in Houston? Where do you work?" Mitch fired question after question, and watched her reaction.

A fearful look entered Annette's face and suddenly she was very anxious to get away. "I don't ever want to see none of y'all again."

Annette ran out the door and this time, didn't take the time to pick up the clothes and put them in bags. She just scooped up everything and tossed it into her car and hightailed it out of there as fast as she could.

"I wonder if she'll even think about the friendship we tried to offer her?" Vann finally spoke.

"I doubt it, Vann," Thomas answered her. "A person like that only understands one thing…getting what they want at any cost."

"Well! It's time to pack up and go home everybody. We've had enough excitement for a while," Rubye said. "Come on, girls." She looked at Katherine, Estelle, and Roxanne.

"Uh, Thomas?" Mitch walked over to where Thomas was sitting. "Would you mind driving my car back and taking the ladies? Vann and I need to talk, so I'd like to ride back with her."

"Sure, man," Thomas answered, then looked at Vann. "As long as that's okay with you, Vann Jo?"

"Yes, that's fine, Thomas," Vann answered in a soft voice.

After everyone else had packed up and left, Mitch looked at her. "Vann, there are some things we need to sort out. I told you I was not going to give up on us and I meant it. I know how I feel about you, but I'm not sure I know what your feelings are for me. The fact that you believe I could do something that despicable tells me you must not think much of my integrity. Can we talk and clear the air so we'll both know where we stand, as well as where we're trying to go?"

"Yes, I suppose so." She led the way to the kitchen and started a pot of coffee. "I guess it's a good thing this happened now so we can figure things out."

"I'll begin by telling you about my relationships with my children's mothers. Beverly and I were married for fifteen years before we had to call it quits. She just couldn't handle the military life. After we split, she continued to try to control my life through our children. It was only after she got married again that she backed off a little. But even now, she still tries to get her two bits in, although the kids are grown.

"I met Katrina, Matthew's mother, at church. By the time I learned what she was really about, she was pregnant with Matthew. I was so ashamed of myself...my actions, that it's only been recently that I decided to get back into church. My relationship with Katrina is strictly that of shared parenthood, although she has pushed for it to be more. She tries to make my life as difficult as she can by trying to manipulate me through Matthew.

"So you see, I have a certain amount of emotional baggage when it comes to women. I've made my share of mistakes, and now I'm so afraid that I'll make another one, that it causes me to do stupid things sometimes. That was the reason why I responded as I did with Annette. I was so afraid she was going to mess things up between us before we even have a chance. Do you understand what I'm saying?"

"Yes, I guess I do understand, but I still disagree with the way you handled it. I would think that you as a judge would know that the best way to deal with people like that is to be upfront. I might have a problem doing that, but you shouldn't. And I would rather you had spoiled the party by exposing what she was doing, than to let her cause misunderstanding and hurt. So, is it my turn? You want to know about my past relationships?"

"Yes, I think that'd be a good idea," Mitch answered, preoccupied with what she had said.

Vann poured them both a cup of coffee, then sat down and began telling him the long story of each of her tragic relationships. "Add my mother's rejection of me and her sudden desire to enter my life when it's apparent her only motive is self preservation, and hopefully you'll get a clear picture of why I've responded the way I did, not only to your proposal, but to Annette's mess as well."

They talked. The coffee pot was empty, and still they talked. Night had long settled around the house and the hour grew late, and still they talked. Hurts from the past came out, fears and concerns for the present and the future, pet peeves, favorite things, most disliked things or habits, idiosyncrasies like which side of the bed they preferred, things other people do that drove them crazy, their hopes, dreams, expectations and uncertainties, and other things were exposed, talked about, sometimes laughed over, but definitely prayed over. It was late when they left the beach house, but they both felt satisfied that a solid understanding of each other had been added to the foundation of their relationship.

chapter twenty

Mitch had known it would eventually happen. The only thing that surprised him was that it had taken this long. Katrina had heard, through Matthew, about Vann. Although he had made it clear that there would never be anything between them except their son, he knew Katrina had maintained the hope of them someday getting married. "For Matthew's sake," she kept insisting. But in the meantime, Mitch knew there had been no shortage of men through her life. He didn't care as long as they posed no threat to his son.

Now, he impatiently paced as he waited for Katrina to bring Matthew to his house for the weekend. He had been prepared to go pick him up as he usually did, but Katrina had nixed it, insisting she would drop him off because she needed to talk to him. Since Matthew was now old enough to make his own way to the car, Mitch's habit was to drive into the parking lot of Katrina's apartment complex, use his cell phone to call Matthew, then wait in the car for him to come out. It worked out well for Mitch since he didn't have to fend off any foolishness from Katrina. But now, as he waited for them to arrive, he prayed and prepared his mind for whatever she had in store for him. He didn't have to think too hard about what she wanted to talk about—Vann…of that he was sure.

His doorbell rang, and when he opened the door, Matthew jumped through the door to hug him and Katrina stepped in, eagerly looking around in curiosity as she did each time on her infrequent visits to his home.

"Oh! You've been decorating!" she exclaimed.

"Vann did it!" Matthew supplied excitedly. "Vann is decorating the whole house," he added.

"Matt, go and watch television for a while," Katrina requested. "I need to talk to your dad."

"I'm hungry! What do you have to eat, Dad?" Matthew grumbled. "Did Vann come over and cook something today?"

"No, son," he answered noticing the angry look on Katrina's face. "But we'll go out in a few minutes and get something. Now please, do as your mom asked."

"Oooo-Kay," Matthew said dejectedly, dragging his feet out of the room.

"Mitch, I want to know who this woman is that you're bringing in here over my child. You know I don't like any and everybody around my son." Katrina wasted no time going on the attack.

"Uh, uh, uh. Now that's a strange comment from someone with a continuous stream of boyfriends in and out, Katrina. All you need to know is that Vann is not just anybody. She's very special to me and in fact, I've asked her to become my wife and I'm praying she'll say yes. She's good for both me and Matt...our lives are better since she's been here. Has Matt complained? Or did he just tell you about her, and you took it from there? At any rate, she's here to stay."

"No, you're not going to have some other woman over here telling my child what to do! Before I let that happen, I'll get a court order to keep him from coming over here. I've been trying to tell you for years that the best thing for Matt is for us to get married so he won't have to be shifted from house to house. But no, you think you're too good for me! Well, you're not going to have things all your way. I'm going to see to that."

Mitch folded his arms and waited for her to finish. When she stopped, he said, "Katrina, think about what you're saying. You cannot have my parental privileges revoked simply because I get married. And if I were you, I'd leave that alone. I know you're aware that you violate that court order every time he's supposed to come to me and you won't let him, or when you leave him here for a week or more when he's only supposed to be here for the weekend. I haven't complained because I love my son and don't want him in the middle of frivolous bickering. I'd love to have our case revisited, and you might be the one who comes out on the losing end."

"Make all the threats you want, but I'm going to check into what I can do to protect my child. That woman could be a child molester or abuser or something. You know you can't be too careful with the people—both men and women—you bring around children."

"Again, let me remind you, that goes both ways. I could say the same thing about you. But you do all the checking you want to on Vann. You might start with the state. She's a volunteer with one of their programs designed to protect children. She's been investigated from head to toe by them. Then you might talk to the couple whose son she raised. He's grown now and still calls her 'Mama'. That's just for starters."

"Huh!" Katrina huffed. "You think you have all the answers, don't you? Well, have you asked your son how he feels about this woman?"

"Matt likes Vann. I'm sure you can tell. She loves children and has been around them enough to know how to relate to them. You don't think I'd marry someone who doesn't like children, do you? You need to get over this pettiness and move on with your life like I'm trying to do, Katrina."

Tears swelled up in her eyes. "Mitch, please! We should be making a home for our son together! Don't do this!" she wailed.

"Not possible, Katrina. I told you that years ago. There has to be a level of mutual trust and respect in any successful relationship. You know as well as I do that it's not there with us. And we won't even talk about love. I don't plan to spend the rest of my life in a war zone. Like I said, the best thing for both of us is to move on."

"We'll see about that," she said, angrily. "If I were you, I wouldn't be making any wedding plans too soon, because you're crazy if you think I'm going to take this lying down." She flounced to the door. "You are in for a fight you don't want."

Shaking his head in disgust, Mitch sat down for a minute to collect himself. He had known Katrina would have a fit when she found out he was seeing someone seriously. Maybe he hadn't tried hard enough to convince her they had no future. "Well, Lord! I leave this in Your hands," he said, before calling Matthew so they could leave for Vann's house for dinner.

Mitch had already sent flowers earlier that day for her birthday and had a gift and card to take to her. She hadn't said a word about her birthday to him, but he had remembered.

While they were eating the delicious meal Vann had prepared, Mitch told her about his plans to visit his parents in Georgia. "I've made it a regular part of my schedule to visit them every few months, just to check on them. Matt will be out of school for the summer in a few weeks and I know you mentioned you wanted to check on your grandmother more often, so I was thinking we could all go. We could take our time on a leisurely drive and do a little sightseeing. I know you just did some touring in the area a few months ago, but I'd like for us to do it together. I want Matt to see a little of historical Charleston, maybe visit a plantation, and then go on to Gullah Island. I hear they have some very nice attractions. Then we could drive on over to the Savannah area and see some of the historical sites there. I'd like to meet your grandmother, and I'd like you to meet my family. And I'm sure they would all like to see Matt. What do you think?"

"That sounds wonderful. I'd love to check on Mama, and she's already said she wants to meet you too. I'm kind of concerned about her. Since her fall and illness, she's talking about being tired a lot lately. But I don't know, Mitch, let me think about it. I've been away from everything quite a bit lately, and I do have responsibilities. I haven't driven to Georgia in years. Since I've gotten older, it's just more practical for me to fly. It sounds like fun though, doesn't it Matt?"

"Uh huh!" Mathew said around a mouth bulging with food. "But Mom might not want me to go unless she goes too, Dad. You know how she is."

"You let me handle your mom, Son. I'm sure it'll be okay," Mitch said in a sober tone.

"You're old?" Matthew asked, looking at Vann questioningly.

"Yes, honey, I am," she answered with a laugh.

"Older than Dad? He's really old!"

"Yep. I'm older than your dad. So I guess that makes me really, *really* old, huh?" She asked, laughing harder.

Matthew nodded his head slowly, "I guess."

Later that night, Vann got a call from her aunt that robbed her of her hard-to-hold-onto peace.

"Vann," Aunt Lu's troubled voice came over the line, "have you talked to Rosetta lately?"

"No, I haven't Aunt Lu. Why?"

"Well, she's still wondering if you're going to help her. I know she's been quiet since Mama got sick, but she said she still needs help. You can't forget about this, Vann. This is your mother."

"I haven't forgotten, Aunt Lu. But you know what's been going on in my life, with Mama's illness and everything. And you did tell me she was doing better."

"She still needs your help, honey. Now you need to give some serious thought to what you're going to do, and when. You can't keep putting it off."

Vann sighed. "Okay, Aunt Lu, but listen, I've got to go. I'll talk to you later."

She hung up the phone with a heavy heart. She had pushed all thought of Rosetta to the back of her mind when she had gone to take care of Mama. But now, here she was in the same place she had been before Mama got sick. "Lord, forgive me. I know I'm being selfish, but I sure do want to go on that trip with Mitch."

They managed to get everything worked out for the trip and a few weeks later, after Matthew's last day of school, they went to pick him up on their way out of town. But when they picked Matthew up, they noticed the clothes he had on were some he had outgrown long ago and were shabby as well.

"Matt, why do you have on those old clothes?" Mitch asked, as soon as he got into the car.

"I don't know. Mom told me to wear these," Matthew answered.

"Well, we'll go back by Vann's house since it's closer, so you can change, okay?" Mitch said, trying to hide his aggravation at Katrina.

But when they went through the bag Katrina had packed, they found nothing but old clothes that were either worn out or too small. There wasn't one decent outfit in there. "We have to go shopping," Mitch said, frustrated. "I can't take my child on a trip with nothing decent to wear."

"We can stop at the mall on the way out of town," Vann said. "Let's just empty everything out of this bag except those things he can use."

Shopping at the mall would have been fun had it been under different circumstances. Mitch worked hard to control his anger, and Vann worked hard to help him.

"Honey, don't let this spoil our trip," she whispered out of Matthew's hearing. "That's what she's hoping will happen. Don't give her the satisfaction."

On the long drive, Vann told Mitch that her grandmother had lived with her in Houston for years, before she'd started demanding to move back to Georgia. They'd tried to talk her out of it, but the old lady wouldn't be satisfied, stating she wanted to live her last days on her own soil.

"I sold one of my houses to pay for the remodeling and repairs on the old house I grew up in," Vann told Mitch. "I wanted it to be a comfortable home for Mama, and a place I could feel comfortable visiting since I knew I would be doing that a lot. Mama's sister and her daughter, Viola, decided to move in with her, so I added a den and another bathroom and bedroom to the three bedroom house. That was five years ago, and it's worked out well. They all look after one another and keep each other company. Mama insisted on putting the deed to the house in my name. She said that after I put my hard-earned money into the place to make it so nice, she didn't want some-body trying to take it away from me after she was gone."

"So you own the house your grandmother lives in, huh?" Mitch asked. "Well, I agree with her, and I'm glad she deeded it over to you. I think I'm going to like the old lady, because she takes care of business. What about your mother, Vann? What's happening on that?" Mitch asked reluctantly, but he needed to know what was going on.

She glanced behind her at Matt sleeping on the back seat. "I...uh...I still haven't made any definite plans to move her...although I've got the room ready for her. But I have been sending money to help her out financially."

"And does that make you feel less guilty about everything?" he asked.

"No. It doesn't," she said softly. "But the guilt did lighten a little when I had to go take care of Mama."

"But what about Rosetta? Is she doing any better?"

"Aunt Lu got after me about putting off making a decision. She said that although Rosetta has been quiet since Mama got sick, she still needs my help, and is waiting on me to make a decision."

"Vann, I don't believe you'll be able to live with yourself if you don't help her." He gave her a brief glance. "This is not easy for me to say, since what I really want is for you to marry me and forget about Rosetta, but we both have to do the right thing. The thing that's going to be in God's will and that will bring us peace."

"Us?" she asked, looking at him with a smile.

"Yeah, babe, *us*. I've already told you I would help you, whatever you decide to do. I just want it to be the right thing."

Vann looked out the window at the passing scenery and sighed. "I know what the Lord is leading me to do. I need to push back my hurt, let His love rule in my heart, and just do it."

"Vann, have you considered that this could be God's way of providing you the opportunity to get to know your mother in this life? You told me how you prayed most of your life for that to happen. Now look how the table has turned—it's her begging you."

"It doesn't mean much because it was brought about by her need, not her desire to know me. It's a hollow victory."

"Maybe," Mitch answered. "But it's still a victory, and don't limit what God is doing. Your mother may think she needs you for one reason, but God may have an altogether different reason for bringing you together."

"I hadn't thought about it like that. But it's still a difficult hurdle to get over."

He reached over and caught her hand. "Babe, you have to forgive her. You know you do. There's no way over that hurdle except through forgiveness. Have you talked to her about it?"

"Yes, but in anger, not in a calm, rational way. And I know you're right. I have to forgive her, but…" she squeezed his hand tightly, "there are years piled up on top of years of this thing festering in my heart; I have to get my own heart right with the Lord. The truth is, I need forgiveness for not forgiving her."

Mitch chuckled. "You have to let the Spirit of God do the work in you. There is nothing too hard for Him, and you know forgiveness is always His will."

chapter twenty-one

It was a wonderful trip. They followed the plan Mitch had prepared and Vann enjoyed every minute of it. And what a joy it was watching her grandmother interacting with Mitch.

While Matthew ran all over the property, trying to climb trees and throwing rocks at the fence posts, Mama quizzed Mitch about everything from his eating habits to every member of his family—whom she happened to know. Then she started in on his past relationships with women. Mitch was honest and upfront about everything, including Katrina's recent threats. After listening quietly, she told him in no uncertain terms that she would talk to the Lord about him and the issue of Katrina, but that if he failed Vann in any way, she would tell her baby exactly what to do to him. "And it won't be comfortable for you, either," she admonished him.

Noticing Vann's hilarious laughter, Mitch squirmed and asked, "Just what is it you'll have her do to me?"

"Just keep in mind what I said, young man, and you won't have to worry about it," the old lady told him.

Vann would always remember the last thing Mama told him: "Young man, my baby's don' been through a whole lotta hurt in her life. She don't need no more hardships heaped on her by nobody else. I'm asking you to see that she's taken care of after I'm gone. If you don't think you can do that, then I'm asking you to go on about your business and leave her alone."

Mitch smiled. "I want to spend the rest of my life with Vann and I've been trying to convince her to marry me and let me take care of her. It's all up to her, but don't worry, I promise you I'll keep an eye on her, even if we don't get married."

"Thank you, young man," she told him. "I can rest easy knowing that."

Mitch's parents were happy to see Mitch and their grandson, and also welcomed Vann with open arms.

"So happy to finally get to meet you," his mother said. "I tell you, he was just miserable when y'all missed each other last Christmas. We wanted him to stay and visit with us a few days, but all he could think about was getting back to Houston to see you."

Vann and Mitch were sitting close on an old-fashioned porch swing. They looked at each other, smiling.

"Yes, we decided we wouldn't be trying to surprise each other again any time soon," Vann stated.

After answering Mitch's questions about their health, they immediately began telling Vann stories about Mitch's childhood escapades. "Did Mitch tell you about the time he broke my gravy boat and then tried to hide it, and ended up getting a whipping?" his mother asked. "All he had to do was tell the truth and that would have been one he could have avoided."

"Judge!" Vann turned to him with a look of amazement. "You lied to your mother? I can't believe you did that." Then she cracked up at the look he gave her.

"I didn't do it, my brother did. But he suckered me into hiding it, and then told Mama I did it. I still owe him for that one," Mitch defended.

"Oh, chile, they was always into something," his mother continued. "Never knew what they would be into next. Trying to ride the bulls and getting thrown, going off in the woods and getting lost, and then claiming they just went camping. I tell you, they were a handful. I still can't believe this one ended up a judge. I'm proud of him though," she said, chuckling.

The conversation turned to what was happening in the community, as they told Mitch about who was sick, who had died, or who had had another child. Mitch's dad finally got around to questioning Vann about her family. "Now, you say Rebecca is your grandmother, huh? I know both of them sisters. Fine Christian women. I know your aunts and uncles too, but I don't know if I remember Rosetta."

Vann laughed. "Join the club, sir. I don't know her either. She was the youngest, which is probably why you don't remember her, and after she left me with my grandparents, that was the last any of the family saw of her."

"Oh!" Mitch's mother exclaimed. "You don't know your mother, chile?" she asked with a shocked look on her face.

"No, ma'am, I don't. I talked to her for the first time last year."

"Uh, uh, uh," she shook her head sadly. "Well, she's missed knowing the beautiful person you turned out to be. She's going to regret that, if she hasn't already."

Mitch squeezed the hand he was holding, and smiled at Vann. "That's what I keep telling her," he said.

"I'm sho' glad you two found each other way off over there in Texas," his father said. "Nothing like being with home folk, and being able to talk about familiar things when you're away from home."

"Yes, we do enjoy each other's company," Vann said, smiling at Mitch again.

"Any wedding plans anytime soon?" His mother asked.

"Mama!" Mitch scolded.

She continued as though she hadn't heard him. "Well, I'll be waiting to hear when the wedding is. Y'all ain't as young as you used to be, and having someone to grow old with is a blessing. Seem like y'all get along with each other pretty well. Ain't no use in putting it off."

"Now, Mama, you are messing around in something that does not concern you," Mitch scolded again. "Just leave all that alone."

"You heard your son, woman," his father chimed in. "But I do think you might be right—for once," he said, making sure he was out of reach of the hand trying to hit him.

"Well, if you must know," Mitch gave Vann a warm look, "I've already asked her to marry me. I'm just waiting for her to say yes."

Mitch's parents then turned questioning looks to Vann.

Matthew was like a bird out of a cage. He ate at Vann's grandmother's house, then swore to Mitch's parents that he was starving to death after just a thirty minute trip. He ran himself to the point of exhaustion chasing after his grandparents' dogs, and just running from one end of the lane leading up to the house to the other. He didn't have that kind of freedom in the city.

Although Vann didn't spend a lot of time with them, Mitch's parents made her promise to come back and see them—even without Mitch.

After returning home, Vann began working on upcoming *High Point* shows. The shows had been going well, and she was actually enjoying doing them. She worked hard to bring interesting topics and speakers to the show, and the Lord had graciously provided

She studied the notes she kept on potential shows and guests. The list included a topic about caring for elderly parents, nursing homes, and other elder care services. "Uh, uh! I can't go there right now. I'd probably start boohooing right there on camera." She went to the next headings—children's issues, women's issues, general health, consumer rights.

"Let's see what we have here—all of these topics are always interesting," she said, perusing the children's issues. "CPS, Children At Risk Agency, adoption and foster care, and the latest child safety tips." All were good, but after calling every agency, she was not able to get a representative lined up for the date the show would be taped. Then she remembered Child Advocates. She snapped her fingers, "Use your resources, girl!"

She called the agency coordinator she worked with, who was excited about the possibility of free publicity for the agency. After checking it out with the agency director, it was a go. They tossed around ideas about the best way to format the show, and decided a panel of guests would probably be better. They would have a child advocate volunteer, a caseworker, and a parent who had been helped through the program.

"Lord, You are so good!" she said, as she finalized plans for the show.

Then, to stay ahead, she planned the next two shows. She called the local school district and obtained a representative who would speak on safety during the summer vacation for one of the shows, and a representative from Parks and Recreation to talk about activities they would be providing over the summer months for the other show.

That done, she outlined the discussion and relevant questions for each of the shows and relaxed. The only thing left to do was prepare her wardrobe for the next taping

Dressed in a black classic pantsuit that she accessorized with red and gold, Vann felt comfortable as the camera lights came on. "Welcome to *High Point*. I'm Vann Sinclair, your host for today. On this show, we'll be discussing a topic that is close to my heart...the welfare of our children. In a perfect world, there would be no need for programs such as this one, but sadly, this is an imperfect world, and many children are in situations that are often detrimental to their well-being, and sometimes, even their lives.

"We have with us three guests who will talk about this wonderful program that comes to the aid of children who are in these situations. First, we have a coordinator from the Child Advocates Agency, who will tell you about the program. Next we have a parent, whose family has benefited from the program, and lastly, we have a volunteer who will talk about her role in rescuing children."

She led the conversation and thanked each guest for their participation. She closed the show with her own customized phrase: "Remember, your High Point may be just one word, one smile, or one touch away."

The next weekend, Vann and Matthew were at Mitch's house relaxing after getting home from church and eating a big meal. Mitch was in his recliner with the Sunday paper and Vann was sitting on the floor in front of the television with Matthew, playing a video game. The doorbell rang, and when Mitch opened the door, Katrina walked in.

"Mom!" Matthew said with a frown when he saw her. "It's not time for me to go home yet. Dad promised to take me to the Kids Zone before bringing me home."

In recent weeks, Katrina had continuously called Mitch, badgering him about his relationship with Vann. Her threats continued—ranging from the ridiculous to the absurd. "Matthew told me she's older than you are. I don't want my child to have to be taking care of some old lady, Mitch. Why in the world would you even consider marrying her?"

Now, as she walked into the room, Katrina barely noticed her son. Her eyes zeroed in on Vann. She had expected old. This woman wasn't old by any stretch of the imagination. She had thought 'fat'. This woman was slender with everything in the right place. She had thought 'gray hair'. But although she had some gray strands, Katrina couldn't criticize, because she had more. She was disappointed to see that the other woman's face was smooth and unlined. Dressed casually in a capri outfit and sandals, she looked vibrant and full of life.

"So... this is the old woman you're messing around with," Katrina stated nastily. "Matthew keeps going on and on about this old woman his daddy is dating. He's really embarrassed about it, and I just wanted to see for myself."

"Matt, go get your things together, Son," Mitch said quietly, wanting to shield him from an unpleasant scene. "We'll go to the Kids Zone another time."

"Aw, man!" Matthew complained, but slowly left the room.

"Katrina, this is Vann Sinclair, the woman I plan to marry. Now unless you can treat her with courtesy and respect, you're not welcome in this house. And I know you're lying about Matthew. He is definitely not embarrassed about anything to do with Vann. He's too busy enjoying the kindness she shows him, and eating the good food she feeds him. She wants to do the right thing for all of us, including Matthew."

" Mitch, *I* want the best for Matthew," Katrina responded. "That's why I'm against you bringing some other woman in here. Matthew needs a stable home environment with both of his parents. I've told you that."

"Katrina...," Mitch took deep breaths, trying to control his anger.

Vann came to stand beside him, and started rubbing his back in a soothing motion. "Mitch, there's no need to get yourself upset. We'll work through this," she said softly.

"I know, babe. But this is all so senseless. And I'm sick and tired of it." His arm went around her and they huddled together, comforting one another.

Katrina covetously watched the interplay between them, as Vann began to speak to her.

"Katrina," Vann said in a soft voice. "I want you to know that I love Matthew very much. But I can assure you that I'd never try to take your place as his mother. He's a wonderful little guy, and I would never do anything to hurt or confuse him."

Katrina's face twisted in anger. "The only thing you can say that I want to hear is that you're getting out of Mitch and Matthew's lives. That would make me real happy. Matthew! Come on!" She turned and walked to the door.

"Katrina," Mitch said with the authority of a judge. "Until you can be civil, please don't come to this house again. Just have my son ready when I come by to pick him up. I don't want to communicate with you in any way. If you have anything to say to me, do it through my attorney."

"You both know where you can go!" Katrina said, casting a hate-filled look at them before walking out the door. "Matthew! I said come on!"

"You know what, babe?" Mitch asked after they hugged Matthew and watched them drive away. "I know without a doubt that it's God's will for us to be together, and I want us to be married before something or someone manages to come between us to destroy what we have. Satan keeps sending people, one after the other—Elliott Shaw, Annette, Rosetta, and now, Katrina—to throw up roadblocks. We can't let that happen, babe. I love you with all my heart. So when are you going to marry me?"

Vann threw her arms around him and hugged him close. "Oh, honey, I love you too, but..." tears filled her eyes at what she was about to say... "but maybe all of these attacks just mean the Lord is trying to tell us that marriage between us is not His will. Have you thought about that?"

"No, honey. Because what we have together is loving, joyful, peaceful, good. You know as well as I do that those things are from God. That's why Satan is trying so hard to kill, rob, and destroy everything."

When Vann left Mitch's house that day, her mind was unsettled. Katrina's arrival had brought an end to their peaceful time together, and it was obvious that Katrina didn't intend to give up.

And...she reminded herself, not only did she have one baby's mama to deal with, she had two. Although she hadn't heard anything from Beverly, Mitch's ex-wife, she fully expected that shoe to fall before it was over. "Lord, this is another path I need guidance on. Because I surely don't know which way to go."

The first thing she did when she entered her house was to check her messages. She became concerned when she saw that Aunt Lu had called three times. "That's strange. I spoke to her right before leaving for church this morning." She pulled her cell phone out of her purse and groaned when she realized she'd forgotten to turn it on after leaving church. Sure enough, there were messages there as well. She felt fear and dread filling her as she hurriedly dialed her aunt's number. Something was wrong!

"Aunt Lu? What's wrong? I see you've called me several times. I...," her aunt interrupted her.

"Vann, where have you been?" her aunt yelled into the phone. "I been calling you for hours! And you didn't even answer your cell phone. What good is having a cell phone if you don't use it, huh?"

"I know, Aunt Lu. I just forgot to turn it back on after church. But what is it? Why were you calling?"

"Well if you would get out of that man's face and stay at home sometime, maybe you wouldn't be forgetting things. It's not like you to be going off somewhere and people can't find you, Vann. Have you lost all your senses over this man? What you need to be remembering is that family is forever, and spend your time trying to help your family. What's gotten into you anyway, missy?"

Vann was silent as hurt from her aunt's words slowly penetrated. How was it wrong for her to finally take a little time to enjoy herself? She finally said, "You are way off-base, Aunt Luberta. And I strongly resent your implication that it's wrong for me to enjoy the company of a man. When have I ever not been available when you needed me? I've always been there for my family, and you know that." As she spoke, anger became a force behind her words.

"Oh, baby, I'm sorry," her aunt groaned. "You didn't deserve that and I certainly didn't have any right to say it. I'm sorry! I guess I'm just letting things get to me."

"You're right, Aunt Lu, I didn't deserve that. Where is it written that I have to be at your beck and call every minute? I realize I've let myself get into that pattern, but as of right now, I'm breaking it. I have as much right as anybody else to live my life and be happy. I'm a human being with feelings and needs just like everybody else. Evidently my family doesn't understand that, and until you do, please don't call me anymore. Good-bye."

"Vann, Vann! I didn't get to..."

Vann quietly hung up the phone. Her heart was racing, and she felt sick to her stomach. She had never imagined herself talking to her beloved Aunt Lu like that. But she had done it. And she didn't regret it—yet. "Lord, if I'm wrong, please forgive me and show me the right way. But I just can't believe that You intended for me to give to others *all* the time. Father, my bucket needs to be filled too."

Fifteen minutes later, Vann's phone rang.

"Vannie, it's Aunt Bernie. I just talked to Lu. Listen, I'm so glad you told that old hag off! You got to get people off your back, honey. I been telling you that for years. This is your time to do new things with your life, but you've got to put old ways of thinking and doing behind you, or you won't ever experience them. Now, you know your aunt is just torn up over how she talked to you, but let her stew awhile before you call her, okay? That's the way to get your message through loud and clear."

Before Vann could respond, Aunt Bernie continued. "She was trying to tell you that Rosetta is in the hospital. She's had a heart attack, and they need somebody from the family to come up there. You can think and pray on it, but in the meantime, you hang tough, and don't let anybody push you into doing something you don't feel comfortable about doing. Okay? Bye."

As usual, Aunt Bernie said what she had to say, and was gone. But at least Vann felt better about what she had said to Aunt Lu.

After taking a few minutes to calm down, Vann dialed Mitch's number, needing to talk to him. "Mitch? I got home and found myself in the middle of a family mess again. I'm so tired of it all, Mitch." Her voice broke. "I just wish they would leave me alone."

"What going on? What's it about? Rosetta?"

"Yes, what else?" she answered. "She's had a heart attack and is in the hospital." She told him about the conversations with her aunts. "I'm so confused right now, I don't know if I was wrong to go off on my aunt like that. I don't think so, but maybe I'm just blinded by my own selfishness."

"Vann, I know for a fact that when you go off on people, they usually have it coming. I'm a personal witness to that," he said, laughing. "Babe, this is another strike by Satan. It's clear to me what's going on. Think about it. Satan is always going to be against God's will."

"Well, I still have to deal with the Rosetta issue. I've put it off too long, and maybe if I hadn't this wouldn't have happened." She didn't want to tell him that the reason she kept putting it off was because she'd been enjoying the time they had been spending together so much. "This latest development with her in the hospital will push me to take action. That's the only thing I'm concerned about right now. And I know the same holds true for Aunt Lu. She just went about it the wrong way."

"She knows that now," Mitch said, laughing. "But Vann, remember, I'm here to help you in any way I can, okay?"

She was quiet for a minute. "Mitch, I need to hang up so I can pray about this. Will you be in prayer with me?"

"You know I will. And honey, let the Lord speak to your heart, and remember what I told you about forgiveness, okay?"

"I'll try. And thank you again for everything." Before she hung up, she said, "Oh! Honey, remember we're invited to Rubye and Thomas' house for a Fourth of July cookout tomorrow."

"I remember, babe. I'm looking forward to it."

Vann hung up with thoughts of Rosetta weighing heavily on her mind, and knew her family troubles would make it difficult for her to enjoy the cookout.

chapter twenty-two

Elliott Shaw was anxiously waiting for the opportunity to rip Savannah up one side and down the other. And he had what he thought was a good reason to do it. In addition to still being angry over her threat to have him arrested, he now knew someone else she had mistreated.

When Annette Gooding had come to him crying uncontrollably over how she had been treated by the good Sister Sinclair and her friends, he had been more than happy to provide a comforting shoulder for her to cry on. After all, Savannah had hurt him too. Goes to show, you think you have people figured out, but you just never know who they are. He had honestly thought Savannah was a meek and mild woman who wouldn't hurt a fly. Apparently, he was mistaken.

He had been calling her and leaving messages for weeks now, and she hadn't bothered to return his calls. He was tempted to go to her house, but couldn't take the chance—she might call the police and his reputation was too important to him. But he would find some way to talk to her, not only about the way she had treated him, but also about the way she had treated Annette. He picked up the phone and left another message. "It's urgent that you call me, Savannah. We really need to talk about a situation involving your friend, Annette."

The next day, his phone rang and it was Savannah. Elliott smiled in glee, relishing the long awaited opportunity to tell her about herself.

"Savannah, I'm glad you finally found the time to call me," Elliott stated, in a snippy voice.

"Well, you did say it was something urgent concerning Annette," Vann responded.

"So that's the only way I can get a response from you, huh? By telling you it's urgent?" Elliott asked, in an unpleasant tone.

Vann sighed, thinking, *why did I do this to myself?* "You know what, Elliott? I don't have time for your snippy insults, so tell me what you want, or hang up, and don't call me again, or I will file an official complaint against you," she stated impatiently.

Elliott wanted to argue, but was afraid she would call the police. She had already shown him she was capable of carrying out her threats. "Do you know Ms. Annette Gooding? Weren't you two friends at one time?"

"Of course I know her, but I wouldn't say we were friends. Why are you asking?"

"She's been telling me how badly you and that judge and your friends treated her. I'm really shocked to hear that, Savannah. I thought you were a better person than that. Has that judge caused you to lose your mind? You're supposed to be a Christian woman, are you not?"

Vann's eyes turned to slits. "I won't argue with you, so get to the point, Elliott?"

"My point is this: I'm not seeing all that self-proclaimed Christianity coming through. You're going around with that judge, mistreating people and doing God only knows what, while ignoring a man who is willing to make a decent woman out of you. I'm saying you need to check yourself, Savannah. No Christian woman would conduct herself like you're doing."

"Lord, have mercy, I've got to hurry and get off this phone with you! It's not worth going into anyway. But I will say this, Elliott. Watch yourself with Annette because she's not all she pretends to be."

"Now you're trying to slander that poor woman. Haven't you done enough to her? She is devastated over the appalling way you treated her. She really had a lot of respect and admiration for the woman she thought you were. That's why she wanted to hang out with you."

"Are you finished? Because that's all I've got to say about you or Annette. I've had sufficient reasons for the way I've dealt with both of you."

"Personally, I think Annette is a very nice woman who you have treated badly, just like you're treating me. And I'm going to take steps to see that both Annette and I are vindicated. You and that judge are going to regret how you've treated us. I promise you that."

"Well, you have a right to your opinion, just as I have a right to mine. So, let's agree. You stay away from me, and I'll be careful not to bother you. But I do feel I need to warn you again—watch yourself with Annette. You can take or leave that advice; however, take what I'm about to say very seriously. If I ever hear a whisper of you and Annette doing anything to slander my name, I am going to sue you for defamation of character. And that doesn't include all that God is going to do to you, because I'm getting ready to pray and ask Him to get into this situation and deal with you. Good night, Elliott."

Mitch was dealing with his own demons. Katrina was still making threats about trying to take away any contact with Matthew if he didn't stop seeing Vann. That didn't worry him...he knew she couldn't do that. But what did worry him were the hateful things she was putting into Matthew's head about Vann.

Each time Matthew came to his house, he had more vile things to say about Vann. Things like: "She's old and decrepit, she ain't my mama and never will be. I don't have to do anything she tells me to, 'cause my mama told me I didn't. Mama told me to kick her if she tries to make me do anything. If it wasn't for Vann, Mama said we could all live together in the same house."

No amount of talking to his son could change what Matthew was saying. Katrina had the time to drill it into him, while Mitch only had him every other weekend if Katrina let him come like he was supposed to. Mitch was so afraid that Matthew would eventually say these things in Vann's presence that he had started taking pains to keep them apart. But for how long? Vann had already started questioning why he didn't bring Matthew around anymore.

His efforts to talk to Katrina also fell on deaf ears. "Katrina, don't you know how damaging it is to teach a child to hate someone? Especially someone who has shown him nothing but love? How is that going to affect his relationship with everyone who crosses his path? Will he be at school kicking teachers for telling him to do something, or calling them bad names? And who's to say he won't eventually turn on you and start treating you the way you're teaching him to treat Vann? Think about what you're doing. And if you don't cut it out, I'm going to ask the court to revisit our case. I don't want my son exposed to your warped way of thinking."

Mitch went to the Lord. "I can't see the way out of this Lord," he prayed, shaking his head in disgust. "Father, I want Your will to be done regarding me and Vann, and I ask that You will not let any weapon that forms against us prosper. Be with us, Father, because we have no other source to look to for guidance. And, Lord, have mercy upon my son, and his mother, and Elliott and Annette, because they all stand in need of Your help."

Mitch sat in his big, beautiful dream house, slumped in trouble. He wanted, no, needed to talk to Vann, but was reluctant to call her because he knew she would ask about Matthew.

"Well, I probably just need to go ahead and tell her what's going on," he admonished himself. "Naw," he decided. "Vann has enough on her plate right now. She doesn't need one more thing to worry about." Vann had told him about her conversation with Elliott Shaw, and how he and that woman, Annette, had joined forces to bring harm to Vann, and probably him too. He wanted to knock the man's block off, and would if he ever had the chance. But right now, he would do as Vann asked, and keep praying for them.

While he was sitting there agonizing over his problem, the phone rang.

"Hey sweetie. How are you?"

Relief and dread hit at the same time. Relief that it wasn't Katrina...dread that Vann might ask about Matthew, as she was prone to do. "Hi, honey," Mitch answered in a pleased tone. "I'm fine, and what about yourself?" he asked, smiling in spite of his double minded concerns. "I was just thinking about you and wishing I could see you." *Well, I was in a way!* he said to the part of his mind that was calling him a liar. "Am I going to see you tonight?"

"If you want to. And I hope so, because I really need to talk to you," Vann answered.

"Do you really, really want to see me? Enough to cook dinner for me?" he asked with a smile.

"Oh! I have to cook in order to see you these days, huh? That sounds kind of messed up to me, sweetie."

"What can I say? I never pretended to be perfect," he said, with a chuckle. Suddenly, he wanted to see her with everything in him. "I'm not going to waste any more time on the phone, I'll get ready and head that way shortly, okay?"

"Yes, but Mitch?" Vann stopped, wondering how to say what she had to. "I just want you to know that I do love you no matter what. Will you keep that in mind?"

"Yes, I will, but I already know this. What's going on? Why are you telling me this over the phone?"

"You'll understand when we talk. In the meantime, I'd better get in the kitchen and find something for you to eat. See you soon!"

He hung up and ran to his bedroom to shower and change clothes. "Thank You, Father...whatever is going on. Maybe she's finally going to tell me she'll marry me. You've been with me so far with this woman, and I trust You'll continue to be with me, even if that's not it. Thank You that I can rely on that, if nothing else."

As they were eating the delicious smothered chicken, green beans, and tossed salad Vann had hurriedly prepared, she noticed that Mitch kept glancing at her expectantly while he ate, waiting for her to tell him what was on her mind. She knew her news would not be what he wanted to hear, and therefore, didn't want to talk until after they finished eating. Why mess up a good meal? Finally, when she noticed he had put his fork down, she laid her own down, propped her chin on folded hands, and looked at him a long time without saying a word.

"Are you going to keep me waiting or tell me what it is you want to talk to me about?" Mitch asked quietly.

Vann smiled. "I'm going to tell you, but this is very hard for me."

"What? Tell me."

She sighed. "I've made some decisions. Some very difficult decisions. About Rosetta, and about...," she hesitated slightly, "about us."

His piercing eyes searched her troubled, light brown ones. She caught her bottom lip between her teeth—a habit she had when she was worried or troubled. "I'm listening, honey, just say it."

"I'm going to Dallas to see about Rosetta. She's still not doing very well. I won't know until after I get there exactly what her condition is."

"When are you going? Remember, I told you I would go with you."

"I know, and I appreciate your offer, but there's no need for you to go. My aunts...Rosetta's sisters...are going with me. I don't know if that's a good thing or not, because they don't get along very well. But the good thing is that Rubye is also going with us. She'll help me keep my sanity in the midst of the craziness."

"You asked Ruybe to go with you before talking to me? When you knew I'd already told you I wanted to go with you?" Anger filled his voice.

"I didn't ask her, she insisted. I was talking to her right after I made the decision to go up there and Rubye jumped right in and said that I wasn't going without her, and I'm so glad she did that. I didn't forget your offer though. I'm sure there'll be plenty that I'll need your help with. This is basically a fact-finding trip to see what needs to be done."

"I still wish you had talked to me first and given me the opportunity to insist on going. I don't know if I like the idea of you wading into that situation without me. There could be legalities involved that you'll need help with. For instance, what about Rosetta's other children? How are they going to react to your being there and taking control of their mother? People are strange creatures. In spite of the fact that they haven't done anything for her, they may take exception to your being there and try to fight you. I'd hate to see you get involved in a mess like that without me there to run interference for you."

"I've thought about all of that, believe me, and I'm not going to fight with anybody. The only issue here is that Rosetta be taken care of. If they want to straighten up and do it, then fine with me. But I can't continue to sit back and do nothing when they're not doing anything. Frankly, I'm praying they *will* step up and do the right thing. After all, she is their mother, which is something I can't bring myself to call her."

His set jaw indicated he was angry. "What else?" he asked tersely. "You mentioned you wanted to talk about us. I don't know why I'm asking, because I can see I've been relegated to a place of unimportance."

"That's not true, Mitch. But I promised you I'd think about your proposal, and Mitch, I love you, and I want to marry you...I just don't know when." He opened his mouth to argue, but she held her hand up to stop him. "I know what you're going to say, and I love you for it. But Mitch, in addition to all the other issues, this situation with Rosetta tips the scale in the negative column, and I believe marriage would be a mistake. That's not to say I don't want it to ever happen...just not now. Like I said, I love you too much to take the chance on all these negative issues destroying us."

Hurt and anger showed in Mitch's face. "I don't believe you, Vann. I don't know if you even know what true love between a man and a woman is. If you did, you would understand that it means sharing the good and the bad times. You would know it hurts me to be left out of sharing this situation with you," he said in a hard tone of voice. "No, Vann. I think you're afraid, and you're using every excuse you can come up with for us not to get married." He stood up from the table. "I guess I'll be going."

She caught his hand. "Mitch! Please don't feel like that. I'm not saying we should totally forget about marriage, just not now."

Mitch pulled away and headed toward the door, where he turned and said, "Vann, you may fool yourself, but you're not fooling me. Somewhere along the line, you convinced yourself that you aren't supposed to get married. Things are never going to be perfect, but even if they were, you would still find an excuse not to marry me." He held his hand up to stop her from interrupting.

"No, no, let me finish. I don't give a darn about how old you are, or whatever is happening in your body, or this situation with your mother, Katrina, or anybody. I love you and I know I want you with me for the rest of my life. Vann, we both know God is able. And we also know He can help us create a new life together, but we have to trust Him. If you're determined to let fear hold you back, then I guess there's nothing more for me to say is there? Thanks for dinner anyway."

Vann's heart sank to her feet as the door slammed behind Mitch. "Oh, God, I hope I haven't made the worst mistake of my life," she said in a sad voice. "Father, I love and need Mitch. Please don't let me lose him through unwise decisions and fear."

chapter twenty-three

Vann's heart was burdened as they started the trip to Dallas. The aunts' petty bickering didn't help. They were barely past the city limits of Houston when Aunt Lu started complaining that she needed to use the bathroom and stretch her legs. Aunt Bernie, true to form, lost no time in scolding her. "You're worse than a child, Lu. We've just barely left home and here you are talking about using the bathroom. Can't you wait until we're at least halfway there?"

"Oh hush, Bernie!" Luberta responded. "You know you have to use it, too. I saw you squirming around over there. The only difference in us is that I'm not ashamed to say so."

Vann and Rubye exchanged looks of determined patience, mixed with amusement, as Vann took the next exit off of the expressway. "That's okay, Aunt Lu. We can all stand to stretch a little. It's not like we're on a schedule or anything, so we can take our time getting there."

"You need to learn how to exercise a little control, Lu," Bernie persisted. "I've learned to do that in my traveling. You can't be stopping to go to the bathroom every thirty minutes."

"And you need to get off of my back, Bernie, and stop looking for every little way to put me down. You've been doing that since we were children, for goodness sake," Lu retaliated.

And you've both reverted to being children! Vann thought to herself, as she pulled into the parking lot of a fast-food restaurant.

"Okay, everybody. Let's refresh ourselves," Vann said, as they climbed out of the SUV and walked slowly to the door. Vann and Rubye went to the counter to order something to drink, while the two older women headed to the ladies room.

239

"Girl, this is going to be a very long ride," Rubye said, with a snicker. "If they can't get along on the way there, what are they going to be like on the way back when they're tired and out of sorts. And are they getting separate hotel rooms? Something tells me that they'd better, or somebody's going to get killed. I don't know what you're going to do with those old women, Vann."

"I don't know what I'm going to do about anything right now," Vann said, laughing.

"Oh, Lord, Vann, something just occurred to me," Rubye said in an agonized tone. "Here I am calling them 'old women', and you know what? Anybody looking at the four of us would describe us as four old women. I don't particularly like the thought of that."

Vann cracked up, laughing. "We are old, Rubye, even though I feel just like I did twenty or thirty years ago."

"Huh," Rubye huffed. "Age is a state of mind, and I ain't claiming being old."

They laughed again, then Rubye's merriment suddenly disappeared. "Vann, what's happening with you and Mitch? I know he's very upset that you didn't let him come with you. But what else is going on?"

"Yes, he's upset over that, but he's more upset over the fact that I told him we need to put off any thought of marriage until I can work through everything. You know that in addition to this situation, I have other concerns as well. Namely, old woman issues, wifely duties, and mess from the past. Mitch is a vibrant man who could have any woman he wants. Frankly, I don't know if I'm the best woman for him, and I don't want to make him so unhappy that he regrets marrying me."

"Vann, other people deal with these kinds of issues all the time. And if those things don't bother Mitch, why are you stressing over them? Give it a chance, girl. If it doesn't work out what have you lost but time that was going to pass anyway?"

"He thinks I've convinced myself that I'm not supposed to get married because of all my past relationship disasters. And he thinks I'm using that as an excuse and not trusting in God to see us through the present situations. Maybe he's right."

"Well, I think Mitch is upset that you didn't choose him...and yourself...to handle first. As long as you keep putting other things, no matter how important they may be, ahead of yourself, you'll always be on the back burner. Do you love Mitch, Vann?"

Without any hesitancy, Vann answered, "Yes...Yes, I do. But I don't know if...." Their conversation was interrupted when the aunts returned from the bathroom—still bickering.

They stopped three more times before reaching Dallas, where they followed the directions to the hospital. Nervousness, dread, and other unidentified emotions filled Vann as she prepared to meet the woman who was her mother for the first time.

Rosetta had been moved from intensive care into a semi-private room, and was feeling much better. The door to the room opened and the group of women walked in. They searched her face, trying to recognize her amidst the tubes and wires, and from her hospital bed, she did the same with them. She hadn't seen her sisters in decades, but she quickly identified them.

"Lu! Bernie!" she mumbled in her weakened voice. Then her eyes flew to the other two women who had entered the room.

Shaky legs barely carried Vann through the door of the hospital room. It would have been traumatic under the best of circumstances, but it was enormously so, seeing the woman who was her mother for the first time, in her extremely ill condition. But even the shock of seeing the frail, pitiful woman with tubes stuck in her body didn't erase the hurt and rejection Vann had felt all of her life.

While her aunts moved farther into the room, Vann closely watched the woman in the bed as her eyes frantically searched each face before settling on Vann. The woman took in everything about Vann, who looked so much like herself, and tears flowed down her face. Vann saw what looked to be relief run across her face, closely followed by something that might have been regret or sadness, which was quickly chased away by a touch of joy—perhaps from the realization that something good had finally come from her long ago frivolous action that had resulted in the child she had tried to forget, because now...hopefully...that child was here to help her.

"Rosie! Oh, Rosie! How are you feeling?" Luberta cried, as she rushed to the bed to give her sister an awkward hug. "Oh Lord, it's been so long, Rosie!" she said, in an emotionally shaken voice as tears ran down her face.

Bernetta followed with uncharacteristic tears flooding her face. "Rosetta, I'm glad to see you!" She too gave her sister as much of a hug as she could, then said in typical Bernie style, "But you know if you weren't in that bed, I'd spank your behind, don't you?"

"Now Bernie, don't start!" Luberta scolded. "She don't need to be hearing that now. We got plenty of time for both of us to do that later," she said with a smile. "Rosie, look who we brought with us." She motioned for Vann to come closer to the bed. "This is Vann, Rosie, but I don't have to tell you that since she looks just like you. Come on, Vann, move up here so she can get a good look at you."

Vann stood rooted to the spot by the door of the hospital room with Rubye, and watched the sisters' emotional reunion.

She recalled every plea and the subsequent heartbreaking disappointment when no response came to the letters she had spent hours writing and rewriting, begging for her mother's love and acceptance. Now, after decades of refusing to even acknowledge the existence of the child she had rejected and abandoned, Rosetta was asking that child for the help she desperately needed, and Vann was suddenly in the tempting position of making the same choices her mother had made.

For months, Vann had been in a conflicting battle. Her desire to tell the woman to get lost and leave her alone, wrestled with the very core of her Christian values—love and forgiveness—which compelled her to walk the walk she had so long confessed.

Rosetta reached toward her, silently indicating her desire to touch her. But the decades of hurt made it impossible for Vann to move. Finally, from a throat clogged with mixed emotions, Vann was able to squeeze out two words. "Hello, Rosetta."

Vann's greeting wrung loud wails out of Rosetta's frail body that she couldn't seem to stop, and broken words poured out. "I'm so sorry! Please forgive me, I'm so sorry. I shouldn't have treated you like that! I know I shouldn't have done you like that. I could have at least answered your letters. I don't have no excuse, except I was just young and foolish. Please forgive me." The weeping that Rosetta couldn't seem to control continued as she reached awkwardly toward Vann.

The words did little to lessen the burden of lifelong rejection, and only made Vann want to retreat and run back to all the good and new things that were happening in her life...a wonderful man who wanted to marry her; her new business venture; and the volunteer work that had thrust her into local stardom...all things she desperately wanted to embrace, experience, and enjoy. Things she did not want to push to the back burner for this woman who she suspected even now, didn't want, but needed her.

Vann didn't respond to the outstretched arms, but stayed where she was, and replied to Rosetta's words. "But you did treat me like that, Rosetta, and long after you were old enough to realize how much your rejection had to hurt. And I was still reaching out for you long after I should have realized you wanted nothing to do with me. I honestly believe you're reaching for me now only because you're desperate for my help, and not because you're sorry."

"Vann!" Aunt Luberta cried out. "Oh Lord, have mercy!" Her shoulders shook as she wept over the traumatic scene taking place between this mother and daughter who were strangers.

Vann closed her eyes, and prayed, "Help me, Father." Tears flowed like small rivers down her face, but she spoke in a voice laced with steel. "But I'm here because I couldn't make the choice you made and ignore your pleas, Rosetta. You see, in spite of the fact that I've yearned for your love all my life and never got it, I do have the love of God in me, and that love compels me to forgive you."

Rosetta wailed again, as her daughter's words hit her in the face like bullets. "I'm so sorry, Vann!" she repeated again. "But...I need you...need you to help me."

"Uh...let's just take things one step at a time." Vann's voice broke as tears made tracks down her face, and finally, she slowly moved to the bed and leaned down to hug the woman. As mother and daughter embraced for the first time, there wasn't a dry eye in the room as all the women broke down in loud weeping.

A nurse came running into the room looking alarmed, and quickly went to the bed to check Rosetta's vital signs.

"I'm alright, nurse," Rosetta said in a tearful voice. "We're just happy to see each other."

"Well you need to calm down," the nurse admonished. "I know you don't want to end up back in ICU."

"Naw, I surely don't," Rosetta answered. "I'll calm down as best I can, but it's going to be hard."

Luberta and Bernetta found chairs and sat down, while Vann and Rubye sat on the empty bed in the room. Rubye held on to Vann's hand tightly and hugged her with the other arm. Rosetta hadn't taken her eyes off of her daughter.

She wiped at the tears on her face with hands that were swollen and misshapen by the ravages of arthritis. "I know I hurt you, Vann, but I sure do hope you can forgive me enough to help me." Her sobs filled the room again as she grappled with the fact that this strong woman, her own child, had been hesitant to even hug her, and that she hadn't deserved the hug that eventually came.

Vann stood up from the other bed and went to stand over Rosetta's bed, then reached down and hugged her again. "Like I said, I do forgive you, Ms. Rosetta. I have to forgive you and love you, and do what I can to help you," Vann whispered softly, through her tears. "You just relax and stop worrying about it." Then she turned and walked briskly from the room with Rubye running after her.

"Ladies room!" Vann managed to whisper. Rubye looked around and was relieved to see one nearby and guided Vann into it. Vann fell apart, as Rubye stood by silently with a comforting arm around her. Hurt and anger from decades of her mother's rejection came out in hard, gut-wrenching sobs. She felt the physical pain as the sobs passed through her body, but the emotional pain causing it was worse.

After long minutes, Vann drew a long, controlling breath, and looked at Rubye through reddened eyes. "I'm so glad you're here with me." She hugged Rubye with all her strength. "I don't know how I would handle this if you weren't here. I thank God for you, my friend."

Rubye hugged her again. "Oh, Vann. You know I wouldn't be anywhere else but here. But even if I wasn't, you'd be okay, because you're a strong woman. I don't know if I would have been able to tell that woman I forgive her, like you just did. You're a wonderful person, Vann. And I'm so glad I know you and have had the opportunity to witness true Christian forgiveness and love. I'll never forget what I just saw, girl. You're something!" Rubye was so touched by the scene she had witnessed that she felt tears flowing again. "I'm sorry, Vann. I'm supposed to be here to support you through this, and here I am, acting like a blubbering idiot."

Vann gave a shaky laugh. "I guess we'd better stop this mutual admiration gig we have going and get out of here. Now that I've gotten through that initial meeting, I don't really know what to do next. Lord, please guide me," she prayed. "I know that You know the path I should take. Please help me walk in love, Lord, and do what I can for that poor woman."

"Amen!" Rubye stated. "He's going to guide you, Vann. He'll show you what to do. And I'll be right here with you, helping you all I can."

"Thanks, Rubye." She sighed. "I guess we'd better get back, huh?"

"You can handle it, honey," Rubye said, encouragingly. "You can handle anything."

Vann knew her hyped-up emotions wouldn't let her rest, so she decided to remain at the hospital with Rosetta. "I might as well start getting to know her," she told her aunts and Rubye, as they left the room and stood in the hallway. "We have some serious issues to get through, so we may as well get started since we don't have a lot of time. She's going to be getting out of the hospital soon, and it needs to be decided where she'll be going. Aunt Lu, do you know how to get in touch with her children? They need to be here to help make that decision."

"Oh, child. I have called them people more times than I can count. I can't reach them. I did leave messages though, telling them they need to come and see about their mother. I haven't heard from them, and the nurses say they haven't seen anyone out here to see Rosetta but the neighbor who called the ambulance."

"Vannie, I wouldn't even consider them in the decision-making process. Evidently, they don't care a thing about their mother," Aunt Bernie said. "You just go ahead and make whatever arrangements you need to make and forget them. You're right, you and Rosetta need to do some talking about a whole lot of things. And me and Lu need to go to the hotel and lay ourselves down."

After Rubye and the aunts left for the hotel, Vann pulled a chair up to the side of the bed and sat down. "Do you need anything?" she asked the woman.

"No, I don't need anything," Rosetta answered. "I'm just glad you're here." She examined Vann's face. "You look like your father's side of the family. He had a lot of Indian blood and you have the same skin tone and hair that he did."

"My aunts think I look like you. I wouldn't know, since I don't know who my father is, but sure would like to," Vann stated, while she eagerly searched Rosetta's face.

Rosetta sighed and turned her head. "No use even dragging up that old stuff now. I think I'm gon' rest awhile."

Disappointed, Vann settled back in the chair with the books Rubye had gone to the gift shop and bought for her. She read awhile, prayed, and tried to nap a little while Rosetta slept, but the traumatic occurrences of the day continued to run through her mind. When she did doze off, the nurse coming in to perform routine procedures on Rosetta, woke her.

"Will the doctor be coming by anytime soon?" Vann asked the nurse.

"Yes, he should be making his rounds around seven-thirty or eight. You probably have time to go downstairs and get something to eat if you want to. The cafeteria closes at nine, and then you'll be stuck with whatever is in the vending machines."

"Thanks, I'll do that," Vann answered.

She had just finished her hamburger when the doctor strolled into the room. Vann introduced herself and waited as he examined Rosetta. Then as he was leaving, she followed him out of the room. She needed to get the full scope of Rosetta's condition.

After her conversation with the doctor, she returned to the room and sat down to resume her reading.

"What did he say?" Rosetta asked.

Vann looked up, surprised. She thought Rosetta had gone back to sleep. "Well, he said you're doing as well as can be expected, and if you keep progressing, you'll be able to be released in a week or so. But he also said that you can't live alone anymore. That you really need to be in a facility where there's around the clock care. So, there are some decisions that need to be made pretty quickly. Personally, I think your children should be included in the decision-making process, but I guess we'll have to do it without them unless they show up soon."

"I already knew I didn't have any business living by myself...look at me!" She held up her hands. "I can hardly even cook for myself, and I can barely walk. I don't have anyone else to depend on for help but my sisters and...you. And I know you don't owe me a thing." Tears slid down the sides of her face.

"Don't worry about it now. Just concentrate on getting better. By the time you're ready to leave, we'll have it all worked out." She noticed the woman trying to shift herself around in the bed. "Are you comfortable? You need me to lower the bed a little?"

"Yes, baby, I do. Thank you."

"You're welcome," Vann said, as she sat back down and settled in for what she knew would be a long night.

"Vann, I know you deserve an explanation of why I did things the way I did," Rosetta said, when she woke up again. "I knew what I was doing to you was wrong, and I've been reminded of that over the years the few times I talked to Mama and my sisters. But what they didn't know was that I was in a bad marriage, and I was too ashamed to tell them. The man I married was mean, controlling, and jealous. I couldn't go nowhere or do nothing without his permission. He was the same way with the children. I tried to make it up to them by spoiling them when he wasn't around, but it wasn't enough. They thought I should have stood up to him more, and when I didn't, they got angry at me. They got as far as they could away from us as soon as they could. I know it was selfishness on my part, but I had to live with the man and I had to make my life as easy as I could for myself."

"You never considered leaving?" Vann asked quietly. "If not for yourself, then for your children?"

Her answer didn't surprise Vann. "No, chile. How was I going to make it with three children by myself? And it wasn't all bad. Me and my husband did have some good times together."

"How long did you tell me he's been dead?" Vann asked quietly.

Rosetta sighed. "He died about five years ago. He left me pretty well off, and I know I should have tried to make things right with my children then, including you, but I was so glad to have the freedom to do what I wanted that I went a little wild. I partied, traveled, and did everything I had always wanted to do. But then my health started failing. Heart trouble, high blood pressure, a bad case of diabetes, surgery a couple of times, then this rheumatoid arthritis that moved all over my body. It was one thing after the other hitting me. My children did come around for a while, but when they realized I wasn't about to give them all my money, they pretty much stopped coming. Now I can see how my own selfishness has affected them. I kept them away from their grandparents and relatives and all the good influences that they should have been exposed to. But I couldn't bring them around my family because then, they would have found out…"

"Then they would have found out about me," Vann said in a flat tone of voice.

"I felt I had to keep the knowledge that they had an older sister from them because…well, you know. I was wrong though. Maybe if they had gotten to know you, you could have helped them learn how to live life the right way. I've made some terrible mistakes."

Vann was quiet, not sure how to respond. Rosetta was still saying things that hurt her to the core, but she was used to that hurt.

"Well, what exactly do you want to happen at this point?"

"I just know I don't want to die alone. And I don't want to die until I can make peace with my children. So far, they haven't even responded to my pleas for help." Tears slid down her face and she started sobbing loudly again. "My own children…the ones that I did everything for, won't even come and see about me, and the very one I threw away is sitting here! Now, ain't that a strange turn of events?" she cried softly.

"No point in worrying about it now, Rosetta," Vann said, quietly. "All you can do is try to do the right thing from now on. And of course, forgive yourself."

"I don't know if I can do that until all my children forgive me."

"What do you plan to do about your home and other possessions? You'll have to decide on that as well. Everything will have to be packed up and disposed of, and the house sold, unless your children want to keep it."

"No, I want to sell it. I won't be able to live there anymore. It's a nice house...might need a little work, but it should bring a nice price. That will give me a little cushion to help out with living expenses."

"Do you have an attorney? Or someone who can handle all of that for you?"

"Yes, in fact, he's supposed to come by here tomorrow. I asked the hospital social worker to call him. I need to get my will updated and take care of some other legal matters. I hope you'll help me with that."

"Of course. But I think your children should also be involved in the decisions."

"I can't wait on them, Vann. I have to do this while I can. I don't know how much longer I'll be here."

"Don't even think like that. You'll be around a long time," Vann said, and hoped she was right.

The next morning, her aunts and Ruybe arrived with their arms full of flowers, snacks, and more books. They were placing the flowers around the room and making themselves comfortable and Vann was again adjusting Rosetta's bed and pillows when the door opened and a woman walked into the room.

She stopped and looked around the room at the other women before her eyes settled on Vann, standing by the bed.

"Who are you?" she asked in a demanding voice, her eyes glued to the face of the woman who looked like her mother.

"I'm Vann Sinclair. And you are?" Vann asked, as she continued trying to make Rosetta as comfortable as possible.

"What are you doing in my mother's room?"

Rosetta looked up in surprise. "Glenda? Girl, I been calling you and the hospital's been calling you trying to let you know I was in here. Where in the world have you been?"

Luberta walked over to the woman. "I'm your aunt, Luberta, the person who's been leaving all those messages for you, and this is your aunt, Bernetta. We're here to check on your mother and see what we can do to help her. And this," she pointed toward Vann, "is your sister."

"Sister? I don't have a sister! And y'all need to get out of here," the woman huffed. But her eyes stayed on the woman standing by her mother's bed.

She was shorter than Vann, heavy set, with short, graying hair, and was dressed in a stylish pantsuit. Unlike Vann, she looked nothing like her mother.

"Glenda," Rosetta said softly, while trying to sit up in the bed. "Honey, this *is* your sister. Your older sister. When I couldn't get in touch with you or your brothers, I called Vann and your aunts and asked them for help."

"You don't owe her any explanations, Rosetta. If she had cared, she would have been here with you," Bernetta said, with much attitude.

"Aunt Bernie," Vann said in a soft, admonishing voice.

"She can't come in here demanding to know who we are, and telling us to get out when she ain't been nowhere around. She's the one who should have been here all along, taking care of her mother," Bernetta said in her no-nonsense voice. "Girl, your mother's been in here nearly two weeks and was in ICU for days, and from what we understand, not one person from her family has showed their face. We had to come all the way from Houston when the hospital said someone from her family needed to be here. So I don't take kindly to anything you got to say."

"I...I've been out of town," Glenda stuttered. "I didn't even know she was in here."

"That is such a sorry excuse, you should have kept it to yourself. And what about your brothers? Where are they? Your mother's been sick for a long time, and in no condition to take care of herself. If her neighbor hadn't happened to go by to check on her, your mother wouldn't be here. So don't you come in here with no attitude! I'll really tell you about yourself." Bernie was in her element.

"Vann sat up in here with her all night after driving from Houston yesterday," Luberta had to get her say in the mix. "It seems to me you could have found some time in the last weeks to at least call and check on her even if you couldn't come see her. Vann has even been sending her money to help out with her medicine. So, I'd say you're the one who needs to be doing some explaining, not us."

"I guess I'll just leave and come back when you all are not here," Glenda said. "I don't have to explain nothing."

"That's fine. But don't you at least want to ask your mother how she's doing?" Bernetta asked.

"I'll just do that later, too," she turned and strutted out of the room.

"Oh my!" Rosetta moaned. "I have really messed things up with my children."

"Well!" Vann stated. "I'm in need of a hot shower, some food, and a soft bed. So I'm going to get out of here for a while and go to the hotel."

A look of fear crossed Rosetta's face. "You coming back, Vann? How long you gon' be gone? I told you, I need your help." Anxiety was evident in her voice.

"I'll be back this evening. If the attorney comes, your sisters can help you with everything. In the meantime, you just try to relax and get some rest. Remember what the doctor told you about your blood pressure."

Vann and Rubye left the aunts there with Rosetta and headed out of the hospital. As they walked through the waiting area, Glenda jumped up from a chair.

"Wait just a minute!" she demanded. "Just who do you think you are? And what are you doing here?" she asked.

"You heard your mother. I'm your sister, and I'm here at your mother's request. Anything else you need to know, I suggest you ask your mother."

"Why you showing up out of nowhere all of the sudden? Where have you been?"

Vann sighed. "I'm sorry, but I'm very tired. I need to go and get some rest. If you want to talk later, I'll be back this evening."

"Well, we are going to talk, you can believe that," Glenda huffed. "Ain't no bunch of strangers gon' come in here taking over when my mother is at the point of death."

"Now *you* wait just a minute!" Vann held up her hand, breathing deeply to stop the anger rising up in her. "Lady, just go talk to your mother and call your brothers. She really needs you all right now, and it's her who needs to explain everything to you, not me. "Let's go, Rubye," she said, turning and walking away from Glenda.

Mitch had been praying, lifting Vann up before the Lord. He was still upset and angry with her, but he loved her and wanted to help her through the painful situation she was in the midst of. Thankfully, Rubye had called him last night to let him know how things were going. When she described the moving scene between Vann and Rosetta, Mitch knew it should have been him there with her, comforting her and being the strength she needed.

Between court sessions, he had alternately called Vann's, then Rubye's, cell phones, hoping to find out what was happening. Frustrated when he didn't reach them, he had continued to pray.

After he recessed for lunch, he called Rubye again, thinking she would be the one he could most likely reach, and when he didn't get her, he called Thomas. He was so relieved when Thomas answered that he couldn't say anything for a second or two.

"Hello! Hello!" he heard Thomas saying, before he could get his voice to work.

"Hey, Thomas. This is Mitch. How are you?"

"Mitch! I'm fine, man. How about yourself?"

"I'm a basket case, Thomas," Mitch said, wearily. "I'm so worried about Vann and how things are going for her that I can't think about anything else. I've called both Vann's and Rubye's cells several times today and left messages, but haven't heard from them. I was just wondering...have you talked to Rubye today?"

"Yes, as a matter of fact, I talked to her a few minutes ago. She's going to call you, man, but evidently things are pretty hectic up there. Rubye's still unsettled over the meeting between Vann and her mother. So you know Vann has to be in a bad way."

"I should be up there with her! I know I should've insisted on going, but I was so upset with her that I let that get in the way. She knew I wanted to be there with her, but asked Rubye to go instead."

"Naw, man," Thomas said, slowly. "You got that wrong. Vann didn't ask Rubye to go with her, it was Rubye who told Vann she was going. And she didn't leave any room for Vann to argue about it. It was a good thing too, because Rubye just told me that Vann definitely needs somebody with her."

Mitch moaned. "I should've done that."

"It's not too late, man. Have you called her? She may be needing to hear from you right about now. You ought to call her, Mitch."

"I've been trying to do that, Thomas, and not getting an answer. Do you know where they're staying?"

"Yes. They're at a Holiday Inn near the hospital. Wait, let me get the number. You may not get them for a while because they are back and forth between the hotel and the hospital, but keep trying, you'll eventually get them."

After stopping at a restaurant to eat, they went to the hotel where Vann showered and fell into bed. She was in a deep sleep when the phone rang. She heard Rubye answer it, then call to her softly, "Vann, Vann, it's Mitch. Do you want to talk to him now or call him back."

"I'll talk to him," she said, reaching for the phone. "Hello, Mitch. How are you?" she asked in a sleepy voice.

"The question is, how are you?" Mitch asked. "Before I go any further, though, Vann, I want to apologize for getting upset with you when you told me you couldn't marry me now. I should have understood and stood by you to help get you through this. And I should have insisted, like Rubye did, on going up there with you. I've been worried sick about you, and angry at myself for letting you down. I hope you'll let me make it up to you. Do you need anything?" Vann was so quiet, he thought she had gone back to sleep. "Vann?"

"I'm here, Mitch," she answered softly. "I'm okay. And you don't have anything to apologize for. I understand why you were upset, but I was really trying to do what's best for everyone. But now, I don't know. Mitch, I'm so happy that Rubye is here with me, but I'm angry with myself for not letting you come too, because I need all the support I can get right now. It's been difficult...I won't lie. But God has been with me through it all, and helped me do what I thought I would never be able to do." She was quiet for a second. "Mitch, I told my...Rosetta...that I forgive her. And amazingly, I meant every word. Mitch, she's very ill and she's in such a pitiful situation, with no one here to help her, that I feel so sorry for her. When she broke down, begging for my forgiveness, I couldn't have possibly done anything else but give it. But frankly, I don't know if she's asking for forgiveness because she needs me, or if she's doing it because she's really sorry. I just know I have to try to do the right thing for her. That's the only way I'll have any peace."

They talked about Rosetta's health, Glenda's reaction to having a sister, and future plans.

"Listen, as much as I would like to keep talking to you, I know you need to get some rest," Mitch declared. "Are you going to stay at the hospital tonight?"

"I don't know right now. I'll see how she's doing and if she wants me to stay. What I'd really like to do is get a good night's sleep, visit her for a while in the morning, then find my way to her house to get an idea of how much work has to be done there."

"Vann, don't wear yourself out. You can always go back up there for that later. Just keep that in mind, alright?"

"Okay, I will," she answered tiredly.

"I'll call you tonight when I think you're back from the hospital. I love you, sweetheart."

"I love you, too," she said softly. "And thanks for calling, Mitch. Bye."

Vann hung up the phone and settled back down to go back to sleep. But Rubye, sitting in the other bed reading, had other ideas.

"You need to marry that man, Vann," Rubye said with a wink, before continuing. "Don't you dare let yourself get so caught up in Rosetta's affairs that you neglect your own. I still maintain that it's not fair for her to expect anything of you. And there are already indications that she's beginning to cling to you. Vann, she'll suck you under if you let her."

"I know, Rubye," Vann answered, sleepily. "But the bottom line is, I don't know how I can walk away and leave her, no matter what the situation is between her and her children. I have to help her and get her settled someplace, at the least."

chapter twenty-four

Fueled by their mutual dislike and thirst for revenge against Vann, Elliott and Annette's alliance grew stronger and they became closer each time they were together. Annette, of course, made sure she used every trick in her extensive arsenal to manipulate Elliott to turn the situation to her advantage. Elliott might not be as good a catch as the judge, but he had enough going for him to make it worth her time and effort to pursue him. She manufactured wild stories about Vann's shortcomings and her offenses against Elliott, which she joyously shared with him to keep his anger alive.

"Hey, Seth. How's it going, man?" Elliott said into the phone. "Haven't talked to you in a while, been kind of busy. You know how that goes."

"Hi, Elliott," Seth responded, amiably. He knew the reason he hadn't talked to Elliott was because the man was still angry with him over not telling him everything he knew about Vann. "I've been running myself. I think I've been on two or three trips with my travel club since the frat event."

"I'm thinking about joining that club and going on some of those trips," Elliott said. "I've got a lady friend who says she likes to travel, also. We both might join."

"Good, good," Seth answered. "Vann's aunt, Bernetta Richardson, is the club coordinator. I'll give her your name and contact information so she can let you know when we start planning the next trip."

"By the way, how are Vann and the judge doing? Have they gotten married yet?" Elliott tried to sound uninterested.

"Nope. But from what I've heard and observed, it's not far off. Mitch Langford is crazy about her. He's the one pushing to get married."

"Hmph! I doubt that!" Elliott exclaimed. "Whoever told you that was just lying."

"As a matter of fact, Mitch himself told me when I ran into him down at the courthouse a while back. He said he'll take her any way he can get her."

"Well, when he finds out what a lowdown and dirty person she is, he's going to back off in a hurry. This lady friend of mine has been telling me some horror stories about Vann and that riotous bunch she runs with. Wild parties down in Galveston at a beach house Vann owns, with all sorts of goings-on, and different men in and out. I tell you it's disgusting, man! And Annette said they treated her like a dog when she didn't want to participate. They threw her clothes out of the house, then wouldn't let her leave until the judge made her lie about something he had done. Man, the woman still cries when she talks about it."

"What wrong did Vann ever do to you, Elliott?" Seth asked, quietly. He knew Elliott was suffering from a bruised ego because Vann had chosen another man over him.

"I told her I was considering asking her to marry me," Elliott said in an angry, complaining voice. "I thought we had an understanding, you know, that we would eventually get together. I even told her I would help manage her little decorating business and the property she owns." Elliott grew angrier as he thought about the opportunity he'd lost to gain control of Savannah's assets. "But what does she do? Goes out and gets with that judge like I hadn't said a word. She's too much of a stupid lowlife to understand what I was offering her."

Seth heard the anger and bitterness in Elliott's voice. The man had lost it. "I wouldn't call her stupid, Elliott," Seth said, heatedly. "I'd say she's one of the smartest women I know. She realized you didn't have her best interest at heart. I don't blame her for telling your behind where to get off."

Elliott had not taken Vann seriously when she warned him not to defame her name. In his arrogance, he didn't think there was anything Savannah could do to hurt him. "All I know is, nobody makes a fool out of Elliott Shaw and she's going to regret how she's treated us. Annette and I are going to bring both her and that judge down, and make them ashamed to even show their faces."

Seth grunted. "You're doing a good enough job of making a fool of yourself, Elliott, and I'd be careful about setting out to do harm to somebody. I'm sure you've heard that old saying, 'dig a ditch for someone else, might as well dig two.' Look, I've got to run, but you think about everything before you start trying to make trouble for Vann. Like I've told you before, that's a godly woman and you don't need to be messing with her."

Mitch was in his garage working on two nightstands he was making for one of his bedrooms. It had been Vann's suggestion, and he wondered why he hadn't thought about it himself. He looked with pride at the matching headboard he had already finished. She had been right, he could do very well if he ever decided to sell some of his work.

Vann. Thoughts about her both delighted and frustrated him. He was glad they had talked and hoped things were okay with them now. He kept rubbing the paint stain into the table he was working on as he talked to the Lord. "Father, how can I convince her to marry me? I believe it's in Your will that we become husband and wife. I need her, and my son needs her...her love, her kindness and gentleness, her warmth and generosity. We both need her to make us better, and to draw us closer to You. Please help me, Father."

The telephone rang, interrupting Mitch's conversation with the Lord. He wiped his hands on a rag before picking up the extension in the garage. "Hello."

"Mitch Langford?" a slightly familiar male voice asked.

"Yes. This is he."

"Judge, this is your frat brother, Seth Conner, remember we had a conversation about Vann Sinclair down at the courthouse one day? I'm a friend of Vann's aunt."

"Yes, of course I remember, Seth. How are you doing?" Mitch answered, curiosity apparent in his voice.

"Well, I'm not real sure I should be making this call, but I have some information that I want to share with you about Vann, Judge," he paused before adding, "and Elliott Shaw."

Mitch's insides tightened. "What about Vann and Shaw?" he asked in a quiet, cautious voice.

"I'm sure you know Elliott has been after Vann, for a long time, in fact. However, ever since he found out some things about her and saw her hosting that television show, he's really been after her." Seth paused, wondering just how much to tell Mitch about Elliott's selfishness. "Well, Mitch, to be honest, Elliott just recently decided that Vann is good enough for someone of his status, and that's why he's all of a sudden wanting to marry her. But of course she told him where he could go."

"Yes, I know all of that, Seth. I told him where he could go as well. So what's going on?"

"Mitch, I spoke with Elliott a while ago, and he told me that he and some woman by the name of Annette were going to bring Vann down, and you too, as a matter of fact. Now, I don't know exactly what they're planning, but I know it's not anything nice. I'm sure you and Vann have done nothing to them, and I felt you should know what's going on so you won't be blindsided by whatever they come up with."

"That's decent of you, man. But I thought you and Shaw were tight."

"Yes, we used to be, but…well, it's not important," Seth said, sadly.

"Thanks, Seth. You don't know how much I appreciate this. You know, I see every kind of corruption from my bench, but man, sometimes people who go to church surpass even that. There are some evil-minded people sitting up in the church house."

"You got that right. But thank the Lord, most of 'em are just like us…trying to live a good Christian life," Seth answered. "Some of us had to grow to that point—I know I did—but I'm glad I grew and continue to grow closer to the Lord."

"Me too, brother. I've made my share of mistakes, too. But I'm determined that with the help of God I'll do better. It just bothers me to know there are people who have been in church for years without a thought to living for the Lord."

"Amen, brother. Amen," Seth replied. "But all we can do is try to tell them, and pray for them. Remember, every tub's got to sit on its own bottom."

Mitch laughed hilariously. "Seth, I haven't heard that in a long time. My grandmother used to tell me that after telling me I was going to burst hell wide open if I didn't get myself straight with the Lord."

Seth laughed before saying, "Those old folk knew how to keep us on the straight and narrow, didn't they? That's why many of us found our way out of darkness." He laughed again before hanging up, more convinced than ever that he had to do something to help Vann and Mitch.

"Lord, what can I do? Give me wisdom, Father." He continued to pray and think on what he could do.

chapter twenty-five

When Vann returned to the hospital that evening, she was experiencing mixed feelings and emotions. Her heart's desire was to do good; however, she couldn't help but think, *Lord, I'm trying not to get weary in well doing, but when is due season for me?*

"Rubye, please pray for me that I'll just do the right thing for everyone...Rosetta, Mitch, myself. You know that's all I want," Vann said, before entering Rosetta's room.

"I'm praying for you, girl," Rubye answered. "Just remember that you deserve some good things out of life too. But if you act crazy and let him, Satan will steal every good thing away from you. You have to do right by yourself, as well as others, Vann."

A spark of memory tried to catch in Vann's mind. Hadn't the man she had met in Charleston told her the same thing?

Rosetta's face brightened when she walked through the door. "Vann! I'm so glad you came back. I was a little afraid that you might not."

"I told you I would, didn't I?" Vann answered, softly. "If I had changed my mind, you would have known. I would have called you."

"I'm just getting to know you, remember? Anyway, I'm glad to see you."

"How are you feeling?" Vann asked, noticing how much better she was looking.

"I'm feeling much better, Vann. I feel like I'm about ready to get out of here, but the doctor said it would still be a few days. Did you get a chance to go by my house?"

"No, she didn't!" Rubye answered before Vann had a chance. "Vann needed to get some rest, so that's what she did." Rubye had a hard time trying to keep from rolling her eyes at the sick woman.

"Oh, that's right. I guess I'm just not thinking."

"What I plan to do is to get a good night's sleep tonight, and go over there in the morning, just to look around and get an idea about what all needs to be done. Then we can go from there," Vann answered.

"Oh, you're not going to stay with me tonight? I was hoping you would," Rosetta said, in a pitiful voice.

"Rosie, I'll stay with you if you want me to," Bernie said. "But I think Vann is right. If you want her to go to your house to see what all needs to be done, she needs to get some rest. Vann ain't no spring chicken, and we don't need to run her so hard that she'll be broken down."

Luberta said, "Vann, I'll go over to Rosie's house with you and Rubye tomorrow and see what we need to do. I know how to make myself useful." She was still angry at Bernetta, whom she had argued with the night before. The two of them had ended up in separate rooms.

"Well, the next thing we need to decide is what to do about Rosetta when she gets out of here. Have you heard from Glenda since this morning?" Vann asked Rosetta. "I spoke to her on the way out of the hospital this morning and told her she needed to come and talk to you."

"No, she ain't been back in here. And she probably won't. Glenda...is...very angry about a lot of things. But I know what I want to do. I would like to go back to Houston with you when the doctor says it okay for me to travel. My children here ain't gon' do nothing for me," Rosetta stated, bitterly. "I just know I don't want to be stuck in some old horrible nursing home, forgotten and being abused by strangers, and I don't want to be alone and sick and dying, either. At least if I move to Houston, I'll have some family there who'll be concerned enough to watch out for me."

It was suddenly very quiet in the room. Although they had all known to expect this, each woman reflected on Rosetta's statement. Rubye groaned inwardly, thinking, *Lord, have mercy on Vann.* Luberta's thoughts were flying all over the place hoping Vann was going to take her in, and she wouldn't have to. Bernetta's mind was busy trying to think of a nursing home they could get her in quickly so Vann wouldn't have to be saddled with her. It hadn't crossed her mind to take her in. Vann could only think, *Oh, Mitch, I'm so sorry.* She knew that until they could arrange for Rosetta's placement in a facility, she would have to take responsibility for her. Rosetta was watching Vann, trying to read from her facial expression how she was taking her announcement.

Vann was the first to finally speak. "Rosetta, I really think you should speak to your children before you make these decisions. I think it's only fair that they be included. After all, they may want you to be near them. And, since they grew up in that house, they may not want to sell it. In fact, it's quite possible that one of them may want to live there. And who knows, when they realize how much you need them, they may shape up and do what's needed. Did you talk to the attorney?"

"Yes, he came by this morning, and I changed everything and made you the executor of my will and gave you the power of attorney over my estate." When Vann gasped in surprise and consternation at this news, Rosetta said, "From what your aunts and grandmother have told me, you're a good businesswoman and well able to take care of everything. I just can't wait around on Glenda. I've called them I don't know how many times, and they haven't even returned the calls. There's no telling when I'll see or hear from them again."

"I wish you hadn't done that." Vann felt an additional weight of responsibility drop onto her shoulders. "I just want things to be done decently and in order, so that no one will be able to accuse me of taking advantage of you and the situation in any way," Vann said, softly.

"Nobody's going to do that, baby. Not while I'm around," Bernie said, forcefully.

"They'd better not!" Rubye said. "Not unless they want to deal with me."

Two days later, Vann, Rubye, and the aunts were headed back to Houston. Vann, with plans to return to Dallas, pack up Rosetta's things, dispose of the household items, and put the house on the market. Rosetta would hopefully be out of the hospital by then and able to take the ride back to Houston. Vann's spirit was low. All she could do was fight back tears and pray, *Lord, what am I going to do about Mitch?*

After getting home, she felt the need to talk to her grandmother. "Hi, Mama. Just calling to check on you. How are you feeling?"

"Oh, sugar, I'm just tired. I just can't seem to rest enough to feel rested, but I'm tolerably well, I guess. So how are you, baby? I've talked to Lu and Bernie and they told me about the trip to Dallas. Sugar, I want you to know that you're doing a good thing, taking Rosetta in, but I'm not too sure it's what you ought to be doing. What about your young man? How is he feeling about all this?"

"He's alright, even though he's upset because I told him I couldn't marry him right now. He's said all along that he would help me with her, but I just don't think it's right to saddle him with that kind of responsibility."

"But if he's willing to do it, why not let him help you? Vann, there has to be a way for you to do both...marry him, and help Rosetta. Have you thought on that any?"

One does not preclude the other. The words popped into her mind and she recalled her conversation with Ben Edmonds again.

"Well, no, I haven't, Mama. Like I said, I just don't think it's fair to Mitch."

"What about you, baby? Is it fair to you? I sho' do regret I pushed you like I did at first. We should have just left you alone and let you make up your own mind, instead of putting all that pressure on you and making you feel guilty about it."

"Mama, I do have a mind and heart of my own. I'm the one who ultimately decided to do this. If it wasn't supposed to happen, there's nothing you or Aunt Lu could have said to make a difference. No, it came down to me and the Lord, and the Lord won. I wasn't going to have any peace unless I helped her."

"Vann, baby, I just hate to see you put your life on hold for Rosetta. She's my child, but to tell you the truth, I'm not sure she'll appreciate it, 'cause she's always been as selfish as she could be. I guess with her being the baby, we all spoiled her and let her have her way too much. But I want you to think about a way you can help her without giving up your own happiness. Bernie mentioned something about a putting her in a place where she could live and have somebody take care of her. She said Rosetta's in too bad a shape for you to be trying to take care of her, so I think that's a good idea."

"Yes, that is what I plan to do, although Rosetta's reason for wanting to stay with me is because she doesn't want to go to a home. But the doctor strongly advises that she be in a health care facility. My only problem is finding a good one, where she'll be well cared for. Hopefully, we'll be able to find one soon."

"Well, I ain't studyin' about what Rosetta wants," the old lady said in an agitated voice. "It's you I want to see settled and happy before I leave this world. Rosetta done made her own bed, and there's nothing nobody can do to help her avoid sleeping in it, because God's law of sowing and reaping is set in motion and going to come to pass. And baby, you can't miss out on what the Lord has for you trying to change that."

Perhaps you are doing something somebody else is responsible for. Ben's words spoke clearly to Vann's mind.

"Now, you just think and pray on this, Vann," her grandmother admonished. I'll be satisfied to go on when I know you're okay. And I truly believe Mitch is a man of his word, and he'll take care of you, just like he promised me."

"Oh, Mama. I hate hearing you talk like that," Vann felt tears filling her eyes. "I just wish…"

"Baby, I'm ready. I told you I'm so tired I can't rest enough. It's time. By the grace of God, I've lived long past what I expected. So you just rejoice over that, and get yourself together so I can go in peace."

"Okay, Mama." Tears slipped down her face as she accepted what her grandmother was saying. "Now you try and rest, okay?"

"Yes, sugar, I'll do that."

Vann immediately called Bernie. "Aunt Bernie? I just had a long talk with Mama. I'm really not liking the way she's talking about leaving here. I know she has to at some point, but…Aunt Bernie, I don't want to think about that happening. She said she couldn't leave in peace unless she knows I'm settled with Mitch."

"I've had that conversation with her, Vannie, and I wholeheartedly agree with her. Not that I'm ready for her to go, but I know it has to happen, baby. And I'm looking at some places to put Rosetta. With all of us looking, I'm sure we'll find a nice, suitable place for her soon, so don't worry. It's just not fair for you to have to deal with this, and have to put off your own plans to do it. It's just not right!"

"It's alright, Aunt Bernie," Vann said, sadly. "I'll deal with it, with God's help."

"You know, Vannie, I think you should go ahead and marry this judge as soon as possible," Bernetta insisted. "Does he have room for Rosetta in his house?"

"Oh yes," Vann answered. "He has a very large house. I'm just reluctant to move Rosetta into it with me. I mean, we'll have enough adjusting to do without that added to the plate. But I will think about it, Aunt Bernie."

"Oh, honey, I'm so glad to hear that. You need to just go on and do it."

Vann hung up after talking to Aunt Bernie, sat there a minute, then started smiling. She was finally clear about what she really wanted...and yes, needed. "Father, I want to marry Mitch and have the kind of marriage that will bring glory to Your name. Now I know, that has to be in accordance with Your will. So I'm going to start taking steps toward that. I know if it's not Your will, You'll stop it. But here I go, Father...I'm taking that first step..." Butterflies fluttered in her stomach. "Be with me, Father."

She sat there a few minutes to get her mind together, then dialed Mitch's number. "Mitch, how are you?"

"Hey, babe. I'm fine, but how are you? You have everything ready for Rosetta?"

"Yes, I'm as ready as I'll get, I guess. But...that's not why I'm calling. Remember when I told you about the kind and wise man I met in Charleston who shared words of wisdom with me?" She continued after he answered, "Well, a lot of it is beginning to come back to me. He said things like, 'You must always remember to be as kind and loving to yourself as you are to others;

sacrifices are rooted in love, sometimes for peace, sometimes for need, but if you keep pouring from a bucket without replenishing it, it will soon be empty, and an empty bucket won't do anyone any good.'"

"Wow! I see what you mean about his words being wise, but have you given them any serious thought?"

"Yes, I'm starting to. It seems as though his words are popping into my thoughts a lot lately." She paused for a second to get her nerve up, then said, "Mitch, you asked me to marry you months ago, and I've been acting like a fool ever since. You were right, sweetheart, I have been afraid to take that step. But God didn't give me a spirit of fear. He gave me power, love, and a sound mind, and those things are leading me to say that I love you with all of my heart, and I want to be your wife. Rosetta will be going into a facility very soon I hope, so that issue will be resolved. As far as all that other mess I was talking about...well, it'll have to work itself out. So...Mitch, will you marry me?"

There was a long silence on the other end, then he said, "I'll be right over."

Fifteen minutes later, Mitch was ringing her doorbell. He rushed in as soon as she opened the door and lifted her off the floor in a tight hug. "Did you mean it, honey? Are you going to marry me?"

"Yes, if you'll still have me," she answered.

He dropped to his knees, holding the beautiful ring in his hand. "Vann Sinclair, I accept your proposal of marriage, and I promise to be the kind of husband that is worthy of your love." He slipped the ring on her finger, then stood and hugged and kissed her.

"How could you even doubt my love for you?" he said, between kisses. "I've never said anything to the contrary. So when? When can we get married?"

"I really don't want to take Rosetta with me to your house. The problem is, there's a waiting list at the places where I really want her."

"Vann, please don't put this off. I want us to get married as soon as possible. If that means my mother-in-law will be moving in along with my bride, then so be it. Please don't make me wait, sweetheart."

"Mitch, look at it like this; we have planning and other things to do to get ready. We have to go through marriage counseling, because Pastor Travis requires it. We have to decide what furniture and household items I'll bring to your place, and you know what a job the packing is. So, it's not like we'll be able to get married next week anyway. While all of that is going on, hopefully God will be working on getting a spot for Rosetta in a facility, and we'll be able to get her settled in there. I don't want you to be thinking about divorcing me a month after the wedding, because of her," she said, laughing.

"Uh, uh," he said, shaking his head, "I'm not going to let you put this off too long, Vann. Two months, honey—surely we can do everything we need to do by then. And I have a surprise for you," he said, with a rueful grin. "I really wanted to wait to tell you about it, but..."

She gave him a doubtful look. "Now, Mitch, you know how those surprises can go. I love surprises, but I'll be just as excited about it now, I promise."

"Well, I was thinking about how both of us need a place to work on our projects. We're both using our garages to do a lot of the work right now, but there's not going to be any room in my garage when you move in, so I decided to build a workshop for us behind my house. It'll be large enough to accommodate both of our projects, and there'll still be plenty of room back there to do whatever else we want to do."

"Oh honey!" She hugged him tightly. "I hadn't even thought about that. I've been so consumed with other issues that I'd pushed everything else to the back burner. Thank you for remembering what I love. I can't wait to see it."

"Well it's not finished yet, but will be soon. We can move Rosetta into the other downstairs bedroom if we haven't found a facility for her before the wedding. So, no more excuses, we're going to do it." He kissed and hugged her close. "I can hardly wait, sweetheart."

Although it was late when Mitch left, Vann couldn't resist calling Rubye. "Hey girl, wake up, I have some news."

"Vann?" Rubye answered, groggily. "What is it? Is something wrong?"

"I'm sorry for calling so late, girl, but I knew you'd want to know that Mitch and I have been making wedding plans."

"Wedding plans?" Rubye was wide awake now. "Vann, when did all of this happen? You didn't mention it when we talked earlier today. What's the date? Where are we having it? Do you want to have a large wedding? Girl, we have so much to do," Rubye said, excitedly.

"Hold on, Rubye, I haven't gotten that far yet. Mitch has given me two months," Vann said, laughing. "I have to get Rosetta here and we have to find a facility to put her in, and pack up my house. So I'm going to be a very busy lady."

"Whoopee!" Rubye yelled, probably scaring her sleeping husband to death. "Girl, I'm so glad God made you see the light. Let's see, it's nearly August already, that means we'll be having your wedding in October. Don't worry about anything...me and the other girls will handle the wedding. I'm going to start planning right now."

"Just keep it small and simple, Rubye. I don't want an elaborate affair. Just close family and friends and maybe a small reception dinner. Do you think you can contain yourself enough to do that?"

"I'll try, Vann. But I'm so happy and excited that it's going to be hard."

"Prayer, Rubye. Much, much prayer, that God will work everything out," Vann said, before hanging up.

The following Tuesday, Vann and Mitch, Rubye and Thomas, and Estelle and Roxanne traveled to Dallas. While Vann and Mitch went to see Rosetta to make arrangements for her discharge the next day, the others began packing up the contents of her house. TreVann arrived in a rented van on Wednesday to help with the process. The group worked exhaustingly the following days, and on Sunday afternoon, they were headed back to Houston with Rosetta and all the personal belongings she wanted to bring, packed into the four vehicles. Her other belongings had been placed in storage and the attorney had instructions to proceed with placing the house on the market.

When they finally had Rosetta's things settled into her room and in Vann's garage, Vann hugged each person tightly. "I don't know what I would have done without you. Thank you so much for all your hard work and help."

The aunts came in carrying large containers of food that the group hungrily delved into, after which, everyone left except Mitch, TreVann, and the aunts. Aunt Bernie lost no time in asking, "Vannie, did you talk to Rosie and explain the situation?"

"Yes, I did, Aunt Bernie. We talked and she decided she still wanted to come."

Bernie turned to Rosetta. "Rosie, I want you to understand that we all...Me, Lu, and Mama, agreed and convinced Vannie that finding a facility for you is the only thing to do."

"Vann explained everything. But I sure do wish I could stay here," Rosetta said looking around the comfortable house. "Vann's got plenty of room here."

"That's not the point, honey," Bernetta answered. "You're too sick for Vann to be trying to care for you. Now, we've managed to get you on the waiting list to live in a very nice independent living facility. You'll have your own little apartment and everything, and there are doctors and nurses on staff around the clock to take care of you if you need them. You'll take therapy every day to help with your arthritis, and when you want to cook your own meals, you can; otherwise, they'll provide them for you. There are all kinds of activities there for you to participate in as well. I'm sure it's the best thing for you. You can come visit us anytime, and of course, we'll be coming by to see you all the time. So don't think you'll be alone. I'm even thinking about putting my name on the list now, so that when I'm ready, they'll have a spot for me."

"I don't care how good you're trying to make it sound, it's still a nursing home and I want to stay here!" Rosetta insisted. "We can hire someone to come in every day and check on me. There's just no need for me to go to a facility."

Luberta said, "Well, maybe when you're better and able to do more for yourself, you can move back in here with Vann. At least you'll have that to look forward to."

An irate look passed between Mitch and TreVann as they listened to the conversation. Mitch squeezed Vann's hand and looked at her, shaking his head.

"No! Now Lu, you know better than that," Bernie stated angrily. "Rosie, Vann is going to make sure you are taken care of, you can count on that. But Vann has this wonderful man patiently waiting to marry her. She's putting off getting married so she can try to get you settled, but personally, I think she's kept him waiting long enough. Living with Vann permanently is not an option."

"I'm not going to abandon you," Vann stated, quietly. "Like we explained to you before you left Dallas, if it was my intent to abandon you, I would have left you there. You can rest assured that I'll always make sure you're alright. However, Mitch and I do have to get on with our plans."

"Vann, I can't believe you're actually going to put your old sick mother out in the cold. Not when we're just getting to know and love one another. And especially not for some man who may or may not be around next year." Rosetta squeezed tears out of her eyes. "I just...know you're not going to forsake me like all my other children are doing. At least they don't claim to be a Christian, like you. A Christian just wouldn't do something heartless and cruel like that to her own mother."

The room sparked with electricity at Rosetta's words. TreVann jumped up and opened his mouth to tell the old lady off, but Vann caught his arm.

"Trevie, Trevie! I'll handle it, honey."

Vann held on to her temper, because for some reason, she wasn't surprised. Years of rejection from Rosetta had taught her not to expect much from the woman who now so freely used the word *mother* to describe herself. She said in a quiet, but firm tone, "Rosetta, you need to think about what you just said. If I weren't a Christian, I wouldn't have given a thought to trying to help you, and you certainly wouldn't be sitting here in my house now. I suggest you remember what you did to me so that you could follow your man, and what you continued doing to me for several decades. You need to think about what you're saying, lady."

Bernie was livid. "Rosetta, I guess you think that because you're here now, you can talk like that and try to change the plan. But we will take your ungrateful behind back to Dallas right now! There's not a person who went up there and helped pack you up to get you here who wouldn't be willing, as tired as they are, to get right back on the road to Dallas and take you back and dump you on your porch."

Witnessing Rosetta's enormous selfishness made Luberta so angry that for once, she agreed with Bernie. "Right about that, Bernie," she stated, angrily. "We can just put her on a bus and send her back, for that matter. You ain't right, Rosie, and I sho' do hate having anything to do with you being here. I think we might have made a big mistake, Lord, have mercy!"

TreVann was fighting mad, and in spite of Vann's objections, he walked over to Rosetta. "Miss Rosetta, this woman is like a mother to me, and I don't take kindly to anybody taking advantage of her. But let me tell you, you better tread carefully, because if I ever hear another hint of ungratefulness coming from you about her, I'll make sure you're out of here quick."

Mitch felt the sting of anger at the woman's blatant attack on his character, but was angrier at her obvious attempt to manipulate Vann's fragile emotions where her mother was concerned. His determination not to say anything and let Vann handle her went out the window.

"Rosetta, if you want to go back to Dallas, we'll see that you get back," Mitch told her coldly. "As the man waiting to marry your daughter, I'll tell you that I don't plan to be anywhere else other than where Vann is for the rest of our lives. See, I love her, and wouldn't do anything to hurt her. Sadly, I don't see any love coming from her pitiful old, long lost mother. All I see is a woman trying to manipulate others for her own benefit."

In the few days she had known Vann, Rosetta had noticed an aura of peace around her that Rosetta didn't understand. And she had also noticed that there was an unusual inner strength in her that was tempered with kindness. There was something else as well that she hadn't been able to identify, but whatever it was, it caused her do some things that Rosetta knew she would never do for anyone—even her other children, whom she loved. Rosetta had always relied on her survival instincts to get what she wanted, but something about Vann told her she might be in for a difficult battle.

And then she had all these people around her, who protected and watched over her like nothing she had ever seen. That boy, TreVann, had been ready to hit her, and Mitch, the man wanting to marry Vann, hadn't been too far behind. Her own sisters—not that she had expected anything else from Bernie, but Lu had always been easy to get around—had shown that they too were willing to throw her out.

She would have to use caution and craftiness to get her way. But she was not going to a nursing home to sit alone and die, of that she would make sure. Now she knew to tackle Vann when she was not surrounded by her warriors.

TreVann turned and hugged Vann and started walking out of the room. "I'll see you in the morning, Auntie," he said quietly.

"You're going to bed already, baby?" Vann asked.

"Yeah, I think I'll watch a little TV." He tossed an angry look back at Rosetta. "Unless you think you might need me for something."

"I'm going to leave too, babe," Mitch said, grabbing her hand and following TreVann out of the family room. As they stood at the door, he said, " I think you and Rosetta need to talk. And stand your ground, honey, because it's apparent she's not going to play fair."

chapter twenty-six

Vann was so upset with Rosetta that she had to go into her bedroom and pray after her aunts left. Rosetta had a rebellious look on her face that told Vann that she still had a fight ahead of her. While talking to the Lord, something occurred to her that she hadn't thought about before...she didn't know if Rosetta was saved or not.

"Oh Lord, I might have moved a disciple of the devil into my home for all I know," she moaned in distress. "Well, there's only one way to find out," she said, getting up from her knees and walking briskly into the family room.

"Rosetta, are you a Christian?" Vann asked, without beating around the bush.

"Yes. I've been a Christian all my life," Rosetta said, defensively. "Why would you ask me something like that?"

"What church do you attend? Or what church did you use to attend before you got sick?"

"I'm a member of Shiloh, down in Georgia. Mama made all of us go to church, and that's where I joined when I was a little girl."

"No, I mean, what church have you attended since then?" Vann asked, her suspicions growing.

"Well, since I've been grown, I've come to believe that all that church stuff is unnecessary. You don't need to go to church to believe in God. Attending church is something men came up with to control people and make money off of them. They ain't nothing but a bunch of slick talking crooks and they ain't getting *my* money."

Vann looked at the woman like she had grown horns. *Oh Lord, have mercy!* she prayed urgently. *Help me, Father. I need Your help right now, Holy Spirit.* She moved closer to Rosetta. "How in the world could you have gotten to this kind of thinking after growing up in your parents' house for seventeen years? I don't care how long you've been away from there, I know you didn't leave there thinking like this."

"Naw, maybe I didn't," Rosetta answered, "but that didn't keep me from learning that there's more than one way to believe. I *chose* to believe this way. I believe in God, don't get me wrong. But I don't believe in all this man-made religion. I can serve God just as well in my own house as I can in some church. I taught my children to think like that too. I don't want some religious crooks taking advantage of them either."

"Help me, Holy Spirit," Vann whispered again, before continuing. "Rosetta, have you ever invited the Lord into your heart?"

"Yes. I told you, I joined church when I was a child," she answered agitatedly.

"No, I don't mean joining church. I mean praying…asking Jesus to come into your heart and become Lord of your life. There's a difference."

"I don't remember doing all of that, but I probably did. And so what if I didn't," Rosetta yelled. "It can't be that big a deal. God knows I believe in Him. That's all that matters."

"And what about God's Son, Jesus Christ? Do you believe in Him? Do you know that He's the only way to God, and to salvation and eternal life? Do you know you need to believe in your heart that Jesus died on the cross to save you from your sins, and to confess your belief in Him in order to be saved?" Vann's heart was beating wildly, as she tried to think of the right thing to say to convince Rosetta of what she needed to do.

"I told you," Rosetta said, her voice getting louder, "I believe in God and He knows how I feel, and if He's as good as

they say, He's not going to let anything bad happen to me."
Rosetta's aggravation was growing.

"Do you know where your spirit will live in eternity after
you die? You have only two choices—heaven or hell."

"I'm going to heaven! I know that. I'm a good person. I ain't
killed nobody!"

"The only way to heaven is through Jesus Christ, Rosetta.
The only way your prayers will be heard is if they're prayed in
the name of Jesus. If you don't know Jesus, and haven't asked
Him to come into your heart, I'm afraid for you, Rosetta,"
Vann said, sadly. "Wait a minute, I have something I want you
to read."

She went and got her Bible and pulled a tract from it. "I
want you to read this before you go to sleep tonight, Rosetta.
It'll explain everything I've been trying to say. And then I want
you to pray in the name of Jesus, and ask God to lead you into
all truth. If you really want it, and pray sincerely, He'll give you
the wisdom to understand."

"So how do you know all of this? And what good has it
done you?" Rosetta asked in a hateful voice.

"I know it because I read and study God's Word, and I go
to church and hear it explained by my pastor. I worship and
praise God, and talk to Him all the time. And to put it bluntly,
if I hadn't done all of those things, I've already told you, there
is no way you would be here in my house, lady. Nobody but the
Lord moved in my heart and gave me the love and compassion
I needed for that to happen, not after all the years you've
ignored my existence. So for no other reason than that, you
need to be trying to pray and thank Him for His goodness. Has
it occurred to you that the reason your other children have no
love or concern for you is that you didn't instill the love of God
in them?"

"Naw, you wrong!" Rosetta's voice rose again. "That has nothing to do with anything."

"Yes, it does! It has something to do with everything, Rosetta!" Vann's heart was broken for the darkness in Rosetta's heart, and before she knew it, she was kneeling beside the woman praying earnestly. "Dear Gracious Master, I come before You in the name of Jesus, seeking Your mercy, grace, and salvation for Rosetta. Father, help her to know that she needs you more than she needs anything or anyone else in this world. Only You have the power to work in her spirit to do what needs to be done to bring her into a right relationship with You. So Father, I pray, save Rosetta tonight through Jesus Christ. Amen"

"Huh!" Rosetta grunted, rejecting the prayer Vann had prayed for her. "What makes you think you're so perfect? You might be on your way to hell yourself for all you know."

"When you start reading the Word, you'll understand. I don't pretend to be perfect by any stretch of the imagination. The Word of God tells us that we've all sinned and fallen short of the glory of God, but it also promises that if we confess our sins, He's faithful to forgive them. And if you keep reading, you'll find out that it is by God's grace that we are saved and not by anything that we can do ourselves. It'll tell you that if you believe in your heart and confess with your mouth that Jesus Christ is Lord, that you'll be saved.

"God loves you, Rosetta," Vann continued, urgently. "And I now know that is the reason why you are here in this house with me right now. God in His mercy, navigated the circumstances to bring you here, so that you could hear what I'm telling you. If He loves you enough to try to save you at this point, He also loves your children enough to save them as well. Perhaps that's been His plan all along, beginning with you leaving me all those years ago. He knew that one day, you would need me to show you and your children the way to Him."

"Huh!" Rosetta grunted.

Vann stood up, wiping the tears from her eyes. "Well, let's get you ready and into bed. But please, before you close your eyes tonight, read this little book. There's a simple prayer in there that I hope you'll pray before you go to sleep. That prayer will make all the difference in the rest of your life on earth, and where you'll spend eternity. I'll be praying that you'll be led to talk to the Lord tonight, Rosetta. I'd go through it with you, but this is a decision you have to make yourself."

Vann continued talking as she assisted Rosetta to the bedroom and helped her get ready for bed. "I'm not going to bug you or harass you about this, but I am going to keep praying for you, and I'm going to ask others to be praying for you, too. This is too important for me not to do that. Good night. I'll see you in the morning."

Vann went back into her bedroom and began making calls. She wanted prayers going up tonight on Rosetta's behalf from as many people as she could contact. Then she fell to her knees and began praying again. "Lord, You are an awesome God. Father, this was not on my famous list," she chuckled, "but apparently it was on Yours. Your Word says that Your thoughts and ways are so much higher than mine. Something I asked for must have opened the door for You to do this work in my life, and in Rosetta's life. And I believe I understand now why You want Rosetta here. Forgive me and cleanse my heart of everything that I'm holding against Rosetta, fill me with Your love and compassion, and help me to be the kind of witness that I need to be to lead her to You. Surely, that is Your higher plan."

Not long after Vann finished praying, TreVann came into her room.

"Trevie? I thought you were in bed. What are you doing up?" Vann asked, turning back the covers on her bed, then going into the adjoining bathroom to start her bath water.

Trevie followed her. "I heard you praying, Auntie, and I know God may have a plan, but I sure hate that you've moved that woman in here. I don't suppose you'd consider taking her back, huh? I'd be willing to drive you back up there to leave her. It would be different if she was a nice person, but she's not, and I really don't like the idea of her being here."

"I know, baby, but it's done and I have to believe the Lord wants her here to get her saved. I can't, in good consciousness, do anything except let Him use me to reach her. We just have to keep praying."

"I suppose," TreVann said, an unconvinced look on his face as he left the room.

Vann followed him into his room and asked, "Baby, are you hungry? Want me to fix you a sandwich or something?"

"Naw, I'm alright," he answered, tiredly. "I'm leaving my door open, though."

Vann laughed. "You need to quit," she said, as she started out of the room. She turned before she went through the door and said, "I'm glad you're here, baby." She left thinking that behind every dark cloud is a silver lining. Trevie was certainly that. But Trevie would have to leave for home in a couple of days, and she might as well face the fact that she would be alone with Rosetta. "Father, I stretch my hands to Thee, no other help I know." She chuckled as the old hymn came to her lips.

In the meantime, Rosetta sat in her room, baffled and angry that she was in the house with a person who was obviously a religious fanatic. She had known Vann was a Christian and planned to use it to her advantage. But she hadn't expected to be bombarded like this on her first night here. And she certainly hadn't expected the woman to tell her she was all but on her way to hell. She picked up the little book from the nightstand and held it in her swollen misshaped hands.

Maybe it wouldn't hurt to read it, she thought. Whatever the outcome, she had no intention of going to any home, no matter how nice they said it was. Not when.... A sharp pain hit her heart and she grabbed her chest. *Oh no! not another heart attack!* The pain finally eased, but it had reminded her of the fragility of her life. And from somewhere, the thought entered her mind that maybe Vann had been right...perhaps there was another reason beyond her own desires for her being here.

Mitch didn't understand how a parent could have such disregard for her own child that she would cast any thought of happiness for that child away, in favor of her own selfish desires. On his drive home, he prayed that the facility would have a space for her soon, so she could get her evil, wicked self out of Vann's house. He was beginning to understand why her other children were so apathetic toward her.

He started praying for Vann, asking the Lord to give her wisdom and strength to deal with Rosetta, and as an afterthought, he prayed for Rosetta, that the Lord would work in her heart and spirit in whatever way she needed. It was obvious that if anyone had ever needed the Lord, Rosetta did.

As soon as Mitch got home, he called Seth. He was concerned about what Elliott Shaw and Annette might be up to.

"Seth? How's it going, brother? I'm just checking to find out if there's anything new regarding Elliott, and if you've thought of anything we can do."

"Yep, I've been thinking on something. Elliott will drop Annette like a hot potato if he thinks all is not aboveboard with this woman. What do you think?"

Mitch rubbed his chin, thoughtfully, and asked, "Seth, didn't you tell me you retired from the police department? What did you do there?"

"Detective...worked homicide for years. Why? What's on your mind?"

"Well, something tells me Annette Gooding might have something to hide. And I was thinking...can you dig into her background a little? If we can find anything, that may be all we need, because you're right, Elliott will run like crazy at the very hint of scandal."

Seth laughed. "Man, I don't know why I didn't think of that myself. And I know a thing or two that Elliott wouldn't like known too. Maybe we can work it from both sides. I'm going to start working on this right now, and I'll get back to you tomorrow when I know something."

The next day, Mitch's heart was light. He thought about his upcoming marriage to the woman he loved, and the wonderful life they would have together because God was with them. It was a long held dream come true. "Thank You, Father," he said with emotion filling his voice. "I know nobody but You are making all this happen."

He was concerned about how Vann was coping with Rosetta, but had held off calling her to give them time to get through the morning. He hoped Vann had been able to rest after her late phone call last night, requesting prayer for Rosetta's salvation. Of course, he hadn't been surprised to hear that Rosetta didn't have a relationship with the Lord. Nobody could be as cold and selfish as she was and have the love of God in their heart.

He also wanted to know if Seth had made any progress in finding out anything about Annette. Seth said he would call, but Mitch was anxious and decided to call him. After dialing the home number, he heard voice mail kick in. He left a message, then dialed the cell phone number. Thankfully, Seth answered.

"Hey, Seth! I know you haven't had a lot of time since we just talked yesterday, but I'm eager to know if you've found out anything."

"Aw, man!" Seth said, jovially. "I surely have. I made a few calls last night and got several friends to start doing some checking. I'm at the station right now, following up on what they found. And man, you were right. She does indeed have a shady past. Annette is a nurse, and does mostly private duty nursing. She's been married three or four times and all the husbands are now dead. I don't know about the others, but there's still a lot of unanswered questions in the last husband's death. The medical examiner said the cause of death was inconclusive and Annette is a person of interest in the investigation. I'm glad she didn't set her sights on me," Seth chuckled.

Mitch didn't share the amusement. "All I can do is thank God for giving me the wisdom to run from her. Well, what do we do now, Seth? I don't particularly like Elliott Shaw, but I'd hate to see him get hurt."

"I've already asked my friends in the department to make me a copy of what they have, and I think there's enough information there to scare Elliott's eyeballs out."

"This is great, Seth. You've been busy and I appreciate it. Are you going to talk to Elliott soon? Oh, man! I'd love to be a fly on the wall when you do."

"I know it. But I get to have all the fun on this one. I'll tell you all about it though. I wish there was some way to have Annette present when I show Elliott this file, but I don't know how to make that happen."

"I think if you can get to Elliott, that'll be more than sufficient. Don't worry about Annette because my guess is that

Elliott is going to take care of her. Now that's another time I'd like to be a fly on the wall," Mitch said, chuckling.

"Me too!" Seth said, joining in the laughter.

Elliott sat, still traumatized, since Seth had shown him the police file on Annette last night. Sitting stiffly in his recliner, he ignored the ringing phone. It had been ringing every few minutes and he knew it was Annette trying to reach him. They were supposed to see each other tonight, but after Seth had delivered his disturbing news, Elliott had been in a state of shock. He couldn't believe that the very things he had always been so fearful of—getting hooked up with an old, no-good woman, and ruining his reputation in the community—had almost happened and that he could've ended up losing a lot more than that.

It further irked him to realize that it had come about only because he was trying to get even with Savannah Sinclair and that judge. Otherwise, he wouldn't have given Annette a second thought. "Umph, umph, umph!" he said, for what must have been the hundredth time. "I knew better! Savannah tried to tell me to watch out for that woman. I don't know why, but she did try to warn me."

The phone rang again. "Hmph! She's persistent, that's for sure. She ought to know by now that I don't want to talk to her, but she probably thinks I'm just another old dumb idiot that she can use to get what she wants." Elliott cringed in embarrassment when he recalled how Seth had witnessed him lose his mind last night. "Oh, Lord," he said, remembering.

Now, he sat alone thinking about how foolish he had been to let himself be taken in by a woman like Annette. The doorbell rang, shocking him out of his stupor. He got up slowly and went to answer it, thinking it was probably Seth coming back to check on him. But when he snatched the door open, he found Annette standing there.

"Hey sweetie! Where have you been? I've been calling you for hours, and you haven't returned any of my calls. What's going on? I don't appreciate being treated like that." As she spoke, Annette pushed past Elliott into the house. "If you're trying to get rid of me, then let me tell you, nobody dumps me until I'm ready. What is your problem anyway?"

"Annette, you get out of my house right now, and don't come back. And you're wrong, lady. I can dump whomever I choose, whenever I choose," Elliott huffed.

"What has gotten into you, Elliott? I thought things were going rather nicely between us. And have you forgotten that we still have to take care of that judge and Vann?" she smiled cunningly. "I'm thinking of some really wicked stuff, and I can hardly wait for it to happen, because I guarantee you, they will be ashamed to show their faces around the city."

"Annette? Just what exactly happened to cause you to hate Savannah and Mitch Langford so much? Why is it so important to do harm to them? You need to answer me, lady. Because it's not my style to run around with dirty, lowdown people who want to hurt people for no good reason."

Surprise wiped all the cunning off of Annette's face. "Whoa! Where is all of this coming from? You want to bring them down as much as I do," she said heatedly.

"Just answer the questions, Annette. And if you can't answer me, I hear the police may have some questions you *can* answer."

Annette's expression changed from shock to anger to the beginning of fright. "You can't threaten me, you old conniving, arrogant, snobbish fool. I know the only reason you been getting with me is because you wanted to get back at Vann for not wanting your old behind. So if I'm dirty and lowdown, you're right there with me, mister. You go ahead and call the police. I'll tell them so many lies that it'll take you a month to get yourself clear. You don't know who you're messing with this time. So you'd better realize that anybody who tries to hurt me will be getting some of that hurt back on themselves." Annette stepped closer to him, "And we can get it on right now, as far as I'm concerned."

The only thing Elliott could think was that he didn't know what she had in that big pocketbook, and he didn't want to find out. The prim and proper Professor Elliott Shaw lost all the refinement and polished sophistication he had groomed in himself over the years, and in his fear and agitation, reverted to the street language he had long left behind.

His knees shook as he said, "Get your...behind out of my house, you ole no-good trash! And you betta not never show your face round here no mo'. You might be don' got away wit killin' some other old stupid dudes, but you sho' ain't killin me! You don't git way from here, I'll kill ya where ya stand right now, you dirty lowdown heifer." Fists drawn back, and in a fighting stance, Elliott was ready to fight.

Annette glared at him before saying, "Okay, I'm going." She walked slowly toward the door, continuing to give Elliott an evil look. "But you better be looking over your shoulder, sucker, because I'm going to get you. Like I said, nobody dumps me and gets away with it! What we were planning for Vann and the judge is nothing compared to what *you're* going to get. I promise you that."

As soon as the door closed, Elliott grabbed his car keys and hurried out the door to the garage. "I gotta put some more locks on these doors and windows. No telling what that woman is going to do because she's capable of anything. I should have listened to Savannah! What in the world was I thinking?" As he drove to the hardware store to buy some heavy-duty locks,

Elliott imagined his good name being dragged through the gutter and felt like crying.

Later as he sat in his secured home, he thought about Savannah. She had been decent enough to try to warn him about Annette. He needed to call her and thank her, especially since he had treated her so badly. But he was ashamed. So the only person he could think to call and tell about his showdown with Annette was Seth.

"Good riddance, Elliott," Seth told him. "She probably won't do anything, but if she does, I guess you'll find out which of your high society, upper echelon friends are really your friends," Seth chuckled. "And I just have to mess with you a little, brother." He chuckled again. "Are you still planning your attack on Vann and Mitch?"

Seth could hardly sit up straight from laughing so hard, because Elliott had hung up on him.

chapter twenty-seven

Rosetta had only been with her a few days, but Vann had found out she was the most hateful, bitter person she had ever encountered. She was reluctant to leave Rosetta at home alone especially for long periods, so she had hired health care providers to come in to take care of her health needs, and to sit with her. On the days when Vann did leave, she almost hated to come back home. The caretakers complained that they had a hard time taking care of Rosetta because she was stubborn and uncooperative. Two of them had already refused to come back, and had to be replaced.

Vann's biggest regret was that the peaceful atmosphere of her home had been shattered, and she missed the tranquility. She also missed the excitement and satisfaction that came from the mental and physical labor that brought forth her creations. But with all the negative energy in the house, her creativity had vanished.

Vann tried without success to talk Rosetta into going to worship services. Rosetta only rolled her eyes and told Vann to get out of her face with that church mess. Rosetta refused to take her medicine when she was supposed to, wanted to eat things she didn't need, and claimed Vann was trying to starve her to death when Vann refused to give them to her. She also complained whenever she noticed Vann getting ready to go anywhere.

"Why you got to be going off somewhere all the time, leaving me sitting up here in this house?" Rosetta rudely questioned. "You think God gon' bless you leaving your own mother alone to do all that other stuff? Huh! I don't. I think you gon' bust hell wide open cause you ain't nothing but a big old hypocrite."

"No, Rosetta, I know I'm not going to hell, because I've accepted the saving grace of Jesus. But I want you to think about what you're saying. I had a life for fifty-something years before I ever knew you. Now regardless of what you think, I'm not going to give up everything in my life just because you suddenly showed up. I can't do that, and if you were a rational person, you'd know it's wrong to expect that. I've asked you to go with me several times, but you say you don't feel like it, or don't want to. And I don't leave you here alone, you always have someone else here with you." She took a deep breath. "Have you talked to the Lord today? If not, maybe you should. You might enjoy the peace and comfort you'll get out of doing that."

As hard as Vann prayed, and stretched her patience to treat Rosetta with kindness, the woman's attitude seemed to get worse instead of better. She constantly found something to complain about, and seemed to get pleasure from calling Vann a hypocrite. The only long term rest Vann got from Rosetta's hatefulness was when TreVann was there.

The first time he had come home and observed her attitude, he had pointed to the door. "You see that door, Ms. Rosetta?" When she nodded, he said, "Well, you're going to be standing on the other side of it real soon if you don't stop being so hateful. Now you can believe me on that." Rosetta believed him, and after that, whenever TreVann was around, she stayed in her room.

Vann scolded TreVann, but deep down, she was laughing at the look on Rosetta's face when he showed her the door.

But TreVann could only stay a few days at a time before he had to go back to Austin.

Vann rejoiced in the good things she had to be thankful for. Mitch was one of them. In addition to the evenings they went to their marriage counseling sessions, he came by most days, bringing flowers, candy, and anything else he could think of, to lift her spirits. He constantly reminded her that their wedding date was drawing closer, and of how much he was looking forward to her being his wife.

One day, while Rosetta was in her bedroom napping, Vann was using the time to make some phone calls. When the beep indicated that a call was waiting, she looked at the area code and saw that the call was from Dallas. Thinking it was about the closing date on Rosetta's house, she quickly ended her conversation to answer it.

"Hello," Vann said, curiously.

"Is this Vann?" a woman asked in a harsh tone.

"Yes, this is Vann. Who is this, please?"

"This is Glenda. And me and my brothers want to know what you've done with our mother. And who gave you permission to sell our home? I just talked to that woman, Luberta, and she told me I needed to talk to you."

Gee, thanks, Aunt Lu. Vann thought. "Your mother is here with me. And I didn't sell your house. Your mother sold her house, and as far as I know, she had every right to do so."

"Where do you live in Houston?" Glenda asked abruptly. "Me and my brothers are coming down there."

"Well, I'm surprised to hear that you're coming all the way to Houston to see your mother when you wouldn't come across town to see her when she was in Dallas. So why exactly are you coming? Are you planning to take her back to Dallas?"

"Look! Just tell me where to come to see my mother. It's not your business why we're coming, unless you've already stolen all her money, because if you have, you're in plenty of trouble. I told you when I saw you at the hospital to leave her alone. Next thing I know you've sold her house and moved her off down there. But you're wrong if you think we're going to let you get away with it. We've already hired a lawyer to get back what rightfully belongs to us."

"I haven't taken anything from your mother, Glenda. If you had talked to your mother like I asked you to, you would know that."

"Like I said, tell me where my mother is. We're getting ready to come down there."

"When do you plan to arrive?" Vann asked. "I need to know so I can make sure we'll be here."

Glenda inhaled, impatiently. "I'll call you when we're on the way, but we'll be getting there sometime this evening."

Vann gave her the address and directions to her house, and was about to ask if she wanted to talk to her mother, but Glenda hung up. Vann immediately called Mitch and told him about the conversation.

"Are they coming to get her?" Mitch asked, hopefully. "I don't believe they give a hoot about their mother, but if they want to take her back, let them have her, and good riddance."

"I think it's just about money, but I'm certainly not opposed to them taking her back to Dallas. Frankly, I'd be willing to pay them to do it at this point," Vann said, laughing.

"And I'd be willing to help you do it," Mitch answered, with a chuckle. "What time are they arriving? I want to be there when they do."

"I don't know, exactly. She said she would call me when they're on the way, but that they'd be here sometime this evening. Oh, Mitch, I'll be so glad when this is over with so my life can get back to normal."

"I know, honey, me too. But, listen, I don't want you taking any abuse from these people. They're obviously after money and whatever else they can get. You tell them and Rosetta that the whole bunch of them can get on back up the highway."

"Don't worry, I'm so fed up with Rosetta that I'm ready to fight. They'll be in for a rude awakening if they come in here messing with me. Listen, I'd better go tell Rosetta they're coming, and call Rubye and the aunts to let them know what's going on. I want everybody to be aware that a war may be about to break out."

"Okay, honey. I'll leave as soon as I can. Are you cooking? Otherwise, I'll pick something up on the way."

"Yes, I guess I'd better, since I'm about to have company. I'll see you in a little bit."

Rosetta's eyes widened in surprise at the news that her children were coming. Before she could stop it, a fleeting hope deep within, that they were coming to take her home, entered her heart. "Did she say why they're coming?" she asked Vann.

"She mentioned something about me stealing your money and selling your house. She said they had gotten a lawyer to get back what belongs to them."

"Oh my goodness!" Rosetta exclaimed, sadness and disappointment filling her heart. "I guess I should have expected that. Well, I'll tell them you ain't took nothing from me, so don't worry about that. I wish they'd just stay where they are if they're coming down here to start trouble. I love my children, but they all have issues. I'm sure you know that already, though."

"I had guessed as much," Vann admitted. "I do think you should give some thought to what they may want. For instance, what if they do want to take you back with them? You need to think about what you want to do."

"Vann, them people ain't coming to get me! If they wanted to do anything for me, they would have done it long ago. Naw, I know I ain't the best person to get along with, but I know I'm in the best place, even though you trying to put me in that facility. At least you want to put me in a good place." Vann was amazed at the almost normal conversation she and Rosetta were having.

Several hours later, the phone rang and it was Glenda, saying they were just hitting the city limits.

"Okay, they're almost here," Vann told the others. Although the atmosphere was one of merriment as they ate, talked, and laughed, they were ready for whatever the group from Dallas came with. Mitch, Rubye, and Thomas had been the first to arrive, followed shortly by the aunts. In addition to the food Vann had prepared, the others had also brought fried chicken and barbeque with all the trimmings.

When the doorbell rang fifteen minutes later, you could hear a pin drop as the noise level fell and the group prepared for the worst. Mitch answered the door and introduced himself.

"Hello, I'm Judge Mitch Langford, Vann's fiancé. Come on in, I'll take you to Rosetta."

"Glenda, Rodney, Sammie!" Rosetta stated, excitedly. "Oh, children, I'm so happy y'all came to see me."

"Well, we just want to know what's going on, and why this woman suddenly showed up and brought you off down here and sold our house," Glenda answered, huffily. It was obvious the stunned looking woman and two men hadn't planned on so many people witnessing the confrontation.

"I'm down here because I want to be," Rosetta answered. "I didn't have nobody to look after me in Dallas, so I called your sister and asked her to come and get me. I sold my house, 'cause I knew I wasn't ever going to be able to live there again. So, why are you all down here?"

"Maybe they've come to get you and take you home, Rosie," Bernie stated, tongue-in-cheek. "I'm your Aunt Bernetta, by the way. I met you at the hospital, remember, Glenda?"

"Yeah, I remember," Glenda answered, sullenly.

"Well? Did you all come to get your mother?" Bernie asked. "She's been mighty unhappy since she got here. But we didn't know what else to do. We couldn't let her stay up there with no one to look after her. But we certainly don't want to interfere if you're finally ready to assume responsibility for her yourselves. Vann is struggling, trying to do everything by herself."

Vann could tell by the looks on their faces that Aunt Bernie was a long way off from their true intentions. Yearning entered her heart. She wanted so much to know and love these people who were her siblings. But as she looked into their closed, angry faces, she knew they would not welcome her. They all must have resembled their father in appearance—short, dark skinned and overweight, she noted. Vann would love to know what their lives were like, what they did for a living, whether or not she had nieces and nephews—everything. But other than the fact that they didn't go to church—which Rosetta *had* told her, she knew she would remain in the dark about them.

"We just want what's ours," Sammie stated, looking at Vann. "Our daddy bought that house and it rightfully belongs to us if anything happens to our mother. And he left some insurance money that belongs to us, too. But for all we know, it could've been spent on this house," he said, looking around Vann's house. "Our daddy didn't mean for no stranger to get what he worked for. We just want what's rightfully ours."

"Sir, you can rest assured that not one penny of your daddy's money was spent on this house," Vann said hotly. "As for your mother's house, the money from the sale of it will be placed into a trust fund that will pay for her upkeep. Nobody's taken anything from you. If that's all you're after, then you can leave now."

"Now, children, you know I gave you your shares of your daddy's money right after he died. That's why you ain't been around lately 'cause you knew I didn't have no more money to give you. But if you want me to, I'll be happy to go back to Dallas with y'all. That's where I'd rather be, but I can't manage by myself. And I surely don't want to go into no nursing home. The money I do have will be controlled by the one who's taking care of me. Now, that's how it is. What you gonna do?" Rosetta stated.

"Well, who is this Vann person anyway?" Rodney asked with a frustrated look. "Glenda said something about her being our sister. Why we just now hearing about this sister? Where she been all this time? Why did she come get you and bring you here? We have a right to know what's happening," he demanded, as he looked around the room.

"I know y'all can understand that," Sammie added.

"Uh-huh!" Glenda put in with attitude. "Anybody with some sense would."

"That's my fault, children," Rosetta said, sadly. "I'm the one who kept the knowledge of Vann away from you. I had her before me and your daddy got married, and y'all know, he would have killed me if he had found out about that. It wasn't Vann that came looking for anything from me. I was the one who called her and begged her to come get me. I just didn't want to be sick and alone."

Mitch stepped into the conversation. "I understand you've hired an attorney to look into all of this for you. Please give him my card and ask him to contact me. I'm not only Vann's fiancé, I'm also her legal counsel and I'll be happy to talk to him or her, whatever the case may be."

Rosetta's feathers were ruffled. "This ain't your business, so you need to stay out of it, because you ain't in the family yet."

"It is his business, because I want him in it," Vann responded. "And if they want to take you home, I think you should go, Rosetta. I don't want you to be unhappy, and obviously, you are, from the way you've been acting. Why don't you take them into the living room, or your bedroom, and talk about it. Then, they can have something to eat."

"Okay, I guess we should do that," Rosetta said slowly. She reached a hand toward Vann for help to stand up and walk into the living room. Vann patiently assisted her, while Glenda and her brothers watched.

A week had passed since Vann's siblings had hightailed it back to Dallas, probably in record time. No one knew what had taken place between them and Rosetta, since she had refused to tell anyone about their conversation. Thirty minutes after they left the room to talk that day, they heard the front door slam, and Rosetta was calling for Vann to come help her. Not even Bernie had been able to browbeat Rosetta into telling them what happened.

Mitch badgered Vann's aunts into coming and sitting with Rosetta more often, instead of simply stopping by for a while and leaving. Vann was able to start going to the fitness center to work off the stress of dealing with Rosetta, and to resume some other pleasurable activities. Some of the enthusiasm she'd had for life, prior to Rosetta's coming, was gradually returning.

Although Vann was glad to have the much needed breaks, Rosetta objected vehemently to them. Just before Aunt Bernie arrived one day to sit with her, Vann and Rosetta got into what had become a regular altercation when Vann was about to leave the house.

"You ain't nothing but a hypocrite!" Rosetta screamed. "You're not too smart either. How can anyone with half a brain believe some man would die for them, and even if He did, how is that going to pay for your sins? Anybody who'd believe that is just stupid!"

"God gives everyone a choice to believe or not to believe," Vann answered, realizing by these attacks that God was working in Rosetta's spirit, and she was fighting it the only way she knew how. "My only responsibility is to make sure you know the truth, then it's up to you to decide what you're going to do with it. Rosetta, you know, and have known all your life, who Jesus is, yet you chose to turn your back on Him in full knowledge. I have peace, Rosetta, but it's obvious you don't, because if you did, you wouldn't keep attacking me about my choice."

"You don't know what you're talking about!" Rosetta shouted. "Why would God let us make our own choice, then punish us for the choice we make? That makes no sense."

"Yes, it does. The Word says He sets before us life and death, blessings and curses. But He's so merciful that He then instructs us to choose life. He's a good God, Rosetta. Again, I ask you to consider giving your heart to Him. You won't regret it."

"Rosie, why are you acting so hateful to us?" Bernetta asked, after she got to Vann's house and made herself comfortable in the family room with Rosetta. "Everybody, especially Vann, is trying to help you, and you are so busy being mean and hateful that you don't realize you ought to be thanking God that we're trying to help you."

Rosetta glared at her. "I'm sick and tired of y'all talking about how hateful I am," she complained. "And what's Vann got to be complaining about. She's got this beautiful house, and all of y'all who love and care about her. She's got the kind of life I always wanted myself, and want for my children, but they ain't even close to having what she has."

"Rosie, just listen to yourself," Bernetta said, a look of disgust on her face. "You talk like Vann is not your child, but she is, Rosie. She's your firstborn child, and even though you have rejected her all this time, she's the only one of your children trying to help you." Bernie shook her head. "I see now that you are actually jealous of her, and you ought to be ashamed of yourself, Rosie, but I guess you don't have it in you. But I'll tell you one thing, you are going to get out of Vann's house with your hateful self, and I don't care if you go to the worst facility there is."

The next Saturday, Aunt Lu called early and told Vann she was coming to sit with Rosetta all day. Vann immediately called Rubye. "Hey, girl, I'm going to be able to get out for a while today, so call the girls and let's get together. I know it's short notice, but that can't be helped. If we can't meet at your house, maybe we can go to Stelle's."

"Great," Rubye stated. "It's been too long since we got together. I'll call you back when I get everything set up and let you know where."

Although the friends talked to one another regularly, they didn't get together as a group often. There was something about being in the company of a group of trusted friends—laughing, crying and eating together—that was refreshing. But things had gotten so hectic that it was difficult for them to get together.

Vann then called Mitch. "Honey, guess what? Aunt Lu's going to sit with Rosetta today, so maybe we can spend some time together."

"Oh, sweetheart, I'm just getting ready to go play a round of golf. I just made the plans, and I'd hate to call back and cancel them. What about later?"

"Perfect. In fact, I was certain that you would be doing that, so I've planned to get together with the girls this morning to have a gab fest. I haven't had an opportunity to do that in a while."

They arranged a time for them to meet at Mitch's house, and talked a little about what they would do with the evening before hanging up.

Rosetta, who had heard her make the calls, couldn't resist taking a jab. "Here you go again! Leaving me sitting here in this house, while you go gallivanting off somewhere having a good time. You think I enjoy sitting in here all the time, not going anywhere but to the doctor? You ain't right, Vann. I keep telling you, you ain't right."

Vann ignored her and happily went about getting ready to go out.

They met at Estelle's house where they settled down to eat the delicious food Rubye and Estelle had somehow managed to get together even with such a short notice, before they started catching up.

Estelle wanted to go first. "I can't wait for you all to hear this," she said, as she gleefully gave them an update on her husband. "We are legally separated, and that divorce attorney Mitch sent me to is his worst nightmare. By the time she finished laying out everything, all his arrogance was gone. No more joint bank accounts, no more coming unannounced to my salons—and she's even fighting against him getting any of them—no more visits to my home with his woman. It was such a relief to see him walk out of the attorney's office with his head hanging down. I'm still rejoicing every time I check *my* bank account and see how it's growing without him messing around with it."

Estelle laughed joyfully. "Now, without my money, he's finding out what I already knew...that girl didn't want nothing but what she could get out of him. He's calling me, complaining about her and wanting to come home. How sweet it is to tell his behind to stop calling my house—which will never be his, since we'll have to sell it and split the profits—because I'm entertaining my boyfriend!" She waved her hand and tossed her long red hair dramatically. The other women screamed, enjoying Estelle's victory.

Roxanne went next. "Ladies, just shoot me if I go running out trying to marry anybody else without praying mightily, and thoroughly checking them out first. I'm not saying I'll never get married again, because I love being married. But I'm not rushing into anything again. The good thing is that after my attorney—Vann, tell Mitch thanks because that sister knows her stuff—by the time she finished with him, he vacated the house without a word, signed the divorce papers, and disappeared. Of course, I don't want to live in the house, so I'm selling it, and having a home built in one of the beautiful new master planned communities. It's turned out fine, but I don't know if I'll ever get over the torment that I went through during that episode," she ended sadly.

"Live and learn, girl. And move on!" Estelle said to Roxanne.

"Well, I don't have any dramatic stories to talk about, thank God." Rubye said. "You all know, my Thomas is his same old self all the time and I wouldn't take anything for him. He promised me that if I went to the Middle East with him so he could make some money, I wouldn't ever want for anything. It was a big sacrifice, and Lord knows, I didn't want to go over there. I had to leave TreVann here with Vann, because he was going into high school and didn't want to come with us. My younger two went kicking and screaming, but I just couldn't leave them behind.

"It was rough, living in a foreign country for ten years. We came home a few times over the years, but I can't tell you how happy I was to land on American soil and know I was here to stay. It did put us ahead financially, so I can't complain. Of course, I don't ask for much, but what Rubye wants, Rubye gets!" She jumped up and did a little dance. The group yelled in victory again. "But, wait a minute," she continued, taking her seat, "unfortunately, that's not the end of the story. We've been asked to go back over there, for two years, they said. However, they said that the first time."

"Rubye!" Vann's heart sank at the thought of her friend leaving again. "Oh Lord, Rubye."

"Well, we haven't decided if we're going, but I think we're leaning more toward *not* going. The political situation is just too unstable over there now, with wars breaking out everywhere. I just don't think it's worth it. But Thomas is looking at the money…that's his main consideration, while mine is living in safety. We'll see who wins. But look! I don't want to put a damper on things, it's not settled yet," she said, smiling.

Katherine was next. "Well, all of you know I've been sick of my husband for years, and nobody knows this but Vann, but I *had* decided to end my marriage and go my own way. Vann told me to pray about it, but all I could see was that he was such a bore—never wanting to go anywhere or do anything. But just when I was about to make my move, and tell him I wanted a divorce, things started happening. First, I woke up one night with chest pains and thought I was about to die. He rushed me to the hospital, they ran tests and discovered I've got heart disease. I went on medication for that, and then shortly after that, I woke up over in the night again and felt like I was on fire. Girls, I was so hot I would have pulled my skin off if I could have. I was naked and still sweating like a pig with the air conditioning blasting. It took me a while to realize I was having the granddaddy of hot flashes. And guess what the man was doing?"

"What?" the others asked, bubbling over with curiosity.

Katherine chuckled. "Have you ever experienced a hot flash that won't stop? I mean a serious hot flash?" They nodded, laughing, because they all understood from personal experience.

"Well, that's what I was in the midst of, and y'all, that man was running around, bringing ice, wet towels, fanning me with everything he could get his hands on, and asking if I wanted to go to the hospital. I think he thought I was dying," she said, breaking out in loud laughing. "I'd had hot flashes before, but that was the first one of that magnitude; however, it wasn't the last by any means. And what does he do? Every time one hits, he's running around, doing whatever he can to cool me off. It is so sweet, that I nearly cry every time I think about it, especially when I consider how I was getting ready to leave him. But the good thing is that I have come to my senses.

"I'd be crazy to leave a man like that. And I've been feeling guilty because when he went through some health problems several years ago, I didn't show him any compassion or support. I feel like the biggest jerk in the world, but I'm thankful to God that I didn't act a fool and leave him. Where am I going to find another man at this point in life who is going to put up with an old, naked woman running all over the house yelling, 'I'm burning up?'"

The picture she painted was enough to cause the other woman to laugh until they cried.

It was Vann's turn, and she hesitated before getting started. "Well, you all know the situation I'm in with Rosetta, so there's no need to get into that. Y'all just pray that a space at that facility opens up quickly because I'm about ready to choke that old woman."

"What facility is that, Vann?" Roxanne asked. "You know my daddy used to own several elderly facilities, and he still knows a lot of people in that industry." She slapped her forehead. "I don't know why I hadn't thought about this before."

Vann named the facility. "I understand why they keep a waiting list because it has a reputation for being one of the best, and it is the one I want her in, but Lord have mercy! I don't know if I'm going to be able to wait much longer. Aunt Bernie wants to throw her anywhere just to get her out of my house, but I can't do that. Not yet anyway."

"I'm going to call him as soon as I get home," Roxanne promised. "Maybe he can make a call or two. And Vann, he'll be glad to do it, after all you did to help me through my ordeal. I didn't want to tell my parents and children about it until it was over. And they really appreciate everything you did."

"I'd hate to bump someone who may have been waiting a longer time than Rosetta, Roxie," Vann said, hesitantly. "but, you know…"

"She'll take all the help she can get!" Rubye quickly said. "If we're talking about fairness here, there is nothing fair about what you're going through, Vann. So you better hush, and accept help from wherever it comes from."

"Amen," Estelle said. "I do understand your wanting to do the right thing, Vann. But God sits high and looks low. He's the One who knows all, and opens doors as He sees fit. Let Him make the decision."

Vann nodded, then laughed. "I tell y'all, trying to get Rosetta up, bathed, and dressed every morning is like doing a day of work on a chain gang. Oh, Lord! And she's gotten worse since her children made their big entrance and exit in the situation."

"Girl, please! We don't want to hear anymore about that woman," Rubye said, laughing. "Hurry up and get to the good news."

Vann paused for a moment. "Okay! Girls, Mitch and I have decided the wedding is going to be in October. I'm actually going to do it, hot flashes, cellulite, wrinkles, and all!"

Estelle jumped up and hugged her, and the others followed suit. "Vann, I am so happy. I feel good about this marriage, and Mitch. God is going to bless you all," Stelle declared.

"Thanks, girls. Not even Rosetta can curb my excitement, because there's finally going to be some new life shaking in these old bones," Vann said, shaking her hips and laughing.

"Yeah!" The women slapped high fives around.

"Now listen, this is really good," Vann said, lowering her voice. "Mitch and Seth told me something last night about Elliott that's going to have you rolling. I know it's gossip, and God forgive me, but y'all already know part of the story."

"Yes, what ever happened with Elliott, Vann? I guess Mitch kicked him totally out of the picture, huh?" Katherine asked.

Rubye jumped in. "Wait! I've got to tell this part, Vann," she said excitedly. "Now girls, just picture this: the 'old geezer' and Annette...together. Get a visual now. Elliott and Annette... getting it on! Need I say more?" she asked, laughing.

The others gave a roar of laughter. "I don't believe it! Elliott and Annette? Naw!" Roxanne said. "That woman is desperate for a man...any man. I must say though, that if two individuals ever deserved each other, they definitely do," she said, laughing harder.

"Well, y'all know what happened in Galveston, so this is the rest of the story," Vann said, laughing. "Annette lost no time in running to Elliott with a lot of lies about what happened. Elliott, of course, was already upset with me for kicking his butt to the curb, so he ate it up. He and Annette got something going...hot and heavy, okay? Elliott popped off to me, then to his frat brother, Seth, about how he and Annette were plotting something against me and Mitch that would make us ashamed to show our faces in public. So Seth and Mitch put their heads together to try to stop them, and found out a lot of interesting things about Annette."

"Girl, you hadn't told me all of this," Rubye said.

"I just found out last night. Anyway, Seth made a special trip to Elliott's house to tell him about what he had found out. There was a lot, but the gist of it was that Annette is a nurse who has been married three or four times, and all the husbands are dead. The police have a file on Annette because there are still questions on the circumstances of her last husband's death. Seth said when Elliott heard all of this, he lost it...meaning he went around the looney bin. He ran around his house like somebody crazy. Threw all of his clothes, food, and even his toiletries out of his house thinking Annette might have poisoned them or put something in them to make him lose his mind. All the while he was ranting about how he was going to get Annette before she could get him."

Loud laughter interrupted Vann and it took a few minutes for the ladies to calm down before she could finish. "Shame on y'all! Okay, where was I? Did I mention he threw out his dishes, linens and even the toilet tissue and the clothes he was wearing?"

Vann could no longer hold her laughter. Tears were running down her face from the effort to contain it, and she couldn't get any more words out. The other women couldn't hear her anyway...they were rolling on the floor, holding their stomachs and laughing their heads off.

"Will y'all quit it!" Vann was finally able to say. "Seth said that when Elliott started stripping out of his clothes, he got out of there fast. But Elliott told him later that when he told Annette to get away from him, she threatened him, and scared him so bad that he went running out and bought new locks for his doors and windows. And now he's fearful about leaving the house, and sits in there in the dark, afraid to turn the lights on, and... "

The laughter erupted again at the thought of the arrogant and snooty professor, hiding in his own house in the dark. A good ten minutes passed before they collected themselves. Every time they thought the laughter was over, one of them would start again, and the others would follow.

"What happened to Annette?" Rubye finally asked, wiping her tears of laughter.

"Evidently Elliott got in some threats of his own, and no one has seen or heard from her since. Seth says Elliott has just about dropped out of everything, even church. He's so afraid people are going to hear about this incident that he's afraid to show his face. I warned Elliott to watch out for Annette, but he didn't listen. I kind of feel sorry for him," Vann finished sadly.

"Oooh! Thank you, Lord Jesus!" Rubye called out. "Lord, we praise You today for Your delivering power. These two people, who set out to dig a ditch for someone else, fell into it themselves. Nobody but You, Lord! Hallelujah!"

"Yes! Praise Him, because He is worthy," Vann said, crying for a different reason now. "And I know He's going to work out this situation with Rosetta. I've concluded that His purpose in all of this is to save Rosetta. She hasn't attended church since she had me and left Georgia. I called you all, remember, and everybody else I could think of the first night she was here, asking for prayer after she told me she didn't believe in Jesus and all that church stuff. I mean her true colors came out. And they've been out in rare form ever since."

"I probably would've had to throw her out," Roxanne stated.

"I've had to pray hard, even after I realized God's purpose in it all. But you know, God is the God of yesterday, today, and forever. I'm certain His plan reaches all the way back to the day she left me behind in Georgia. He knew then, that she was going to need me to show her the path to Him. She hasn't taken the path as far as I know, but I've made sure she knows it," Vann said, a sad smile on her face. "So, please continue praying, because Rosetta needs those prayers badly to be able to overcome whatever is keeping her from accepting the Lord.

"And now ladies, although it's been great, I have to get out of here. Mitch is probably back at home and waiting for me, and I'm not going to keep him waiting any longer. I'm just like a bird out of a cage today and I'm going to enjoy every bit of this freedom."

"You go on, girl. And don't worry, we're getting ready to plan an out of this world wedding and reception for you and Mitch," Rubye told her.

Vann hugged her friends. "Now, ladies, nothing elaborate, please, just close friends and family," she said, before making her exit.

As soon as she left, Rubye said, "Don't pay any attention to what Vann said. We're going to do it up. She's been too good a friend to all of us to plan some little old insignificant affair. No, this is going to be one to remember."

Mitch was happy he would have Vann to himself for a few hours. He couldn't decide whether to take her someplace special for dinner, or to just spend a quiet evening at home. *I'll let Vann make the decision,* he thought.

Mitch's mind went to the troubling conversation he'd had last weekend with Matthew. "Don't you like Vann?" he had asked.

"I guess, but I really like the food she used to fix for me. How come she doesn't fix any food for us anymore? Is it because Mom was mean to her?" Matthew asked.

"No, son, that's not the reason. Vann's mother is staying with her for a while, and she's old and very sick, so Vann has been busy taking care of her. And I'm going to be honest, Son, I haven't wanted you around Vann since you've started saying all those ugly things about her. I don't want you to hurt her feelings like that."

Head down in shame, Matthew said, "Mom told me to say those things and to be mean to her, too, so she would go away."

"I know that, Son, but you're old enough to figure some things out for yourself, and you should always remember that God wants us to treat everyone with love, just as He always does with us."

"Are you still going to marry her? And is she going to live here with you?" Matthew asked.

"Yep. We are going to be married real soon, and she's going to be moving in here with me, since my house is larger than hers. So when you come over, she'll be here to fix you whatever you want to eat."

"What's going to happen to her mother? Is she going to die soon?"

"Well, let's hope not. She's going to live in a place where they can take care of her."

"Oh. Is it that lady I met when we went on the trip? You know, the one who lives with the other two ladies."

"No, that was Vann's grandmother. The lady who is living with Vann now is her mother." Mitch was surprised by all of Matthew's questions, but tried to answer them all, even though he knew Katrina would probably be picking Matthew's brain about everything they talked about.

"You know, Son, you don't have to tell your mother everything we talk about. You know she doesn't like Vann, and telling her anything about Vann will only make it worse. I want you to understand that Vann is not the reason your mother and I didn't get married, Son. We didn't get married because we don't love each other, we don't believe in the same things, and we don't get along. It wouldn't be happy and peaceful like it is when Vann is here. But we both love you very much, you understand what I'm saying?"

"Yeah, but Mom says it would be different if we all lived together," Matthew argued.

"That's not true, Son. Just think about it. Are we happy now, when we don't live together?"

"No. You're always arguing and fighting," Matthew said, laughing.

"Right. And we don't even see each other that much. Can you imagine what it would be like if we all lived together? None of us would be happy. I just want you to think about all of those mean things you've been saying about Vann, and realize that your mother is telling you all of those things because she's angry."

Mitch shook his head sadly as he concluded that what it would probably come down to was his and Vann's love against Katrina's hate-filled teaching, since the boy's mother was such a strong influence in his life. He could only pray that God's love would prevail.

As Mitch thought about it, he realized his son was in the middle of a conflict, and being squeezed from every side. He felt badly about it, but didn't know what else to do except to show him all the love he could.

Breaking out of his thoughts, Mitch looked at the clock...again. "Vann should be here by now," he said in a disgruntled voice. He was a little miffed anyway that she hadn't called him before making plans to get with her girls. Maybe if she had called earlier, he wouldn't have made plans and they could have had the entire day together. But if he'd been thinking, he would have called her first, before he made other plans, so he couldn't blame her. "Honestly, Lord. I'll be so happy when this is over and we're married. Then we won't have to work so hard to spend time together."

"Where *is* she?" He was anxiously headed to the phone to call her when the doorbell rang. "Finally," he said, going to answer it, a big smile covering his face.

chapter twenty-eight

A few days later, Vann answered the phone and heard Roxanne's excited voice on the other end. "Vann, guess what? Daddy's managed to get you an opening at that facility you want your mother in. She can move in next week. Isn't that great? I'm so glad, Vann."

Vann screamed joyously and moved out of earshot of Rosetta, who was sitting in front of the television, watching soaps. "Oh, hallelujah! Thank you, Roxie, and tell your dad I love him. You don't know how much this means to me. I was starting to fear I would have to take her with me to Mitch's house, and I gotta tell you, although Mitch had graciously offered to let her stay with us, now he's so put out with her that the only thing he's talking about is sending her back to Dallas."

"Huh! I understand," Roxie said, laughing. "You need to go over to the facility and pay the deposit and get everything set up for Rosetta, because next week, your only concern will be getting ready for your wedding. Well, I gotta run. Rubye has me working on something."

"Thanks again, Roxie, and about the wedding...remember, I don't want anything extravagant, now. You need to remind the others."

"Yeah, yeah, I know. Bye now."

Vann hung up, feeling as if a giant boulder had been lifted from her shoulders. Rosetta had been with her a month. September had arrived, and October, the month she would be married, loomed just around the corner. Thank God it would be a small affair that wouldn't require much, if her friends were following her wishes.

Knowing what Rosetta's response would be, Vann decided she would give her the news later because the first thing Vann wanted to do was praise God for answering her prayers. She went into her bedroom, closed the door, and fell to her knees.

"Father, I can't thank You enough for opening up a space for Rosetta at that facility. Lord, You know I want to do the right thing for her, and I believe this is it, even though I know she disagrees. Father, I've talked to her about Your salvation, and I've talked to You about it as well. Now Lord, I know it's in Your hands, and I leave it there.

"Father, guide us as we make this transition. Let everything go well, and grant that when Rosetta sees the place, she'll like it and want to live there. Forgive us Father, if someone has been displaced or delayed in any way due to Rosetta getting in, and Lord, please work it out for them in a way that will ultimately bless them. And Father, let there be someone at that place who will water and nourish the seeds of Your Word that I've sown in Rosetta, so that in Your own time, You can bring forth the harvest. Thank You, Father.

"Now Lord, I thank You again for sending Mitch into my life. And Father, as we prepare and draw closer to our marriage, I ask that You walk before us and make every crooked place straight. Then walk with us and work in us, Father, that Your love will flow through us to each other, and Father, we need You to walk behind us and keep all harm, danger, and evil away. Let our marriage bring glory to Your kingdom and be a blessing to those around us. Lead us, guide us, direct and protect us, Father, for only You know what lies ahead. I give You all the praise and glory right now, Lord, because I know You have all power in earth and heaven to give us the victory in these things. In Jesus' name. Amen."

❖ ❖ ❖

They set the wedding ceremony for the third Sunday in October, right after church services. Vann liked that plan, thinking, *Perfect! we can simply wait until everyone leaves except our family and friends, and do it without anyone else being the wiser.* Rubye was the first to tip her off to how far things had gone awry. Vann had intended to wear a nice suit she already had for the ceremony, but Rubye insisted on going shopping to buy her a wedding outfit.

After trying on several outfits, they finally found it. The long, beaded, off-white dress with a sexy back double pleat split came with a matching three quarter length jacket, with an identical double pleat in the back.

When she tried the outfit on in the store, Rubye gave a little scream and said, "Oh yeah, this is it. You look gorgeous."

Vann agreed.

They managed to find the perfect off-white sling back shoes that were adorned with similar beads, and in a small specialty shop, found the perfect purse and hat to complete the outfit.

The next tip off came when Thomas called her and wanted to know when they were leaving for the honeymoon. "Just so we know how to plan the reception. Since we don't know exactly how long the wedding ceremony will last, we don't want to have to rush the reception if y'all have to leave to catch a flight."

"No big reception, Thomas. Just a small dinner with family and friends. Nothing more than that, okay?"

"Yeah, I got it, Vann Jo," Thomas said, and hurried off the phone, wanting to kick himself and thinking, *That call should have been made to Mitch.*

Rosetta had been in the facility for nearly two weeks, and Vann hadn't missed a day coming to see her. On each visit, Vann would bring Rosetta a bowl of fruit, a comfortable gown, underwear, lipstick, or something thoughtful.

"It's not so bad," Rosetta grudgingly admitted to Vann. "I have everything I need and I'm receiving excellent care. I can sit in my own apartment and watch television or I can go out to the lounge when I want some company. I was angry at you at first, but now I realize you did what you thought was right. And you know what? A whole lot of people have been left here and forgotten, but at least you and my sisters come see me. They say I'm lucky to have a daughter who cares enough to come see me, and always bring me something.

"And guess what?" Rosetta continued. "They watch you on television, and they think it's great that I have a daughter who is a television star, and who is so nice too. They say that most people in your position woulda just stuck me out here and left me," Rosetta nodded her head, smiling.

Vann smiled too, happy to hear she was liking the place. "I'm happy that you seem to be enjoying yourself, Rosetta. I'll stop worrying so much now."

"Vann, I've been doing a lot of thinking since I've been here. Just being so close to people who are here one day and gone the next, made me pull out the Bible and the books you made sure I brought with me, and I'm reading them too.

"It was a little rough at first," she admitted, thinking back to her first days there, when her stubbornness had made it a difficult adjustment.

After Vann and Rosetta's sisters had gotten her settled and left, the administrator had come in to welcome her and tell her what to expect. "Now, Mrs. Smith, this is an excellent facility, and you can expect to receive the best for your health care needs. But I want you to know that the quality of your stay here rests entirely with you.

"We'll do everything we can to accommodate your needs and make you comfortable, but we expect you to give our staff the same courtesy they give you. If that doesn't happen, you'll find yourself having to do without the services you would normally receive. For instance, when the worker comes to assist you in the morning with your hygiene needs, you need to cooperate. If they ask for your wishes regarding meals, you need to give them an answer. Are you understanding me, Mrs. Smith?"

"Yes, I guess so," Rosetta answered sullenly.

"Very good, then."

"Well, what if they come to help me with my bath and I'm not ready, can I tell them to come back later?" Rosetta asked.

"I'm sorry, but no. If that happens, you'll have to go without that service that day because others are waiting. We'll be assessing your health needs continuously, and if we have to adjust your level of assistance, we'll do that."

"Huh!" Rosetta had said to herself when the woman left. "I'm paying them good money so they better not be messing with me."

But the next day, she found herself awkwardly trying to bathe by herself with painful arthritic fingers after she told the worker she wasn't ready and to come back later. The worker never did come back. The message had been sent...loud and clear.

"I miss Vann," she had wailed, tears running down her face. "But it's never going to be the same, and I have to accept that or my last days on earth are going to be harder than they have to be."

Now she said, "Vann I know you're trying as hard as you can to make me as comfortable as possible, and I know I don't deserve that, because I've been so hateful to you all of your life. I hope the Lord will forgive me, and help me." Her face lit up, "And I've been trying to pray, too."

"I'm so happy to hear that, Rosetta," Vann said, her eyes brimming with tears. "And I want you to know that God is more concerned with what's in your heart than He is with the words you say. So keep seeking Him, and He's going to answer the desires in your heart."

Rosetta looked away from Vann and said, "I know you want to find out about your daddy, and how all of that happened. And I guess I do owe you some kind of explanation. I was engaged to the man I married, and your daddy was already in the army. After I graduated, I went to live with my aunt in Atlanta to go to beauty school. I was working in a little café in the evenings, and that's where I ran into your daddy. We knew each other from school, and we were both glad to see someone from home. Anyway, he offered to drive me home one night, and well…one thing led to another. He left right after it happened on his way to military service.

"I never did go back home. I stayed in Atlanta, had the baby, and told my aunt to do whatever she wanted with it, because I didn't want my fiancé to find out. My aunt called Mama, and she came and took you home with her. She tried to talk me into keeping you, but I had my mind made up about what I wanted to do. A baby would have messed up everything. So, I pushed that whole episode to the back of my mind, and went on with my plans."

Vann's eyes were filled with tears again. "Well, at least I finally know that. What about the man? What happened to him? Who is he?" she asked.

"That ain't even important for you to know at this point," Rosetta said, a stubborn look on her face. "I think he got killed in the war anyway."

Tears slid down Vann's face. "Rosetta, I would still like to know who he was," Vann pleaded.

"Ain't no use for you to know all that," Rosetta said in a cold voice. "He never even knowed you were born, so even if he was alive, he wouldn't be interested in finding out after all these years. That's all I got to say about it. I told you what I did 'cause I knew you wanted to know. Don't make me sorry I did."

Vann wiped at her tears, knowing it was useless to plead with Rosetta anymore.

chapter twenty-nine

Her wedding day finally arrived. Vann could barely contain her excitement throughout the worship service, just thinking about the fact that she was about to be Mitch's wife. She tried to control the big grin she knew covered her face, but it seemed everyone around her wore one just as big as hers. Well, she had always heard, smiles are contagious.

When Vann was ready to leave the room she had used to change into her wedding attire, the plan was that she would meet Mitch in the sanctuary where their pastor, family, and friends were waiting. But Estelle came in to hover over her hair and makeup, getting on Vann's nerves, and then Rubye grabbed her and led her to the front of the church where Trevie stood, grinning. "Wow! Auntie, you look great. I'm honored to escort you down the aisle," he told her.

"What? Boy, I'm just going to walk back into the church and meet Mitch at the altar, I don't need an escort." She looked around, realizing there were still a lot of people milling around. "What are all these people still doing here?" she whispered. "I thought we gave them plenty of time to clear out."

The double doors leading into the sanctuary suddenly opened and organ music began to play. Trevie led her to the opening, and when she looked inside, she almost fainted. A beautiful wedding arch had been placed at the front of the church, and floral arrangements had been placed at the end of each pew. A white runner led to the altar and the church was full of people. In fact, it looked as if no one had left. Two little girls waited for the cue to start scattering flowers along the aisle. "Oh my goodness!" Vann said, in a shocked voice.

TreVann tucked her hand under his arm and slowly pulled her along with him through the door. Through her tears she saw Mitch, a big smile on his face, standing at the altar with a man she didn't recognize. She had no way of knowing that the man was Mitch's brother, who had flown in that morning and surprised him. Her eyes went to the left side, where she saw all of her girlfriends, Cy and Sylvia, the aunts and other family members, and a double look convinced her that the almost unrecognizable woman sitting in a wheelchair at the end of the front pew was Rosetta. "Lord have mercy!" she mumbled. She quickly looked to the right and saw Seth, Mitch's children—including Matthew, some of Mitch's coworkers and frat brothers, and oh Lord, were those Mitch's parents smiling at her?

"Oh, y'all are in so much trouble," she whispered through clinched teeth to Trevie. He merely squeezed her hand and made sure she kept walking as the musicians played and began singing, 'He's Been Faithful, So Faithful to Me', which was one of her favorite songs.

Mitch took her trembling hand into his, and smiled down at her. "You look beautiful," he whispered.

"You too," she whispered back, smiling up at him.

"They're up here whispering love words to each other, y'all," Pastor Travis said to the congregation. "Bring those pretty chairs they decorated up here, so they can sit down. This is a real joy, and I'm going to take my time even though I know y'all are hungry, but just bear with me a little while. The caterers are preparing as I speak, and we're going to feed you." After Vann and Mitch sat down, the pastor continued. "Sister Vann, I want you to know they almost had to tape my mouth up to keep me from spilling everything. I was so excited, I just wanted to tell it all. My wife was deep in the planning process, and every time she would tell me something new, I'd want to call you. I didn't know my wife knew all those words she threatened me with," he said, laughing along with everybody.

"This precious couple and I have been talking over the last several weeks, and I'm just as happy as I can be to join them in marriage. They're both mature Christians, have their heads on straight, know who and what they want for the rest of their lives, and most importantly, they love each other.

"Sister Vann has been taking care of her mother, who happens to be here today, while she has continued to take care of her church responsibilities. She works around this church, helping out in the office and in the pantry, teaching Sunday school, and participating in our prayer meetings—even when she can't be present, she listens in and prays with us over the speaker phone.

"And as often as I see her and talk to her, I didn't know Sister Vann even had marriage on her mind until a few weeks ago. I should have known something was going on when she called and asked me for insight on how to make godly decisions. She said she was preparing a lesson for her class, but that she needed it too. I should have asked some questions about what decisions she was trying to make, but I didn't. But guess who did? You got it! My wife. She was on the phone with Vann before I knew it, getting the scoop.

"I haven't known Mitch personally very long, but I do know of his reputation as a criminal judge who rules with integrity and fairness." He stopped and chuckled. "Did y'all know they met in his courtroom?" He chuckled more. "Sister Vann was there trying to help some little children, and she got into it with the Judge so bad that he threatened to throw her in jail. Sister Vann must have really been carrying on down there."

The pastor was now laughing hard, and so was the church. "But she was on the Lord's assignment, defending the little ones. Anyway, Mitch saw what kind of woman she was, and he was hooked. He told me he had been praying for a wife, but when he saw Vann, he was praying for one specific woman. And the rest, as they say, is history.

"So today, I want to say a few words about the faithfulness of God. They already know He's been faithful to them, and now their desire is to be just as faithful to Him and to each other." He paused. "Let me give you a perfect example of God's faithfulness. Shortly after their courtroom altercation, Mitch had already started praying. Well, he decided to tag along to a retirement reception one evening with a friend who told him he could come, eat, and leave. But he was unaware of who the honoree was. Imagine his surprise when he realized it was Sister Vann, …and hers, when she saw him there." He cracked up, laughing.

"God is awesome, y'all. I keep telling you that. The Word of God tells us that His mercies are new every morning, and His faithfulness to us is great. So, I encourage you to use this couple as your inspiration. And when you're ready to quit or give up on some dream or desire you may have, remember Vann and Mitch, who are just starting their lives together after waiting not years, but decades to find one another."

"Oh, praise You, Father, You're so good!" a voice called out loudly, obviously in tears. Others joined in, praising God, thanking Him for His goodness. Soon, tears and praises were flowing all over the church.

The pastor continued with tears in his eyes, "They have reminded me of a thing or two about waiting on God." He stopped and looked down at them. "You have ministered to me and reminded me of His faithfulness, and I appreciate it, because pastors get a little weary sometimes too." He wiped at the tears in his eyes. "I'm just so happy for you, and now let me do what God has ordained me to do—joyfully join you together in holy matrimony."

Vann and Mitch had nearly gone through the entire box of Kleenex someone had handed to them by the time the pastor led them through their vows and pronounced them man and wife.

Imagining her tear-stained eyes and smeared makeup, Vann whispered to Mitch as they walked down the aisle together, and were escorted to the church reception hall, "I know I look a mess."

"No, you look wonderful, as always, and I love you," he whispered back, as he hugged and kissed her.

chapter thirty

Katrina literally dumped Matthew on their doorstep immediately after they returned from their Bahamian honeymoon.

"He ain't coming to visit," she explained, vengefully, "he's coming to stay, so deal with it."

Vann was thrown into a tizzy! And to make matters worse, Katrina had done a good job coaching him, and the ten-year-old simply oozed hostility toward her and treated her with as much contempt as his preadolescent mind could muster.

Vann couldn't help but wonder what she had gotten herself into. She loved Mitch, but the ongoing battles with Matthew were a continuation of those she had just escaped from with Rosetta, and she felt so weary she didn't even know if she wanted to keep trying.

"It'll work out, honey," Mitch told her every night in the quietness of their bedroom. But it didn't seem to get any better.

"Lord! What should I do?" Vann cried out to the Father constantly. "I've gone from one hostile person to another one, with barely a chance to even catch my breath."

Then, two weeks after he came to live with them, the school called to inform her that Matthew was in trouble at school—again! But this time, they were sending him home. After calling Mitch, who was in court and couldn't leave, she had no choice but to go to the school to pick him up herself.

She apologized to the assistant principal, grabbed the boy, and hurriedly left the school. They didn't say a word to each other all the way home, after he asked, "Where's my daddy?"

"He's at work," she answered, "where he usually is at this time of day. He'll be home as soon as he can, but I wouldn't be real anxious for him to get there if I were you."

They entered the house and Vann asked him if he was hungry and fixed him a sandwich. She told him to go to his room when he finished it, then went to the workshop Mitch had had built for them. But she did more praying than working.

"Father, the devil is trying to destroy our home. Please let Your presence, peace, and power fill this house, and may Your love and all of the fruit of the Spirit be so strong in this place that the devil will have to leave. In Jesus' name, I thank You for all You're going to do. Amen."

After dinner, which was tension-filled because of the impending showdown between Mitch and Matthew, Vann escaped to the serenity of their bedroom. She ran a hot bath, pouring a generous portion of her favorite scented bath oil into it, stripped and slipped into the large tub, while upstairs, her husband and his son were having a loud discussion.

"Ahhhhh! Now this is just what I needed," she said, as she stepped into the hot water. "Thank you, Lord. I don't take any good thing for granted." She closed her eyes and tried to relax and concentrate on God's goodness.

She had been sitting there a while when the door opened abruptly and her husband walked in.

"Ever heard of knocking?" she asked in annoyance, startled by his entrance.

"You look very relaxed," he said, walking toward the tub.

"I am! So get out," she answered irritably.

"And let you have all this fun by yourself? I don't think so." He quickly stripped and stepped into the tub with her.

"Can't a woman find any peace in this house?" she asked, but suddenly she was so hot she was glad to be sitting in the tub of water. *Must be a hot flash,* she thought.

"Not as long as you're the wife and I'm the husband," he answered, pulling her close.

"So how did things go with Matthew?" she asked, trying to cool down.

He sighed, "I don't know. I talk, I yell, I even plead with him. But I can't seem to get through. The thing is, Matthew has been placed in the middle and is having to decide where his loyalty should be. It's causing all sorts of conflicting emotions in the kid. So it's no wonder he's acting out at school and with you. I don't know how we're going to overcome all the ugly things Katrina has fed him, but we have to keep trying because it's certainly doing a good job of disrupting our home, and that means Katrina's winning."

"Well, I guess Matthew needs to know that nothing he says or does will make any difference," Vann said, quietly.

"Yes. As hard as it may be, we have to convince him that no matter what, we're staying married. I told him that and asked him if he wanted to go back and live with his mother. As of now, she still has custody, even though I've already asked my attorney to petition the court to have custody transferred to us." He kissed the side of her neck, and pulled her closer.

"What did Matthew say?" Vann reached up and stroked his tension-filled face as she spoke.

"Hmmmph! Now this is going to surprise you more than it did me," Mitch answered. "He put a serious look on his little face, was quiet for a while, then told me he'd have to think about it."

"What? I can't believe that. I thought that was what his acting out was about. That he doesn't want to be here."

"Yeah, I did too. But I don't think he expected me to offer to take him back. He knows that I've wanted custody of him for years."

"Well, what do you think it is, honey?"

"I just don't know! I do know that Katrina is still coaching him when he goes to her on the weekend, but I don't know how to stop her except to cut off all contact between them, and that probably wouldn't help matters much. Unfortunately, Matt's not strong enough yet to stand up to his mother or to go without seeing her regularly."

Vann sighed, "We just have to keep praying and asking God to take control. He'll work everything out."

"Thanks, honey. I know how hard this is on you, but I don't know what I would do without you." He continued planting kisses on her face and neck.

"You wouldn't be having this problem if you didn't have me."

"That may or may not be true, but I don't want to talk about Matthew anymore. He's taken up enough of our time and spoiled our day. I'm not going to let him spoil the night, okay? Let's just enjoy spending time with each other now, babe."

That night, from a deep, restful sleep, Vann heard the phone ringing and groaned when Mitch eased his arm from around her to answer it. "Hello," he mumbled in a sleep-filled voice. A few seconds later, he said, "Oh God. Hold on a minute. Baby." He shook her gently. "Honey, telephone."

Vann knew then that another nightmare had invaded her hard-to-hold-onto happiness. "What?" she asked. "Who is it?"

"It's Bernie. She needs to talk to you," Mitch answered, not wanting to be the one to deliver the news that he knew would be devastating to her.

"Aunt Bernie? What is it? What's going on?"

"Now, Vannie, you know I wouldn't be calling you at this time of night if something hadn't happened. It's Mama, Vannie. I just got a call from Georgia. She's gone, Vannie. She took sick and they rushed her to the hospital, but they couldn't save her. She passed away about an hour ago. I haven't called Lu yet, and I'll leave it to you to tell Rosetta in the morning. I'll talk to you tomorrow and we can start making arrangements. Bye."

"Bye, Aunt Bernie," she said softly and hung up the phone. "Mama. My mama's gone, Mitch. Oh God, my mama's gone," she cried in his arms.

"I know, babe. But she told us she was just waiting for you to get settled, remember? She was a woman of her word until the end. And think about how long you've had her, honey. Now is the time to rejoice because she lived a long, good life."

Vann saw Rosetta totally lose her composure when, mere hours later, she went to the facility, took Rosetta's gnarled fingers into hers, and gently told her that her mother had died.

Rosetta lost it. "Oh no! Oh Lord, my mama done died and I didn't even tell her how sorry I am for the way I've acted all these years," she cried. "Lord, I didn't treat my mama and daddy right, leaving them with that baby, and running off like I did. And I never told them I was sorry about that. I didn't even go back to see her. I didn't even go to Papa's funeral. Oh Lord, I'm so sorry." She sobbed so uncontrollably that Vann pushed the intercom button, which had a worker running into the room in a matter of minutes.

"My mother just got the news that her mother passed away. I think she may need something to help calm her down," Vann explained.

"Vann, I have to go to that funeral, " Rosetta wailed. "I just have to."

"I don't know if you're up for that kind of trip, Rosetta. Why don't we ask the doctor about it?"

Of course, the doctor agreed with Vann that Rosetta wasn't able to make the trip, much to her displeasure.

Twenty-four hours later, Vann and Aunt Bernie were boarding a plane to Savannah to complete the funeral arrangements already started by phone. Mitch was unable to get off work, but would leave after work on Friday. He wouldn't make the wake on Friday evening but would be there for the services on Saturday morning.

Throughout the process of finalizing the arrangements, preparing the program, and dealing with the usual issues, Vann remained dry-eyed, strong, and calm, knowing Mama would want that. But she felt an aloneness she had never felt before, and knew it was because she had lost the person who had been so dear to her all of her life. She went to the Lord in prayer.

"Father, I'm grateful to You for leaving Mama here with me so long. She's been the only parent I had for most of my life. But Lord, now she's gone, and it's left such a big hole in my heart, but I know You don't make mistakes. So Father, I ask that You be a refuge and a strength for me in this time of trouble.

"I've seen Your merciful hand at work in my life, and I thank You for giving me Mitch after I gave up on ever having a husband, and for fulfilling Your promise to restore that which has been devoured by sending Rosetta back into my life. I pray she will eventually become the mother that was lost to me so many years ago. And I also pray that before I die, I will at least know who my father was.

"Now, Lord, see us through this time of great loss, and let Your grace be sufficient and Your strength made perfect in this weakness I'm now feeling. I thank You and give You praise for everything—past, present, and future. In Jesus' name, Amen."

Vann was okay until Saturday morning when she received a call from Mitch.

"Babe, you doing okay?" he asked, tiredly.

"Yes, but where are you? I was starting to get worried," Vann said, a sinking feeling in her stomach.

"Sweetheart, I hate to tell you this, but nothing has changed since last night. The plane is still grounded in Charlotte. They're hoping the weather will break soon, but for now, we're just sitting here."

Vann numbly hung up the phone and quickly lost all the composure she had maintained. She curled up in the bed there in the hotel room she had reserved for them, and wailed. She managed to pull herself together to get dressed and drive the rental car to the house, where she met the rest of the family. But her emotions were hanging by a fragile thread. *Oh Lord, I need Mitch with me, please let him get here,* she silently prayed.

The limo arrived to pick up the family. *Still no Mitch.* She climbed out of the limo when they reached the church. *Still no Mitch.* She walked stiffly down the aisle and took a seat on the end of the front pew. *Still no Mitch.* The service started and she sat there, silent tears running down her face through it all. *Still no Mitch.*

It was during the final viewing that Vann, head down, Kleenex pressed to her eyes, felt someone slip an arm around her. "It's alright, babe. I'm here," Mitch whispered.

She looked up and saw not only Mitch, but TreVann, Rubye, Thomas, and Estelle leaning over her. She threw her arms around them and gave up the hard-held control, letting her sobs fly.

That release, and the presence of Mitch and the others, restored her composure and once again, she was calm, strong, at peace. Until...

As they were leaving the cemetery, a man walked up to Vann and just stood there, staring down at her, a strange expression on his face. He was tall, looked to be seventy-ish, and had the same skin tone and hair that Vann had. Mitch and TreVann, who stood with Vann between them, gave the man a hard look.

"Miss, I'm Ted Lightfoot. I know you don't know who I am," he said, in an emotionally shaky voice. "And I'm sorry to be telling you on this occasion, but...I'm your father. I sure would like to talk to you before you leave. Is that possible?"

Vann, Mitch, and for once, TreVann, all stood there, mouths open, speechless, while the man continued. "I'm sorry, I know this is a shock, but would it be alright if I stopped by your grandmother's house a little later? I...I...promise not to take up too much of your time, but I do need to talk to you." He looked at Vann with hopeful eyes.

Vann's eyes flew to Mitch before they settled back on the man. "I've just buried my only parent, and this day is hard enough without hearing this. Sorry, I've had about all I can take today."

TreVann stepped between Vann and the man, "You heard her, mister. You need to get to stepping."

"Wait a minute, Trevie," Mitch stated. He knew Vann was on emotional overload, and was concerned that she might regret a rash decision. He said, "I'm Mitch Langford, Vann's husband. Uh...Mr. Lightfoot, now is not a good time. My wife needs some time to get through this occasion and to rest and relax a little."

"I understand, and I really hate to intrude at a time like this, but it's important that I talk to you before you leave. There are some things I need to say to you." He looked at Vann as he spoke.

Vann slumped against Mitch, shaking her head. "I'm sorry, that's not possible at this time, Mr. Lightfoot," Mitch told the man as he dug into his pocket for a card and scribbled his cell phone number on the back of it. "Maybe she'll feel like talking to you later, but not right now. We have to be going."

"Whoo!" TreVann exclaimed as they walked away from Ted Lightfoot. "Who needs a television with you around, Auntie? We can just tune in to your life to get all the excitement we want. I'll be doggone! Who would have thought this would ever happen," he said, shaking his head.

"Trevie, we're going to the hotel and rest a little. What are you going to do? Go to the hotel, or to the house?" Mitch asked.

"I'm going to the hotel and change clothes, then I'm going on over to the house with the others. They've already left to go to the hotel to change. I'm ready to chow down on some good food," TreVann told them with a smile.

"Okay. Tell everyone we'll be over later, will you?" Mitch said, as they got into his rental car, and drove the short distance to the hotel.

It was much later when Vann and Mitch arrived at the house, which of course was still packed with people. Vann was still messed up over what had happened at the cemetery with the man, Ted Lightfoot. And coming to the house without Mama there to talk to about it made it especially hard. When she saw all the people still there, she wanted to turn around and go back to the hotel, but knew she was expected to show her face.

They had only been there long enough to speak to everyone, have plates piled high with food pressed into their hands, and find a quiet corner in which to sit down, when the aunts came walking up, curious expressions on their faces.

"Eat your food, baby," Aunt Lu ordered. "And tell us about this man Trevie said is claiming to be your daddy. Rosetta kept his identity to herself all these years, but where has he been and why hasn't he said something before now? I tell you, all kinds of crazy people come out of the woodwork when somebody dies. He's probably thinking you might get a little something. Uh, uh, uh!"

"I don't know anything, other than what he said at the cemetery," Vann answered. "To be honest, I'm not interested in anymore long lost parents showing up right now. But Mitch told him to call us later."

While she spoke, Ted Lightfoot walked quietly up to the group and hearing her last comments, said, "I know what you told me, and I hope you'll forgive me for showing up here like this, but I just couldn't let you leave without talking to you and letting you know that I never knew about you. I was hoping we'd have a chance to talk alone, but I guess it's just as well that I say what I've got to say to you all."

"Well, where have you been all these years? And what happened to you when Rosetta came up pregnant? Didn't you at least wonder about whether the child was yours?" Bernie asked.

"I've lived away from here for years and just recently moved back. Rosetta and I...we were just kids, you know...just messing around. There was nothing serious between us. Rosetta, if I remember correctly, was crazy about some other dude and all she wanted to do was marry him, and I was getting ready to leave for the army. We just got to fooling around one night and things went too far. It didn't mean anything to either one of us. I left town the next week and forgot all about it."

Vann, remembering what Rosetta had told her, said, "I don't care how old you happen to be, it's never good to hear that neither of your parents wanted you."

"That's not true!" Ted heatedly objected. "If I had known about you, I would have wanted you. But honestly, I had no idea. I'm not proud of myself for never thinking about it, but I left for the army a few days after we were together, and two months later, I was on my way overseas to fight in the Korean war. I got shot up real bad, and I didn't even know I was in the world for a long time.

"Your grandmother was concerned when she learned you were getting ready to marry a man from this area. She knew it was a possibility that the guy could have been your brother or cousin. That's when she called Rosetta and demanded to know your daddy's name. She was good enough to try to do the right thing after talking to Rosetta, and finally got in touch with me."

"And why are you presenting yourself here now?" Mitch asked.

"Vann, your grandmother asked me not to say anything until you got some situation with your mother settled. She said you already had a plate full of trouble with Rosetta and didn't need any more. That is the only reason I hadn't looked you up. I've been wanting to contact you ever since I learned about this.

"Vann, I don't have any other children that I know of, and if I have a chance to get to know you before I leave this world, then I want to do so. I just couldn't let you come down here and be this close to me, and not say anything. I've been trying to get my nerve up to say something to you all week. I knew I had to do it today, before you leave. If your mother didn't do right by you, I'm sorry, but please don't blame me. Believe me, if I had known I had a daughter, I would have proudly claimed you. You're all the close family I have left in this world beside two brothers and an elderly aunt, who is my mother's youngest sister."

Luberta sniffed. "Lord Jesus! I don't know what to think about this! I don't expect no better from Rosetta, but Mama should have said something when she found out. She didn't have no business keeping something like this to herself."

"She did say something, Lu," Bernie said. "She was content knowing there were three other people who knew the identity of Vann's father...me, Rosetta and this man. Rosie's been too busy being hateful to say anything, and Mama told me not to. No sense in Vann knowing anything about this if the man didn't plan on doing anything about it."

"Mama told you?" Luberta exclaimed loudly. "Now see. That wasn't right. I love Vann just as much as anybody, and there was no reason to keep this from me. I don't want to see Vann hurt anymore either."

"Lu, you know you can't keep nothing for long," Bernie said. "Mama was afraid you would end up saying something to Vann about it and Vann didn't need that at the time."

"I wouldn't have done that!" Luberta screamed. But she knew her mother and sister had been right about her as usual.

"How do we know you're really her father?" Mitch interceded. "We don't know anything about you, and Rosetta can't be trusted as far as I'm concerned. We need some proof, and then based on where you've been all these years, I might not want you anywhere around my wife. You might not mean her anymore good than her mother."

"There are tests we can take that will tell us the truth. And I don't mean no harm to anybody. I'm a Christian man, and all I want is to live the rest of my life in peace with God and others. I wouldn't do anything to hurt my own child," Ted Lightfoot proclaimed, looking directly at Vann. "There's no doubt in my mind about who you are. You look just like my mother. I have pictures of her I'd like to show you."

"That's funny," Vann said, "everyone else thinks I look just like my mother."

"That's because they haven't seen the other side. I guarantee you, you look like the Lightfoots," Ted said, smiling proudly. "I can't wait for you to meet my family. My aunt is going to have a fit when she sees you."

"We'll see," Mitch responded. "Vann's been under enough pressure the last few months without adding this. You'll have to wait a little longer."

"Do you mind if I call you in the meantime, Vann?" Ted asked anxiously. "Maybe even fly to Houston to see you? You have to understand that I'm not getting any younger."

"We'll have to see about any visits, Mr. Lightfoot," Vann told him. "But I guess it'll be okay for you to call. My husband is right, though. I've been through quite a bit lately, and that includes taking on responsibility for Rosetta's care. I just can't take on any new trouble right now. I hope you understand what I'm saying."

"There won't be any trouble, Vann. I promise you that. I know you can't call me dad, but I'd appreciate it if you would at least call me Ted, so that I'll know you don't think of me as a stranger. I guess I'll have to live with whatever you wish for now. But I sure was hoping you'd agree to meet my family before you leave. I'm really anxious for them to see you."

"Where do you live?" Mitch asked. "We'll be leaving here shortly to go see my folks. If it's not too far out of the way, maybe we can come by for a few minutes." He looked at Vann. "Do you want to do that, honey?"

"I guess it'll be okay," Vann said, as Ted quickly handed her a piece of paper with his address and phone number already written on it.

"I was trusting that you would say that," he told Vann, smiling. "I guess I'll leave and let you finish eating," he pointed to her plate of food that had gotten cold a long time ago.

Vann and Mitch decided to go straight to Ted's house when they left her mama's house, and to go see his parents the next morning, before catching their flight back home.

When they found the nice, well-kept house, located about thirty miles away, the door opened before they could get out of the car and Ted was coming down the steps to meet them.

"I'm so glad you came," he said to Vann. "Come on in and meet your family."

Vann didn't know what to expect, so she prayed silently, asking God to let His will be done, and that no one would end up getting hurt if it turned out she was not his daughter. She needn't have worried.

The minute she stepped through the door, an older lady cried, "Mary, oh Lord, it's Mary! Lord Jesus, let me hug you." She reached for Vann from the wheelchair she was sitting in. Vann went across the room and hugged the old lady, then said, "I'm Savannah, but everyone calls me Vann. Who is Mary?"

"Mary was your grandmother, Vann," Ted told her. "But didn't I tell you that you look just like her? This is my aunt, Leona, and my brothers, Charles and James Lightfoot."

The brothers stood and shook Vann and Mitch's hands. "Glad to meet y'all," they both said, but their eyes never left Vann. "You look just like our mother," Charles said. "It's amazing."

"Sure enough do," James added. "Ted told us that everyone thinks you look like your mother, but if that's true, she and my mother must have looked a lot alike."

Ted, in the meantime, had produced a scrapbook full of pictures, which he thrust into her hands. "Here, look at these pictures," he said.

But before Vann could open the book, he put a framed picture in her hand. A man and woman she assumed were Ted's parents, smiled at her from the picture. She gasped when she looked at the woman. She saw her face in the picture—her eyes, her mouth and smile, her nose—everything. "Oh goodness, she looks just like me," Vann exclaimed.

"No, sweetheart, you look like her," Ted said, gently. "You are my daughter, and her granddaughter."

"She would have been so happy to know she had a grand-child," Leona said, sadly. "That woman should have told Ted," she said, an angry look briefly crossing her face. "But we have to remember that God knows best. If He had wanted it to happen, it would have."

Ted went to get iced tea for everyone, and while Vann looked through the scrapbook filled with pictures, she answered questions about her life—where she lived, her family, what she did for a living.

"I want to get to know you and your family, Vann," Ted told her again. "I'll come to Houston to see y'all as soon as you tell me it's okay."

She was convinced that Ted was her father when they left. But she hadn't decided whether it was a good thing.

chapter thirty-one

Mitch had left Matt with Katrina while they were in Georgia, and strangely, with little complaint from her. It didn't occur to him to question why she had been so cooperative.

He dropped Vann off at home and headed over to Katrina's to pick up Matthew. As he drove, he prayed that Matthew's initial acceptance of Vann would be restored to what it was before Katrina poisoned his mind, and that they would finally become a family.

As was his custom, he called from his cell phone when he arrived, prepared to wait for Matt to come out of the apartment. Red flags immediately went up when Katrina insisted he come in. Mitch was tired from the trip and in no mood for her foolishness.

"Katrina, I don't have time for any of your mess. Just send my son out, because I'm not coming in there," he told her.

"I have to talk to you about something, Mitch," Katrina responded. "I'll let you win this one today, but be warned, we are going to talk soon."

A few minutes later, the door opened, and Matthew came running out. "Dad! I'm glad you're here 'cause I'm ready to go home. Why didn't you let me go to Georgia with you and Vann? I've been to funerals before," he complained.

"We just felt you would be happy spending a few days with your mother, Matt. And to be honest, we didn't know what to expect down there, but we knew it was going to be hectic. But we're back, so let's go home. You have school tomorrow."

"Did Vann cook something? I'm hungry."

"No, Son, she's tired from the trip. We'd better stop and pick something up, or you'll have to make a sandwich or something."

"Okay. McDonald's!" he said, always happy for an excuse to eat fast food, which he didn't get often now that he lived with them. "But I sure hope Vann cooks something good tomorrow."

When they got home, Mitch told Vann about his encounter with Katrina while Matt took his bath and got ready for bed. "I don't know what she's up to, but you can guess it's nothing good."

"You know what that's about, Mitch," Vann stated, quietly. "Katrina thought she was going to ruin our marriage by sending Matt over here to disrupt things, and now she realizes that's not going to happen. But the main thing is, she's realized that the child support checks she's been getting from you will stop since Matt is now living with us. It'll be interesting to see what her next move is because you know she has one."

"You're right, babe. I guess we need to be ready."

The phone rang as they were preparing for bed. "Hello," Mitch answered, and after hearing the voice on the other end, his whole facial expression changed. "What do you want and why are you calling my house?"

Vann was surprised by the tone of Mitch's voice. It was unusual for him to respond so negatively.

"Now, why in the world should I let you speak to my wife? The last I heard, you were plotting something to hurt her. I'm not going to let you upset her, so you're going to have to deal with me."

Vann waited, curiosity eating at her, while Mitch listened. She had figured out that it was Elliott Shaw on the phone. Why was he calling?

"Okay, I'll let you talk to her, but I'm going to be on the extension, and if you say anything out of the way to her, you'll have me to deal with, you hear me?"

Vann picked up the phone and spoke cautiously into it. "Hello, Elliott. What do you want?"

"Savannah, I know I don't have any right to be calling you," Elliott said in a sincere tone Vann had never heard before. "But I wanted to tell you how sorry I was to hear about your grandmother passing, and I wanted to apologize for all I've said and done against you. You were right about everything, Savannah, and if I'd had a lick of sense, I would have listened. That woman, Annette, is no good, just like you told me." He paused before continuing. "Well, I also want to congratulate you, and wish you and your husband much happiness."

"Thank you, Elliott," Vann said in a cheerful voice. "I appreciate that. By the way, I haven't seen you at church lately. What's happening there?" Seth had told them Elliott refused to leave his house unless it was absolutely necessary.

"I can't come back until I get this situation with Annette cleared up. I've resigned from the deacon board and everything else. This thing has messed me up and disrupted my whole life, and I don't know if I'll ever be the same. Truthfully, I guess I don't want to be the same, but I have issues to settle that's for sure. Just pray for me." His voice cracked and Vann wondered if he was crying.

"I'll be doing that, Elliott, but let me say this. Many times when trouble comes, Satan convinces us to stay away from the church, when in fact, those are the times we need the prayers and support of our church family the most. So let me encourage you to come to church if you don't do anything else."

"You're a good woman, Savannah, and I hope your husband knows that. You never did even pretend to go along with my efforts to…you know. I just wish…"

"I know I have a good wife, Mr. Shaw," Mitch interrupted. "Now, my wife has had a long, hard week, and needs to get some rest. We appreciate your well wishes, and hope everything works out for you. Goodnight, sir."

"Mitch," Vann scolded, after they had hung up, "he was just trying to apologize."

"He did, and he said all he needed to say," Mitch said, finality ringing in his voice. "I have no desire to talk about Elliott Shaw. He's old enough to know what he needs to do, and nobody can tell him anything. It's between him and the Lord. Now come here, woman. You have a husband who needs your attention."

"Mitch, I've been thinking about something ever since we left Georgia," she said, settling into his arms.

"What's that, honey?" Mitch asked, even though talking was the last thing on his mind.

"All my life, at every milestone occasion, I wanted my parents, or my mother, to be there, cheering me on, sharing in the moment, you know? But that never happened. And now that I have you to share things with, what happens? First, my mother shows up at my wedding, and then, who shows up at the next biggest thing—Mama's funeral—my nonexistent, never mentioned, daddy. Isn't it strange how life works?

"Rosetta has brought mostly nothing but trouble to me, but I know why God sent her into my life. Now I'm trying to figure out why He's sending Ted. I sure hope he's not bringing trouble, Mitch. I don't know if I can stand anymore than what Rosetta has brought."

"Baby, God's not going to send anything into your life that He's not able to help you handle. You've taken care of Rosetta, you've witnessed to her, and told her what she needs to do about her salvation. It's all in the Lord's hands now. As far as Ted goes, I can just say that you have to give him a chance. Did you see the look on his face when he introduced you to his family? He had tears in his eyes. I thought he was going to break down right there. We can't judge him by Rosetta. They are definitely two different people. Just wait and see what the Lord is going to do. He might have a double blessing in store."

When Vann visited Rosetta the day after returning from Georgia, she found her with eyes red from crying.

"What's wrong? Are you still upset over not going to the funeral?" Vann asked her.

"Bernie just left here and she said some things that...well, that just made me see myself for who I am," Rosetta sniffed and wiped at the tears running down her face.

"What kinds of things?" Vann asked curiously.

"Well, for one, she told me I didn't have no business being upset over not being able to go to Mama's funeral since I didn't worry about going to see her when she was living, and that when Daddy died, I didn't go to his funeral either. And she said I expect too much from you, and don't deserve nothing you're doing for me. She got after me about being so mean and hateful to you. She told me Ted Lightfoot came to you and told you he was your daddy, and that he didn't know about you, but he loves you and is anxious for y'all to get to know each other. When I asked her if he was going to try and take you away from me because of what I did, she said she wished he would because my only concern is what you can do for me, and his concern is what he can do for you."

She covered her face and boohooed. "Bernie asked me how I got so messed up, and that's the question I've been asking myself since she left. How did I get so messed up? That question just keeps ringing in my head," she cried.

"Oh." Vann didn't know what to say. Bernetta had only told the truth.

Rosetta tearfully continued. "Bernie said there's some things I need to say to you before something happens, and Vann...,"

Rosetta had to stop, as her shoulders shook with sobs. "Vann, I want you to know that I'm sincerely sorry for abandoning you like I did. At the time, you were just something that interfered with my plans. And I guess that's all I ever thought about you. There's no way I can make it up to you, but I sure do wish I could." She sobbed uncontrollably again.

"I've been praying and asking the Lord to forgive me, and to save me. I prayed that prayer you're always trying to get me to pray. And I wish I could tell you that I love you, but I can't tell you that because I never did let any love for you grow in my heart."

Vann was crying at this point. "That's okay."

"It took me getting into this condition to realize what I threw away. And when I get to the point where I can, I'll tell you that I love you with all of my heart. Not just for what you're doing for me, but because you're my child," she continued sobbing, but quietly.

Vann wiped at the tears streaming down her face. "I'm just happy that you're talking to the Lord, and getting it straight with Him. Mama would be so happy."

"Can...can I go to church with you sometimes? They have a service here for those who want to go, but it's not the same. I enjoyed hearing that pastor talking about the Lord at your wedding. I sure would like to hear some more, and maybe I can join the church if they'll take me. I need to join another church since I may not ever get back to Georgia to go to that one."

"That's wonderful, Rosetta. Mitch and I will be happy to take you to church whenever you want to go," Vann told her. "Why don't we plan for Sundsay?"

When she left Rosetta, Vann sat in her car, talking to the Lord. "Father, I thank You and praise You for what You're doing in Rosetta's heart. And Lord, forgive me for not being as patient with her as I should be. I promise Lord, I'll do better if you me give the chance. Thank You for everything You've done, and all that You will do, Father. In Jesus' name. Amen."

She could hardly wait to tell Mitch about what had happened, and quickly dialed his work number, but was disappointed when his voice mail came on. She left a message, knowing he would hear the joy she was feeling.

Vann left Rosetta's facility in a rush to get home and get ready for her *High Point* show tapings. She was planning to do tapings for two shows, so two different outfits were necessary. After making sure she had everything she needed, she was getting ready to walk out the door when the telephone rang. She grunted with impatience and ran to see who was calling. She didn't recognize the number and decided not to answer it. She quickly got into her SUV and was backing out of the garage when her cell phone started ringing. Thinking it was probably Mitch calling her back, she fished the phone out of her purse and looked at the display window. It was the same number that had come up on her home phone. Curiosity got the best of her and she pushed the button to accept the call.

"Is this Mrs. Langford?" a woman's voice asked.

"Yes, it is. Who is this?"

"Hold on just a minute!"

"Vann? Could you please come get me?" Matthew's broken plea registered in her ear. "Please?"

"Matthew? Matthew, where in the world are you? You're supposed to be at your mother's."

"I am, Vann. But Mom had to leave and go to work, and her boyfriend threw me out of the house. He…"

"What? Matthew, what did you…?" She had been about to ask what he had said or done, but now wasn't the time. "Matthew, honey, did you call your mother?"

"Yes, but she didn't answer. I called Dad too, but he couldn't answer cause he's in court. I called Grandma and Aunt Fran, too. They told me to call you."

Why?! Obviously, Matthew had tried everyone he could think of and she was the last resort. "Matthew, where are you now?" she asked as questions flew through her mind.

"I'm next door at the neighbor's apartment."

"How did you know my cell phone number?"

"Daddy gave it to me and told me to memorize it just in case I needed to call you. Are you coming, Vann?"

"Yes, honey. I'm on my way. I'll be there in a few minutes."

"Okay. Are you almost around the corner?"

"Not yet. Just hang on."

"Okay."

She pulled into the parking lot of the apartment complex a few minutes later, and quickly ran to the apartment.

Matthew must have heard her heels clicking on the sidewalk. The door opposite his mother's flew open and he ran out and to her immense surprise, threw his arms around her, sobbing wildly.

A woman followed him out and invited them into her apartment. "It's a dirty shame the way that creep manhandled this kid. I don't know what he would have done if I hadn't threatened to call the police."

"Oh Lord! Matthew, what happened, honey?"

"I was hungry, and I wanted to fix a sandwich, and he told me I couldn't. Then, I told him my mother told me I could. And he said he didn't care what my mother said. So I was going to fix a sandwich anyway. It's my mom's house, not his! And then he grabbed me by my shirt and pulled me to the door and pushed me out. He shook me hard, and pushed me again and told me not to come back."

Matthew was crying again, and Vann was shaking angrily. She couldn't stand the thought of any child being pushed around like that. She tried to call Mitch, but got his voice mail again. "I don't know what to do," she told the neighbor. "I'm in a hurry to get to work, but I can't take him without his shoes and coat."

"Okay, wait a minute." The neighbor went to the phone and called apartment security. "Security is on the way. Just give him a few minutes," she said, after hanging up.

Vann thanked the neighbor profusely for her help.

The guard arrived in a few minutes, and after Vann explained the situation to him, he knocked hard on the door. "Security!" he yelled, loudly.

When the door opened, she looked up at the man, noting how big he was. "Sir, Matthew needs to get his shoes and coat out of there," Vann told him.

"Who are you?" the man asked in a belligerent voice, looking her up and down.

"I'm his stepmother, not that it's any of your business."

"And it ain't none of your business what goes on in my house. Y'all need to get off my porch."

"From what I've heard, you're already in trouble for abusing this child, mister," the guard said, "so I suggest you let him get his belongings."

The man weighed what the guard had told him in his mind, and said, "He can gon' on and get his stuff. Ain't no problem." He moved out of the door.

Vann asked the guard to wait while she and Matthew went into the apartment. "Matt, get your coat and shoes and whatever else you want, and hurry, because we need to go."

Matthew shot past her into his room and came back a few minutes later with his shoes, coat, and Game Boy. He shot the man a dirty look before jumping behind Vann.

"I want you to know this is not over, mister. When this child's father, Judge Langford, hears about how you've treated him, he's going to want some answers," Vann told him as they left the apartment.

"Judge Langford?" the man called after her, a different look now on his face.

"Yeah, my dad!" Matthew said, struggling into his shoes and coat.

"Come on, Matt." She caught his hand and walked to her SUV. He hopped into the backseat when she opened the door and started sniffling again. She grabbed a handful of Kleenex from the box she kept in the truck and mopped his face, talking to him as she did. "It's okay, sweetie. You're alright now. We'll stop and get you something to eat and then we have to go to the television station for a while. By the time we finish there, your dad will be on his way home."

"Okay," he answered in a quiet voice.

She got him settled in the green room with his food, cautioning him to be careful, then went into the studio to do her tapings. She pushed the incident to the back of her mind, so she could concentrate, but she was still angry and baffled. Why would Katrina leave her child with such a cruel person?

By the time she finished and went to get Matthew, he had fallen asleep on one of the chairs. He was in such a deep sleep that Vann wondered how much sleep the child had been getting the couple of days he had been at his mother's.

She stepped out of the room and went into the ladies' room and dialed Mitch's cell phone.

"Mitch?"

"Yeah, honey. What in the world is going on? Katrina has left several hysterical messages on my phone. Something about you coming over there and taking Matthew without her permission."

"Lord! Give me strength!" Vann cried out. "Now, Mitch! See! This is exactly why I don't like getting involved in this kind of mess! Matthew called me from a neighbor's to tell me Katrina's boyfriend put him out of the house. So I *did* go over there and get him, then we came to the studio, which is where we still are. And Mitch, he's sleeping so deeply, I really hate to wake him up."

"Well, Katrina lied because she knows I'm getting ready to beat some people down, including her. Matthew's not going back over there. Ever."

"Mitch, we'll be on our way home in a few minutes. Are you heading that way?" She was afraid of what his answer would be. She didn't want him going to Katrina's and forcing a confrontation with that big dude.

"I'm going to go have a talk with Katrina and her boyfriend first. Then I'll be on home."

"No, baby. Please don't go over there. Let it alone for now. They're waiting on you, and no telling what they'll do. You have to deal with people like that with a cool head. Come on home now. Your child needs to see you. He's pretty upset. You can deal with them later."

Mitch was quiet for a minute. "Right now I'm so angry, I can't think straight. But I guess what you're saying makes sense. I'm on my way home. I'll see you when you get there." Another pause, "And sweetheart? Thank you for everything you've done for Matthew today. Hopefully, this will help him understand some things. But I just want you to know how much I love and appreciate you."

"I love you too, honey. And you need to check on your petition to get custody as soon as possible."

"I've already done that, and the custody hearing will be in two weeks. I feel justified in demanding full custody, and after this, I don't think I'll have any trouble. We'll talk about it when I get home. I'll see you in a little while."

chapter thirty-two

It was the day before Thanksgiving and all was well in Vann's world. She had plenty to be thankful for and was trying not to let the bad weather dampen her high spirits.

It had been stormy and raining all week. "Oh my goodness! This rain just won't go away!" Vann noted sadly as she looked out of the kitchen window. She so wanted their first Thanksgiving together to be special. She kept adding things to the menu and was now up to three different meats and every traditional side dish and dessert she could think of. Her plans to go grocery shopping on Monday had been delayed until Tuesday, and then put off until today, and still had to be accomplished in between storms. She and Matthew had been out twice already today, picking up things for the meal, and on the last trip, they had picked up Rosetta, who was to spend the night. Now as she looked out at the downpour, she worried that Mitch wouldn't be able to get home through the flooded streets.

She pulled the pan of cornbread out of the oven, thinking it would be perfect by the time she was ready to make the stuffing. She was trying to get as much as possible done on the off chance the weather would break and they would be able to go to Thanksgiving Worship Service tonight.

She heard the garage door opening. "Matthew? Is that you messing with the garage door?" she called.

"No, ma'am," Matthew answered from his place in front of the television where he was playing a video game.

Before she could get to the door leading into the garage to see what was happening, it opened and Mitch stepped inside.

"Hey, babe," he said, placing his briefcase on the small table next to the door, and turning to kiss her. "It sure smells good in here."

"Hi! What are you doing home? It's only three o'clock."

"Why? Aren't you glad to see me?" he asked, smiling.

"Yes, indeed. I was just watching the weather and worrying about whether you would be able to make it home."

"Whoo! It is bad out there, and there's no sign it's going to let up any time soon. So they shut everything down for the rest of the day and told us to go home. They didn't have to tell me twice! I was out of the door as soon as the words were out of their mouth."

"Good. You can help me. I still need to wash the greens and I wanted to get that done in case we go to church tonight."

"Honey, you've got plenty of time, because we're not going anywhere tonight. The weather advisory says that if you don't have to get out, to stay put. So we're in for the day."

"Oh well, fine with me," Vann said, with a smile. She loved having her family settled safely at home when the weather was bad.

"Hey, Matt! What are you doing, man? Like I have to ask," he said, noting the ever-present Game Boy in Matt's hands. "Did you take care of your chores today?"

"Yes, sir. I did everything I was supposed to do, and I helped make the pies too, didn't I, Vann?"

"Yes, sweetie, you sure did," she looked at him with a smile. "You've been a big help today."

"How're you doing, Rosetta? You feeling alright?" Mitch asked. Rosetta was sitting at the kitchen table, awkwardly smearing icing on a cake. She was making a mess, but she wanted to help and Vann didn't have the heart to reject her offer.

"Yes, Mitch, I'm doing alright. This weather's not helping my arthritis very much, but that can't be helped. So they closed down the courts? I didn't know they ever did that."

"Yep. On the day before a holiday, nobody wants to take the chance of not being able to get home, or wherever they're planning to go. And this weather is apparently not going to let up."

"Well, I'm glad we're all in here where it's dry and comfortable. I surely do hate we can't make it to church tonight, though. I was looking forward to that sermon the pastor said he was going to preach."

"Have you heard from TreVann, honey?" Mitch asked. "I hear the weather is pretty bad in Austin, too. I wonder if he's going to be able to make it here."

"No, I haven't heard from him today, but maybe Rubye has. As much as I want to see him, I kind of hope he'll stay at home. This is definitely not traveling weather, especially with all the people who'll be on the roads between now and tomorrow."

"Well, Mike and Alicia are still planning to be here. I talked to them this morning. Of course, if this keeps up, they won't be able to make it either. The forecast says it will let up a little tomorrow morning, then the sky is going to open up again tomorrow afternoon."

"Oh, dear," Vann said. "That doesn't sound too encouraging. I'm going to call TreVann and tell him not to be trying to get here if it keeps storming like this. And he certainly doesn't need to be getting on a plane."

"I'm sure he knows that, babe," Mitch told her. He hugged her from behind and kissed the side of her face. "I'll go change clothes, then I'll be back to help wash the greens, okay?"

"Thanks, honey. They'll be waiting right here."

Thursday morning, Mitch's children with their toddlers in tow, managed to get to the house and were comfortably settled in the family room watching the Thanksgiving parades on television. Vann was busy putting the finishing touches on the meal and playing with the toddlers, when she heard a cell phone ringing.

Mike pulled his cell phone out and answered it. He sat up excitedly. "Mom! Was your flight ever able to get out?"

After listening for what seemed a long while, he said, "Oh no! That's terrible. Do you know how long? Oh wow! Well, do you need anything? Oh. Okay, I guess we can try to get out there. But you know a lot of the streets are already flooding. No, it's not raining now, but it's supposed to start up again later on today. Yeah, okay. We'll come right now."

He disconnected the call and told everyone, "That was Mom. Their plane got rerouted to Houston last night because of the weather. They've been sitting out there at the airport for hours. She called when they got in, but was thinking their plane would be able to take off at any time. Now she's found out the flight is delayed indefinitely, so she wants us to see if we can get out to the airport so she can see the kids and we can visit a little. Come on, let's go," he told Alicia, as he gathered up the babies. "Maybe we can get back before it starts raining again. Don't eat up everything, squirt," he said to Matthew.

Two hours later, the phone rang, and Mitch picked it up. "Mike? What's going on? Where are you? You probably should be headed back here before it gets too bad. It's already starting to rain again."

"Hey, Dad! Listen, I need to ask you something," Mike said.

"What?" Mitch asked, a feeling of dread washing over him. He knew it wouldn't be good.

"Well, their flight is still cancelled indefinitely. It's so crowded, there's hardly walking room in the waiting areas.

They'll probably be stuck here all night and into tomorrow. So, I was wondering if it was okay to bring them home for dinner. Then after dinner, I'll take them on over to my place."

"I don't know, Son." He glanced at Vann, who was busy setting the table for the gigantic dinner they were getting ready to eat. "That might be kind of awkward for everybody. Does your mother know you're making this call?"

"No. I thought I'd better ask before I mentioned it. Do you think Vann will mind? I mean if it's going to cause a problem, just forget it."

"Hold on, let me ask Vann." He walked into the dinning room where Vann was, and pushed the mute button. "Uh, honey. This is Mike on the phone. He says that Beverly and her husband's flight is still indefinitely cancelled and they'll probably be spending the day and all night in the airport because both the airport here, and the one in Memphis, are closed down due to weather conditions. He wants to know if he can invite them to dinner, then he's going to take them on to his place. What do you think?"

She frowned, "What can I say?" Vann saw her plans for a special Thanksgiving dinner disappearing. "I don't see how we can say no, since it would be inhospitable to do so under the circumstances. So, I guess you can tell him it's okay."

Forty-five minutes later, they arrived and Vann greeted them and told them dinner would be ready shortly.

All through dinner, Vann noticed Beverly watching her and Mitch's interaction with each other with avid interest. Vann started praying in her spirit. *Lord, let Your peace be upon this house.* Surely the woman couldn't have a problem with Mitch re-marrying. He hadn't been her husband for nearly twenty years.

Surprisingly, the meal went well, and Vann was delighted to see most of the food disappearing. She looked around the table at the strange assortment of people and could only feel amazement at how the Lord had arranged it. Beverly's husband kept them laughing about the extremes they had gone to, trying to sleep in the airport, and kept thanking them for the good meal and a place to really relax.

After the meal, Vann's hopes fell when she heard a thunderstorm overhead and knew that it would be impossible for them to leave anytime soon. "Lord, just be in me for whatever I need right now," she prayed. "Help me to appropriate all the fruit of Your Holy Spirit."

"Beverly, I know you all have to be exhausted, and probably want to freshen up a bit. You're welcome to use one of the bedrooms to rest. And if you want to take a shower, feel free. Maybe by that time, you'll hear something about your flight," Vann offered.

Beverly's husband, Henry, spoke up, "Vann, we'd appreciate that. We are tired and travel worn. A shower and rest would be great. Just show us the way. Come on, Bev."

Vann led the way upstairs where she showed them into a guestroom and pointed out the bathroom and linen closet where they could find fresh towels. As she turned to leave, Beverly stopped her.

"How did you and Mitch meet?" she questioned. "Are you an attorney also?"

"No, but we did meet in court," Vann answered. And when she saw Beverly's eyebrow arch inquiringly, she explained the circumstances that led to them getting together.

"Interesting." She lowered her voice to keep her husband, who had gone to the bathroom, from overhearing. "You know, Mitch was my first love, and I'll always love him. I know now I should have stayed with him. I've regretted leaving him a number of times."

Vann smiled. "Well, I don't plan to ever make that mistake. Mitch is a very sweet man, and I love him very much," Vann said as she turned to leave.

A little later, Vann escaped into her bedroom to relax. She had a houseful of people who, from the looks of it, wouldn't be leaving anytime soon, and she needed to regroup. She lay across the bed and reflected on the day. It wasn't long before Mitch followed her with a concerned look. "Honey, you okay?" he asked, laying down beside her.

"Yes, I'm fine, but I do have something to say to you."

"What is that?"

"If you have any more baby mamas hidden anywhere, you'd better keep them there!"

Mitch laughed, "No, sweetheart. I don't have any more. I promise you."

Everyone ended up staying the whole night, and as they coordinated sleeping arrangements, which was no big deal with the house being as large as it was, Vann and Mitch joked about their strange collection of house guests before they went to sleep.

Before leaving the next morning, Beverly thanked them for their hospitality. "And please Vann, keep an eye on my children and grandchildren. I'll be calling from time to time to just check and see how things are going if that's okay."

"That'll be fine," Vann told her with a smile.

After Beverly, with husband, children, and grandchildren, left for the airport to catch a midday flight, and Rosetta and Matthew settled down in front of the television, Vann collapsed in relief in the bedroom with Mitch. "You know, honey, I so wanted our first Thanksgiving together to be special," Vann bemoaned.

"It was special, babe," Mitch said, thoughtfully. "Very special. Special in ways I don't care to remember, but special...really, really, special. Yes, it was so special that I..."

"Shut up, you nut!" Vann said, hitting him playfully with a pillow. "For Christmas, we're going to keep it very simple... nobody but you and me, and catered food."

"That's fine with me, but knowing you, we'll have a house full of people again."

"You think you know me so well, but you just watch. That's not going to happen."

"I do know you, babe, and that's why I know what I'm talking about."

chapter thirty-three

Mitch had reluctantly permitted Matthew to spend the weekend with his mother, and was returning to pick him up Sunday evening. He had left Vann talking easily with Ted, who had been calling on a regular basis, at first talking only to Mitch until Vann had finally felt ready to deal with a newfound daddy. Unless he was mistaken, he heard her telling Ted that, yes, it would be okay for him to spend Christmas with them.

It wouldn't be Ted's first visit. The week after Thanksgiving, he had flown to Houston, insisting on a DNA test to prove to Vann she was really his daughter, although Ted was already convinced she was. During his three day stay, he told them about his life. It turned out he was Retired Colonel Theodore Lightfoot, with an impressive military career. After he retired, he and his wife spent several years traveling around the world, before her health broke. After that, his time had been devoted to taking care of her.

Unfortunately, they had not had any children. She had eventually passed away, and Ted had simply existed in a fog until a few years ago, when he had decided to move back to Georgia to be near the little family he had left. His siblings had only had one child each, and both children were deceased. His aunt, now in her late nineties, had outlived all three of her children.

Mitch reflected on Vann's newly discovered parents on the way to pick up Matthew. It had been a long time coming, but thank God it happened. The funny thing was that the parents were now circling each other like roosters with their feathers ruffled, afraid one would get ahead of the other in Vann's affection. "I love it!" Mitch had told Vann. "You know that Scripture about God doing exceeding, abundantly above all we can ask, think, or hope?" When she nodded, he said, "Well, we are definitely seeing that happen. God is truly faithful."

Mitch pulled into Katrina's apartment complex and called to tell Matthew that he was waiting for him outside, but Katrina answered the phone and told him to come in because they needed to talk.

"Oh no, not this again," Mitch groaned. "Katrina, I'm not coming in there, so just send my son out."

"He's not here. He doesn't need to be here to hear this conversation."

"Well, where is he? Because I'm not coming in there."

"You'll sit out there all night then. I just want to talk to you, Mitch. You owe me that much courtesy."

Disgruntled, Mitch slowly got out of the car and went to her door. "Okay, what is it you want to talk about, Katrina?" he demanded as soon as she opened the door.

"I know I told you that Matthew would be living with you, but I've thought about it and decided that's not the best thing for him. He needs to be with his mother."

Mitch saw red, as anger hit him. "What does Matt have to say about that? The last time he and I talked about it, he told me he wanted to stay with us. I doubt you've even considered what he wants, Katrina. You must have given it a lot of thought before you literally dumped him on my doorstep. Now, why the change all of a sudden?"

"It's my prerogative to change my mind," she answered in a spiteful voice.

"I know what this is about," Mitch said, looking at her coldly. "You've realized the child support money is not coming anymore, haven't you? That's the reason for this sudden change of heart. Or is it that you've received notice about the custody hearing, as well as the charges I filed against you and your boyfriend for child abuse and endangerment? I know you didn't expect me to just forget that, because Matt sure hasn't."

"Well as of now, I still have custody, and until that changes, everything will resume as ordered under the current court order," she huffed. "So you can leave because Matthew's not going with you."

"Not until I see my son," Mitch said, angrily, "so you get my son here immediately."

Katrina saw that he meant it, and went to the phone to make a call. While they waited for Matthew, Mitch said, "I will not have my son jerked around like this anymore. There'll be no more of these games, and you *will* follow the current order, as well as the new one, to the letter."

"I wouldn't be too overly confident if I were you, or I'll fix it so you'll never see him."

"You might try. We'll let the court rule on who he should live with. I've requested full custody, and the court will take everything you've done into consideration, and talk to Matthew about which parent he wants to live with. But at this point, I believe I can provide the better home for him."

Matt came running through the door from across the complex and into his daddy's arms. "Dad! I'm ready to go, I just have to get my stuff."

"Wait a minute, Matt," Mitch searched for the right words. "Uh...listen son, your mother has changed her mind. She wants you to come back and live with her again."

"Do I have to, Dad?" Matthew asked, tears gathering in his eyes. "I'll come visit you, Mom, but I want to stay with Dad, please!"

Mitch felt tears stinging his eyes as he heard his son begging to live with him. "For the time being, Matt, you have to stay here. But I promise, I'm already doing everything I can to fix it so you will live with me. In the meantime, you can still come on weekends and holidays, and we'll have a lot of fun then, okay?"

Matthew wiped the fast running tears from his face. "Okay. But all my clothes and stuff are still at home...I mean at your house."

"We'll bring it to you tomorrow, and you'll go to school this week, and before you know it, it'll be Friday and I'll be back to get you for the weekend. How does that sound?"

"Okay," Matthew said resignedly. "Can I come stay with you and Vann when I get out for Christmas?"

"Maybe some of the time, but since you spent Thanksgiving with us, you'll probably have to spend Christmas with your mother. You understand? So you can talk to her and see when it'll be okay for you to come, and we'll come get you." Mitch was praying they would have full custody by then, and it would be a moot point, but he didn't mention it to the child.

Matthew immediately turned to his mother and said, "Mom, I want to go to Dad's house for Christmas. Papa Ted said he was going to take me shopping and to some other neat places."

"Who is Papa Ted?" Katrina asked suspiciously.

"Vann's dad," Mitch answered. "He and Matt have become good friends."

"Well, we'll have to see Matt, because your grandmother and the rest of the family are expecting you to spend Christmas with us."

Matthew hung his head, as he fought back tears. He wanted to be in the warmth and love of his dad and Vann's home. "I'm going to pray about it," he said, surprising his mother again.

"Pray about it? Where in the world..." She stopped, realizing that the only place Matthew could have learned that was in Mitch's home.

"I have to go, Matt," Mitch told him. "But I'll see you tomorrow evening. Do you have clean clothes to wear to school tomorrow? Remember what Vann told you about always wearing clean underwear?" he asked, smiling.

Matthew laughed. "Yeah. She said if I get in an accident and had to pull my clothes off, I would be embarrassed if I had on dirty underwear. I still have some clean clothes that I brought with me. Mom said Vann always packs too much."

"Well, I guess it's a good thing she does, huh? I'll see you tomorrow, Son."

Mitch sat in his car for a long time as he worked to control the anger he felt toward Katrina and the tears that fell from his eyes. It hurt him badly to leave Matthew there, when he wanted so badly to go home. He couldn't wait for the custody hearing, which had been rescheduled once, and prayed all would go the way he hoped it would. He slowly drove away from the apartment complex, his heart heavy.

chapter thirty-four

Vann was surprised at how much she missed Matthew, and her heart felt heavy at how much it had hurt Mitch for Katrina to change her mind and decide to reclaim him. But the attorney didn't think they'd have a problem getting full custody as long as Matthew wanted to live with them.

Christmas was less than two weeks away and Vann was in the midst of last-minute preparations, decorating, and shopping. Ted would be coming in a few days and she was actually looking forward to seeing him again. TreVann had called earlier that day, asking if his room was ready. He had visited, but hadn't stayed overnight with her since she'd moved to Mitch's house. Vann happily told him that his room was always ready, and then began a whirlwind of activities to make it so.

They had found out the night before that Matthew was giving Katrina such a hard time, that she had finally agreed to let him spend his holiday break with them, so he would be back home on the weekend.

Vann had asked her aunts to take Rosetta for Christmas when she'd planned to celebrate with just Mitch and herself. But Rosetta, like Matthew, threw a fit and demanded to come to Vann's house, stating that was where she was supposed to be, and besides, she had to watch Ted to keep him from trying to take her child. *Child?*

So, before they knew it, they had acquired a full house for their first Christmas together. Oh, well.

As Vann sat making lists and thinking about all she had to do to get ready, the phone rang. "Hey, girl, what are you doing?"

"Rubye! I'm sitting here making list after list of things I have to do to get ready for Christmas. You know, it's so funny. I decided after Thanksgiving, that Christmas would be just me and Mitch...alone. Mitch told me I was dreaming when I was talking about it, and he was absolutely right. But it's all good. Did Trevie tell you he plans to come? He called, wanting to know if his room was ready," Vann said, laughing.

"Yes, I talked to him. And that's one reason I'm calling. The other kids are spending the holidays with friends, and Thomas and I will be on our own. So add us to your list and tell me what you want us to bring, because we're coming to your house."

Vann laughed harder, "Good! You can bring the desserts, and ask Thomas to do one of his fabulous smoked briskets. I've already got a ham and a turkey, so that should be plenty of meats, unless he wants to do some ribs, too. It's up to him. I'll take care of the side dishes and everything else. I am so excited, Rubye! This is getting better and better."

That evening when Mitch got home, Vann told him how their guest list and meal had expanded, and he looked kind of sheepish. "Uh, babe...I forgot to tell you...I was talking to Seth yesterday, and he told me he would be spending Christmas alone, so I sort of invited him to come by and eat with us."

"That's fine. I'd love to have Seth. We have to remember to have something under the tree for him. I'd better put it on my list now," she said, looking through several pieces of paper to find the gift list.

"And I think Mike and Alicia have just about decided they're not going to their mother's, so they'll most likely be here too," Mitch started laughing. "Didn't you say something about us spending this Christmas alone? What happened to that?"

"I don't know," she said in amusement. "I was kind of looking forward to it, but then people started inviting themselves, and I didn't have the heart to tell anyone no. It looks like we're going to have a packed house."

"To be honest, I think I'm going to enjoy that," Mitch said, quietly. "I've had too many holidays when I wished for someone to share them with, and I'm finally getting my wish. And I'm glad we have the kind of home where people feel welcome and want to come and visit."

"Me too, honey," Vann said. "You know, since last Christmas, I've lost Mama, who was the most important person in my life for so long, and I really thought I would be a little sad and depressed, because I usually spent Christmas with her. But look how God has been faithful in giving me a wonderful husband, both of my parents, and many others to make my life full and rich. God is so good."

"Yes, He is. And I have to tell you, this is shaping up to be the best Christmas I've had in a very long time. We are truly blessed, sweetheart. And we'll have plenty of days to spend with just the two of us. And every day that we're together is a special day. Remember that."

"Ooooow! Honey, you're making me cry," Vann said, wiping at the tears in her eyes.

The week leading up to Christmas, the judge finally scheduled the custody hearing, much to Mitch's relief. Matthew spent thirty minutes talking to the judge alone. When they came out of the private session, the judge sent Matt out of the room, then told them how the child had pleaded with her to let him stay with his dad and Vann.

"He told me that when his mother's boyfriends come over, he feels like he's in the way, and is often sent to stay somewhere else. He told me how his mother taught him to be ugly to his stepmother, but he didn't want to be because he loves her. He told me about the time his mother's boyfriend put him out of the house without his coat and shoes and his stepmom had to come get him," she cut her eyes to Katrina. "Failure to protect children from abuse is a crime, and I will provide Matthew's statement to the D.A.'s office for the case that is now pending on that incident," then she resumed recalling her conversation with Matthew. "He said he loves his mother too, but he feels like his home is with his dad and stepmother, and that is where he wants to be. And ladies and gentlemen," the judge announced firmly, "that is where he is going. The mother will have one weekend per month and some holiday visitation rights that will be spelled out in the order. We'll see how that works out," she cut her eyes to Katrina again. "That is my ruling."

Christmas was wonderful! They did, in fact, have a full house. In addition to all the people they were expecting, Seth called and asked if he could bring Elliott. "I know all the history," Seth said, "but the man is really in pitiful shape, and needs to be around people who will show him the love of God." Seth had then convinced Elliott to come, telling him Vann and Mitch would love to have him.

When Seth arrived with a much thinner, unhealthy-looking, Elliott, he took Vann and Mitch aside and explained how he'd called the week before to check on Elliott, and found out he was sitting home alone. "I'm really concerned about him. His health is not good, and he's a different man now. We know he brought the trouble on himself, but he still needs help," Seth told them. "And I hope I didn't overstep the boundaries of our friendship by asking you guys if he could come today, but I just felt sorry for him."

"Of course not," Vann said, shocked at Elliott's appearance. Gone was the arrogant, snooty, overbearing attitude, and in its place was a quiet, unsure, pitiful man. "Hey, Elliott, come on in and make yourself at home," she and Mitch said to Elliott, who was understandably unsure of his welcome.

By the end of the day, the game room upstairs had lively games going on. Ted, Seth, Elliott, and Thomas had a loud domino game going, while Mitch, Trevie, Mike, and Alicia's boyfriend, were in the midst of a card game. Downstairs in the family room, the women had camped out in front of the television watching tear-jerking Christmas movies.

Matthew and the babies had a ball running from group to group, eating their little hearts out, and enjoying their bounty of gifts. Matt, of course, was anxious to get outside to ride his new bicycle.

Even Rosetta mellowed out and got along with everyone...a miracle in itself. Of course, there was way too much food, and everyone left with foil wrapped plates piled high with leftovers. The good thing was that everyone who was supposed to, went home. Even Rosetta was dropped off at the facility by Rubye and Thomas, leaving Ted the opportunity to enjoy his new family without her interference.

Things finally settled down somewhat as the year drew to an end. Vann was gradually getting back into her routine, and was loving the new workspace Mitch had built for them. She was in the midst of planning a new lineup of shows for *High Point,* but considering what she could cut from her schedule, since they now had full custody of Matthew and his numerous activities to keep them busy.

chapter thirty-five

The Saturday after New Year's Day rolled around as a mild and sunshiny day. Matthew was spending the weekend with his mother, who had made a complete about-face since losing custody of her son.

Katrina had cried as she listened to the judge talk about her son's pleas to live with his father. Now, whenever she called to talk to Matt, she was as nice as could be. Matt told them she had a new boyfriend who seemed nice. Their only hope was that he would treat Matt well whenever he visited.

Now, Mitch was getting ready to go play a round of golf with Thomas, while Vann was preparing for a gab session with her friends, who were meeting at her house. She groaned when the phone rang, knowing she didn't have time to get into a conversation with a long-winded person. "Hello?" she answered in a brisk voice.

"May I speak to Vann?" a slightly familiar voice asked.

"This is Vann. Who's calling please?"

"This is Glenda. Where's my mother?"

"Oh. Glenda, how are you? Your mother is in an assisted-living facility, and doing well. Do you want her number? I'm sure she'll be happy to hear from you."

"Yes, give me the number. Me and my brothers are still planning to look into you moving her down there and selling our property. So, you're not off the hook."

"You'll have to talk to my legal counsel about that," Vann answered. "But I sure do wish we could sit down sometime and just talk about everything. After all, we are siblings, and I'd love to get to know you and my brothers."

Silence. Then, "I'll have to think about that. We'll see."

Vann gave her the number, then said, "Okay, well, at least come and visit your mother. She's not going to be here always, you know. You should treasure the time you have left to spend with her."

"Bye," Glenda said abruptly, and hung up.

"Oh my," Vann said to Mitch. "That was Glenda, and we just had a very strange conversation."

Mitch laughed. "You know what, honey? Something tells me life will never be dull or boring for us. Just think about it: Rosetta's and Ted's arrival into your life and their constant battling for your affections; Katrina's wishy-washy ways; Glenda and her brothers' threats, and the possibility that God will eventually bring you all together; Beverly's nosiness; Matthew running through the house, yelling 'yuck' every time he sees us kissing, plus all the activities he'll be involved in that will keep us busy; Mike and Alicia and the grandbabies; TreVann's pending marriage and plans to move back here; the aunts and their cantankerous ways...oh Lord!

"Throw in our new extended family of Seth and Elliott, whom I don't think we'll be getting rid of anytime soon...." Ted, Seth, and Elliott had formed a friendship and started hanging out together. "Then there's the decorating and wood-working projects, your television program, our church activities...and everything else life is certain to deliver into our lives. Do you think these old bodies are up to the challenges?"

"Baby, as long as we're trusting in the Lord's faithfulness, we can handle anything. We might be old, but thankfully, God sends new life and new mercies to these old bodies every morning," Vann answered.

"Speaking of new life, how is Ted enjoying his new apartment? Are you sure you're okay with him moving here to be near us?"

"Absolutely," Vann answered. "For the first time in my life, I have a doting parent, and just think, I'll be surrounded by three generations of men who adore me," she said, smiling widely. "And it's wonderful to see how crazy Ted and Matt are about each other, and I think they're good for one another. They both seem to need what the other has to give."

"Like I said, never a dull moment," Mitch said, laughing.

"You'd better get going, Judge, or you're going to be late."

"You're just trying to get me out of here before those women get here." He hugged her close. "But you know, Thomas and I have been known to crash that hen party."

"Now, you don't want to do that, Judge. You might get thrown out of here."

"Nope." He kissed her and hugged her closer. "I'd just recommend that we sit down and negotiate. I'm sure we could come to some sort of agreement."

"Hmmm, I guess we could, Judge. On the other hand, there's always that other promise that I never did get to keep. I know you don't want me to do that, now do you?" she said, kissing him sweetly. "Now go!"

"I could throw you in jail for contempt, but then I'd have to come and get you. So, I guess I'll just leave." He gave her another hug and kiss and started out the door. "How long are they going to be here, anyway? When can I come home?"

Vann slammed the door without answering.

Her friends toured the house and workshop, ate the sumptuous food Vann had prepared, then settled down to talk. It had been a while since they had gotten together, so they were all anxious to get updates on what was going on in everyone's life.

Vann, of course, was the object of much curiosity, and therefore, the questions started coming to her first. "How is married life, girl? How are things going with Rosetta and the arrival of your long lost daddy? How is motherhood working out? What about your siblings? When are you going to have some new pieces ready? Do you think Mitch will make me an entertainment cabinet like yours? Can you make me an ensemble for my bedroom?"

Smiling, Vann began talking. "I'm probably the only fifty-something-year-old woman in the world to acquire a husband, birth parents, three children, and two grandchildren all in the same year." She gave a joyful laugh. "A year or so ago, I wouldn't have believed how my life has now changed. So many new things...and not just meeting Mitch and getting married, but my decorating projects and the television show, Rosetta and Ted entering my life—it's just amazing. Not everything has been good or pleasant, but God has brought me through it.

"Amazingly, Matthew loves to follow me around and loves my cooking. Ted has moved here to be near us, and he's one of the best things that's happened in my life. Rosetta is still...Rosetta, but she finally accepted Christ into her life, and she's trying to do better. My sister, Glenda, has called a few times on one pretext or another, and Mitch and I are praying she'll eventually come around. I don't know about her brothers.

"But through it all, God had been so good. He keeps showing me that although I can't change the past, He will restore some things, and add some new things...good things... that will make up the difference." Her eyes were shiny with tears. "The only thing that can't be restored is Mama, who I wish was still here to share everything with me. But somehow, I believe she knows, and is smiling." Vann told them about Thanksgiving, and then about Christmas and the full house of people she had ended up having. Of course, they frowned on Elliott showing up.

Vann shook her head, "God has taught me a lot about forgiveness. It's very hard to do, but it's not an option. You either forgive or you live in disobedience, and you ain't gonna have no peace, so you might as well go on and forgive and move on. If you could see Elliott now, you would feel sorry for him. And I doubt if Annette has ended up much better. Anyway, enough about me. Now, Rubye, you've kept us waiting long enough on this Mideast thing. Are you going or not?"

"Not!" Rubye said, laughing. "We just made the decision final yesterday. Thomas did have dollar signs in his eyes when they told him how much money he would make, but after thinking about it, he agreed that money ain't everything. It's just too unsafe over there. And it was going to be hard for us to leave our children again, as well as all of our friends who are like family to us. Our business is doing so well and has so much potential to do better when Thomas is able to work it full time. That's the next news...Thomas has decided to retire and work with me in the business. So, no, we're here to stay."

The rest of them clapped and expressed their joy at the news. Roxanne wanted to go next. "Girls, I'm loving my new house. I was able to customize everything to fit my taste, and I'm enjoying just settling in and making it my own. And instead of looking for a new husband, I've decided to start a new career...something that I'll enjoy doing. I've already started taking classes. I'm envious of Vann and all of her new things, and I've been thinking—if God did it for her, He'll do it for me. And He gave her a husband on top of everything else. So, I'm going for it!"

"So, what's your new career?" Vann asked.

"Real estate. When I was looking at houses, I fell in love with going into different houses, and seeing all the options that people have today. And I think I'd like to help people find the right places to live that fit their lifestyle. Single family homes, condos, patio homes…there are so many choices that it's easy to get confused about what's best for you. I think I'll be good at it."

"You will," Vann said, encouragingly. "What about you, Katherine? You're about to be left on the old job by yourself."

"Oh no, I'm not. My husband and I are planning to move out of the city…still close enough to stay connected to our family and friends…but far enough out that we can have enough land to grow a big garden and keep y'all supplied with all the greens, okra, tomatoes, and peppers you can eat, and so we can have all the flowers we want. He's been talking about doing this for years, but as y'all know, I had other things on my mind. But you know, I'm like Roxie. After looking at all the new and good things that happened when Vann decided to make some changes in her life, I decided to do it too. We tend to get into these ruts and think we have to stay there, when there's all this big old world out there, full of all kinds of new things to explore and do. Well, my retirement papers are already being processed, and we've begun looking for a place. Sorry, Roxie, but you won't be ready in time to handle that for us," she said, smiling. "But, girls, I am so excited. My husband and I are doing well since we started planning and doing things together, and he's even agreed to do a little traveling with me."

The women clapped and high fives went around the room. "Wow!" Rubye said. "And I thought I would have the most exciting news. This is wonderful! What's going on with you, Stelle? Anything new?"

"I do have some news, although it's not as exciting as what I've heard from everyone else, but it's good." Stelle looked at

Vann, who already knew, and smiled. "I have a new male interest, girls! And it's looking good! I've known him for years, and his wife, who died a few years ago, used to be one of my clients. He owns several beauty supply places and has always been very nice to me. When he found out I had split with my husband, he called and asked me out, but I was too emotionally washed out to consider it. But I'm together now, and we've been seeing a lot of each other. My ex-husband tried to come back, but he was quickly shown the door. Like Vann said, it doesn't make sense to go back and dig in stinking garbage after you've gotten rid of it." They all screamed with laughter, and shook their heads in agreement.

"No, I'm moving on," Stelle continued. "My business is going well and I'm happy with my life right now. Roxie, you go on and pursue this real estate thing. I might be your first customer, because I'm truly thinking about downsizing to a nice condo in the future."

The telephone rang and Vann excused herself to answer it. She came back smiling a few minutes later. "That was my husband wanting to know if we're about done, because he's ready to come home. I had to almost throw him out of here this morning."

"Say no more, girl," Rubye said, laughing. "We need to get out of here, girls, …remember these people are still newlyweds." Grabbing purses, they left in a hurry.

Vann watched them leave and sat down with a smile of contentment. "Father, thank You for Your faithfulness. I am definitely out of the rut."

"It is of the LORD's mercies that we are not consumed,
because his compassions fail not. They are new every
morning: great is thy faithfulness."

Lamentations 3:22–23 KJV

Reading Guide

1. How do both Mitch and Vann exemplify the biblical call to "do justice and love kindness" (Micah 6:8 ESV) in their chosen vocations?

2. Vann has quite a set of girlfriends! Who are the women you spend time with? How would you describe your relationships with them—and their relationships with each other? In what ways are those friendships a support and encouragement to you? In what ways are they an outreach ministry in themselves?

3. Vann has learned to be content in her present state, an allusion to Philippians 4:11. What is your current state—and to what extent are you content in it? What do you think would increase your contentment?

4. Vann often feels pulled in too many directions, juggling the demands of so many people. How do you juggle your commitments to work, family, ministry, friends, community, and self? Which area is most likely to suffer and why?

5. Elliott makes a lot of foolish assumptions about Vann based on her age, gender, and apparent "lower-class" status. What assumptions do you make about people? What do others assume about you? What are the drawbacks of such assumptions?

6. After an upsetting day, Vann sat back and considered the years of her life—the good and the bad, the blessings and the challenges. What do you see when you look back over your life? Where do you see God's hand at work?

7. Aunt Lu asks Vann to think of her mother like anyone else in need—but Vann isn't sure she can do that. Why? What about family relationships might make them more difficult than relationships with strangers? (Compare the parable of the prodigal son in Luke 15:11–32 with the parable of the good Samaritan in Luke 10:25–37)

8. Vann admits to God that she isn't sure what the right thing to do is—or if she even *wants* to know. What do you think is the right choice? Why? How would you counsel a friend in Vann's position?

9. Is TreVann right about his godmother and her too-soft heart? When have your attempts to practice Christian compassion and kindness been taken advantage of? When have you failed to practice such compassion—and why?

10. "Are you ready?" the preacher asked, and Mitch leaped to respond. What are you getting ready for? Are you ready now to respond? Why or why not?

11. Vann and Mitchell finally take time to put all their relational history on the table after the incident with Annette. We all have histories—for better and worse. What kind of relationship baggage do you carry today—with a parent, a sibling, a former spouse or ex-lover, a child? In what ways is that history a blessing? How is it a burden?

12. Forgiveness is always God's will, Mitch tells Vann. But they both know it isn't easy to do. Read some of Jesus' words about forgiveness in Matthew 6:9–15; 18:21–22; and Luke 17:1–5. In what relationships do you need God to increase your faith to enable you to forgive?

13. Vann is overwhelmed by the choices set before her—related to her birth mother and to a future with Mitch in particular. Rubye suggests that she should have settled the latter before the former. What do you think? What would be the pros and cons of each choice? How do *you* make decisions when your relationships and commitments conflict?

14. Seth tries to speak truth to Elliott; Rubye challenges Vann to be wise. Whom in your life can you trust to tell you the truth and give you wise counsel? (See Proverbs 7:4; 17:17; 18:24; 27:5–6, 9.)

15. Rosetta maintains that she is a Christian but that she doesn't need church or "man-made religion." How do you define your faith? In what context do you act it out? How important is a community of faith (i.e., a church family) to your Christian walk? Why?

16. Rosetta is a particularly difficult person to deal with, but the choices that face Vann and her aunts face many of us with aging relatives. How do you make decisions about caring for an aging parent, grandparent, aunt, or uncle—while also honoring the need

to care for yourself and other family members (spouse, children, etc.)? What biblical principles or verses guide your decisions?

17. Contrast Vann's grief with Rosetta's when Mama dies. In what ways have you experienced the difference between grief for someone who is well-loved and someone with whom you have unresolved baggage? How does your faith in God get you through both kinds of loss?

18. Vann feels like she is living in a soap opera and it's overwhelming. When have you felt that way? To whom do you turn when you need someone stable or trustworthy or wise? Consider these Scriptures when you need an anchor in your storm: Psalms 23; 42; 62:5; 121; Romans 8:31–35.

19. Mitch and Vann's first Thanksgiving was "special" to say the least! Describe your craziest family holiday and how you managed to make it through.

20. Vann and her girlfriends share laughter and praise over the changes in their lives over recent months. They remark that change can be hard, but it's often necessary to pull a person out of a rut. What part of your life is a rut? In what life transitions do you see good change? Where do you see God's faithfulness at work in your life? (Lamentations 3:22–23).

Prayer of Salvation

God loves you—no matter who you are, no matter what your past. God loves you so much that He gave His one and only begotten Son for you. The Bible tells us that "...whoever believes in him shall not perish but have eternal life" (John 3:16 NIV). Jesus laid down His life and rose again so that we could spend eternity with Him in heaven and experience His absolute best on earth. If you would like to receive Jesus into your life, say the following prayer out loud and mean it from your heart.

Heavenly Father, I come to You admitting that I am a sinner. Right now, I choose to turn away from sin, and I ask You to cleanse me of all unrighteousness. I believe that Your Son, Jesus, died on the cross to take away my sins. I also believe that He rose again from the dead so that I might be forgiven of my sins and made righteous through faith in Him. I call upon the name of Jesus Christ to be the Savior and Lord of my life. Jesus, I choose to follow You and ask that You fill me with the power of the Holy Spirit. I declare that right now I am a child of God. I am free from sin and full of the righteousness of God. I am saved in Jesus' name. Amen.